The

The House of Lyall

by

Doris Davidson

BIRLINN

This edition published in 2006 by
Birlinn Limited
West Newington House
10 Newington Road
Edinburgh EH9 1QS

www.birlinn.co.uk

ISBN10: 1 84158 472 X
ISBN13: 978 1 84158 472 0

Originally published in 2000 by HarperCollins*Publishers*

British Library Cataloguing-in-Publication Data
A Catalogue record for this book is available from
the British Library

Printed and bound by Antony Rowe Ltd, Chippenham

To Jimmy – chief cook, cleaner and bottlewasher since I started writing. Until then, I had no idea that husbands could come in so handy. They can't half hide their lights under bushels.

Thanks to Susan Opie, my editor, who sorted out the muddle in which I managed to find myself. *The House of Lyall* would have been far less readable without her help.

Part One

1894–1903

Chapter One

It had never crossed Marion Cheyne's mind before, but then she had never seen so much money before, and she didn't recognize what she was feeling as temptation, never having come across that before, either. So her hand was as steady as a rock when she picked up five sovereigns and dropped them into the pocket of the apron which enveloped her from neck to feet. Some inborn sense of preservation, however, made her stir the silver and copper around the remaining golden coins with her finger, so it wouldn't be noticeable at first glance that any had been removed from the shallow china dish. This was actually meant to hold bonbons, but Mr Moodie deposited his small change in it every night – farthings, ha'pennies and pennies as a rule, with the odd thrupenny or sixpenny bit amongst them, sometimes even a shilling or a florin, but never gold, and certainly never a heap of gold like today.

Finished here, she walked to the door, but the telltale jingle accompanying each step made her stop to tie the coins tightly inside her handkerchief; then to be doubly sure they would not betray her, she stuffed the solid little bundle into the pocket of her drawers. This act of secrecy, an admittance that what she had done was wrong, didn't bother her as much as it should have done. If the gentry were as stupid as leave big amounts of money lying about, they deserved to be robbed.

Not that the Moodies were true gentry. Even if their house stood on its own, hidden from curious eyes by the spreading trees that had given it its name, Oak Cottage wasn't much different from the rest of the houses on that stretch of the turnpike – most of them built of the pink granite quarried in Peterhead. Of course, he *was* manager of the North of Scotland Bank's branch in the Square, and went to work every morning in a black suit and a white shirt with a winged collar, and a moleskin hat jammed on his head, but that didn't give him the right to think he was better than his neighbours. Apart from Mary McKay – who was employed by the council to assess the old and infirm inhabitants of Tipperton with a view to putting them in the poor's house – they were mainly shopkeepers, and most of them could buy and sell him.

Her mind returning to matters in hand, Marion realized that she would be under suspicion the minute he discovered the loss of his five pounds – there were only herself and the mistress who could have taken them, and he wouldn't blame his wife. Well, it didn't matter, for Marion Cheyne would be well away by the time he came home. She'd been thinking of leaving anyway. It wasn't that Mr Moodie had done anything out of place, but with him sleeping in a different room from his wife, their servant was taking no chances of being roped in as his bed-warmer . . . or maybe worse! She would be fifteen next week, old enough to fend for herself, so why shouldn't she go to Aberdeen and look for a better job? No one would miss her at home – her father was too much taken up with his new wife to care a docken about his daughter, and Moll, her step-mother, couldn't stand the sight of her, which didn't really matter because *she* hated her. They'd already got rid of her young brother by sending him to work for a horse-breeder in England somewhere, though it had pleased Kenny, for he'd always been mad about horses and wanted to be a jockey some day.

When Marion went into the kitchen, Mrs Moodie was dampening the first lot of clothes they had washed earlier and rolling them up for her servant to iron in the afternoon with the rest. The girl had nothing against the woman, but she could feel her cheeks reddening at the thought of what lay hidden under her skirts, so when her mistress looked up and said solicitously, 'You look flushed, Marion. I hope you're not coming down with something,' she was quick with her reply.

'I'm not feeling very well.'

The result was surprisingly gratifying. 'You had better go home,' Mrs Moodie said, 'and don't come in tomorrow unless you feel better.'

Presented with a perfect means of escape, Marion had the sense to take advantage of it, and within minutes was walking through the back gate and round on to the drive. It had happened so quickly she had no time to make plans, but one thing she did know – she couldn't go home. Her stepmother would see she wasn't really ill, and would go on and on at her till she was trapped into saying something she shouldn't. If she owned up to the stealing, she would be hauled back to Oak Cottage to confess. The only thing she could do to avoid that was to go with just what

5

she was wearing, but the five sovereigns, now beginning to weigh on her conscience as well as on her hip, would be enough to pay her fare and buy some new clothes.

Squaring her shoulders, she flung her head back, and with her long copper-coloured hair streaming out behind her, she strode out as if she hadn't a care in the world. And neither she had, she assured herself, for she had burned her boats and there was no use worrying. As she walked past the cemetery, she remembered some boys at school telling her the spirits of the dead lurked near the gates to catch sinners and criminals, and even though it was only ten to eleven on a bright October morning, icy shivers ran down her spine and her heart seemed to be beating inside her mouth. Terrified, she pulled up her skirts and sprinted well past the danger area, until common sense told her she was being daft. Only bairns believed in ghosts. There were no such things, in the cemetery or anywhere else.

She slowed down a bit, but kept running because the track branching off to the left led down to the sawmill where her father worked and she wanted to get past as quickly as possible. She couldn't chance being seen by any of his workmates or their wives, though there wasn't much risk of that with all the trees in between the cottages and the road. In a valiant effort to bolster her conscience, she started to whistle – her poor dead mother used to say that whistling maidens and crowing hens weren't lucky, but it had never broken her of the habit – stopping only when she neared the first houses in the village proper. She didn't want to draw attention to herself in case any of her stepmother's cronies saw her. She had often moaned that the whole of Tipperton might as well be a burial ground for all the life there was in it, but today she was thankful that it was so.

Long before she came to the smiddy she could smell the smoke, and feel the heat of the almost molten metal, and hear the clang as the smith shaped another horseshoe. She used to watch him on her way home from school, fascinated by his skill yet shuddering at the thought of the agony the horses must suffer when he shod them, but this time she hurried quietly past.

Reaching the crossroads, she dithered over whether to turn left over the river in the hope of being picked up by a carter taking a load of vegetables to Aberdeen – she didn't know when the coach ran, and in any case, she could hardly stand about here where everybody would see her – or to turn right and make for the railway station. She would certainly be out of sight there, for it was well out of the village and she had often played there with the other bairns in the school holidays. The sight of a stranger getting off was a source of endless diversion and speculation for them.

It occurred to Marion that a train for Aberdeen came through about half-past eleven. She wouldn't have long to wait, and she had more than enough money to pay the rail fare, so she turned right.

She was on heckle-pins while she passed the shops, but strangely, there weren't many women about that morning, and nobody she knew. Then she remembered that it was Monday, washing day for most housewives – she couldn't have timed this better if she'd tried.

There was quite a commotion inside and outside the Mart, where farmers from miles around came to buy and sell beasts and grain, and to have a news with old friends, but she didn't recognize any of them and, in any case, they were all too busy to notice her. In another few hundred yards, she hurried past the tall, grim building which had a brass plate on its gate proclaiming it to be 'Tipperton Institution for the Aged, Destitute and Incurable', an awful grand name for what everybody in the place knew was really the poor's house, only steps away from the entrance to the station.

She was about to turn in, congratulating herself on getting there without being seen, when, coming towards her, she spied a sight familiar to the whole village: Mary McKay on her bicycle, her hat jammed down on her head, her skirts flapping about her legs. She was the very last person Marion wanted to see, a terrible gossip who kept everybody informed about everybody else's business except her own and, crossing her fingers, the girl prayed she would go past without stopping. No such luck!

'What are you doing up here at this time of day, Marion Cheyne?' Mary asked breathlessly, as she drew up alongside.

'Mrs Moodie sent me with a message to . . .' the girl cast about for a name that would sound plausible, '. . . to Miss Fraser up the moorie.'

The nurse noticed her hesitation but did not remark on it. 'I'll not waste your time, then, for she'll be expecting you back.'

Unaware that the woman had suspiciously moved into the lane to the poor's house from where she could check unseen whether she carried on along the road to the moor, Marion turned into the station with relief that nobody would know where she had gone. Tipperton being little more than a halt, there was only one railway employee. Dod Cooper was station master, issuer and collector of tickets, porter, signalman, post office sorter and general dogsbody . . . but not a nosy parker. He kept his tongue between his teeth, as the saying went, and Marion was sure that he wouldn't say anything to her father or anybody else about her presence at the station.

Glancing at the big clock on the back wall of the wooden shelter, she saw that she had still ten minutes to wait, and to pass the time and keep out of sight, she paid a visit to the WC, which reminded her to resurrect what was the sum total of her possessions . . . five gold pieces. Then she caught sight of her reflection in the mirror – her face white and strained, her hazel eyes wide and anxious, her coppery hair carfuffled from hauling off her big apron before she left Oak Cottage. She hadn't a comb, so the only thing she could do was to run her fingers through the tangles until they looked smooth. Thank goodness her hair was dead straight, and so easily tamed. Moistening a corner of her handkerchief with her tongue, she scrubbed her cheeks to bring some colour back into them, and was quite pleased with the result. Surely Dod Cooper wouldn't notice anything strange about her now.

Ten minutes later, after concocting a lie about why she had handed over a sovereign for a ticket that cost less than a shilling – she said one of her aunties had given it to her so she'd have something to spend when she went to Dundee to see her mother's other sister – Marion almost collapsed into a seat in an empty compartment. Not a soul knew where she was going . . . even Dod Cooper couldn't tell the bobbies if they started asking, for he thought she would buy another ticket in Aberdeen to take her to Dundee. She could hardly believe how easy it had been, right from the beginning, as if fate had guided her, encouraged her, and she hadn't strayed far off the straight and narrow when all was said and done. She had grasped at an opportunity, and who could blame her for that?

Her thoughts now ventured further ahead. She hadn't had the cash for very long, but it gave her a feeling of power, of not being at anybody's beck and call. It was a good feeling, and she wanted to be like this all her life. It wouldn't be easy to get a position where she would come in contact with the upper classes in Aberdeen, but she was prepared to work her way up until she landed amongst people with lots of money, and then . . . then she could marry a rich man and live in luxury until she died. Love didn't come into her scheme of things – though it would be nice if it did turn up somewhere along the way. Whatever, in future Marion Cheyne would make sure that her every action would be to her own advantage.

When Alfie Cheyne went home at midday, looking much older than his forty-one years after six hours' hard work at the mill, his wife, nudging thirty but with the hourglass figure of a twenty-year-old due to the tight lacing of her stays, was not her usual flirtatious self.

'That lassie o' yours has run off.'

His greying brows plummeted. 'Run off? Dinna speak daft, wumman! She's at the Moodies' where she's supposed to be . . . is she nae?'

'She left there this morning. She was goin' into the station this foreneen when Mary McKay saw her, an' she never come oot again, for Mary waited half an hour an' more, so she said. An' when she went up an' asked Dod Cooper, he hummed an' hawed then said she was awa' to Dundee. So I went an' asked Mrs Moodie if she kent onything about it, an' she said there was money missing.'

'But my Marion wouldna steal!' Alfie gasped.

'Well, Mr Moodie had left twelve sovereigns for his wife to pay for a new table an' chairs she was gettin' delivered, an' when the cart came from Aberdeen an' she went to pay the man, there was only seven left. Marion must have ta'en the other five, for there was naebody else there. Oh, she'd said she wasna feeling well, an' Mrs Moodie sent her hame, but she didna come back here.'

Her triumphant sneer annoyed Alfie. Why had she thrust this worry on him when all he wanted was to eat his dinner in peace and have a wee nap before he went back to work? He'd got precious little sleep at nights since he'd wed Moll. He'd thought he was the luckiest man on God's earth the first month or so, and told himself many a man would give his right arm to change places with him, but by Govie, you could get too much of a good thing.

'Have you nothing to say about her?' Moll demanded suddenly.

'What can I say?' he mumbled. 'If it was her that took that money, an' it looks like she must have . . .' He halted, rubbing his hand over his wiry beard. 'If it was just a shillin' or two, it wouldna be so bad, but five sovereigns! That's near what I get for a twelve-month slaving in the mill an' filling my lungs wi' sawdust.' Thinking that it might be as well to keep on his wife's good side – he might fare a lot worse if he got her dander up – he said quite decidedly, 'Well, a' I can say is good riddance to her!'

That made her beam with pleasure. 'It'll just be me an' you, noo, Alfie.'

He nodded. 'Aye, Moll, just you an' me.' And if she carried on the way she'd been doing, he thought morosely, he'd be a wizened old man before he was fifty, his manhood drained off him. Looking at it from the other side, though, she was a damned good-looking wench who knew how to please a man, and there were worse ways to end his days than taking full advantage of what was legally his.

'You'll be ready for your stovies now, then?'

She had almost purred the words, and Alfie's saliva was flowing as he watched her filling a bowl with creamy milk, heaping his plate and then sticking a quarter of oatcakes in the middle. This was the traditional way to eat this dish, the milk being necessary to wash down the dry triangle of oatcake and barely moist stoved potatoes. For dinners like this every day he would gladly put up with Moll's nightly appetite.

Something else struck him as he took a quick sip of milk to clear his gritty mouth. 'Are the Moodies going to report her to the bobby?' he asked, wiping his moustache and picking up his fork.

'She says he'll likely want to, but she's goin' to tell him it was his ain fault for leaving so much money where Marion could get her hands on it, an' ony young girl would have been tempted. Eat that up afore they're caul' now, for I've got a apple dumpling for after.'

When Marion came out of Aberdeen railway station, her ears were assaulted by the bustle and din, and her nose by

12

the strong smell of fish. Not that she didn't like fish – she got it once a week at home – but she wasn't accustomed to the stink of it all around her. Horses clopped over the granite setts, their carts piled high with wooden fish boxes leaking streams of brine on the road, or loaded with big beer barrels looking as though they would come toppling over at any minute. The leather-aproned carters whistled blithely, and mostly untunefully, as they flicked the reins to show their trusty steeds who was master.

Errand boys flashed past her on their bicycles as she stood gaping, the parcels in the baskets on their handle-bars wobbling precariously when they rounded the corner, bells shrilling in warning. The pedestrians must have been aware of the danger, but the women were more concerned with striving to hold their skirts down against the wind, which made Marion recall a rhyme one of the old men in Tipperton had taught her brother.

The devil sent the wind to blow the ladies' dresses
    high,
But God was just and sent the dust to blind the bad
    man's eye.

Eight-year-old Kenny had kept chanting it till their father had given him a good clout on the lug. Memories of Kenny made Marion think fully about what she had done. If she hadn't run off – if you could call going on a train running off – she could have gone back and returned the five sovereigns before anybody noticed they were gone, but it was too late now. She had left her home and would have to stay in this huge unfriendly city, and she had no idea of where to go or what to do, though it might be wise to get away from the horrible stink of fish.

She had noticed that most of the carts coming from her right were empty, while the ones going in the opposite direction were piled high, so it didn't take very much gumption to tell that the docks were to her left. To be certain, however, she went to the edge of the pavement and craned her neck leftwards. Yes, she could see an array of masts with their sails tied up, so there *were* ships there, loading or unloading.

She set off now away from them, turning a corner in seconds and going up a street of shops with houses above them, but even with money in her pocket, she resolutely kept her eyes away from the windows; she might need every penny before she got settled.

At the top of the hill, a black and white tiled sign on the wall of the last granite building told her this was Bridge Street, which didn't surprise her, though there was no water under the bridge she'd just crossed, only another road. The thoroughfare she had reached – it was the only way to describe it, it was so grand – was Union Street, according to the nameplate on the far side, and having heard of that before, she knew it was more or less the backbone of Aberdeen.

Curiosity overcoming all her other senses now, Marion turned right and wandered round several of the large shops, stores really, and it was very much later when, emerging from one absolute wonderland, she caught sight of a clock on a building some way ahead. Twenty-five past five! No wonder it was getting dark and her belly was rumbling. She'd had nothing to eat since breakfast time. She was considering going back to the last place she'd walked round, where she'd seen people sitting having meals at the tables, when it dawned on her that all the shops she could see were now emptying before the doors were closed for the day.

Disappointed, and hungry, she trudged on, Union Street changing to Castle Street and widening into a kind of large square, which soon narrowed again and became Justice Street. Halfway down here, wonder of wonders, she came across a pie shop, where several men in working clothes were waiting to be served. They were obviously buying things to eat somewhere else, and came out in ones and twos, each carrying so large a bundle that it looked as if they were preparing for a siege, but she went inside when one of them politely held the door open for her.

The short stout man behind the counter saw her perplexed expression. 'They're night shift at the gas works,' he informed her. 'If you want, you can sit down an' eat yours here,' he added kindly. 'You look worn oot.'

'I've been walking a lot,' she admitted, sinking down gratefully on one of the benches at the side. She was even more grateful when he set a plate down on the stained table in front of her, for there was a large mouth-watering pie on it, smothered in gravy and a big mound of juicy peas. There was also a big chunk of bread on the side for mopping up the last drops of moisture.

'Was you makin' for some place in partikler?' the man asked, having no one else to serve at that moment.

Dog-tired physically, Marion was as alert as ever mentally. 'I was supposed to be goin' to my auntie in

Bridge Street,' she fibbed, naming the first place that came to mind, 'but she wasna in. She musta forgot I was comin', so I've been shovin' in time till I was sure she'd have to be hame for my uncle's supper. But, if she hadna minded aboot me, she'd only be cookin' for the two o' them, and that's why I come in here.'

The man nodded, satisfied that she wasn't in any kind of trouble, but the entrance of more customers took his attention off her. When a quarter of an hour later, she stood up to leave, he said solicitously, 'You'll manage to find yer wey back to yer auntie?'

'I'll go back the wey I come,' Marion assured him, holding out a shilling because she didn't know how much he charged.

He waved it away. 'Na, na, lass, that's a' richt.'

'But I must pay for the pie.'

'My treat, m'dear. Us Aberdonians are nae as mean as folk mak' oot.'

'Well, thank you very much then.' It crossed her mind to ask if he needed any help in the shop, but he'd been so good to her already it wouldn't be right to take advantage of his good nature.

Of course, she did not go back the way she had come, but went on down Justice Street, then turned into Constitution Street, lined with an assortment of houses, big and small, but sadly she discovered in a few minutes that it took her down to the beach. It was much darker now, with just a scattering of tiny stars twinkling over the wide expanse of water. She'd heard more than one person in Tipperton saying that it didn't matter what kind of weather it was, or what time of day, when you went to Aberdeen beach you'd be sure to find other folk there, but *she* couldn't see a blessed soul!

October was long past the season when the well-off from Glasgow and Edinburgh took holidays, and who on earth would come here at the back end of the year if they didn't have to? Well, she was too tired to trail back to find a place to stay the night, but she'd have to have a rest. She'd feel better in the morning, more able to look for lodgings, and maybe a job, though she did have enough money to keep her going for a few weeks – months if she was careful.

She was lucky to find, a short way along the front, a three-sided brick erection, likely for the use of mothers or nannies to keep a watch on their children playing on the sands, which afforded some shelter although it was fully exposed to the icy night wind howling in across the North Sea from the Arctic. It was bitterly cold, but she was so exhausted that she did eventually fall into a deep sleep from which she was rudely awakened in a few short hours by the screaming of the gulls circling overhead, probably hoping she'd some scraps to give them.

'You're unlucky this time,' she shouted at them to scare them off. 'I haven't anything for myself to eat, so you'd better go and look somewhere else.'

Standing up was an almost impossible task. Her whole body felt as if it were frozen stiff, and once on her feet, she stood looking miserably around her. With the dawning of the day came the realization that she would never survive if she didn't find somewhere to live, and she didn't know how to do that. She'd made a dreadful mistake when she ran away from Tipperton, an even worse when she stole the money. Was this God's way of warning her that unless she went back and confessed to her crime, He would have to punish her? Deciding that it was better late than never to do the right thing, she still felt a great reluctance to move. Why didn't she just lie down again and let the elements finish her off?

But Marion was not a pessimist by nature, and it wasn't long before she shook off her despondency. Far better to face up to her sin than cause trouble by practically committing suicide on a deserted beach.

Nevertheless, by the time she had retraced her steps of the day before, her feet and legs still aching agonizingly, her spirits had taken another downward spiral. How could she face the Moodies again, after the banker's wife had been so kind to her? And what about her father? He'd never been a violent man, though he'd often given her brother a wallop when he misbehaved, so what if he lost his temper with her? What she had done was an awful lot worse than anything Kenny ever had.

To stop her imagining the leathering she would get, Marion came to a halt to find out where she was. Without noticing, she had got back to Union Street and, if her memory served her right, she wasn't far from the top of Bridge Street. Should she go home . . . or not? Still a child at heart, she gave herself a choice. If the next street she came to was Bridge Street, she'd go down to the station. If it wasn't, she wouldn't. That was fair, wasn't it? Surely God wouldn't argue with that?

Not sure whether to be pleased or not, she found that the next street was indeed Bridge Street and, resigned to her fate now, she turned down it, her steps determined. At the entrance to the station, however, she was assailed by sudden misgivings. She had told Dod Cooper at Tipperton that she was going to her auntie in Dundee, and maybe that's what she *should* do. Her mother's sister did live there, and it would be a lot easier to confess to Auntie Bella than to her father.

Unfortunately, after running down the steps and going to the ticket office, she was told that trains from there ran north only, and she'd have to go to the station at the other side of Guild Street to get a train to the south. She trailed back up to the street level, turning left as the ticket man had directed her, but – although it was only a matter of crossing the street and going along a wee bit – by the time she reached the LNER station, she was confused and completely demoralized once again.

After taking a few faltering steps, she came to a trembling halt with tears streaming down her cheeks and her hands over her ears to blot out the cacophony around her. She stood thus for at least five minutes, nobody taking any notice of her until a gentle hand on her shoulder made her look up into the concerned face of a young man in a flat black hat and a priest's flowing robe.

'Are you lost, my child?' he asked. 'Where do you want to go?'

Marion couldn't answer that. She *was* lost, but not in the sense that he meant. 'I've run away,' she whispered at last, compelled by his calling to tell him at least part of the truth. But not wanting him to be under any misapprehension, she added, 'I'm not a Catholic.'

'Priests help all God's creatures,' he smiled, 'even if they are not Roman Catholics. What is your religion, my dear?'

'I went to the parish church at hame.'

'Can't I persuade you to go home again?' At her tearful, mute shake of the head, he took her by the arm. 'If you have nowhere to stay, the Church of Scotland, like us, runs a place where young girls may have a bed for the night. Would you like me to show you where it is?'

They had just turned into Bridge Street when he said, 'I haven't asked your name yet. Mine is Father Bernard.'

Marion wished that hers was more in keeping with the life she wanted to lead, and with a feeling of destroying all bridges behind her, she said, 'My name's Mar . . . Marianne . . . Marianne Cheyne.' It wasn't such an awful lie. She had just changed one letter and added another two, but it sounded so much better. It was just a pity she hadn't thought of changing her last name as well.

'Would you be looking for work, Marianne?'

'I've been in service before.'

'I wasn't suggesting you go into service. I know some ladies who run a children's wear shop in Holburn Street, and they have been speaking of taking on a smart young girl to help them. Would you manage that?'

'I'm sure I could.'

'I shall take you there first.' Father Bernard took her across the street and up a long flight of stone steps. 'It's shorter this way than going by Union Street,' he smiled, as they made their breathless way to the top.

After passing a beautifully turreted granite building which she took to be a castle but which he told her was the main post office, he led her into a narrow street which eventually led them out on to Holburn Street, where the shop was.

While they walked, he told her a little about the ladies who ran it. 'There are three unmarried sisters, but

Miss Esther keeps house for Miss Emily and Miss Edith. They live in Strawberry Bank.'

'What a lovely name for a house!' Marianne exclaimed.

'Strawberry Bank is the name of the street,' he grinned. 'Miss Esther, the youngest, seems quite happy to be the homemaker. Miss Edith, the brains behind the business, is the eldest, and Miss Emily, the middle one, is the quietest. They are dear ladies, all three.'

The sign above the shop window read 'E. & E. Rennie, Children's Outfitters'. The two elderly ladies within raised their heads when the doorbell tinkled, their faces lighting up when they saw the priest. 'Father Bernard!' they chorused. 'How nice to see you.'

Marianne lost track of the order of events then, everything happened so quickly, but when she lay down that night in the attic room in the Rennies' cottage in Strawberry Bank, she had an assistant's job, she had two serviceable serge skirts and two plain blouses for work, and was also the proud possessor of a barathea skirt, and a cream silk blouse for Sundays . . . with a frill at the neck. These had been purchased for her by Miss Esther on Miss Edith's instructions after Marianne told them that she had run away from home without any clothes because her father's new wife made her life unbearable.

As the priest had said, they were dear ladies, all three. Miss Esther was inclined to twitter a bit, probably because she was on her own all day and was glad to have someone to talk to. She was plumper than the other two, the result of testing her cooking for seasoning, likely. Her rosy face was round, her full lips nearly always turned up in a smile.

Her white hair was often rather untidy, except on Sundays, she said, when Miss Edith put in her hairpins for her so that they would not fall out in church. Miss Esther could be classed as happy-go-lucky, Marianne decided.

Miss Emily was indeed the quiet one, listening to what her sisters said when she was at home, yet able to keep up lengthy conversations with customers in the shop, or maybe it just seemed that way and it was the customers who did most of the talking. Not only was she the middle of the three in age, she was also middle in height, about two inches taller than Miss Esther, who was barely five feet, but shorter than Miss Edith, who was about five feet six. Miss Emily, although she had a pleasant heart-shaped face, was inclined to be rather prim and occasionally showed her displeasure by gripping in her mouth if anyone made a remark which she considered not in the best of taste. She was slim, but not too thin, and particular about her appearance, her black dresses immaculate and the soft, silvery coil of hair on the crown of her head with never one strand out of place. Miss Emily was . . . well, daintily quiet was the only description for her.

Miss Edith had the strongest personality. She had a long face with clean-cut features and sharp blue eyes. Her hair, dragged back into a tight bun at the nape of her neck, was steel-grey, and her body was verging on the scraggy. Her words were clipped when she spoke, she gave the impression of being stern and forbidding at times, but Marianne soon got to know that it was just a veneer. Miss Edith was a sheep in wolves' clothing.

Marianne didn't feel that she had deceived the Rennies. They were pleased to have an assistant – they would have fitted her out with clothes for the shop anyway – and she would work hard to repay them. Best of all, she still had four pounds nineteen shillings plus a few coppers left of the five sovereigns. She had better hang on to that in case . . . well, just in case. But come what may, she wouldn't dream of stealing from her benefactors, or whatever the female version of that was.

She had been really lucky this time. God had given her a wee taste of what he could do to her if she ever stole again . . . but she wouldn't have to, would she? She'd been weak yesterday but she felt different now. She would work hard and make something of herself, do anything she had to, to make a success of her life – but she wouldn't do anything dishonest.

Chapter Two

Trade had been very brisk in the weeks leading up to Christmas, but the lull during the first three months of 1895 gave the Rennies and their assistant time to clean shelves and glass cases properly and arrange their replenished stocks to Miss Edith's satisfaction. It being found that Marianne had a penchant for setting out an eye-catching window display, she was allowed to carry out this important task at least once a week, more often if any of the items on show were removed and sold, which became a more regular occurrence as March came to an end and April brought sunshine along with its showers.

The shop was extremely busy on Saturdays, but as Marianne – this was how she always thought of herself now – decided one Saturday in early April, while she went to fetch another batch of white wool from the storeroom at the back, the premises were so tiny that even four customers filled the shop and six made it look crowded. There had been a steady stream all afternoon today, though those who had to wait to be served showed no impatience. In fact, the eyes of the young mothers or elderly grandmothers were usually caught by something other than what they had come to buy, which meant extra sales, and was it any wonder with the Rennie sisters being so obliging and polite, no matter what?

They darted about their little emporium like birds, from counter to shelves, or to drawers, or to stands, even to the window display, and didn't mind laying out dozens of items for someone to choose from, be they expensive christening robes (lovingly and beautifully stitched by Miss Esther), or the cheap woollen mittens and bootees knitted by Miss Emily in the evenings while Miss Edith wrote up the books.

Marianne could still scarcely believe her luck in being part of it. The Kennies had taken her completely under their collective wing; they had given her room and board as well as wages, and they were so clearly glad of the extra pair of hands in the shop that they never made her feel under any obligation to them. They had taught her by example how to deal patiently with members of the public bent on being difficult, although there were very few of them; how to remove – surreptitiously and with no change in gracious manner – sticky little fingers that were exploring the garments within their reach; how to suggest, without making it too obvious, that a pale green coat and hat set would suit ginger (this word was never mentioned, of course) hair much better than a bright scarlet.

It was all very exciting to Marianne, but the most exciting thing that had happened to her was meeting Andrew. When the three sisters had been in such a state of chirping nervousness about the nephew who was coming for Christmas dinner, she had known he was someone really special. Miss Esther had told her he was the son of their darling brother Edward, who had gone to live in Edinburgh many years before.

'Sadly,' she had continued, 'he died not long after his only child was born, and Annette, his wife, was so afraid that anything would happen to Andrew that she hardly let him out of her sight. We didn't see him at all when he was a child, but we met him at her funeral, and again . . . oh, it must have been last August, when he came to tell us he had been accepted for Aberdeen University and would be starting there at the beginning of October. He can't really have had time to settle down, yet he's coming to visit us already. He's a dear boy.'

Believing that anyone under fifty would be a boy to Miss Esther, Marianne had paid little heed to this, but Andrew had definitely been under fifty, more than thirty years under, and his clear grey eyes had lit up when they fell on her. Marianne, not long fifteen, had felt deeply flattered by the warmth of his smile when Miss Edith introduced them, and the strength of his handclasp had made her heart speed up in a fluttery manner for the very first time in her life.

Concentrating on every word spoken in case she missed any relevant information about him, she'd learned that he was eighteen, a first-year law student. By dint of an arch question asked by one of his aunts, Marianne had even got to know that as yet he had no lady-friend, and the knowing look exchanged by Miss Esther and Miss Emily had not escaped her; they were planning some matchmaking in a year or two, with her as the lucky girl.

Andrew had turned down his aunts' frequent invitations to Sunday tea by saying he hoped they would understand that he had to study every minute he could, but he did promise to take an afternoon and evening off at Easter, which was why, at five to one on the afternoon of Easter Sunday, Marianne was sitting decorously on the edge of the sofa so as to make a good impression. At the other end sat Miss Esther, strands of fluffy white already escaping from the chignon Miss Edith wanted her to adopt but which wouldn't stay pinned, her blue eyes expectant, cheeks flushed, hands fidgeting ever so slightly against the dark blue crepe of her Sunday dress. Still persisting in tasting what she cooked, Miss Esther's girth had gradually increased, and Marianne couldn't help thinking that she would soon be a proper roly-poly . . . though that was a bit unkind.

The other two sisters were occupying the armchairs by the fireside, consciously or not staking their claim as breadwinners to the best seats, but while Miss Emily – a faint wave at the front of her immaculate silver coiffure – nervously crossed and uncrossed her black-stockinged legs under cover of her skirt, Miss Edith appeared to be in perfect control of her emotions. She had hidden the deep hollow at her neck with a stand-up collar, but she could do nothing to camouflage the hollows in her cheeks, which made her long narrow nose appear even longer and more pointed. Children with vivid imaginations would see her as a witch, Marianne reflected, especially in that black bombazine dress which did nothing for her. It fell straight from shoulder to hips, her bust, if she had one, lost under heavy tucks of material.

A barely discernible tic at her jawline, however, showed that she was not as composed as she looked, and Marianne couldn't help but pity all three sisters. The nervousness, the preparations for the elaborate meal and the production of best china and tablecloth, and all because there would be an unaccustomed male presence in the house – a young man who likely had to eat off unmatched china in his room at the varsity. Still, as he had proved the last time he was here, Andrew Rennie was a perfect gentleman who wouldn't spoil his aunts' pleasure by telling them so.

He arrived at one o'clock exactly, making Marianne suspect that he had waited outside so as not to be early. That was the kind of boy he was, she mused, wondering if gaining his degree and then training to become a solicitor would make him rich enough for her to consider as a future husband. She liked the way his brown hair waved at the front, and his neat, rather gingery moustache; she loved his grey eyes and the strong lines of his face. He was a good bit taller than she was, at least seven inches more than her five feet three, and very handsome. She wouldn't mind marrying him . . . but she wasn't going to jump at the first boy she met. There was plenty of time yet, and who knew, she might come across somebody with more money than Andrew could ever earn. In any case, once he was soliciting, or whatever solicitors did, he wouldn't want to tie himself to a country quine with little education.

During lunch, he told his aunts about life in Marischal College and Marianne found herself transported to a magic world of books, of lectures, of theses demanded on time by grim-faced professors. Then his expression lightened, and he made them laugh about the tricks his fellow students got up to, especially how they got the prescribed work done and still had time to go out and enjoy themselves. 'They take it in turns to do the research and revision, and then they all make copies with slight variations.'

'Oh, Andrew!' exclaimed Miss Edith. 'I hope you do not take part in those deceptions?'

'No, Aunt Edith,' he assured her. 'I appreciate my good fortune in being given the chance to make something of myself, although I have a struggle to get through the work in time.'

'I am glad to hear that you behave honourably.'

It was Miss Esther who said, when they were clearing the table, 'It is too nice a day for young people to be cooped up inside. Why don't you take Marianne for a walk, Andrew?'

He jumped to his feet eagerly. 'I would love to, Aunt Esther, but perhaps she does not care much for walking?'

The girl stood up quickly. 'I do, I love it.'

'She is only fifteen, remember,' Miss Edith cautioned him. 'Do you think it seemly to . . . ?'

'Seemly my foot!' exclaimed Miss Esther. 'Her head is screwed on the right way, and Andrew knows how to behave. I am not suggesting he takes her to the Tivoli, or anything like that.'

It was the first time Marianne had heard any of the sisters arguing and she hoped that they wouldn't end up fighting, but Andrew led her outside before anything else was said. 'Don't take it to heart,' he smiled. 'I do not think their disagreement will last long.'

'I dinna like the idea of them quarrelling over me,' she murmured.

'They're not really quarrelling, and what would you rather do? Go back and sit with them, or walk along the Dee with me?'

'That's nae fair,' she smiled. 'You ken fine I'd rather walk with you, wherever you take me.'

'We might meet some of my fellow students. Quite a few take their lady-friends that way, as well.'

Marianne wondered if he realized what he had said. Did he really want her to be his lady-friend? Or did he mean lady friend, which wasn't the same at all? She didn't ask; the thought of meeting other boys, whether alone or accompanied by lady-friends, was too exciting to jeopardize.

There were indeed several couples promenading when they reached the path which ran along the riverbank, but no one Andrew knew. 'I hope you won't be bored with just my company,' he smiled, after they had been ambling along for about fifteen minutes. 'I'm often accused of being a dull old stick.'

'Oh, you're nae dull,' she protested automatically.

'It's what comes of not knowing any girls, and I get the feeling you haven't known any boys, so we can learn together . . . if you like?'

'Learn what together?'

He laughed at her wary expression. 'Nothing bad. Just the art of making conversation with the opposite sex.'

Relieved that this was all he had in mind, she said, 'I didna ken there was an art to that.'

'There's an art to everything, Marianne, and it would help us to find out more about each other.'

She had no intention of telling him anything about herself, other than giving him the 'cruel stepmother' reason for her leaving home, but as time passed, with him confiding that he hoped to set up a law firm of his own eventually, she let it slip that she wanted to marry someone rich. As soon as she said it, she wished that she hadn't.

'I suppose you think I'm awful?'

He took her hand and stroked it gently. 'Not at all, my dear. It is probably every girl's dream to marry money, but the majority never do. They fall in love with a boy who hasn't a penny to his name, and live in a poky little house, and raise a large family on next to nothing. . .'

'. . . and they end up hating each other,' she burst out. 'I've seen it happening time and again at hame.'

'It doesn't always happen like that. Didn't your parents keep on loving each other until your mother died?'

She considered briefly. 'I never heard her saying she loved him, but I suppose she must have, deep down, and he was that cut up when she died I was sure he loved her.' After a pause, she added, somewhat bitterly, 'But it didna take him long to find another wife.'

His grasp tightened. 'It's different for men. Most women can face years and years of widowhood, but a man needs someone . . . to care for him, to look after his children . . . to satisfy his needs. Do you know what I mean, Marianne?'

She coloured and snatched her hand away, her outrage making her speak in the dialect she had been doing her best to forget. 'Aye, I ken, and I'm sure decent men dinna speak to young girls about things like that.'

'I'm sorry. I told you I had never had anything to do with girls. I was only trying to save you pinning your hopes on a dream which may never materialize, but I'm beginning to suspect that you are one of those people who will succeed in everything you set out to do. I will not, however, cast it up if you do marry a poor man.'

31

They said nothing for some time, and she found it very pleasant to be walking so close to him, the gentle sound of water lapping against the bank disturbed occasionally by the screech of the swans sailing majestically a little farther upstream. If he wanted her to be his lady-friend . . .

'Well, well! Rennie, you secretive old dog!'

The strident voice startled them both, their heads swivelling to see who was talking. A broad young man in grey breeches, and with a peaked cap set on his head at an absurd angle, had come up behind them.

'Oh, it's you,' Andrew said unenthusiastically.

'Won't you introduce me to your paramour?' Without waiting, the other man turned to Marianne with his hand outstretched. 'My name is Douglas Martin, and this . . . is Vi . . . um . . .' He looked enquiringly at his companion with a barely suppressed lewd giggle.

'Vi Collie,' she supplied, rolling her eyes sideways.

Shaking the proffered hands one after the other, Marianne murmured, 'Pleased to meet you.' There was something about Douglas Martin she didn't like, but since he seemed to be Andrew's friend, she would do her best to be polite to him . . . and the common-looking girl clinging to his arm like a sticky-willow. It dawned on her that Andrew hadn't introduced her to them, and she hoped he wasn't ashamed of her.

Catching her accusing eye, he looked at the other man and said, very coldly, 'This is Marianne Cheyne. She works in my aunts' shop.'

The underlying message was received and acted upon. 'Ah . . . yes . . .' Douglas mumbled, moving away. 'We'd better be getting on, eh, Vi?'

When the ill-matched pair were out of earshot, Marianne asked, 'Why did he go off so suddenly? Did he not want to speak to a girl who works in a shop? That Vi looked as if she . . .'

Andrew laughed at her confusion. 'Yes, Martin is a snob of the highest degree, yet it wouldn't surprise me in the least if he had spent most of last night with her.'

She was shocked. 'Do students do that sort of thing? Have you?'

'Have I been with a lady of the streets? Not yet, but I sometimes feel I should, just once, to see . . . to learn . . . the ropes.'

They both laughed, he self-consciously, she in embarrassment, and they turned to maske their way back to Strawberry Bank.

At his Aunt Esther's behest, Andrew's visits became weekly once his preliminary examinations were past, and throughout the summer, he and Marianne went out walking every Sunday afternoon if the weather was suitable. Sometimes, they met other students who stopped and were introduced to Marianne, who was pleased that they seemed as decent and polite as Andrew was. In fact, she was quite attracted to one in particular, and when they happened to run into Stephen Grant too many times to be coincidental, Andrew didn't seem to mind. 'You've made a conquest,' he teased, making her blush.

Nevertheless, it was well into September before this was proved to be true. As Marianne waited for Miss Edith to lock up the shop one night, with Miss Emily fussing silently round her sister as usual, she was astonished to see the lean six-footer standing in the next doorway. When he came forward, she said timidly, 'Miss Edith, Miss Emily, this is Andrew's friend Stephen Grant.'

'You are his aunts, I believe,' he smiled, showing a dimple in each cheek. 'I hope you don't mind if I ask your permission to take Marianne out one evening? Andrew will vouch that I do not drink, and I have no other vices which would blacken me in your eyes.'

Marianne held her breath, but she need not have worried. Both sisters were bowled over by his boyish charm, and Miss Edith, the decision-maker, was beaming as she said, 'We have no objection to you taking Marianne out for a short walk occasionally, Mr Grant, as long as you do not keep her out late. You may call for her at half-past seven tomorrow night.'

Taking this correctly as a dismissal, Stephen gave a small bow, cast a delighted glance at Marianne and walked away. Before she had time to make up her mind whether to be pleased at his dexterity in dealing with the elderly ladies or offended that he hadn't asked her first, Miss Edith said, 'He seems a very agreeable young man. I take it you like him, Marianne?'

'I don't know him very well, but I've nothing against him.'

'I don't know what Andrew's going to say about this,' Miss Emily put in. 'I thought he and Marianne –'

Miss Edith tutted impatiently. 'She is too young to be serious about any one boy – it will do her good to get to know others. She can come to no harm as long as we vet her escorts.'

Too young – as Miss Edith had said – to appreciate what could happen to her, or to have any deep romantic thoughts about either Stephen or Andrew, Marianne slept soundly that night, and did not feel at all nervous about the assignation until about five minutes before Stephen was due.

When the expected knock came, Miss Edith motioned her to stay where she was and went to the door herself. 'Ah, good evening, Mr Grant. You must come in and meet my youngest sister, and then we will hinder you no longer.'

'They all like you,' Marianne told him a few minutes later, as they walked away from Strawberry Bank. 'You made a good impression on them.'

'Your aunts are dear old souls,' he smiled.

She didn't correct him. What difference did it make if he'd made a wrong assumption? 'Have you seen Andrew today?' she asked.

Blushing, Stephen looked squarely at her. 'I made a point of seeing him. I didn't want him to think I was keeping our meeting a secret.'

'What did he say?' she asked conversationally, although she wasn't really interested in what Andrew had said. It had nothing to do with him who she went out with.

'He said he was glad someone else was taking an interest in you.'

This put a different slant on things. How dare Andrew palm her off like that? Had he another girl in mind for himself? She couldn't let Stephen see that she was angry, however. It wasn't his fault.

They kept on walking and talking, her anger faded, and the more she was in his company, the more she came to like him. When he told her that his father was one of the top surgeons at the Infirmary and his mother had been a Drummond of Drumtocher, she could tell that he wasn't just trying to impress her.

'Are your parents still alive?' he asked her then.

The abrupt question took her by surprise. If she told the truth, he would want to know where her father lived and what he worked at, and she couldn't tell him about the ramshackle house where she had been born and brought up, the sawdust from the mill lying thick over the bits of furniture her mother had dusted lovingly several times a day until her lungs had been contaminated. 'They both. . . died,' she said presently. 'That's why I had to come to Aberdeen.'

'Where did you live before that?'

'We'd a lovely big house in its own grounds.' For a moment, she felt sick at the lies she was concocting, but she had started now and it was quite good fun really. Carried away by her imagination, she went on, forgetting to be careful with her speech, 'It had oak trees a' roon' it, an' it had six lums an' a orchard at the back, an'. . .' Her inventiveness giving out, she looked guiltily round into Stephen's face.

Fortunately, he thought he understood the reason for her sudden stop. 'I'm sorry, I shouldn't have made you speak about it. I can see you still haven't got over losing your parents and your home.'

She dropped her eyes in a suitably overcome way, and they walked on for a time without saying anything. They were in Albyn Place, where each house was a veritable palace to Marianne, when Stephen observed, 'D'you see this house we're just coming to? That's where I live.'

She was shocked. He couldn't live in a place like this? It was huge! There were dozens of lums, and turrets at the corners, with tiny leaded windows which wouldn't let in much light but were real quaint; there was a curved drive up to the entrance; it was too big to be called a door. Before she had time to absorb any more details, they had passed the vantage point and her view was obscured.

'That's funny-looking trees,' she observed, never having seen anything like them, their feathery branches sweeping down to the ground.

'I can't remember the Latin name for them,' Stephen smiled, 'but most people call them monkey puzzles. I hope you don't think I took you this way to boast about my home, it was just that it's a pleasant way to get out of town – right out Queen's Road.'

Queen's Road being a continuation of Albyn Place, she had to agree with that. All the houses they passed before they came to the open countryside were every bit as grand as the Grants', and all built from the silver granite taken out of Rubislaw Quarry, so Stephen told her when he took her up the grassy bank to show her the vast, gaping hole. It was so deep that her legs started trembling and she felt a sickness deep in her stomach, and she was extremely grateful that he didn't make her stand so near the edge for long.

They had been walking for almost an hour when he asked, 'Do you want to sit on this dyke for a minute?'

She shook her head. 'I'd like a wee seat to rest my feet, but I'd best be getting back.'

'Yes, if you're late, your aunts might not let you come out with me again, and we can't have that.'

Until then, Stephen had been doing most of the talking, mainly about his fellow students and their squabbles, and had told her how disappointed he had been at not getting into Oxford, which had made her realize the vast difference between them, and when he asked which kind of books she read, she was too ashamed to confess that she couldn't read very well.

'What kind of books do you like?' she countered, hedging.

He shrugged wryly. 'I used to like Sheridan and I quite liked Oscar Wilde's stuff, but I don't get time to read anything these days except law books . . . so dry they turn your brain to sawdust.' Then he laughed. 'I expect you're like my mother. She loves novels – romances and tragedies, you know. She cried all the way through Mrs Wood's *East Lynne*.'

'So did I, and I love romances, and all.' Marianne hadn't read any novels, romantic or otherwise, but if Stephen's mother loved them . . .

'How old are you, Marianne? I didn't think of asking before.'

'I'll be sixteen next month.' His involuntary gasp, 'God, you're only a baby,' made her ask, 'How aul' are you?'

'I was twenty-one in July.'

From then on, Marianne could sense a difference in him, and tried to think what had caused it. Did he think she was too young for him? Or had he seen through her attempt to sound well read?

At her door in Strawberry Bank, he remarked, very correctly and not at all convincingly, 'Thank you for walking with me, Marianne, I have enjoyed your company, and no doubt I shall see you again some time. Good night.'

She managed to hide her disappointment that he so clearly didn't want to take her out again. 'Good night, Stephen.' She had to force her legs to move as she went into the house, only to find that her ordeal was just beginning, because the sisters were waiting eagerly to hear how she and Stephen had got on together. Too vain to say something had gone wrong, she told them about the first half of the evening, letting them believe that things had been the same on the way home, and, urged to tell them as much about his house as she could, she embellished her description until they were satisfied and she was free to go to bed.

Miss Esther and Miss Emily retired to their room happy that their young friend had enjoyed her entire evening, but Miss Edith, sharper and more observant, had a feeling that this was not the case. Sorry for the girl, she kept her suspicions to herself.

Marianne felt reluctant to go out with Andrew the following Sunday, but once away from the house, and sure that he would be sympathetic, she asked him if Stephen Grant had said anything to him about her.

'He didn't say anything about anything. Why? Didn't you get on together?'

'We did at first, then . . . oh, I dinna ken what happened. I couldna tell him the names of any books because I've never read any, and then he asked how old I was, and after that, he hardly spoke.'

Andrew pursed his mouth for a moment. 'Would you like me to tell you the novels my mother used to read?'

'Would you, Andrew? I hated having to read books when I was at the school, but I might enjoy novels with good stories. Another thing, though – maybe he didna . . . didn't like the way I speak.'

'You have a very broad country accent,' Andrew smiled, 'but that's nothing to be ashamed of.'

'I hear myself broader than folk in the town, and I dinna ken any big words. And when I get mixed up, it gets worse. Could you help me with that, and all?'

'You want me to prepare you to be a lady, is that what you mean?'

'If I do find a rich husband, I wouldn't want to let him down by not speaking proper.'

'If he loved you, he wouldn't care how you talked.'

She shook her head. 'Like I told you before, I'm not interested in love. Will you help me, Andrew?'

'All right, I'll give you lessons in speech and deportment, so that you will be able to hold your head up in any company. I'll make you read certain books in set times, and I'll give you others to help you to improve your vocabulary. But once we start, young lady, we'll go on until I'm satisfied with you, so there must be no complaining.'

'I won't complain, Andrew, and I'm really grateful. I'll show that Stephen Grant I'm as good as him . . . and his mother.'

'Ah, so you're doing it for him, are you? Well, I can promise you that when we are finished, you can set your sights much higher than Stephen Grant.'

Her eyes were dancing, her face agog with enthusiasm for what she hoped to accomplish. 'I'll maybe end up among royalty,' she giggled, her expression sobering when she saw how Andrew was looking at her.

'I'd prefer if you stayed just the way you are right now,' he said softly.

Chapter Three

At first, Marianne's eagerness to improve herself had amused Andrew, but, looking back, he was amazed by her quick assimilation of all he had taught her over the past year. He had given her a list of books he thought would appeal to her as well as add to her vocabulary, and by the middle of 1896, there was a marked improvement in her self-confidence, especially when she was introduced to his friends. What bothered him was that they obviously liked talking with her and lingered on while he wished them at the other end of the earth. But he could not tell her so. She clearly didn't feel the same way about him as he did about her.

Another summer coming to an end, the weather turned progressively colder. Sunshine gave way to winds and showers, then to mists and rain and then to sleet and snow . . . accompanied by gales. The young people did not forego their afternoon walks unless the weather was too bad, but come Marianne's third November in Aberdeen, they were more often inside than out. This put a temporary end to the lessons, but Marianne surprised the sisters by her newly acquired ability to enter into discussions on current affairs. As Miss Edith observed, 'Andrew has worked wonders. Except when she is under stress, Marianne has practically lost her country accent, and she can carry herself quite gracefully. And she has grown since she came here; she is almost as tall as he is now.'

'I think they're a perfect couple,' Miss Esther beamed, 'just made for each other.'

'No, no,' cautioned Miss Emily. 'I think that our Maid Marianne is looking for someone with better prospects than Andrew.'

Very much out of character, Miss Edith gave a long sigh. 'Can't you see that he already loves her? I am afraid she will break his heart, not deliberately, but he will be hurt, nevertheless.'

Sighing too, Miss Esther murmured hopefully, 'She is young yet. By the time she is old enough for marriage . . .' The return of the young people at that moment put an end to their conjecturing.

It soon became noticeable, to Marianne herself as well as to her benefactresses, that her relationship with Andrew had changed; although they were still just friends, a new element had crept in of his wanting to touch her, to brush hands or shoulders, to sit closer to her on the sofa, which made Miss Esther nod happily.

Marianne herself did not know how she felt about it. While she liked the way that she sometimes caught Andrew looking at her, his eyes soft with admiration . . . or more? . . . it made her uneasy. She had now made the acquaintance of several of the students who were at Marischal College with him, and she was hoping that one of them would ask her out so that she could make some comparisons. She did wonder how Andrew would take it, but surely he'd want her to enjoy herself? A few hours of innocent pleasure – what would be wrong with that?

Andrew sprung his surprise as soon as he arrived on the first Sunday in December. 'There's a Hogmanay Ball being laid on for the Law Faculty,' he announced, his eyes going round the four smiling faces. 'I want to go, but . . . I need a partner.'

'Take Marianne,' beamed Miss Esther. 'She won't have to worry about a ballgown, because there's plenty of time for me to – '

'I can't let you make one for me!' the girl gasped, scarlet-faced.

Miss Edith, the decision-maker, stepped in. 'That is not the point in question, Marianne. Do you really want to go, or do you feel that you had better go for the sake of appearance, since most of Andrew's friends will have seen him out walking with you?'

'I want to go,' Marianne cried, 'but it'll be an awful lot of work for you and such an expense . . .'

Miss Esther stood up. 'I was not meaning to make a dress. I am sure one of the old gowns in the trunk in our cellar would fit without too much alteration. Emily, will you come down with me to hold the candle while I look?'

After her sisters left the room, Miss Edith got to her feet. 'I may as well go with them. I would quite like to see our gowns again. Mamma had them made for our one and only ball, but . . .' She shrugged this off as though she did not regret it, but her wry smile and rather sad eyes told a different story.

'Your one and only ball?' echoed Marianne. 'Why was that?'

'Father did not approve of dancing, but he was away at the time when Lavinia Tennant – Father Bernard's mother, you know – invited us to her twenty-first birthday ball, so Mamma let us accept. She said we would never meet any young men otherwise, but when Father came home and found out, he locked the gowns up in his old trunk, and took it down to the cellar. Then Mamma died, and . . . well, we didn't feel like dancing after that, and by the time Father passed on, we were all past marrying age.' Miss Edith dashed away the solitary tear that had edged over her bottom eyelid as she closed the door behind her.

'I don't think I'd better go to the ball with you, Andrew,' Marianne whispered. 'It would likely upset them to see me wearing . . .'

He came towards her, eyes wide and pleading. 'Please, Marianne? I can't go unaccompanied. Please?'

A flash of irritation made her say, 'You just want me to come with you because you can't find another partner, that's all! Why don't you ask that Vi, or one of the other ladies of the street? You told me once you wanted to – '

He stepped back like a wounded animal and lashed out in the only way he knew how. 'Maybe I will.'

'Go ahead, then, and see if I care!'

'Oh, how stupid I've been, thinking you . . . liked me a little bit.'

Her conscience smote her. 'I do like you, Andrew! Quite a lot! But I don't want to bring back bad memories to your aunts, they've been so good to me. Can't you understand that?'

'Yes, of course I do, and I'm sorry. All right, if you think even one of them will be upset if you wear her dress, I won't try to make you change your mind.'

They left it at that, and he sat down to await his aunts' return.

The elderly ladies, whispering excitedly, came in with their arms empty and explained that they had taken the dresses up to Marianne's room. 'You can try them on when you go to bed,' Miss Edith told her.

Andrew smiled broadly. 'I get the impression you don't want me to see them.'

'Of course we don't, not yet!' declared Miss Esther, who was now harbouring secret dreams of him taking one look at the girl in her chosen gown and being so overcome by love that he would gather her into his arms and shower her with kisses in front of them all.

Pretending to be offended, he got to his feet. 'I suppose I'd better get out of the way.'

'You don't need to leave yet,' Marianne protested, although she was desperate to see the gowns.

'I have a lot of revision to do for the end-of-term assessments,' he assured her. 'I wasn't intending to stay anyway.'

As she had been doing for some weeks, she saw him to the door, but tonight, instead of his usual joking farewell gesture of tipping his forelock, he took her hand in both of his. 'Choose the dress you want, Marianne, and don't worry about the aunts. They're not as vulnerable as they look; they're really tough old birds.'

'I still wouldn't want to hurt them,' she said gently. 'You wouldn't be angry if I didn't go with you, would you?'

'I wouldn't be angry,' he said softly, 'I'd be broken-hearted.'

His eyes held the same strange look she had noticed briefly before; a serious look that she couldn't have described if anyone had asked her; a look which, combined with the squeezing of her hand, had made her heart speed up, her stomach turn over with a pain that wasn't a pain, the kind of feeling she welcomed and wished would never go away. Hoping that he was about to kiss her on the mouth, she was disappointed when he raised her hands to his lips. 'Good night, my dear Marianne,' he murmured.

'Good night, Andrew.' She closed the door and leaned against it. She couldn't be falling in love with him? She couldn't be! She certainly hadn't counted on anything like that! The rich man of her dreams still hadn't materialized . . . but he would!

When she went back to the parlour, Miss Esther said, 'Shall we go to your room now?' and at Marianne's nod, they all trooped upstairs.

When she saw the array of shimmering loveliness spread across her bed, she gasped with awe and glanced helplessly from one to the other of the elderly ladies. 'I'll never be able to choose one.'

'We will leave you to try them on,' Miss Edith said, in the brisk manner she used in the shop, pushing her sisters towards the door.

'Yes, take your time, dear,' Miss Esther smiled. 'Move around and see how you feel in them. Nothing is worse than spending a whole evening in something uncomfortable.'

Miss Emily nodded. 'When you've picked the one you feel happiest with, Esther will do any alterations it needs.'

Ignoring the smell of camphor emanating from the gowns, Marianne tried to judge, while she tried them on in an imaginative euphoria, which suited her best. First, she wriggled into Esther's soft peach – tulle underlined with stiff taffeta – with layers of ruffles looped round the hem of the huge skirt, and so narrow in the waist that she would have to be laced in very tightly before the buttons down the back would fasten; Miss Esther must have been much slimmer when she was young. Holding the back together as she twirled in front of the long cheval mirror, she gasped at the way the yards and yards of material moulded into her body instead of looking bulky as she had believed they would. She had never given a thought to her figure before, but her curvacious reflection elated her – this was the one!

In case Miss Esther's sisters would be offended, she decided to try on theirs too, and so, lifting the deep rose which had been Miss Emily's, she slipped it over her head and turned back to the mirror. It was not a girl she saw this time, but a tall, elegant woman, the décolletage displaying every inch of her neck and shoulders . . . and most of her bosom. The front of the skirt flowed to the floor, but the back was padded out by a bustle, not big, but enough to be a talking point these days. She considered for a short time and came to the conclusion that she didn't have the nerve – nor the figure, if it came to that – to wear this gown. Maybe when she was older . . . ?

The ice-blue creation that was Miss Edith's seemed at first glance to be too cold a colour, not what Marion had thought would appeal to her, but as soon as she put it on and pirouetted to get an idea of how it looked from behind, she knew that *this* really was the one. There was just a shadow of cleavage showing at the bust, much more demure, though the bodice was constructed so as to make the most of small breasts. From the waist, which was not quite so small as the peach, the skirt billowed out over a wide crinoline. It was . . . oh, perfect didn't do it justice, but it was the best word she could come up with.

A quiet tap at her door made her call, 'Come in.'

Miss Edith opened the door and asked, 'Have you decided yet? Please don't laugh at my haste, but I had to find out.'

'I'm not laughing. They're all lovely, but I'm going for yours.' Although Marianne had told Andrew she would give up the idea of going to the ball if any of his aunts seemed distressed, she knew now that she wasn't so self-sacrificing. Whatever happened, she would be there as his partner.

Miss Edith, however, did not appear at all distressed. 'Do you not think it too old-fashioned?' she asked, as she began to fasten the tiny cloth buttons. 'Crinolines of this size were going out even when I wore it, and that's . . . great heavens, almost forty years ago!'

Marianne shook her head. 'I don't care how old-fashioned it is!'

'It certainly suits you . . . much better than it did me.' Miss Edith said nothing more until she had done up the whole twenty-four, then she stepped back to get a better view. 'You look exactly like one of the illustrations in a fairy-tale book we once had.'

She called for her sisters to come and see, and when they ran in, Miss Esther clapped her hands in delight. 'Oh, Marianne! You're like the fairy in –'

'I've told her,' Miss Edith said drily, but smiled just the same.

'I hope nobody's offended because I've chosen this one,' Marianne murmured. 'I couldn't make up my mind when

I saw them first, but this one fits me best. It won't need any alterations.'

Miss Emily gave a long deep sigh. 'Seeing you standing there like a graceful swan . . . it takes me back –'

Not wanting any of them to become nostalgic, Marianne interrupted, 'I can't get over what a difference a dress can make.'

'People used to say, "Manners maketh man",' Miss Esther smiled, 'but our mamma always added, ". . . and the proper clothes maketh woman."

'I can't get over Father taking the trouble to put camphor in the trunk when he packed these away,' Emily observed. 'I was afraid they would be moth-eaten, but they look as good as new. We shall have to give them a good airing to get rid of the smell of the mothballs, and we should hang them in a closet so that Marianne can have the use of any of them any time she wants. Andrew will probably take her to other balls.'

'That's true,' Miss Esther beamed. 'Oh, this is all so romantic.'

Edith brought their matchmaking to a halt. 'If not Andrew, someone else. We must not rush the girl into anything, and I think she wants to get to bed now.'

She helped Marianne out of the blue gown while her sisters went out with theirs over their arms. Crossing to the door carrying hers, she said, gently, 'Those two have made up their minds that you and Andrew are right for each other, and I have the feeling that he would agree, but you must not marry him just to please us, or because you feel you owe us something. Think of your own happiness, my dear.'

'Thank you for understanding, Miss Edith.' Marianne sat down on the bed when the door clicked. In spite of being so tired, and so excited, she had to think. She liked Andrew, was possibly on the verge of loving him, but she wanted more than that. She wanted wealth, a standing in society. She wanted to be the wife of a man with power, a man other people looked up to and admired. Andrew would never fit that bill: he was too honest, too considerate of his fellow men and women. He might be successful as a solicitor, but he would never make a name for himself at that or anything else.

Feeling suddenly chilly in her undergarments, she stood up to change into her nightie, then got into bed and snuggled down. In her last thoughts before sleep claimed her, she pictured her spectacular entry to the ballroom on Andrew's arm in the magnificent ice-blue gown, imagined all eyes turning to watch her progress into the room, conjured up dozens of handsome, eligible bachelors begging her to dance, gold cravat pins gleaming a few inches above the chains of their gold pocket watches.

Drifting off into slumber, her dreams followed the same pattern, and strangely, in the morning she could remember them distinctly.

When she was thirteen, there had been a special celebration put on in Tipperton for some occasion now forgotten, and her mother had allowed her to stay to watch the dancing after the concert. Marianne had been enthralled by the energetic Lancers and in her dreams had seen herself performing the intricate steps with this stranger or that, their eyes telling how much they were attracted to her, her crinoline floating out around her. Each time the music had come to an end, her partner – a new one every time – had taken her to another room on the pretext of finding her a comfortable seat. Then her supple body had been pressed against a manly chest, firm hands going round her waist, but each time she'd looked up to smile at a hopefully prospective suitor, it had been Andrew's face she'd seen, his lips within a fraction of hers.

During breakfast, she assured herself that he'd been the one she'd seen because he was the only man she knew for certain would be there. He was too shy to kiss her; it was more likely to be Stephen Grant or any one of the men she had been introduced to over the past year and a half.

It could even be the boy – the rich man – who was to be her future husband. She didn't have a picture of him in her mind; she didn't care what he looked like . . . as long as he was taller than she was. She was five feet seven already and maybe hadn't stopped growing, so he might need to be over six feet.

Tall and wealthy? Surely that wasn't expecting too much? He didn't need to be handsome.

Chapter Four

In order to be seen at her best, on the evening of the ball Marianne waited until Miss Esther, chirping delightedly, had taken Andrew inside before she came slowly down the stairs. His stunned expression, the admiration which sprang to his eyes, more than compensated for the awkwardness of holding up a crinoline so that she wouldn't fall over it, but the shocked faces of his aunts told her that her petticoats were showing. Well, it was better to be a little immodest, she thought, in some irritation, than to pitch headlong down the stairs and display a much more intimate garment.

Miss Esther sidled up to her before she reached the floor. 'Let me remove the hoop,' she whispered. 'I had quite forgotten that Edith had trouble with it. All I have to do is snip the holding stitches, so it will not take long.'

'No,' Marianne whispered back, 'I want it left in. It's a talking point, isn't it? No one else'll have one.'

'That is true. Well, if you are sure.'

Miss Esther helped her down the last two steps, where Miss Edith flung a hooded cloak round her shoulders, and before Andrew led her out, all three sisters kissed her on the cheek. She needed Andrew's assistance to negotiate the high step of the cab he had waiting, but once up, she had the presence of mind to lift the back of the hoop before she sat down, albeit rather gingerly.

When Marianne finally walked majestically into the Mitchell Hall on Andrew's arm, her reception was all that she had hoped for . . . at first. All eyes turned to her, and those of each young man brightened at the sight of her fairy-tale loveliness. Savouring this, it took her a few minutes to realize that the girls – there as partners to the law students – were whispering to each other, and giggling as they pointed at her. One of them – all skin and bone in a hobble-skirted gown – didn't bother to lower her voice. 'Doesn't she know these things have been out of fashion for decades? My grandmother speaks about wearing them when *she* was a girl, for goodness' sake.'

This raised a laugh from the girls standing nearest to her, until they caught sight of Andrew's scowl. 'I think I should take you home,' he said loudly to Marianne. 'I don't want you mixing with these ill-mannered people.'

Sick at heart, but determined not to show it, she shook off the hand he had laid on her arm. 'It's all right, Andrew,' she declared as staunchly as she could. 'They can't help being badly brought up, and they didn't bother me. In any case, I don't need to go anywhere near them. They'll be in the minority here, I'm sure.'

The girls' mouths gaped, their eyes widened in shock, but several of the young men clapped their approval at her show of spirit, and Andrew was left standing at the side while she went off with one after another of those clamouring to claim a dance. As in her dream, she was often asked to go to another room, a secluded room, to have a rest after an energetic romp, but she always said that Andrew was her escort and asked to be returned to where he was waiting.

'I'm sorry,' she puffed, nearly an hour after they had arrived. 'I don't like saying no when somebody asks me, so if you want to dance with me, you'll have to make a stand against them.'

He had been watching her closely while she was on the floor, noting her too brilliant eyes, her deeply flushed cheeks, the white around her pinched nostrils, all of which gave the lie to the impression she was trying to give, that of enjoying herself. 'I'd prefer if you'd sit this one out with me,' he said.

'Oh, thank you, Andrew,' she said gratefully. 'It's been an awful strain.'

'It must have been.' He could not let her know that he was well aware of the effort she had been putting into appearing free of care.

During one of the previous dances, he had looked for a place to take her if he got the chance, and led her now to the little alcove he had found. It was screened from the rest of the hall by two large plants in tubs, and even better, as far as he was concerned, the only place to sit was a small chaise longue.

Flopping down in utter exhaustion, Marianne was horrified that the crinoline made the front of her skirt shoot into the air. She looked at Andrew in dismay. 'I should have listened to Miss Esther,' she wailed. 'She wanted to take the hoop out, but I wouldn't let her. I thought . . .'

His heart went out to her when he saw the tears in her eyes, and he longed to hold her, to stroke the soft coppery hair one of his aunts must have dressed for her, it was so beautifully pinned up. But he did not want to take advantage of her present vulnerability. He tried to think of an answer to her latest problem – it wouldn't do for her to be caught in such an undignified position – and then he took hold of both her hands. 'I'll pull you up, but you'll have to be careful when you sit down again.'

With Marianne decently covered, he felt free to sit down beside her. 'I wish I hadn't made you come,' he murmured, taking her hand. 'I had no idea that any girl could be so rude about another's dress. In any case, I thought you looked . . .' He paused, swallowed, and then said reverently, 'I had never seen anything so beautiful in all my life as the picture you made walking down my aunts' stairs.'

'Oh, Andrew.' It was all she could say with her throat so tight.

'And I'm sure all the men here tonight felt exactly the same when they saw you come in. You outshone every girl in the hall. That's what was wrong. That girl was jealous. It was a compliment, really, when you come to think of it.'

'Was it? Are you sure?'

'Yes, I'm sure. And the rush of men to dance with you, that was a compliment too. Now, have you rested enough, or do you want to dry your eyes and give me at least one dance before I take you home?'

Turning towards him, she leaned forward and kissed his cheek. 'You're such a dear, Andrew. I'm sorry I neglected you, and I feel better now.'

As soon as they emerged from their haven, Marianne was besieged once more, but she shook her head. 'This dance is Andrew's.'

When the military two-step was over, they made for the seats round the wall, and noticing two young men heading in her direction, Marianne waved them away.

'I won't hold you to the next dance if you –' Andrew began, but she broke in, 'I want to dance with you.'

Waiting for the music to start again, she let her eyes rove round the hall and when she noticed a small knot of girls at the opposite side looking up flirtatiously at a tall, fair-haired young man, who was paying no attention to them, she gave Andrew a nudge. 'D'you know who he is?'

'I can't see his face, but he must have more charisma than I have,' Andrew grinned. 'Girls do not mill round me like that. Do you want me to find somebody to introduce you?'

'Oh, no! I'd be too embarrassed.'

The next dance was stopped before the end, so that everyone could hear the bells chime midnight, and after the hand-shaking and well-wishing had died down, most of the men kissed their partners, and so Andrew felt emboldened to kiss his. 'Happy New Year, dear Marianne,' he murmured bashfully, taking her in his arms.

As with several other couples, the first kiss was quickly followed by another of longer duration, and when Andrew drew away, he was confused by the depth of his feelings and too shy to declare himself.

Striving to understand her own emotions, Marianne said breathily, 'We'd better get off the floor before . . .' Not knowing why she wanted to sit down, she broke off.

Acutely conscious of each other now, they sat through the next dance without uttering a word, but at last Andrew said, 'I think I should be getting you home, in case the aunts are worrying.'

When he helped her to her feet, she said, 'I'd like to walk home, if that's all right? My head needs clearing.'

'Mine, too.'

Although the night air was bitterly cold and frost was glittering on the granite setts of the street, they ambled along silently for quite a time before Andrew summoned enough courage to say what was on his mind. 'Marianne,' he began, 'we've known each other for two years, and I was drawn to you from the very first. No, don't say anything yet,' he warned, as she opened her mouth, 'I want to get it off my chest, and I need to know where I stand. I said "drawn to you", but I really fell in love with you the minute I saw you. I meant to wait till I'd something to offer you, until I had set up as a solicitor, which won't be for a few years yet, but I know my aunts would be pleased if you . . . if we . . .'

They had stopped walking, and Marianne put her hand up and stroked his cheek. 'We're too young to make our minds up on something as serious as marriage, Andrew.'

'We could just be engaged . . . and my mind was made up months ago.'

'It might change in a few years, and if you remember, I told you on our very first walk I was going to marry a rich man. Maybe you thought that was a silly girlish dream, but I still mean it.'

He eyed her mournfully. 'So you don't love me?'

'Maybe I do, maybe I don't. I just don't know, Andrew.'

'If you did, you'd know,' he said, his voice throbbing with the pain eating at his innards. 'I fall asleep every night thinking of you, and I wake every morning thinking of you, and I think of you every minute of the day. That's love, Marianne!'

'I often think of you, Andrew, and if you went away, I'd really miss you, it would probably make me miserable for a long time, but I can't be sure if it's love or not. I'm sorry.'

'It's all right,' he said gruffly, although clearly it wasn't. 'We'd better go.'

Pulling up the hood of Miss Edith's cloak, she held the body of it closely around her. 'I didn't mean to hurt you, Andrew,' she told him as they walked on again. 'I told you the truth, but remember, as your aunts keep saying, I'm only seventeen. I do like you an awful lot, more than anybody I've met yet, and maybe I will fall in love with you and marry you . . . some day.'

'What about the rich man you're looking for?' he sneered.

'If I meet one and he asks me to marry him, I'll say yes. You see, Andrew, I never had any money to spend, that's why –' Her hand flew to her mouth, but after a moment, she went on, 'I may as well tell you.'

For the very first time, she confessed to being a thief, and was most surprised when Andrew said, 'Not many young girls would have denied the temptation when confronted by a heap of sovereigns like that; most of them would have taken the lot. But tell me, what did you spend them on? What did you reward yourself with as a counter-effect to your guilt?'

She drew a deep breath. 'Do you know something, Andrew? I never did feel truly guilty. I thought it served Mr Moodie right for leaving his cash lying about, and all I bought was the railway ticket to Aberdeen. I still have four

59

pounds, nineteen shillings and a few coppers left. Now, how does your love stand up to what I did?'

Coming to an abrupt halt, he grabbed her by the arms and turned her round to face him. 'I don't condone it, Marianne, but my love for you is strong enough to withstand any sin you care to commit. Don't forget that, do you hear? Even if our paths diverge in the future, any time you are in trouble, you have only to come to me. I will always be there for you.'

Feeling humbled, tears came to her eyes. 'Andrew, I'm all mixed up. When you say things like that my heart aches with what I suppose is love, and I want you to kiss me, but you won't want to . . .'

'I'll always want to, my darling.' His kiss was tender, a pledge of undying devotion. 'I've been a fool tonight. I shouldn't have said anything; it was much too soon. You must wipe it from your mind and not let it spoil the close companionship we had before.'

When they reached Strawberry Bank, his aunts wanted to know how their evening had gone, and only Miss Edith saw the shadows in Andrew's eyes, the heightened colour in Marianne's cheeks, as they described the four-piece ensemble which had provided the music for the more sedate dances, and the three students who had volunteered to play, with gusto, for the others. At last, putting an end to the questions still being asked by her sisters, she shooed the young man away and ordered the girl to bed.

'Something went wrong,' she whispered to Miss Esther when Miss Emily had also gone upstairs. 'Something they kept from us.'

Miss Esther frowned. 'They said they had a marvellous time.'

'Yes, and maybe they did, most of the time,' Miss Edith nodded, 'but they were definitely holding something back.'

Her sister eyed her thoughtfully. 'Would it have been the crinoline? Remember the trouble you had with it?'

Miss Edith smiled triumphantly. 'That's it! Marianne must have had trouble sitting down. I just hope she was not as bad as I was – even my drawers were in full view, if you recall.'

'They would have been embarrassed, but they would have got over it quickly. I'm sure they enjoyed themselves as much as they said.'

Marianne heard the murmur of their voices as they said good night and went into their separate rooms, but she knew that she wouldn't sleep. How could she, after what had been said earlier? It was all very well for Andrew to tell her to put it out of her mind, but she'd been cruel to him, hurt him badly, yet, in spite of that and the theft she had confessed to, he still swore that he loved her, would love her for ever. How could anybody love like that? If he landed in trouble by committing a crime and came to her for help, would she stand by him? She didn't think she would! But then, she had never professed to love him – that was the difference.

She wasn't interested in love. She wanted the safety, the power, of money around her, the wherewithal to buy enough clothes to fill closet after closet – and have some little saleswoman falling over herself to give advice on the proper outfit for the occasion. She could do without cuddles and kisses, she hadn't had many up to now anyway . . . though she'd the feeling she could grow to like Andrew's. But he could never take her into the realms of the upper classes, where no one would ever dare speak to her the way that stuck-up pig of a girl had tonight. If it hadn't been for that, she might have let herself be swept away by his declaration of love.

She was getting weak.

The New Year of 1897 was only days old when the snow started, and for the next three weeks there were no walks for Marianne and Andrew, which, if they were perfectly honest, was a relief to both of them. By the time the storm came to an end, and the streets had cleared, the two upsetting episodes of the night of the ball were past history and were never mentioned, and Marianne and Andrew slipped back naturally into the easy relationship they had had before.

Marianne, however, was still longing for a chance to compare him with another man . . . or more than one . . . and so, if they met any of his friends when they were out, she deliberately flirted with them. Her efforts came to fruition one Sunday early in March, when they ran into Douglas Martin, whom she had met only once before, with his common 'friend', Vi.

He was with a young man this time, one who greeted Andrew like a long-lost friend. 'Oh, Rennie, you don't know how glad I am to see you. Could I possibly have a few words with you, or . . .' He tailed off, looking apologetically at Marianne. 'I'm sorry. I didn't realize . . .'

'I don't mind,' she assured him, walking on to give them privacy.

Douglas seemed to have the same idea, because he hurried to catch up with her. 'You don't mind if I keep you company until they . . . ?'

She smiled encouragingly. 'I don't mind.'

He waited until they were well away from their companions before he said in a low voice, 'I've seen you out with Rennie a lot, though you haven't seen me, and I hoped I'd get a chance to speak to you on your own some time. Maybe I'm saying something I shouldn't – if you and Rennie are . . . I don't want to trespass.'

She was mystified, but intrigued. 'Andrew and I are only friends.'

Thank God! I'll have to grab my chance, so . . . will you come out with me tomorrow night?'

She did not take long to consider. She couldn't say she cared for him much, but Andrew had told her some time ago that Douglas Martin had given up Law and was now studying for the ministry, so an evening out with him would be interesting . . . yes, it would be very interesting. 'I'd love to,' she murmured.

'Seven o'clock at the Junction?'

'All right, but I might be a few minutes late. I don't finish work till six.'

'I'll wait,' he grinned, turning as the other two came alongside.

They split into their original pairs, and Marianne's curiosity made her ask, 'What did that fellow want with you, Andrew?'

'He wants me to help him with some written work he should have handed in, so I said I'd go over it with him tomorrow night.' He hesitated for a moment, then said, 'What was Martin saying to you? You looked very serious.'

'He asked me to go out with him tomorrow night and I said yes.' Why should she keep it a secret? There was nothing to hide.

Andrew's open face closed abruptly. 'I'd rather you didn't go, Marianne.'

She felt outraged at his attitude. 'You don't own me, Andrew Rennie! I'll go out with anybody I want!'

'But I know what he's like. Remember the kind of girl he was with when – ?'

'I know you said she was a lady of the streets, but that doesn't mean Douglas is a . . .' Not knowing the word 'libertine', she stopped.

'He boasts about the girls he's . . .' Too much of a gentleman to repeat the things the other man said, Andrew ended lamely, '. . . been out with.'

She thought she knew what he meant. 'I can look after myself. You should know by this time I'm not a shrinking violet.'

He said no more, though aware that she had no idea what men like Douglas Martin could do, and she wouldn't believe him if he told her.

Monday was several degrees colder than Sunday yet Marianne's temperature was higher than usual. Andrew wasn't the only one who had shown displeasure at her making a tryst with another man: all three of his aunts had let her see how they felt at some time during the day, but she didn't try to defend herself. They didn't own her either, and they couldn't interfere in her private life.

Supper that night was eaten in an uncomfortable silence, but neither the sisters' stony glances nor occasional accusing looks made any difference to Marianne, and when the time came for her to set off, she decided that she couldn't keep up the animosity any longer.

'I know what I'm doing,' she said as she put on her jacket.

Miss Edith's mouth twisted in disbelief. 'You are far too young to know what some young men can do. You have only ever been out with Andrew, who is a proper gentleman. He would never –'

'I was out once with Stephen, remember?' Marianne pouted. 'Douglas is a nice boy, too.' Andrew had made her suspect that Douglas wasn't as decent as he or Stephen Grant were, but that was half the fun of going out with him, as far as she was concerned. She wanted to find out what he would do, and she would easily stop him if he tried to do anything wrong.

Miss Esther took over the cautioning. 'Be careful, Marianne dear. I remember, when I was about your age, a boy –' Her face turning deep crimson, she came to an abrupt halt, then went on, her voice trembling a little, 'No, no. You do not want to hear that.'

'Times have changed,' Marianne murmured. 'Things are different nowadays.'

'Not all that much,' Miss Esther said sadly. 'So be on your guard.'

Miss Emily added a rider. 'It is best not to let boys know how you feel; it only encourages them.'

'Do not let him keep you out too late,' was Miss Edith's farewell.

Douglas was waiting at the Junction, where Holburn Street met Union Street. 'I thought of taking you to see the show at the Music Hall,' he observed. 'It's a bit too cold for a walk, isn't it?'

If they were in a hall among other people, Marianne thought, he wouldn't have the chance to do anything to her, wrong or otherwise, and she dared to say quietly, 'I'd rather go for a walk, if you don't mind?'

They set off into the dimly lit evening.

Smiling at the effort her sisters were making to camouflage their tiredness, Miss Edith remarked, 'For goodness' sake, off you go to bed, the two of you. I'll wait until Marianne comes in.'

They jumped up with surprising alacrity, Miss Esther saying, 'I seem to need more and more sleep as I grow older.'

Stifling a yawn with her hand, Miss Emily nodded. 'I am the same.'

As the eldest, Miss Edith shook her head reprovingly. 'If you give in to your years, senility will come on you all the sooner.'

Miss Emily paused at the door. 'Oh, do you think we should not. . . ?'

'One early night will not harm you, but do not make a habit of it.'

Edith lay back against the cushions of what had been their father's seat, a wide, leather-covered armchair with a high, buttoned back. She was concerned for their protégée.

Marianne looked older than seventeen and she had no experience of the big, harsh world, where men, even young men, lay in wait for those such as her, to ravish them, to defile them and leave them afraid to trust any other man. She cast her mind back almost forty years. She had been seventeen, the same age as Marianne, when she met Sandy Raitt. She would never forget him. Sandy! He had been so handsome in his blue uniform, and looked such a gentleman that even her father had been taken in . . .

The elderly lady was startled out of quite a deep sleep by the silvery chimes of the domed clock on the mantel shelf. Eleven o'clock! What could have happened to Marianne? Wide awake again and, in her anxiety for the girl, more finely tuned to any noises, Edith became aware of a sound outside in the street. Thank heaven! But it was far too late for Marianne to be staying out with a boy! She would have to be told . . . but why hadn't she come in?

Absolute silence fell again, and after another five minutes, Edith could stand it no longer. She had to find out what was going on.

Striding to the front door, she opened it quietly and was astonished that she could see no one in the flickering light of the gaslamp a few yards along. Thinking that she must have heard a cat prowling about, she was on the point of going back inside when her eye was drawn to a slight movement to her right.

'Is that you, Marianne?' she said softly, not wishing to rouse her sisters.

Skirts rustling, a figure trailed round from the side of the cottage. 'Good gracious!' Edith exclaimed. 'What were you doing round there?'

'I was . . . I was waiting . . . for you to go to bed.' The unsteady words ended in a torrent of tears, and Marianne gladly allowed herself to be led inside.

Her story came out as if she were in a trance; the walk down to the river and along the banks. 'He wasn't doing anything bad,' she went on, gulping, 'till we came to the cemetery . . .'

'Trinity,' murmured Miss Edith, wondering what was coming.

'Is that what it's called? Well, he took me over and pulled me inside the gate . . . I was scared to go . . . and then he . . . started . . .'

'I can guess, my dear. Do not distress yourself by telling me.'

But now she had started, Marianne felt compelled to get it all out. 'He was only kissing me at first, and stroking my neck, but something aboot him made me fear't, so I started fightin' him aff, but it was like fightin' a raging bull and I couldna stop him – nae even when he started touchin' me on my . . . bosom. But when he lifted my skirts and tried to force me down on the ground, I went right mad.'

Her voice was rising, so Miss Edith grasped her hand. 'My dear girl, I know exactly what happened. It happened to me once, when I was about your age.' She gave a tight smile at the incredulity on the white face. 'I was quite pretty in those days and I was very lucky that the boy did not make me pregnant, otherwise my father would have thrown me out. The best thing for you to do now is to give yourself a thorough wash . . . down there, and go to bed. We can do nothing else but wait until –'

'You don't understand!' Marianne cried. 'I didn't let him! You see, I've always been scared of cemeteries, and it was being so close to the gravestones as much as him mauling me . . . that helped me to . . .'

'You actually stopped him?' Miss Edith could scarcely believe it.

'I twisted awa' and kicked him right in the balls! An' when he was holdin' himsel' and swearin' like a trooper, I took to my heels and ran.'

Her eyes wide with shock at the coarseness which had come from the trembling young mouth, Miss Edith over-looked it since the girl was in such a state. 'All I can say is thank heaven you got away from him. It was a brave thing you did, but you might easily have been overpowered. Your escape was lucky indeed! Now, off you go to bed, but remember, do not arrange to meet any more boys until I have vetted them. Good night, my dear. You are quite safe now.'

'Good night, Miss Edith.' Marianne stood up and, on impulse, bent down and kissed her cheek. 'Thank you for not being angry with me.'

'Is that why you waited outside? You were afraid I would be angry? I am angry at the boy for taking advantage of a naïve young girl, but it was not your fault, although . . .' she paused for a moment, a twinkle in her eyes, '. . . we tried to warn you, if you remember? But we must let bygones be bygones. I shall never mention it again, not even to my sisters . . . and especially not to Andrew.'

Miss Edith did some thinking while she made sure that the fire was left safe before she went to bed. Was it fate that had made the seducer choose a graveyard in which to perpetrate his vile deed? Had Marianne been given divine protection? Or was it sheer good luck? Whatever the reason, her ordeal had not been as bad as it could have been. At least it was over. She would not have the worry of waiting to see if her show came. Nor was she suffering from a broken heart, as she, Edith, had been, for she had loved Sandy Raitt. They had kept company for almost three months while he was stationed in the Torry Point Battery, close to Girdleness Lighthouse – he had been one of the first volunteers who made up the Aberdeenshire Royal Garrison Artillery – but after that night, she had neither seen nor heard of him again.

She laid down the poker and straightened up. He had professed to love her, which was why she hadn't stopped him . . . and it hadn't been an altogether dreadful experience because she loved him. Even after all those years, there was still a soft spot for him in her memory. She may be an old maid, but unlike many of the breed, she *had* tasted of the sweet fruit which was forbidden to unmarried girls.

One pleasant Sunday afternoon in late March, when Marianne was walking along the beach promenade with Andrew, the sea looking much more friendly than on her first visit, she was surprised to see Stephen Grant coming towards them. She hadn't seen him since the night he dropped her like a hot brick, a year and a half ago, and she was elated by the change in his expression when he heard her talking in such a refined manner. She laid it on thickly. 'It's so nice to see you again, Stephen,' she gushed. 'I often wondered if I had done something to offend you.'

'I've b-been b-busy swotting,' he stammered.

'All the time?' Her eyes twinkled mischievously, causing Andrew to step in to save his friend embarrassment. 'Pay no attention to her, Stephen. She is just teasing.'

'May I walk along with you?' Stephen mumbled. 'Dick Thorne started off with me, then he met a girl he knew, and –'

'You're very welcome to join us,' Marianne smiled.

For a time, conversation centred round the weather, always a good talking point, then Stephen looked hopefully at Andrew. 'My parents are abroad until the middle of July and I was thinking of asking some friends to dinner one night next week – Dick and his girl if they'll come, another three chaps with partners, and there's my young sister and me, of course. Would you and Marianne care to come? Our cook is a true gem, so you'd be guaranteed a sumptuous meal.'

Before Andrew could answer one way or the other, Marianne said, 'We'd love to come, wouldn't we, Andrew?'

'Yes, thank you, Stephen. We'd be delighted.'

'I'll let you know which day when I've got everything arranged.'

Satisfied that his invitation had been accepted, Stephen bade them good night and left them, and Andrew turned to Marianne. 'What are you playing at?' he demanded disapprovingly. 'I'd have thought you wouldn't want anything to do with him after he –'

'He lives in one of the biggest houses in Albyn Place.'

'Oh!' His face fell. 'Is he rich enough for you, then?'

'His father is. Oh, I just want to see inside their mansion.'

'But you wouldn't say no if Stephen popped the question? He's not a brilliant student, you know, and he'll probably end up being an ordinary solicitor like me, with hardly enough money coming in to keep himself, never mind a wife.'

'He'll still have a wealthy father,' she retorted, 'and a mother out of the top drawer. I never made any bones about what I wanted, Andrew. You've known that all along.'

'Yes, you're quite right.' He appeared chastened now, and held his head down for most of the way back to Strawberry Bank.

When they neared the house, he mumbled, 'Will you please tell my aunts I've a lot of notes to write up? I can't face them right now.'

'I'll tell them, and . . . Andrew, I'm sorry. Anyway, Stephen might not want to marry me. He was quick enough to drop me before. It's a long way from dinner to marriage and maybe he asked us to make up the numbers.'

'Oh, he already has his eye on you. I'm sure the "dinner for friends" was a spur-of-the-moment thing just to get you into his home.'

Marianne deemed it wisest not to continue on that topic. 'Will I see you next Sunday?' she begged.

'If you want me to come.'

'Of course I want you to come. I'll always be your friend, no matter who I marry.'

He turned away hastily, making her regret being so insensitive. He had made it clear so often that he didn't want to be just her friend.

When she went in, she passed on Andrew's message and then pleaded a headache so that she could go to bed. She didn't care that his aunts would suspect something was wrong between them – she couldn't please everybody and she wasn't going to try. She would please herself. It was her life, after all.

The doubts started creeping in after she undressed and lay down. Was she being foolish? She knew nothing about Stephen Grant except that he was an out-and-out snob, so his parents would likely forbid him to marry the likes of her. Why couldn't she be content to marry Andrew when he'd got his degree? She would be better off than she was now, financially and emotionally, because nobody else would ever love her as much as he did. And she . . . nearly loved him. It hurt to think there might come a time when she would no longer see him. It would depend on the partner she chose, though not many husbands would permit their wives to remain so friendly with another man.

It all depended . . . it all depended . . . was it to be Stephen? Or Andrew? Or somebody she hadn't yet met?

Chapter Five

'Andrew is asking for trouble,' Miss Esther remarked. 'Marianne will meet a different kind of people at Albyn Place.'

Miss Edith shrugged. 'He is afraid that if he doesn't take her, she might come to resent him for spoiling her chances.'

Miss Esther said no more, but when Andrew said the next Sunday that the dinner was to be on Wednesday, his pale face and sad eyes pierced her heart and she longed to reassure him. As she whispered to Miss Emily when they went to bed, 'She cannot possibly meet anyone nicer than he is, so he need not upset himself.'

On the evening of the dinner, wishing that she had something more elegant to wear, Marianne put on a skirt and blouse she had bought the previous summer and, it still being cold in the evenings, she was forced to cover the pastel pink with a muddy-grey woollen cardigan, felted after being washed so often. She didn't care so much that her well-worn coat was bordering on the threadbare – she would be taking that off – but while Andrew walked with her to Albyn Place, she wondered if anything would be said about her lack of dress sense. But surely Fate couldn't be so cruel as to have the horrible girl of the Hogmanay Ball at Stephen's house tonight?

She soon discovered that Fate could. Stephen himself admitted them to his home and detailed his sister, Myra, to show Marianne where to leave her coat. Then, when she was taken into the drawing room, the first person she saw was the stuck-up pig, as she had designated her.

Only too conscious of her matted cardigan, Marianne stepped forward to shake hands when Myra made the introductions. 'Marianne, meet Sybil and Barty, and Ethel and Richard. Hamish and his partner haven't arrived yet.'

Taking in only one of the names, Marianne sat down in the chair Myra indicated. So she was called Sybil, was she? Well, if she started anything here, she would get more than she expected. Another man coming in at that moment, there was a renewed flurry of hand-shaking, and when that was over, Sybil leaned across her partner and said to the girl on his other side, in a clear voice that echoed round the room, 'Do you see what I see? It's the crinoline creature from the ball – and she is no better dressed for the occasion tonight than she was then.'

Her blood boiling, Marianne strove to keep calm. 'We do not all have the money to dress in the height of fashion,' she said quietly, into the deathly hush that had fallen. 'I have to work for a living, though I don't suppose you'll ever know what that means.'

Sybil turned a scarlet face towards her. 'You . . . you . . . insolent . . . guttersnipe!' Barty, her partner, tried to calm her, but she went on, 'Who do you think you are talking to?'

'To a bad-mannered, spoiled bairn that should ken better!' Marianne spat out, the speech lessons forgotten in

75

her white-hot anger, the good impression she had wanted to create killed off in the first few minutes. 'I'm nae as well-educated as you, but I wouldna dream of doing to onybody what you just done to me!'

Tears stinging her eyelids, she stood up to go to look for Andrew, who had disappeared somewhere with Stephen, and the tall, fair-haired stranger who had come in behind her stepped aside to let her pass. 'Good for you!' he murmured, patting her on the back. 'I have been dying to take Sybil down a few pegs for a long time.'

Recovering some of her equilibrium as he followed her out of the room, Marianne sighed, 'But being a gentleman, you couldn't, so it fell to an ignorant peasant like me.'

'No, no, do not degrade yourself like that. I just wish I had your spirit.' After closing the drawing-room door behind him, he gave her arm a brief, reassuring squeeze. 'I do not suppose you will feel like staying here now, so if you go and fetch your coat, I shall take you home.'

Still too upset to think, she was halfway to Strawberry Bank with him when she exclaimed, 'Oh, Andrew'll be wondering where I am! And what about your partner?'

One corner of his mouth lifted in a smile. 'She had not come out of the cloakroom when we left, but I should think they have both been told by this time that I whisked you away. And if it was Andrew who was talking to Stephen on the stairs, Hester won't mind being left with him. The question is – will he mind being left with her?'

'No, I don't think so.' She knew Andrew would be hurt that she had run out on him, but she couldn't have stayed a minute longer.

'Perhaps I had better introduce myself. Hamish Lyall, your very good servant, Miss . . . ?'

'Marianne Cheyne,' she laughed.

'Are you and Andrew . . . ?'

'We're just good friends. I work in his aunts' shop, and I've got a room in their house.'

'I hope you do not think me too bold on such short acquaintance, Miss Cheyne, but I would be honoured if you let me treat you to a meal one night, to make up for tonight's disaster.'

'But it wasn't your fault, and I don't know –'

'I will ask your employers' permission, if you think it necessary.'

Her temper having completely cooled, she looked at him appraisingly. He was very tall and not particularly handsome, but he was dressed in the latest style – a cut-away coat and brimmed hat, which must have cost a pretty penny. Slim, with a longish, leanish face and straight blond hair combed well back, his chin was clean-shaven, but his top lip sported a neat moustache. She was sure that this was the first time she had seen him, yet there was something familiar about him.

'Have we met before, Mr Lyall?' she asked.

'Not met, exactly,' he smiled, 'although I have seen you before. At the Hogmanay Ball,' he added, noticing her perplexity.

It came to her suddenly. He was the man who had been surrounded by adoring girls! Well, well! If she were to be seen out with *him*, it would be one in the eye for the obnoxious Sybil. 'You don't have to ask anybody's permission,' she said. 'I'll be happy to go for a meal with you, thank you for asking me . . . and for rescuing me.'

'May I call for you tomorrow at . . . half-past seven?'

'Half-past seven's fine. Good night, Mr Lyall.'

'Hamish, please . . . if you will allow me to call you Marianne?'

'Good night . . . Hamish,' she smiled.

The sisters were surprised to see Marianne home so early, and although she confined her tale to Sybil's nasty remarks of that night and did not mention her criticism of the crinoline, they were outraged that anyone could treat their protégée in such a barbaric manner.

They were still discussing it when the door opened and Andrew came in, having run all the way from Albyn Place. 'I'm sorry,' he panted. 'I was having a quiet chat with Stephen and I didn't know what had happened until we came downstairs.'

Miss Edith gave a start. 'Then who took you home, Marianne, if it wasn't Andrew?'

'One of the other guests,' she smiled. 'His name's Hamish Lyall, and he's very nice. He's taking me for a meal tomorrow night.'

Andrew's concerned face turned an even deeper shade of red. 'Is that what he said his name was?'

'Oh, no!' Miss Esther fluttered. 'Did he give a false name?'

Marianne's stomach plunged. She might have known he was too good to be true. 'What *is* his name, then?'

Andrew was obviously reluctant to tell her, so she repeated, 'What *is* his name, Andrew? Tell me!'

He looked at the floor for a few seconds. 'It wasn't really a false name,' he mumbled, then stared defiantly at her. 'He didn't tell you his full name, that's all. He's the

Honourable Hamish Bruce-Lyall, and his father is Lord Glendarril, an old friend of Stephen's father.'

Miss Edith was first to recover. 'Ah, yes. I have read about the Bruce-Lyall family, and if my memory serves me correctly, there were twin sons. One suffered from some kind of debilitating disease and died when he was still quite young, and it would appear that Hamish stands to inherit the title.'

Miss Esther clasped her hands together in pleasure. 'Our Marianne will be sharing a table with an honourable tomorrow night.'

'Fancy that!' Miss Emily looked awestruck.

'Yes, just fancy!' Andrew said dolefully. 'I'll have to go now.'

'But neither of you could have had anything to eat?' Miss Esther was a willing hostess. 'We have enough ham and vegetables left over to make a decent meal for two.'

'I couldn't eat a thing,' he muttered. 'Thank you all the same.'

'Neither could I,' Marianne said. 'I'll see you to the door.'

Outside, she started to apologize, but Andrew had worked himself into what bordered on a frenzy of jealousy. 'You could have waited for me. I came down a few minutes later, but you had found your rich man! Is he the one, Marianne? Is an honourable good enough for you? I don't believe you could do much better than him. He will be a lord one day!'

Marianne's temper flared once more. 'Andrew Rennie! I didn't know who he was. I only agreed to see him once because I thought it'd be bad manners to refuse when he'd rescued me from your snob friends, but if he asks me to meet him a second time . . . or a third or fourth, I will! I'm sure he would never sneer at me, for he's honourable in every sense of the word, and you needn't think I'll take a walk with you on Sundays again, for I won't!'

She slammed inside, and barged past the sisters, who looked at each other in dismay as she stamped upstairs.

'Oh dear!' moaned Miss Esther. 'It looks like Andrew has put his foot in it somehow.'

Miss Emily was wringing her hands. 'Poor boy! Poor boy!'

'Perhaps we should consider this more,' Miss Edith observed wisely. 'Is it fair of us to want Marianne to stick to Andrew if she will be happier with young Bruce-Lyall?'

Her head on one side, Miss Emily murmured, 'But she only met him tonight.'

'It could be love at first sight,' romantic Miss Esther put in.

Miss Edith snorted. I think it is love of money with Marianne. I've had the feeling, from little things she let drop, that she has always wanted a rich husband. I hoped that she was growing out of it, but Andrew's jealousy, understandable though it is to us, may have pushed her into this other man's arms.'

Miss Edith was very near the truth. Marianne had wounded Andrew by what she had done, but he had wounded her every bit as much. She had expected him to sympathize, not to upbraid her for making her escape from a terrible situation with the only person available. Andrew had left her on her own with a roomful of strangers and he hadn't been there when she needed him, after all his promises. She couldn't rely on him, whereas Hamish knew the right thing to do at the right time . . . and he *was* rather nice. Besides, according to Miss Edith, he had a lineage to be proud of, and *she* hadn't objected to him as a suitor.

In the dining room of the comfortable inn where he had a room, Hamish told Marianne that Ma Cameron – as the hostess was affectionately known – was famed for the meals she provided. 'I always stay here when I'm in Aberdeen overnight, though I don't like leaving home for long these days. My father's health is none too good, and –'

'Hamish,' she interrupted, 'why didn't you tell me who you were? I got an awful shock when Andrew said your father was a lord.'

He smiled enigmatically. 'He came to check if you got home safely? Did he think I would seduce you on the way?'

Shocked, she said, 'He wouldn't have thought anything like that.'

'But he wasn't pleased?'

'No.'

'Is he in love with you?'

'He says he loves me.'

'Do you love him?'

'Why are you asking all these –'

'Do you?'

'I don't know.'

He leaned back now. 'I am pleased to hear that, Marianne. You would certainly know if you *were* in love with him, and it encourages me to . . . get to know you better, if I may?'

Overwhelmed by astonishment as well as shyness, she could only whisper, 'I've no objection.'

So Hamish called for Marianne every Thursday for three weeks, taking her first to His Majesty's Theatre where her awe at the magnificence of her surroundings was dispelled as soon as the first act came on. She was totally unaware of Hamish, who spent his time watching her rather than the performers on stage. In the second week, he introduced her to the Music Hall, where, although the acts were of much the same standard – men and women singing or dancing, jugglers juggling with an assortment of items – the sketches were humorous instead of dramatic, and the interior was not quite so impressive.

The third week saw her at the Tivoli, laughing at the jokes delivered at speed by the comedians and the slightly naughty ditties sung by women – one dressed as a man – who encouraged the audience to join in the choruses. There were also some acrobats, young men and girls in scanty costumes contorting their bodies in unbelievable ways. She loved every minute, as she told her escort while he walked her home.

'I must apologize for the rowdiness of the audience,' Hamish said. 'The people up in the gods are a rough bunch – that's the top tier of seats,' he added in explanation.

'Oh, I didn't mind that,' she smiled, 'though I did wonder at first why they were shouting. You've opened my eyes to things I never knew went on, you know.'

He gave a sad little smile. 'Perhaps that was not such a good thing, but next Thursday, if you will allow me, it would give me great pleasure to take you to Ma Cameron's for a meal.'

'But you took me there already – to make up for the meal I missed at Albyn Place, and you've taken me to all these other places, so you've more than made up for –'

'None the less, I need an opportunity to talk to you properly, to ask –'

He broke off, but she was so involved in thinking of all the things she had to tell the Rennies that it didn't occur to her to wonder what he meant to ask.

As he had done every week, he bade her good night at her door and waited until she went inside before walking away. Marianne always felt uncomfortable about that – it made her feel self-conscious to know his eyes were on her every step. But as she had known they would be, the sisters were waiting eagerly to hear where she and Hamish had gone that night, so it was some time before she managed to get to bed, to dream, naturally, of all the wonderful things she had seen.

There was something different about Hamish, Marianne thought the following Thursday as they sat down in Mrs Cameron's dining room. His face was just a trifle flushed, his voice was pitched a little higher as if he were excited about something and, recalling that he'd said he would have something to ask her, she waited for him to ask.

She was beginning to think he had forgotten, or had changed his mind and wasn't going to bother, when he said, hesitantly, 'Marianne, when I asked you a few weeks ago if you were in love with Andrew, you did not know. Have you come to any conclusion yet?'

She shook her head. 'I haven't given it any more thought, but like you said before, if I *was* in love with him, I would know, so I suppose I'm not.'

'Good! That enables me to come to something I have been mulling over since the night I met you. If I asked you to marry me, what would you say?'

She grinned now, sure that he was joking. 'I'd say you were drunk . . . or mad . . . or both.'

There was no answering humour on his face. 'I am neither,' he said gravely. 'My father is obsessed with getting me married so that he will know, before he dies, that I have a son to succeed me. To let you understand, the title always goes to the next *legitimate* male – even those born through the female line – and he is afraid that . . .' Hamish halted briefly, then changed what he had been about to say. 'He has also stipulated that I find a woman who is fit enough in mind and body to be the perfect mother, and who will be less likely to give birth to puny weaklings – his words. You see, with so much inbreeding over the centuries, very few of my ancestors lived to a ripe old age . . . indeed, some were bordering on idiocy.'

'Oh, surely not!'

He clicked his tongue. 'Not literally perhaps, but quite near. I am making heavy weather of this, I am afraid, and I have said enough at present. I will give you ten days to think it over, and if you are interested, we can discuss it further.'

'Yes, I need time. I don't know what to think right now, my mind's in a complete whirl.'

Hamish laughed. 'I had better take you home.'

On the way, Marianne was too stunned to speak and was thankful that he expected no answers to the inconsequential remarks he was making. But when they reached the end of her street, he said, 'I shall meet you here at the

84

same time a week on Saturday . . . so be ready with your answer.'

When she went in, her benefactresses were waiting anxiously to hear how she had fared, so she described the inn, the room, the food she had eaten and some of the things they had talked about, but she could not bring herself to tell them about Hamish's proposal. She was still too dazed by it.

Unable, even after two whole days, to make up her mind, Marianne felt the need to discuss it with someone, and during a restless Saturday night, she hoped that Andrew would turn up the next day, to see his aunts, if not Marianne herself. She had never made any secret of her ambition, and surely he'd have got over his pique by then – he might even be pleased that she had got the chance to fulfil her dream – and she had always been able to tell him more than she could tell his aunts.

Unfortunately, she rose on Sunday morning to the sound of heavy rain battering against her window, and although she put up a silent prayer that it would clear by lunchtime, it had not eased off at all by the time Andrew arrived. She had meant to ask his advice and be guided by it, but it seemed that there would be no opportunity for private talk.

When he came into the parlour, however, and Marianne saw how pale and drawn he was, she was quite glad that she would be unable to discuss anything with him. It would be too cruel to let him believe, even for a few minutes, that she wasn't sure. She had been offered the chance of a lifetime – how many girls got the opportunity of being a real lady with a title? – and even if there were no family fortune, how could she turn the rest down? Her very position would give her access to the wealth she craved, and a title would give her power.

She tried, by addressing most of her remarks to him, to let Andrew see that she was still friends with him, and she wasn't the only one who was relieved to see him brighten as the afternoon wore on. The weather had faired by the time he was leaving in the evening, so she walked a little way with him, 'to blow the cobwebs off me'.

As soon as they were outside, Andrew sighed, 'I shouldn't have said what I did when I last saw you, and I'm truly sorry, Marianne. I was angry at you for leaving without me, and when I learned who had seen you home, I was afraid you would prefer him to me, might even see him again. But that does not excuse me for . . .'

'Andrew,' Marianne said softly, 'you've nothing to be sorry for.' She hesitated, then added, 'I'd better tell you, though . . . he has asked me to marry him.'

He grabbed her arms and pulled her roughly to a halt. 'I thought you only dined with him once?'

'I thought that would be all, but it was more than that and he proposed last Thursday and gave me ten days to think about it. I've thought and thought . . . well, I'm going to accept.'

'But you can't, Marianne! You don't know anything about him!'

'I know enough.'

'Oh God, Marianne! You can't do this! You know I love you, and you can't love him!'

Her heart was cramping at the anguish in his eyes, but she said stoutly, 'Who said anything about love? I told you a long

86

time ago I didn't care about love. He wants me to . . . give him the son he's got to have to continue the Bruce-Lyall line.'

'Good God! Do you realize what you are saying, Marianne? He must know dozens of suitable girls; he doesn't need you. Not like I do.'

'Andrew, my mind's made up. I've always said I wanted a rich man, but even if he's not rich, I'll still marry him for the title.'

He flung her from him. 'I'd better not argue any more. I thought I could have persuaded you to . . . but when I asked Stephen, he said the Bruce-Lyalls were one of the wealthiest families in Scotland.'

'There you are!' she snapped, rubbing her arms where his nails had dug in. 'It seems I picked well, after all.'

Chests heaving with the anger they felt, they glared at each other for several moments before Marianne said, with a catch in her throat, 'Andrew, I know you don't think much of me now, but I still want you for a friend. You're the only one I could turn to if –'

'You're beginning to have doubts?'

'No, I don't have any doubts, but even the best marriages go wrong sometimes, and I'd like to know I had someone . . .'

'Oh, Marianne!' The words were wrung from him. 'I let you down on that evening at Stephen's, but I'll never let you down again. I'll always be there for you. I'll run at your bidding, and I'll do anything you want, whatever it is. I'll never stop loving you.'

She was surprised by the tears which sprang to her eyes. 'I wish it could be different, Andrew dear. I wish I could love you like you deserve to be loved.'

He put his hand up to dry her cheek. 'Tell me something, Marianne. Do you love Bruce-Lyall?'

'No, I don't love him, but I do like him and he can make my dreams come true. Can't you feel happy for me about that?'

He held her face between his hands now. 'I do, Marianne, though I would feel happier if I had been the one to make your dreams come true.' His lips touched hers lightly. 'It does help a little to know that you do not love him either, but it is still going . . .' A slight tremble in his voice made him clear his throat determinedly. 'Do not forget, if you ever need me you have only to let me know.'

'Thank you, Andrew. I won't forget, but why don't you find another girl? You must know some.'

'None of them can compare with you,' he sighed.

'That's just because you don't want to compare them. I'd better go back now, or else your aunts will be thinking I'm lost.'

Because Marianne had taken almost half an hour to come back from seeing Andrew to the end of the street, two of his aunts had presumed they had made up their quarrel, and so were not averse to the girl meeting Hamish again.

'It will do her good to mix with people like that,' Miss Emily said, feeling free to state her opinion because she knew that Miss Esther felt the same.

'It should do us good, too,' the youngest sister pointed out. 'He must have young married friends who might need a layette for a coming infant, or want to buy something for a toddler.'

Perspicacious Miss Edith said nothing. She knew that something had happened between their nephew and the girl, something drastic, which had not been resolved. She also wished she knew how to stop Marianne from seeing more of young Bruce-Lyall; a liaison between them could be dangerous. Marianne's head could easily be turned by the thought of having a title and acting the gracious lady . . . and where would that leave poor Andrew?

On Saturday, Marianne was rather pleased that Hamish had asked Ma Cameron if they could have dinner served in his room, away from the possible eavesdropping of her other customers, but he waited until their meal was over before he broached the important subject. 'Have you made your decision yet?'

'Didn't you say there were further details to discuss?' she hedged.

He looked at her over the rim of his brandy glass. 'I think we could safely leave the other details until you give me your answer. I have already told you my reason for marrying you, so you should be under no misapprehension.'

She felt a twinge of what she hoped was '*mis*'-apprehension. There was something here that she couldn't fathom, something he was keeping from her, but surely nothing bad? There was no love between them, she was content to have it that way, and there couldn't be anything else unless . . . 'Are you preparing me for a divorce after I give you the son you want?'

'Oh no, my dear, nothing like that. Our marriage will last until the day one of us dies . . . as long as you are happy with it.'

It wasn't a truly satisfactory answer, suggesting as it did that she might not be happy, but the lure of becoming a member of one of the wealthiest families in Scotland was too great. 'I have decided, Hamish. I'll marry you whenever you want.'

He poured himself another brandy and gestured to her to lift her glass. 'We will drink to that and then we can get down to business.'

She took a small sip, shuddering as the spirits set her throat on fire, and watched in amazement when he tossed his down in one go like a dose of cough linctus, and poured another.

The brandy seemed to help him to present his case. First, I had better tell you that my mother was not at all happy about this, but my father made her see that it is best . . . all round, and so you will be summoned to Glendarril very shortly.'

'To see if I pass muster?' Marianne was outraged at being ordered, not invited, to meet his parents.

'There is no suggestion of passing muster,' Hamish smiled. 'I have made my choice and they will stand by that. As is only natural, my mother wants to meet you and you will be expected to live with us so that she can prepare you for – ' he broke off, his tone softening. 'I can tell by your terrified expression that I am not explaining things very well.'

'It *is* a bit terrifying,' she admitted. 'You know I don't exactly shine when I meet snobs . . .' Her hand flew to her mouth. 'Oh, I don't mean your parents or their friends are snobs. How could I, when I haven't even met any of them yet?'

Hamish did not appear in the least put out. 'They *are* snobs, my dear Marianne,' he grinned, 'my mother the worst of all. But you will soon learn how to talk to them, and to the servants. That is why Mother wants you to move in with us as soon as you can. It will take her time to arrange the wedding to her liking, with goodness knows how many guests – five hundred, I shouldn't be surprised.'

'So many? And what about my wedding dress? Miss Esther will want to make it . . .'

'Mother will whip you up to London or Edinburgh for an exclusive, if I know her. There will be no need for you nor Andrew's aunts to worry about anything. It will all be taken care of – invitations, your whole trousseau, the brides-maids' dresses, the floral arrangements, the wedding break-fast, the hiring of the musicians.' He stopped, laughing at her bemused face. 'Yes, I know every step, every inch of the way to the altar. A young friend of the family was married last year, and Mother wouldn't let the bride's mother – her closest friend – do a single thing. She took over the wed-ding completely, and I must say, she did a wonderful job.'

'I never dreamed it would be anything like that,' Marianne sighed, 'but it's maybe good that your mother will be choosing my wedding gown. You know how some people criticize my taste in clothes.'

'Shall I tell you something?' Hamish murmured, slur-ring the words ever so slightly. 'It was hearing you stand up to Sybil at Hogmanay that started me thinking . . .'

'Oh,' she gasped. 'You saw that business as well, did you?'

'That's when I began to consider you as a wife, and when I told Father how you fended off Sybil and her cronies, he agreed that you would be ideal for our purpose, but I knew nothing about you – your name nor where you lived. So I could hardly believe my luck when I saw you at Albyn Place. Now, I had better take you home.'

Hamish got to his feet and came round to pull Marianne's chair back for her, and when she was standing in front of him, he muttered, 'I suppose I should have kissed you earlier, when you accepted me?'

'It doesn't matter,' she said, although she *was* quite disappointed that he hadn't, then or now.

'You will be receiving a letter from my mother in a few days, I suppose, to tell you when she expects to see you.'

'You'll have to meet the Rennies before I leave them. Will you come in with me tonight?'

'I have had a little too much to drink tonight, I am afraid. I do not want them to get a wrong impression, because I do not normally indulge, but . . . well, I had to boost my courage. I do, however, want very much to meet them. Shall I come tomorrow?'

'I'll let them know, though I'm sure it'll be all right.'

He left her at the end of her street, and Marianne went in to tell the sisters of her good fortune. They should be pleased for her . . . unless they couldn't forgive her for not marrying Andrew.

When the summons arrived, Marianne was awestruck. The coat of arms itself at centre top was very impressive, and the gold deckled edging, but it was the embossed heading at the right-hand side which took her breath away. Castle Lyall, Glendarril! Hamish hadn't said he lived in a castle and Miss Edith hadn't mentioned it.

But everything was going to be all right. In the ten days since he had met them, Hamish had charmed his way into three elderly female hearts, Miss Edith's being the last to succumb. Even Andrew, sure that he would hate the man as soon as he was introduced to him, had admitted to her that Hamish was a decent fellow.

Marianne was relieved that there was no sign of rivalry between them. In fact, they got on so well that she hoped Hamish wouldn't object to her inviting Andrew to the castle occasionally after the wedding. She couldn't bring their friendship to an end and leave him as if he meant nothing to her. It wasn't true. She had *always* felt something for him . . . though it wasn't love.

Chapter Six

On the southbound train, Marianne felt quite down-hearted. She had hoped to be sent off with good wishes ringing in her ears, but at the station Miss Esther and Miss Emily had barely touched the tips of her fingers with theirs before they turned away, and when Miss Edith stepped forward her opening words were anything but encouraging. 'I trust you have considered all aspects of the union you are determined to make? You will be far removed from your friends – '

'When I came to Aberdeen,' Marianne butted in cautiously, 'I was all alone and I didn't know a soul. I wouldn't have known what to do if it hadn't been for that priest.'

'Ah yes, Father Bernard. When his mother was alive, she was a great friend of ours, and we all missed him when he took up his missionary post in East Africa. But you are unlikely to meet anyone like him in a long glen with little habitation, according to what I have read.'

'I'll have proper relations, though.' Realizing that she might have offended Miss Edith, Marianne hurried on, 'I've thought of you and your sisters as my aunts as much as Andrew's, but when I marry Hamish, I'll have a mother and a father – just in-laws, I know, but still relations – as well as a husband. I won't forget you, though. I'll come and visit you as often as I can.'

Miss Edith – stern, inflexible, disapproving Miss Edith – swallowed her emotion before she said, her voice quavering ever so slightly, 'I will pray for your happiness, Marianne.'

'I know *you* will, but I wish Miss Esther and Miss Emily could see past the ends of their noses.'

'It is their love for Andrew that they can not see past, but I am sure that in the fullness of time they will forgive you for breaking his heart.' The noise of steam pressure building up made Miss Edith step back, satisfied by Marianne's stricken face that the last barb at least should make her think again.

The girl held out her hand in appeal – to be understood, to assure these dear ladies of her love for them – and cried out, 'I'll write to let you know the arrangements for the wedding.'

The guard's whistle shrilling, the two younger sisters turned back to see her being borne away, and three hands kept waving until they were out of Marianne's sight. Only then did she sit down. There was so much to think about, so much had happened in so short a time, that she still couldn't take everything in.

First, there had been the strange proposal and Andrew's reaction when he'd been told, then her acceptance – with no sign of elation from Hamish – and how the Rennies had taken her decision. Perhaps she had gone the wrong way about telling them, but she'd had no time to plan it, and finding an easy way was impossible. She had announced it the minute she'd walked into the house . . . thrown it at them defiantly.

'I'm going to marry Hamish!'

There were three separate gasps, holding different degrees of horrified astonishment, and then Miss Edith – why was it always Miss Edith? – her nose twitching, said, 'It is obvious that you have been drinking, Marianne. I can smell the brandy on your breath, but you should have thought before coming out with a remark like that. It was enough to give any of us a heart attack. If it was meant as a joke, it was in very poor taste.'

'It's not a joke,' she burst out, thinking fleetingly that Miss Edith's heart would not be so easily attacked. 'He asked me last week and I said yes tonight. That's why we had the brandy.' Hamish had ordered the brandy before she gave him her answer, but it made no difference. It was a good excuse.

Miss Esther's hand had jumped to her chest. 'Oh dear! My heart's still thumping with the shock,' she wailed. 'You can't marry anyone else, Marianne! You love Andrew . . . don't you?'

'Yes, I do love him . . . like a brother.'

'Unfortunately, he does not look on you as a sister.' It was Miss Edith again, her eyes and voice holding a sharp censure now. 'I have never seen any boy love a girl as much as he loves you. Does he know about this . . . charade?'

'It's not a charade. I told him on Sunday, and . . . well, I suppose he took it the way you'd expect him to take it.'

'Poor boy!' murmured Miss Emily, dabbing her eyes with a square of lace-edged lawn.

'It's so cruel!' moaned Miss Esther.

'You don't need to tell me I'm being cruel! I know that perfectly well, and I wish it could have been different!'

'When is this wedding to be?' Miss Edith asked. 'Will there be time for you to see sense and change your mind?'

'I won't change my mind! You'll likely be worse shocked when I tell you I'm marrying him because it won't be long till he has a title. I suppose I'd be happy if I married Andrew but . . . having wealth and a standing in society, I'll be ecstatic!'

Miss Edith shook her head. 'Wordly possessions are not everything, and I have not heard you say that you love young Bruce-Lyall. The prestige of being even the highest lady in the land is worth nothing if there is no love there. Perhaps it would satisfy you for a year or so, then the rot would set in.'

Marianne was almost weeping with the futility of trying to explain. 'I haven't known him long, but I do like him an awful lot.'

'I grant you that he is nice, but does he like you "an awful lot"?' Miss Edith's lips were almost in a sneer.

'Yes, he does!' Marianne burst out. 'So you see!'

The argument had ended there, Marianne recalled. It was evident that the sisters had not understood what they were meant to see, and, to be quite honest, neither did she now. Hamish had only said that he admired her spirit. He had never mentioned liking, let alone loving. But she didn't want love. She'd be more than content to spend his money in exclusive gown salons, or having her clothes made specially for her by a world-renowned . . . whatever dressmakers were called in high circles. Nobody would ever laugh at her again for what she was wearing.

People would bow and scrape to her. Men would worship at her feet . . .

The train drawing to a screeching halt, she was laughing as she looked out to see where she was. Stonehaven. Halfway there.

The short stop, the stir of the small station, the different accent she could hear, though this was only fifteen miles or so south of Aberdeen, all served to wrench her mind away from the pleasant plane it had reached. Her thoughts went now to Andrew. Poor, dear Andrew. She would miss him, truly miss him. An ache for him was already beginning deep down inside her. Would it lessen as time went past, or would it be a case of absence making the heart grow fonder? Would she come to regret being so impetuous? Should she back out before it was too late?

She banged her fist on the window frame. No, she wasn't going to back out! She had made her choice, she had survived the ordeal of wounding the four people she cared for most so that she could have a wonderful new life – the life she'd had her heart set on since she'd seen a heap of sovereigns lying in a dish. And whatever she had to suffer in future years – supposing the Bruce-Lyall family lost every ha'penny and she was forced to go out to work again – she'd have been part of Society with a capital S for a while, and she would never go crawling to anybody. She would never admit she'd been wrong.

The next stop was Laurencekirk, another fifteen miles farther on. As soon as Marianne stepped down on to the platform, a porter – or possibly he held down all the jobs like Dod Cooper at Tipperton – came forward, touching his hat respectfully. 'Miss Cheyne? His Lordship's carriage is waiting. I'll take your luggage out for you.'

He did his best to hide his surprise at learning she had only the valise she was carrying, but it was obvious that he thought she fell far short of the usual standard of visitors to Castle Lyall.

'Thank you,' she said, as graciously as she could. She was tempted to add 'my man', but decided that such an embellishment would best be kept until she was actually married to Hamish.

She followed him out to the waiting carriage, where the coachman, a man about forty with an almost completely bald head, also stared doubtfully at her, but the coat of arms on the door gave her fast-sinking morale a great boost. The coachman, looking down on her from his lofty perch as the railway employee helped her aboard, was just a servant, *her* servant . . . or would be very soon.

Nothing was said while the high-stepping horse trotted out of the village at a gentle pace, turning, without any directions from the man, into a much rougher side road marked 'Glendarril'. Proceeding into the glen, they came, in what she judged to be about three miles at least, to a wide, low building with a high, smoking chimney stack. She didn't like to ask what it was, but when they passed it, she saw a huge sign above the gates – 'Glendarril Woollen Mill'. So that was how the Bruce-Lyalls made their money? She hadn't given a single thought to that before now.

They penetrated deeper and deeper into the narrow glen, lined for the next few miles by silver birch and horse chestnut trees, with a wealth of wild flowers growing around them – ragged robins, lords-and-ladies, small blue orchids, bluebells swaying in the gentle breeze. The road was climbing, she realized, and with the thinning out of the trees she could see dozens of sheep grazing on the hills rising on either side, and beyond them, in the distance, the snow-capped peaks of mountains pierced the sky. With so little sign of habitation as yet, Marianne had a strange feeling that they had left civilization behind, and she wondered how much further they had to go. Eventually they came to some small cottages, each with a neat strip of garden in front, and, she could see as they approached at an angle, a stretch of cultivated ground at the rear. She brightened now, and felt considerably better when she saw another cluster of houses and farther on, a small church with a large bell in its tiny steeple. Alongside, within the area of yew trees which surrounded the kirkyard, poked the chimneys of what she took to be the manse.

'That's the school,' the coachman announced shortly, pointing to what looked like another cottage on their left. He gave a cackle at her astonishment. 'It's the dominie's house, and all.'

Tipperton having had a large population of children, sometimes nearly a hundred and fifty at a time, its two-storeyed granite school had a good-sized, separate building at the side for the headmaster. The County Council employed one assistant for him, usually a product of Aberdeen University who had failed to graduate, and another helper known as a pupil-teacher, unpaid because he or she was learning a profession. So this tiny place seemed to be most inadequate.

'Just a dominie for the whole school?' she asked. 'No other teachers?'

'No teachers, just Mr Wink.' He turned round and grinned at her. 'Is that no' a funny name for a dominie? William Wink. He's been here all his life, and he's awfae good wi' the bairns. There's only five the noo – Jeannie and Maggie McDonald, wee Kirsty Bain, Chae Rattray and . . . oh, aye! The dominie's ain laddie, Peter. He's mair like his mother than his father, though! Mistress Wink wouldna be pleased if she kent folk ca' the dominie Wee Willie Winkie behind his back, for she thinks she's better than . . . oh!' His large brown hand thumped the side of the carriage. 'I shouldna say that to you, for I hear tell you're Master Hamish's intended?'

So caught up in his gossip, Marianne had practically forgotten how she would appear to the men and women on the estate. It wouldn't do for the future Mrs Bruce-Lyall to be seen hobnobbing with any of them, least of all the coachman. 'Yes,' she said, primly. 'We are engaged to be married, Mr . . . um . . .'

'I'm Carnie, miss. Just Carnie.'

'Carnie. I'll remember that.'

The next small collection of buildings boasted a shop, actually the front room of one of the houses, and judging by the vast selection of items packed into the window, it sold everything. One much larger house stood out from the others.

'That's the doctor's,' Carnie told her. 'Auld Dr Tyler retired just six month ago, and some folk havena got used to Robert Mowatt treating their ills, for he was born and brought up here in the glen and they still think of him as a laddie.'

In another hundred yards, the horse turned, once more of its own accord, into a wide drive with huge metal gryphons perched atop the gateposts, one on each side of the entrance. She knew they were gryphons because she had come across them in one of the books Andrew had given her to read to broaden her knowledge. But Andrew had no place in her mind here. Her eyes were drinking in as much as they could as she was borne between two lines of larch trees, their feathery boughs caressing the edge of the long curved drive. They were lovely to look at, though she couldn't help thinking that more daylight would filter through if there were fewer of them.

She hadn't realized that they were still going uphill until they emerged into an area of landscaped gardens that took her breath away with their splendour, neat low hedges breaking the huge expanses of lawns on the down slope into symmetrical designs, with flowerbeds in regular patterns. And then she saw it – the castle itself.

Her initial impression was one of disappointment. This wasn't the fairy-tale castle she had imagined, with quaint turrets and tall thin windows where an imprisoned Rapunzel might have let her hair down for her lover to climb. It seemed to have been built quite haphazardly, with no definite plan, and it was much smaller than she had expected. On closer inspection when they drew nearer, however, she found that it had been built in a series of wings, and stanchions, and – glory be! – there *were* some turrets after all, almost out of sight among the welter of stonework. It must be an awful old place, she decided, for it was just built of big boulders, probably carried down from the mountains and added to at various times. It wasn't nearly as grand as Balmoral – where Andrew had once taken her on the train – which was granite-built and sparkled in the sun as if it were studded with diamonds. But that had been rebuilt for Queen Victoria by her loving Prince Albert, God rest his soul, and Marianne Cheyne shouldn't be critical of Castle Lyall. At least it *was* a castle!

The horse came to a standstill at the steps up to a massive oaken door, and Carnie jumped to the ground to come hurrying round to help his passenger down, but Marianne was too rapt in discovering all she could about the higgledy-piggledy building to notice him. When she did, she got to her feet but was sidetracked by turning her head and seeing the panorama on that side of her. From this high vantage point, looking over the larches they had passed on the way up, she saw the mountains much better, range after range, some so tall that, judging by the amount of snow huddling in the passes between them even in May, it must come at least halfway down them in winter. What she could see of the most distant seemed to be truncated masses of dark blue rising mistily to blend into the hovering cumuli, but the lower slopes of the nearer ranges tended to be brown, probably with dead heather, for it wouldn't burst into glorious purple until August or September.

She shifted her attention to the foothills – nearer but still miles off – green for most of their height from the grass and undergrowth where there were no pines and firs, and from the trees themselves up as far as the tree-line.

She was surprised at how much she remembered of the natural history books Andrew had given her. Brought up in the heart of an area of low-lying farmland, windswept and bare, she had never seen mountains like these, and what she used to think were hills had been little more than mounds, touched with white only in the severest winters.

'Are you ready, miss?'

Carnie's voice brought her out of her reverie, and grasping his rough hand, she let him half lift her down on to the gravel driveway. Only then did the front door open, but it wasn't Hamish who stood waiting to welcome her, and she climbed the dozen or so steps with a heavy heart. If he couldn't come to the station to meet her, he should at least have been here to welcome her.

'Her Ladyship is waiting to receive you,' announced the stiffly erect maid, black-clad apart from a strip of white lace round her head.

'Thank you.'

'You're a bit late.'

Marianne wasn't going to start by apologizing for anything . . . to anyone. She followed the woman along a corridor until she halted outside one of the oak-panelled doors. After giving a small tap, the servant opened it just wide enough for Marianne to walk through, and closed it silently behind her, leaving her to stand uncertainly.

The elegant woman sitting in a chair by the window stared at her, giving her no indication of what she was expected to do. If this was meant to cow the girl, however, it had the opposite effect. Marianne reacted to the cavalier treatment by deciding not to knuckle under. At some date in the future, *she* would be Lady Glendarril and this ill-mannered woman in her silk dress and rope of pearls (for she *was* ill-mannered, even though she was an aristocrat) would be a dowager.

Smiling at this comforting thought, Marianne advanced into the room, and held out her hand. 'You must be Hamish's mother? I *was* expecting him to come to meet me at Laurencekirk – or at least one of the family – but it seems none of you has even a nodding acquaintance with mannerly behaviour.'

The last part came out before she realized what she was saying. She had no right to speak to a titled lady like that, and although she derived great satisfaction from seeing the woman's jaw drop as far as it would go, she whirled round in dismay at a sound behind her. The man in the door-way, however – quite short and unheathily thin, wearing old corduroy trousers and a battered tweed hat and jacket – wasn't scowling at her as she deserved, but was softly clapping his hands.

'Good for you!' He grinned at her impishly. 'Hamish said you had a lot of spunk. I am his father, in case you were wondering.'

'I thought you must be,' Marianne smiled, still deter-mined never to fall into the trap of apologizing. 'I'm very pleased to meet you.' She turned again to his wife, and this time, after a slight hesitation, her hand was touched by the heavily ringed fingers. 'I'm pleased to meet you, and all, Lady Glendarril,' she smiled, doing her best to put things right between them. She should have thought before saying what she had; she would be wise not to make an enemy of her future mother-in-law.

Lord Glendarril looked accusingly at his lady. 'Hamish said he was going to collect Marianne. Where is he?'

'I have had frightful indigestion since Sunday – I didn't tell you, Hector, in case it alarmed you – so I asked him to get some magnesia for me from the pharmacist in Montrose. He left early enough to be back in time to meet . . . the train.'

Her husband frowned. 'You did not need to send him to Montrose, surely? Robert could have given you something?'

She glared at him defiantly. 'I always get it from Montrose, but I have just remembered . . . the old man died some weeks ago, and I do not know if anyone has taken over from him yet.'

Marianne glanced at the man to see if he had been fooled by this blatant ploy to keep Hamish from going to the station, and was glad to see that his lips were compressed in a thin hard line.

When he caught her eye, he said, 'Would you like me to show you round some of the gardens, my dear? Or are you too tired after your journey?'

'No, it wasn't far and I'd love to see the gardens.'

He waited until they were clear of the house before he said, in a low voice, 'I am afraid that Lady Glendarril is against Hamish taking you as his wife.'

'I gathered that.'

'Since our other son died, she has pinned all her hopes on Hamish, and even if he wanted to marry one of the royal princesses, his mother would not consider her good enough. In any case, I have always believed that this family needs a new strain in it to set healthier blood running through its veins, and when he told me how well you had stood up to a girl who was nasty to you, I knew you were the one for us.'

'Well, I'm prepared to do my duty as his wife . . .' She decided to be brutally honest – there was something about this man that demanded it. 'I suppose he told you that love was never mentioned between us, so you won't be surprised to know I'm marrying him for the money?'

His expression saddened. 'I was afraid of that . . . but perhaps . . . in time you will . . .' He broke off. 'We should go back. Hamish is probably here and will be wondering where you are.'

While they strolled along he said, 'My wife is a woman who likes her own way, and I would advise you not to cross swords with her. For instance, however much you want the wedding to be to your liking, let her arrange it. She will derive great pleasure from letting it be known that she was responsible for everything. She has her mind set on making a great splash, the kind of show she was denied herself because her father, titled although he was, could not afford it. It was a pity you got off to such a bad start with her, but I am sure she will come round to you. Ah, here is Hamish now, and I would be obliged if you kept our little talk a secret.'

The length – and strength – of Hamish's apologies for not meeting her did much to soothe Marianne's ruffled feelings. It wasn't his fault that his mother had manipulated him. What was more, she had most likely smothered him with love after his twin died, and she would be to blame for Hamish being the way he was now. That was something *she'd* have to remember, Marianne told herself, when her son came along . . . When she arrived she had been pleased that both Hamish and his father were casually dressed, remembering her previous dress mistakes, but when she entered the dining room at seven that evening and saw them in evening dress and Lady Glendarril in a beautifully embroidered gown, with her greying hair coiled up in a deep swathe, Marianne's heart sank.

The maid assigned to Marianne had asked about a dress but Marianne hadn't understood the situation and had shrugged off – foolishly, she now knew – suggestions that she change.

The woman pounced on her immediately. 'Why have you not changed? Did Hamish not tell you that we always dress for dinner?'

Hamish jumped to his feet. 'I'm sorry, Marianne, I didn't think.'

'It wouldn't have mattered anyway,' she shrugged, struggling to keep her temper under control. 'I don't have any dresses – just blouses and skirts.' And not many of them, she thought sadly.

He came over and took her hand, squeezing it comfortingly as he led her gently to her place. Unfortunately, his seat was at the opposite side of the table and during the meal, he scarcely had a chance to say a word to her, his mother skilfully manoeuvring the conversation to exclude the interloper. Trying not to show how hurt she was, the girl took the opportunity to study as much of the room as she could see without twisting round. Facing her was a fireplace so immense that you could roast an ox in it, she thought, then smiled as she realized that any roasting of oxen or other beasts would be done in the kitchen, not in the dining room. The andirons, the poker, tongs and long-handled shovel, looked to be made of silver but surely they couldn't be? Heat would melt silver, wouldn't it?

The two magnificent portraits on either side of the chimney breast must be Bruce-Lyall ancestors. The man, resplendent in a maroon velvet jacket with a cream cravat at the neck, had a look of the present Lord Glendarril – the same penetrating blue eyes and silver hair receding from his deep forehead; the same brownish eyebrows and bushy moustache, though the beard was much bushier – his father, or grandfather? The woman at the other side would be his mother, or grandmother. Her attire was more sombre, her black dress, moulded to her body, showing a bust of large proportions. Her long face was sharply featured and her hair was metallic grey, pulled severely back off her face. The one redeeming feature in what would otherwise be a mundane representation of a serious, plain woman, was the twinkle, the sparkle, the artist had caught in her grey eyes.

Hoping that no one had noticed her absorption with the portraits, Marianne stole a glance at Hamish, and was astonished to find him looking at her with the same sparkling twinkle in his eyes, more blue than grey. His mother seeking his attention again, he turned away at once, and Marianne was free to continue her appraisal of the room.

Above the mantelshelf was another portrait, a younger man posing in a bright red uniform, his blond hair partly covered by a shako with a red hackle at the side. He was so like Lord Glendarril that he must be his brother.

To her left, she saw a pair of smaller paintings on the wall at right angles to the fireplace wall, again of a man and woman she took to be husband and wife, dressed in what could only be Regency style, very elegant and ornate. Beside the door, she noticed for the first time a row of miniatures, oval in shape and with narrow gold frames. She came to the conclusion that the only way she would find out who was who would be to ask Hamish . . . if she could get him away from his mother long enough.

By the time dinner was over, the strain was beginning to tell on Marianne, and when Lady Glendarril remarked on how tired she looked, she gladly took up Hamish's suggestion that she go to bed. She did need a rest, and a good night's sleep would help her to withstand all the jibes the woman cared to make tomorrow.

Chapter Seven

Perhaps it was the euphoria of organizing on such a large scale in such a short time, or perhaps Lady Glendarril had been warned by her husband to be more friendly towards her future daughter-in-law, but whichever it was, Marianne was very thankful that the woman grew less antagonistic towards her as the days went past. The only friction, a slight contretemps, was the compiling of the guest list for the wedding.

'Have you decided whom you wish to invite?' Clarice asked. 'If you have, I would like a list of the names and addresses as soon as possible . . . not more than two hundred, if you can avoid it.'

Marianne burst out laughing. 'I can give you my list right now, Lady Glendarril.' She stretched over for a piece of paper and a pencil, wrote for a minute or so and then handed it over.

Clarice scowled. 'I do not appreciate your sense of humour.'

'It wasn't meant to be funny. I just want to ask four people to my wedding, that's all, and surely there's nothing wrong in that?'

'But have you no other relatives?'

111

The smile was wiped off Marianne's face. 'No, and the Rennies are no relation either.' She hesitated, wondering if she should divulge her early life to this out-and-out snob, and came to the conclusion that the least said about it the better. She had given Andrew the four sovereigns and the silver and copper before she left Aberdeen and asked him to put them in his church collection, and that, as far as she was concerned, was the end of that! Her conscience was clear . . . though she still had to account for her non-relationship to the Rennies.

'They're just three sisters who took me in when I arrived in Aberdeen, homeless and friendless after I ran away from my cruel stepmother. They gave me a job in their shop and a room in their house.'

Lady Glendarril gasped. 'When Hamish told me about you, I asked my solicitor to make inquiries about them, to satisfy myself of your . . . and he said that their father had been a sea captain who had left them some money when he died. This was how they bought their shop – selling children's wear? – which, I understand, is quite successful. I had no idea . . . Hamish let me believe that they were your aunts –'

'They're Andrew's aunts,' Marianne interrupted, 'and maybe Hamish didn't realize –' She broke off, then murmured, 'I'm sorry, but they're the only real friends I've ever had.'

'But,' floundered the older woman, 'you must know a few girls . . . ?'

Marianne snorted. 'Them that I met would be the last folk I'd invite.'

'But there are already more than a hundred and fifty on my list.'

Hector stepped in now, his eyes resting pityingly on Marianne before he addressed his wife.

'You must crop your list, Clarice. Why can you not settle for the quiet ceremony Hamish said he would prefer?'

Quite clearly averse to the idea of having to tone down her plans, but an aristocrat to her fingertips, she ignored his last question. 'I presume you will want to invite the Mowatts, the Peats and the Winks?'

This annoyed him further. 'We must ask the whole glen,' he scowled. 'The workers would be deeply hurt if they were not allowed to see their future laird being married.'

'Then I shall have to book Brechin Cathedral instead of St Giles,' she declared, giving a resigned sigh, 'and we shall have to provide transport for them. In the face of that, you must at least let me invite all my relatives.'

'Just your sisters and their husbands,' he stipulated. 'That makes four for you and four for Marianne, and I suppose to be fair we should invite four of Hamish's friends too.'

'I did ask him, but he said there was no one in particular that he wanted to ask.'

Marianne was disappointed at the turn events had taken. She didn't want to be married in a small place like Brechin, even though it *was* in a cathedral. She wanted to be the main attraction at a big society wedding in St Giles, the most prestigious place of worship in Scotland's capital city. On the other hand, though, now she came to think of it, she might make more of an impact as a big fish in a small pond.

When Hamish came home that evening from a trip to Aberdeen, he was pleased to be told of the change in wedding plans. 'That suits me,' he grinned. 'I was not at

113

all keen on us being the focus of all eyes in Edinburgh, were you, Marianne?'

'Not really.' She had actually been looking forward to seeing the bystanders' mouths drop open in reverence at her beauty, to having them whisper to each other that she was the next Lady Glendarril . . . but surely it would still happen like that, if on a smaller scale. After all, she could make a proper splash when she accompanied her husband and his parents to London for the Queen's Jubilee on 22 June. Lady Glendarril had promised to help her choose some dresses for that occasion, too, and it was to be only two weeks after her own big day. She was bound to meet hordes of the nobility there.

Excitement pulsed throughout the castle as the young Master's wedding drew nearer. The servants were avidly looking forward to the trip to Brechin in the laird's crested carriages and being guests in the cathedral along with the nobs. By early June, Lady Glendarril had taken Marianne to Edinburgh several times to select and fit a gown for the bride, and an outfit for herself, and although Marianne had been given no choice in hers, she didn't care. The creation her future mother-in-law had plumped for was absolutely perfect. Its foundation was a plain ivory silk shift, and at the final fitting, when her waist was confined in a high corset which pushed up her bosom, Marianne was delighted with her new figure. The frothy Chantilly lace overdress had dozens of minuscule seed pearls sewn on, and the matching train trailed yards behind her as she paraded around the small salon in the Royal Mile, which, according to Lady Glendarril, was patronized by all the royal princesses when they were at Holyrood.

It was at the final fitting, when Marianne first saw the headdress – which could have passed for a tiara with a veil – that she wondered if she would ever have the dress sense that Hamish's mother seemed to have, a talent for instinctively going for what was most suitable . . . and most expensive.

While Lady Glendarril was having some last-minute alterations done to her own ensemble – a straight, powder-blue dress with a long jacket to be worn with a huge straw hat with deeper blue fringing round the brim – Marianne was taken to another room for silk underwear, silk stockings and ivory-coloured satin shoes.

'Nobody'll see what I've got on underneath,' she laughed.

The assistant who was attending to her – the manageress was fussing around Lady Glendarril – did not smile. 'Knowing that she is dressed to perfection, underneath as well as on top, gives a bride confidence.'

Her hands slid down the hour-glass figure, then up again to make a small tweak at the neckline which then showed less bust.

On the return journey in the train, Marianne noticed that her companion looked deathly pale and beads of sweat were sitting on her upper lip – though it would offend her dignity to be told so. 'Are you all right, Lady Glendarril?' she asked anxiously.

'To be honest, Marianne, no, I am not. A dreadful tiredness came over me after we had lunch, and it has grown worse and worse.'

'You should have told me. We could have come home hours ago.'

'I did not want to have to come back again.'

She said no more, but Marianne kept a wary eye on her, watching for any further sign of exhaustion or illness, and she was glad when Lady Glendarril's eyelids drooped. A short sleep should help her.

When they arrived at Laurencekirk station, she was relieved to see Hamish standing on the platform. He came forward to give them a hand down, and then helped them into the landau while Carnie saw to their parcels.

'Your mother's not feeling well,' Marianne whispered. 'I think we should stop at the doctor's.'

But the woman had heard. 'You will do no such thing,' she said weakly. 'It has been a long day and I am very tired, that is all. I will be back to normal by morning.'

Her personal maid having been given the day off and not expected back until 10 p.m., Marianne saw Lady Glendarril to bed as soon as they entered the castle, and his Lordship himself carried up a tea-tray to her. 'She does not want anything,' he said, when he came down five minutes later. 'And that is most unlike her.'

Marianne tried to stop him fretting. 'I'm tired myself, and I'm a lot younger than she is. Leave her to sleep.'

Immediately after dinner, when Lord Glendarril took himself off to bed, the girl looked at her young man apologetically. 'I hope you won't be offended, Hamish, but I'll have to get some sleep, too.'

'I'd like to talk to you for a few minutes first.'

'Make it quick, then. I'm dropping on my feet.'

His eyes averted from her, he said, 'I trust that you still want to go ahead with the wedding? I know that you do not love me, and I wondered if you had changed your mind . . .'

She sighed. 'You told me why you wanted me to marry you, Hamish, and I told you why I accepted you. It is a business arrangement – agreeable to both parties – nothing more than that.'

'Yes, but . . . 'He hesitated, then burst out, 'I had the feeling you were in love with Andrew Rennie, so if you want to carry on seeing him after we're married, I won't –'

'I *will* carry on seeing him, Hamish, but I'm not in love with him either. I don't need anybody to love, I'll be quite happy the way we'll be . . .' She paused briefly then sighed. 'Now, if that's all you wanted to talk about, can I go to bed?'

'Yes, of course.' He held his hand out and squeezed hers briefly as she stood up. 'Thank you for being so honest with me, my dear, and remember, if ever you do fall in love, I shall sort something out.'

'Divorce, you mean?'

'Oh, no! Divorce would be unthinkable for a Bruce-Lyall, but we could arrange something, I'm sure. Something that would suit both of us. Now, off you go!'

The early morning peace of Castle Lyall was shattered by a loud wail of anguish. 'No! No! Oh dear God, no!'

Marianne jumped out of bed and, not stopping to put on a wrap, hurried along the corridor. Servants were appearing in various kinds of night attire, converging at the point where Lord Glendarril, wild-eyed and ashencheeked, was standing in his nightwear at the door of his wife's room.

Gripping his silk dressing robe together on top of a nightshirt that was too short to hide his bare legs, Hamish pushed to the front and grabbed his father's arm with his free hand. 'What's wrong?'

'Your mother! I came to see how she was, and she did not answer me. I think she . . . is dead!'

This galvanized the entire gathering into action. Carnie said, 'I'll get the doctor,' and he dashed downstairs. His wife, the cook – her hair hanging like a grey-flecked black blanket down her back instead of being pinned neatly on top of her head as it was normally seen – gathered her staff together to go down to make some tea and have some sustenance ready for his Lordship and his family; the chamber maids – looking uncomfortable in the dozens of little rags they had put in their hair in order to curl it – looked at each other in helpless blankness until Mrs Carnie told them to light the fires in all the public rooms and to have them spotless for the many callers who were certain to come. She also took one look at the mistress's personal maid and said, 'You'd better come down and all, Thomson, and get some brandy in you afore you land on the floor in a faint.'

The gardener and his underlings went to waken the young lads who slept in a room above the stables, so that they could get the other carriages and equipment ready before Carnie came back.

Having had a quick but close look at his mother to make sure that she really had stopped breathing, Hamish turned to Marianne. 'I'll take my father downstairs and give him a dram to steady his nerves, and I'd be obliged if you'll stay with Mother until the doctor comes. You won't be frightened, will you? Thomson is in no fit state but I could send up one of the other –'

Despite the chattering of her teeth, Marianne said bravely, 'No, I'll be all right; it's your father that needs the attention now.'

She watched him helping the older man as far as the landing, then turned round and advanced slowly into the chamber of death. She made it to a chair and, her knees refusing to bend, sat down with a thump. She had no idea when Lady Glendarril had died, but already there was that unmistakable sense of another presence in the room. She'd had the very same feeling after her own mother died, and hadn't been comforted by a neighbour's doom-laden observation, 'It's the Grim Reaper letting you ken he's been.'

When the doctor arrived, almost an hour later because he had been at a difficult confinement, Marianne was stiff with cold and fear, and was glad to be packed off to bed with a sleeping powder. She was asleep in no time and heard nothing of the ensuing commotion, or the visits Hamish made to check on her.

It was late afternoon when she came to her senses again, and she lay for some minutes remembering and conjecturing. This was Tuesday and the wedding had been planned for Saturday, but no doubt it would have to be postponed. It was ludicrous, she knew, but she couldn't help feeling that Lady Glendarril had planned this as well, hoping the wait until the end of the recognized period of mourning would make her change her mind about marrying Hamish.

But Marianne Cheyne certainly wasn't going to give up the chance of the best marriage she would ever be offered, and if she did have to wait a year, she would hold out for St Giles and resurrect Lady Glendarril's original guest list. Best of all, she would ask Andrew to find out the addresses of those horrible girls who had belittled her in Aberdeen and invite them all, rub their snooty noses in the splendour of her wedding gown and her castle home. Yet, even with the thought of an Edinburgh wedding enabling her to get her own back on Sybil and friends, she didn't really want to wait. She would rather be married sooner than later.

She got out of bed languorously and went over to the washstand where the willow-pattern ewer had been filled with water, probably hot at the time but now stone cold. Pouring some into the matching bowl, she splashed her face several times, which took her breath away but gave her the invigoration she needed. Selecting one of the lawn blouses Clarice had bought for her on their first visit to Edinburgh, she dressed herself with more care than usual, because she could hear strange voices wafting up, and guessed that the house would already be full of people come to pay their respects to the dead woman.

She discovered that they were well past the respects stage, and had progressed to airing their views on when the wedding should now take place. No one noticed her as she circumnavigated the large group in the ballroom, her ears taking in every argument put forward for the postponement of the wedding, yet hoping that someone would advocate letting it go ahead as planned. After a time, concluding that this was too much to hope for, she moved into the vast library – walls lined with shelf after shelf of leather-bound tomes, with busts of famous authors placed in a seemingly random manner on all available surfaces – where another heated discussion was going on.

Those assembled here were clearly relatives of Lady Glendarril, her sisters and their husbands amongst them, likely, who were not afraid of saying what they thought, no matter what. Here, also, were Hamish and his father, both scarlet in the face and looking ready to erupt at any moment.

'Oh, no, Jarvis!' exclaimed one whale-boned, silver-haired matron to a man who may or may not have been her husband. 'They cannot be married as soon as that. Three months is not nearly long enough for –'

'A year at least,' agreed another high-bosomed lady who could have been her twin. 'And it should be St Giles, like poor dear Clarice wanted. I simply cannot understand why she cancelled that. It was so inconsiderate! I had my dress made long before the letter came to say she had changed it to Brechin and we were not invited after all.'

Hector could contain himself no longer. 'No, and you will still not be invited, Priscilla, whatever I decide. And I hope all of you heard that! Whatever *I* decide, I said, for it is my decision that counts, not what any of you think. I have been mulling it over ever since you descended on my house like a plague of locusts and I am sure Hamish and –' He broke off to look round, then, spotting Marianne hovering near the door, he held out his hand to her. 'Come here, my dear, and tell me what you think of *my* idea.'

He put his arm round her shoulders when she went to him. 'I see no reason to postpone the wedding for a year, not even three months. We could have the funeral on Friday and the wedding could go ahead in Brechin on Saturday as planned. *Or* . . . and this is what I believe we *should* do . . . we can have both wedding and funeral on Saturday in our own kirk here in the glen.'

Shocked gasps and dismayed exclamations greeted this. 'Hector, you simply can *not* have a wedding and a funeral . . .'

'It isn't done, Hector, old boy.' This from a stout man with such a purple complexion that Marianne feared he was about to have a heart attack there and then.

Hector looked at her. 'What do you think, my dear? Would you be willing to . . . Do you feel you could cope with that?'

'I'll do whatever you say,' she quavered, 'as long as Hamish –'

Her bridegroom-to-be drew in a long breath and let it out noisily. 'I don't see why not, if Duncan doesn't object. The Reverend Duncan Peat,' he added, for the benefit of those not familiar with the name.

'Duncan won't object,' Hector said, waving his hand airily. 'He is a product of the glen.'

At this, several dissenting voices pointed out that his place of birth should have no bearing on his beliefs, and Hamish waited for silence before he said, 'My father financed him while he studied for the ministry.'

Embarrassed that his largesse had been made public, Hector mumbled, 'That does not mean I expect him to kowtow to me. He is quite free to refuse to conduct one or other of the ceremonies, or both if he so wishes, but he holds liberal views. I think he will agree.'

With barely concealed ill grace, the members of this gathering split into small groups to discuss the matter further, although some, out of curiosity, followed their host to the ballroom, where, with his arm still round Marianne, he made his announcement again. It was received in exactly the same way as before.

Head held high, and leaving his son to deal with irate relatives and friends, Hector shepherded the girl upstairs to the room where his wife lay, and only then gave way to his true feelings. 'Clarice, oh, Clarice,' he moaned, plumping down on a tapestry-cushioned chair. 'I know you tried to be a good wife to me, but I'd have been happier if you had not tried to run my life. If I had let you, you would have strangled me with affection like you did Hamish. That was why I went away so often – to get away from you. I felt free when I was in Edinburgh and London, free to find a woman to give me release from the eternal frustration of bowing to your wishes.'

Somewhat shocked and very embarrassed by what he was admitting, Marianne let him ramble on. It was probably the best thing he could do.

'You would have been hurt and puzzled, Clarice, by the length of time I spent in the arms of those ladies of the streets, but I was determined not to be like my ancestors, most of whom, according to legend, were more interested in other men than in women. Mind you, for a time in my teens, at school, I did have a preference for masculine company, but once I left I did not take long to discover the delights girls could provide.'

He took his handkerchief out to mop his perspiring face, and as he returned it to his breast pocket, he muttered, 'I should not have betrayed my wife. Thank God she never knew.'

He fell silent, and Marianne still couldn't think of anything to say. She wished with all her heart that she could sneak out and leave him to his tortured thoughts, but she couldn't bring herself to move. She was hardly aware of Hamish coming in almost twenty minutes later, but gratefully accepted his arm to help her to stand. When he took her into her own room, she said, 'You should get your father out of there. It's not good for him.'

'I'll see to him in a minute, but I wanted to tell you Miss Glover has told the chamber maids to make rooms ready for those relatives who live furthest away. If they do not arrive until tomorrow, they will likely want to stay over until Saturday. I sent the trap for Duncan Peat and he came up with a solution that everyone finally agreed to. He'll have the funeral service first so that those not invited to the wedding can leave before it starts, but . . .' he stopped with a wry smile, 'I am afraid they will all stay on out of curiosity, though there won't be many asked back to the house. Marianne, are you still sure about this?'

'I'm still sure, though I wish it was all over. Now, for any sake, Hamish, go to your father.'

Left alone, she sank back on her bed to think. The society wedding in St Giles she had longed for was only a pipe dream now. She had been prepared to settle for making a ripple at Brechin, and that, too, had been knocked on the head. Nevertheless, being married in a wee kirk in a sparsely populated glen, with members of the nobility mixing with the castle staff and estate workers, would most likely be unique particularly since it was to follow a funeral where some of the mourners would be wedding guests once the coffin was interred in the kirkyard. It would be a talking point for years, Marianne mused happily.

Her first priority would be to let Andrew and his aunts know of this latest development. They had declined to attend at either St Giles or Brechin Cathedral – no doubt they felt such places would be too grand for them – but surely they wouldn't refuse to come to a wee kirk where most of the people in the pews would be workers in the Glendarril mill and their families, and tenants of the wee crofts on the estate. The four Rennies would have to come! They were her only guests . . . and she had the feeling she would need them.

Chapter Eight

'Well, I never!' exclaimed Edith Rennie in some irritation, when she read the short note Marianne had enclosed with her letter to Andrew. 'How can she and Hamish be so callous?'

Esther was not quite so quick to criticize. 'They could hardly have carried on with their original arrangements . . . not with a death in the family.'

Edith nodded vehemently. 'That is precisely what I meant. They should be showing more respect and not turning his mother's funeral into some sort of circus. His father must be cut to the quick that they have not cancelled the wedding . . . nor even postponed it.'

'I gather from what she said in her letter to me,' Andrew put in, 'that it was Lord Glendarril himself who suggested it, Aunt Edith. She said he was angry at his wife's relatives for dictating that the couple should wait anything from three months to a year.'

Esther and Emily exchanged troubled glances, but it was left to Edith to ask the question. 'Andrew, you do not think . . . ? Marianne could not be . . . ? Surely Lady Glendarril would not have let her son make free with the girl?'

Amused by her spinsterish euphemistic term for reduction as much as by her calculated refusal to use any of the words usually associated with pregnancy, Andrew was still appalled at the suggestion that this was the reason for the hasty tying of the knot. 'Oh no, I shouldn't think that!'

'Poor girl,' murmured Emily, joining into the discussion at last. 'Marianne was so happy . . . and now . . . oh dear!'

Esther nodded. 'Yes, immediately after she becomes Hamish's wife, she will have to stand at his mother's graveside and comfort him! Solemnizing a marriage and consecrating a body to the grave at more or less the same time sounds very heathenish to me, and it does not bode well for their future happiness.'

Knowing why Marianne was marrying Hamish, Andrew let out a deep sigh. Even before the unexpected death of the bridegroom's mother, he had not foreseen the girl being truly happy on her wedding day, never mind in the future, and as it was . . . 'It's the other way round, Aunt Esther. They have arranged to have the wedding ceremony after the burial, and I'm sure Marianne will cope, whatever happens.'

Edith regarded him shrewdly. 'You are not thinking of attending, are you, Andrew?'

He gave an apologetic smile. 'I thought she might need someone on her side, someone she could turn to if anything goes wrong. She has nobody down there, nobody at all.'

Edith was about to point out that she had Hamish, but something in her nephew's eyes stopped her.

'If there's any bad feeling amongst the mourners,' he carried on, 'and I fear there will be since Lord Glendarril has stipulated that only the estate workers will be looked on as wedding guests, Marianne will need me . . . all of us, Aunt Edith. That's why she wrote. We are invited back to the castle afterwards as her guests . . . her *only* guests.'

'In that case, we had better accept, but it scarcely gives us time to find clothes suitable for both ceremonies – a Herculean task.'

When Andrew was leaving, Edith walked a little way along the street with him, and he guessed she meant to give him a lecture. Her first words proved him right.

'I hope you have thought carefully about what you are doing, Andrew. I know how you feel about Marianne, and I am rather afraid that watching her being joined in holy matrimony to another man will be too much for you.'

'It's because I love her that I want to be there for her, though it'll turn the knife deeper into my heart. I'll never stop loving her, Aunt Edith, so I'll have to get used to her being someone else's wife. I'm a grown man now so stop worrying about me. Marianne said one of their carriages would pick us up at Laurencekirk station if we did decide to go, so I'll send her a telegram to let her know we will be there.'

Before she turned away, his aunt stroked his cheek. 'You are a dear boy, Andrew, and I hope with all my heart that some day you will find a –'

He interrupted her there, to stop her hoping for the impossible. 'We have to take the nine forty train on Saturday forenoon, so I'll meet you at the station around half-past.'

Saturday dawned bright and fair, but the tension at Castle Lyall became more fraught as the morning progressed, resentment running high amongst those who had stayed overnight and still had not been invited as guests at the wedding. Fortunately, Lord Glendarril had taken the precaution of having Carnie and his wife set up tables in the ballroom as well as in the dining room, so that his relatives – a few ancient aunts and spinster cousins – and the army of relations on his wife's side could be kept separate while they had breakfast . . . not that it was really necessary. The majority on both sides agreed that the wedding should have been put off, and all were outraged that they had been ordered to leave after the interment. They whispered to each other that Hector's loss had temporarily deranged his mind – why else would he ban them from the wedding reception? – but one look at his set face prevented even the most stout-hearted from saying anything.

Marianne, aware of the atmosphere there would be downstairs, kept to her room – she was nervous enough without getting involved in any arguments – but she was quite glad when Lord Glendarril himself appeared with a cup of tea after her breakfast tray had been removed untouched.

'You need something in your stomach to see you through this day,' he said, sitting down on the edge of her bed. 'How are you feeling?'

'Not as bad as I thought I'd be.'

'Only another few hours to go and then we can relax. We will still have the reception to get through, of course, but the workers will likely clear the tables of food in no time, and I have told them there will be no dancing or celebrating afterwards . . . not in the castle. I have made

129

several crates of spirits and porter available to them, and what they do in the privacy of their own homes – or in the school hall – is up to them. I know some people think I am showing no respect for Clarice, but I have had to steel myself, and I know I shall give way when everything is over.'

'It would be only natural,' Marianne murmured although privately wondering how natural anything could be in such an unnatural situation.

'Natural, perhaps, but as a Bruce-Lyall, I cannot let that sort of weakness be seen by the minions. I must say, I have been impressed by how Hamish has been taking his mother's death. He was so devoted to her I would have thought . . . but he must have more backbone than I gave him credit for.'

He laid her empty cup on the table by the bed and patted her hand. 'I suspect that he, too, will give way when the pressure is off, so you will have to be strong for him, my dear.'

'I will,' she promised. 'I know it sounds awful, but I didn't know your wife very long, so I'm not so affected as everybody else.'

'That is good. After today, you will take her place as Lady of the . . . but we will say no more about that at present. I shall send Thomson up to help you dress. She will be *your* personal maid now.'

Something he hadn't considered before suddenly struck him. 'Um, Marianne, I trust you will wear the wedding gown Clarice chose?'

'Oh, Lord Glendarril, I couldn't turn up at her funeral dressed like that! What would folk say?'

He gave a half-smile. 'My dear girl, we Bruce-Lyalls do not give a damn for what people say, especially the upstart

130

nouveaux riches who bore their way into everything. As for *my* workers, every man, woman and child is dependent on me for the roofs over their heads, for the food they eat, for the clothes they wear. Not that I ever cast that up to them, but whatever they think of today's arrangements, they are unlikely to voice their opinions aloud.'

'But I wouldn't feel right about it myself,' Marianne pointed out. 'I could wear the navy costume she had made for me, that would –'

'You cannot get married in a navy costume!' he frowned. 'I know how these women's minds work. They will be wishing they could have seen the wonderful gown our maids told them about.' He tapped his fingers on the jamb of the door for a few seconds then brightened. 'I know! I shall tell Thomson to pack it carefully in its box, and one of the young lads can take it to the church as soon as possible. You will wear your navy costume when you leave here, but after the funeral, she will help you to change in the vestry, and I guarantee that you will cause quite a stir when you walk down the aisle.'

That settled it for Marianne. He was arranging it so that she could have her big moment after all, although she would have preferred more people – especially more of the aristocracy – to witness it. But why was he rushing the wedding like this? Was he afraid that Hamish might change his mind, or was he afraid that he, himself, would die unexpectedly?

Andrew was astonished when Hamish himself met them at the station. 'I got orders from Marianne to take you to the house first because she has something to ask your aunts.'

After being helped into the impressive landau, the ladies settled back to enjoy the scenery, and Hamish turned to face the other man. 'I have something to ask you, too, Andrew. I would be honoured if you would act as best man for me. I'm glad you could come, and since we are keeping the numbers to a minimum . . .'

'Of course, and I'll be honoured to do it.' Nevertheless, Andrew's heart was aching at the thought of what this would entail.

His aunts were much happier at what Marianne asked of them. She had decided, when she first knew they were definitely coming, to ask Andrew if he would give her away, but Hamish had appropriated him to be best man, and she had enquired of the minister if she could have a woman to take over this duty.

Duncan Peat had said he didn't see why not, although it was most unusual, and so she had asked Miss Edith to do this, and Miss Emily and Miss Esther to be bridesmaids.

The small church was absolutely packed for the funeral service, with many of the gentry left fuming outside. The hymns were played on a small wheezy harmonium by an elderly woman who seemed to be crouching over the keyboard as her feet pedalled madly, but the music could be heard even above the lusty singing. After Duncan Peat spoke a fitting eulogy for the laird's wife, he put up a shorter prayer than usual before the last hymn was sung. The six pallbearers now stepped to the front and hoisted the brass-handled coffin up on their shoulders. In a slow march, they carried it outside to where the beadle, who was also gravedigger, had the family lair – the largest and most ostentatious in the kirkyard with a huge marble angel standing guard at its head – open to receive its latest occupant.

Still frightened of cemeteries and gravestones, Marianne kept her eyes on Hamish, and saw his pallor change to a horrible grey. Alarmed that he was going to faint and fall into the grave, she was about to run forward to him when she noticed that his father was exactly the same colour. She should have expected it. After all, they were saying goodbye to a woman they had loved. She herself, mindful of what she had to do immediately after the service, had purposely kept in the background, and when the Reverend Duncan Peat ended his closing prayer, she signed to her maid and to Esther and Emily to follow her to the vestry.

Some ten minutes later, she was asking, 'Do I look all right? Is my veil on straight?'

Thomson, a small woman in her late forties, seemed to be struck dumb by the transformation of the robust young girl into this elegant woman, but Miss Esther breathed, 'You are absolutely lovely, my dear. I do not think I have ever seen a more beautiful bride.'

Thomson slipped out to give the organist the signal and then sat in the seat Mrs Carnie had kept for her. When the Wedding March rang out, Marianne made sure that her two maids of honour had a firm grip of her long train before going forth to link arms with Miss Edith, who had been waiting just inside the church door for her moment of glory.

The little procession moved slowly and gracefully down the aisle – Miss Esther and Miss Emily in the midnight-blue shantung dresses they had considered suitable for both funeral and wedding, though they had not known beforehand that they would be bridesmaids, and Miss Edith regally tall and erect in a clerical-grey moire two piece, as if she had known she was to act as 'father of the bride'. The gasps from those in the rear pews were enough to make all heads swivel in order to have a good look at the bride, the girl who had flouted convention by wearing a gown fit for a princess when she should be in unrelieved black to show respect for the woman who had died before becoming her mother-in-law.

As though to the manor born, Marianne kept her head aloft and her step slow and measured. She knew that this day would be spoken of in the glen for many years, and hoped that these women would not hold it against her. Surely they would realize that she'd had no option?

'You are very quiet, Andrew,' Edith observed when they were homeward bound in the early evening. 'I hope that you are not –'

'I'm all right, Aunt Edith. I must admit it was an ordeal, but not quite as bad as I expected. I was really proud of you three, though. You carried out your duties to perfection.'

As he had hoped, this took their minds off him, and they proceeded to discuss the funeral, the wedding, the meal, the friendliness of the glen folk, leaving him free for his own thoughts. The sight of Marianne walking so determinedly down that aisle would have amused him in other circumstances, but he had been overcome with love for her, she looked so ethereal, so virginal, swathed in yards of ivory lace, and he had been hard pressed not to fold her in his arms and defy anyone to take her away from him. But . . . she was not his!

He had known, of course, that Marianne did not love Hamish – which was what had made it easier for him to bear his heartache – but he hadn't realized until today that Hamish did not love her. Hamish had stood like a statue while she came nearer, had shown no sign of emotion when she reached him, had not had the slightest tremor in his voice when he made his vows. The minister had to tell him to kiss his bride, and the kiss itself was a token gesture. Andrew didn't know whether to be glad at Hamish's lack of response or sorry for Marianne. Most girls would want to be loved, for that love to be proved in front of the congregation, but Marianne was not most girls. The thing was, would she be satisfied to spend the rest of her life with a man who had come across as completely indifferent to her?

There was a suggestion of dawn in the sky, yet Marianne Bruce-Lyall was still lying wide awake, remembering, conjecturing, but not, for one single moment, regretting. She had savoured to the full the impact she had made. Apart from the thrill she had got from the audible reactions in the church to her gown, there had been the standing inside the ballroom to be introduced to the handful of relatives present and better still, to every resident of the glen. Although nothing specific had been said or done, she had been left with the distinct impression that Hamish's kinfolk looked down on her, but the estate workers, those she would be most likely to come in contact with, had made her feel welcome amongst them . . . as their better.

Her mind now went over her leave-taking of the Rennies. She had expected Miss Emily and Miss Esther to be weepy, but she had been astonished that Edith had openly dabbed her eyes and then hugged her closely. 'You know I wish you happiness, Marianne dear,' she had whispered, 'but I would like you to look on us as aunts to whom you can come if you need advice, or if . . .'

Her voice breaking there, Marianne had said shakily, 'Thank you, I'll not forget.'

Then Andrew had taken her hand, his eyes dark with the hurt she had inflicted on him. 'I'm truly sorry, Andrew,' she'd murmured, his pain reaching out to clamp around her heart.

His finger had risen to dash away the tear that she couldn't stop edging out. 'No tears, my dear,' he'd told her. 'I am happy that your wish came true, and I sincerely hope that you will find happiness as well as contentment in your new life . . . but remember, Marianne, if things do not work out the way you envisaged, I will gladly come and take you away from him.'

Before she realized what he was doing, he had swept her into his arms and given her a kiss that came within a hair's-breadth of being passionate. Then, with a stifled moan, he had jumped on the landau and it had moved away. She had gone back to Hamish, who had been standing in the doorway to give her privacy to say her goodbyes. He'd looked even greyer than before, despite the feverish spot in his cheeks.

'There's still a few left,' he'd muttered, 'but my father is helping them to gather all the left-overs . . . Ah, here they come.'

The few he mentioned – about ten over-happy men and perhaps six women – had reached the foot of the curved steps as the first of the traps returned, and Marianne had had to smile when she'd noticed the boxes that clinked being loaded much more carefully than the ones which presumably held the left-overs from the meal.

'Thank you for everything, your Lordship,' the oldest man had grinned and, after shaking his employer's hand, he'd turned to Marianne. 'My best wishes to you and your man, m'lady, and dinna tak' lang to gi'e us the heir we need.'

The sturdy woman who was obviously his wife had pulled at his sleeve. 'Behave yoursel', Tarn! Get up on the coach, for ony sake.'

The drive empty at last, Hector had turned unsteadily, and Marianne had helped him up the steps, smiling as she noticed how high he was lifting each foot, as if uncertain where to set it down. Recalling having seen Dick, his valet, staggering around in an advanced stage of inebriation quite early on, she'd realized that the servant would be totally incapable by this time of attending to his master. 'Will Hamish help you get undressed?' she'd asked her father-in-law inside.

'I can manage to take off my own clothes,' he'd said, but it was the bridal couple themselves who had half carried him up to his room, where, giving up all pretence of joviality, he'd sat down on his bed with tears streaming down his face. Never having seen a grown man cry, Marianne had felt most uncomfortable. 'I'll leave you to deal with him,' she had whispered to Hamish, and withdrew before he could say anything.

She'd felt pleased to have the chance to undress without being seen, but had forgotten that she could not unfasten the hooks and eyes down the back by herself and she had not wanted to ring for Thomson. Sighing, she'd sat down at her dressing table to wait for her bridegroom.

It had been twenty minutes before he'd appeared. 'Too much whisky made Father very emotional,' he'd muttered, 'but he's fast asleep now.'

'That's the best thing for him. Hamish, will you help me out of this gown?'

When he'd come closer, she'd seen that his face was ravaged by tears. 'Hamish, I'm sorry. I should have known how upset you'd be. I'll ring for Thomson.'

'I'll manage!' With what was almost a grunt, he'd grabbed her by the shoulders and spun her round with her back to him, so that he could undo the tiny fasteners. Letting her go abruptly when they were all open, he'd burst into tears and she'd thought it best to let him get it out of his system. Eventually, he had said brokenly, 'I am truly sorry, Marianne. I don't know what you must think of me, but I couldn't help it.'

Knowing that he was ashamed of himself for giving way, she'd tried to reassure him. 'I was the same when my mother died. Everybody's the same. After all, your mother's the person who feeds you and takes care of you when you're small . . .'

'I can't even use that as an excuse,' he'd hiccuped. 'My brother and I had a succession of nurses to feed us and care for us.'

She could have bitten her tongue out. 'Your mother gave birth to you, Hamish, and there's always a close bond between children and their mothers, especially boys, I've been told.'

138

'Perhaps that is it, then. Ever since my brother died, I have felt it my duty to make it up to her. She was almost inconsolable at the time, and made such a fuss of me after she recovered.' He'd stopped, and there was a long pause before he had whispered, 'I know what you are expecting of me, Marianne, but I can't, not tonight!'

'I understand,' she'd soothed, but to his rapidly retreating back.

It shouldn't have come as any surprise to her, but she could not help feeling let down. It was their wedding night and he had left her in this huge bed on her own.

Because of the ill-feeling he had engendered by having the wedding immediately after the funeral, Hector had decided to offer a kind of sop to the offended relatives who had stayed all night.

Sitting down to breakfast the following morning, he looked around the table with a somewhat shamed expression. 'I have been thinking more clearly since my beloved wife was laid to rest,' he said sadly, wiping away a non-existent tear, 'and I realize that I ought to have listened to . . .' He cleared his throat noisily. 'I should have let Hamish and Marianne postpone their marriage as they wanted to, but what is done can not be undone, and I pledge, before all of you here, that my entire household will observe the customary full year of mourning. We will not, therefore, attend the Queen's Jubilee on the twenty-second as we had planned.'

The satisfied murmurs proved that his strategy had worked. Only Marianne's disappointed expression pricked his conscience and, as soon as he got her alone, he murmured, 'I am very sorry, my dear. I know how much you were looking forward to going to London to join the celebrations, but it is best that we do not flout convention again.'

Marianne nodded her head. 'I *am* disappointed, but I do understand. I heard Lady Glendarril's two . . . cousins, I think, say yesterday that they were shocked at you for . . .'

'If I tried to count the times I have shocked Eunice and Rosemary over the years,' he chuckled, 'it would be in the hundreds, perhaps even the thousands. They are sour old maids – they were sour even when they were young. It would have done them the world of good if one of their brother's friends had ravished them.'

Marianne's smile vanished when Hector went on, 'Speaking of which, I hope you will soon be telling me that I am going to be a grandfather.' He clasped her hand tightly for a second and then walked away.

Wondering what he would have said if she told him what had happened the night before, Marianne went upstairs to the room where she had lain alone in the darkness. The vast bed had curtains all round, which she intended to remove as soon as she could. She had left them open last night, but she had still felt as though they were smothering her when she tried to get some sleep.

When would Hamish come to her bed and make them truly husband and wife? Surely he wasn't such a Mammy's boy that he'd take weeks to get over her death?

She took a deep breath. What was the good of looking on the black side? It was early days yet.

Moll Cheyne had waited impatiently all forenoon for her husband to come home, and the minute

140

he walked in, she burst out, 'Have you seen the day's paper, Alfie?'

'I havena time to sit about readin' papers,' he growled, setting his hard backside on the equally hard chair at the table. 'I hardly get time to draw breath.'

Always worried that the sawdust he breathed in would eventually clog his lungs completely, Moll let him finish his soup before she handed him the *Aberdeen Journal* and pointed to the photographs accompanying a prominent article. It had been written by a cub reporter on the *Observer* – the local paper for Laurencekirk and most of the county of Kincardine – whose editor had deemed the Bruce-Lyall funeral-cum-wedding worthy of much wider circulation.

Peering at the pictures short-sightedly, Alfie suddenly exclaimed, 'Lord preserve us! It's my Marion!'

'Read it,' his wife urged. 'Read it an' see why she's never wrote or let us ken where she was.'

Still only concerned with the photographs, he studied the first – a host of black-clad men and women over-shadowed by a girl in a dark costume standing at the rear of the group but in the foreground of the picture – then read out the caption: 'Marianne Cheyne is one of the mourners at the burial of Lady Glendarril of Castle Lyall, in Glendarril churchyard on Saturday.' Alfie's head shot up. 'She must be in service at the castle.'

Moll shook her head then pushed back the greasy lock of hair that had fallen over her face. 'It doesna say ony-thing aboot her bein' in service, but maybe that's where she met him.' Her husband's puzzled expression made her snap, 'Get on, Alfie!'

141

His eyes moved slowly to the other picture – the same girl emerging from a church wearing a wedding gown and accompanied by a tall young man with a sombre expression. '"The Honourable Hamish Bruce-Lyall leaving Glendarril church on Saturday with his bride, the former Miss Marianne Cheyne,"' Alfie read out. His brows crawled together in puzzlement. 'There's some mistake here. It says the frunial was on Saturday, so the wedding couldna have been on Saturday an' all?'

Moll stood up. 'For ony sake, read it a'!' She moved over to the fire to make a pot of tea for him. It's all he would feel like after reading the rest.

At last, Alfie took a look at the headline: 'GLEN MINISTER CONDUCTS WEDDING IMMEDIATELY AFTER FUNERAL OF GROOM'S MOTHER.'

The reporter may just have been learning his profession, but he knew how to attract attention . . . and how to hold it. Much was made of the fact that Marianne had been befriended by the Rennies when she arrived in Aberdeen, and that she had shown her gratitude by asking them to take on the duties of bridesmaids and of giving her away. This information had been gleaned mostly from those of Hector's relatives who had been denied the privilege of being wedding guests, and thus were loud in condemnation of Hamish and Marianne for not cancelling their marriage, but the journalist had taken great pains to cast no slur on the bridal couple. In fact, he made it appear that Clarice herself had begged them before she died not to change their plans, and that they had agreed reluctantly.

This was how he explained the seriousness of their expressions after the nuptials were tied, creating a tide of

142

sympathy for them by saying that each anniversary of their wedding would remind them of Lady Glendarril's death. He ended with, 'And so, as the Honourable Hamish Bruce-Lyall and his bride start married life with sorrow dimming the joy they should be sharing, let us wish them every happiness for the future.'

Alfie laid down the newspaper as Moll set an enamel mug of tea before him. 'Well?' she demanded.

'Well, what?' Alfie was not particularly bright at the best of times, but what he had just read had completely flummoxed him.

'Are you to be writin' to her?'

'Writin' to her? What the devil for?'

'For God's sake, Alfie! Can you nae see what this means? Here's us, countin' every ha'penny an' never having enough to go round, and there's her, rollin' in it!'

He banged his clenched fist on the table top, making the tea splash out of both mugs. 'If you think I'd beg fae my ain lassie, you're softer in the heid than I thought you were.'

'But she's got plenty, an' you *are* her father.'

'I used to wonder what had became o' her, an' I'm pleased she made something o' hersel', but a father's supposed to provide for his bairn, nae the other wey roon'.'

'Aye, well, but . . . maybe we should let her ken the Moodies never did nothin' aboot that money she took, an' tell her she's welcome back ony time she –'

Alfie's face darkened even further. 'She'll nae be welcome back! I'm having nae trock wi' a thief though she *is* my ain lassie. And dinna you think on writing to her, for you'll nae get me to speak to her supposing she's got the nerve to show her face here!'

143

Recognizing that nothing would make him change his mind, Moll gave up, but she cut out the item about the wedding and hid it away for future reference. Should Alfie ever have to stop working because of his chest, she would write and ask Marion – Marianne, as she called herself now – for help . . . but she wouldn't tell him.

After all the house guests had left, Hector joined the young couple in the Blue Room and said quietly, 'Do you remember me saying you would have to take Clarice's place as mistress of the castle, Marianne? Now, because of her death, I cannot let you take a honeymoon, but I will allow you one week to spend as much time with Hamish as you wish. After that, I expect you to acquaint yourself with the layout of the castle, and what goes on behind the scenes, so to speak. You will probably have noticed that the running of the every day household matters is in Miss Glover's capable hands, but if you do not like her, it will be up to you to find a replacement, and that goes for all the members of our staff. Mrs Carnie is an excellent cook, but if you and she do not get on –'

'I'm sure I'll get on with Mrs Carnie,' Marianne interrupted, 'and Miss Glover.'

'Roberta Glover can be a bit abrupt at times, but she knows her job inside out, and she'll keep you right if there is anything you are not sure of. And now,' he went on, getting to his feet, 'if you two young things do not mind, I must go to bed. I still feel a little off colour after yesterday. I do not make a habit of getting drunk, as Hamish will verify, but whisky was the only thing to numb the ache. Sorrow is not the best of bedfellows.'

144

'No, indeed,' observed Hamish.

And Marianne said, 'We won't be long in going to bed, either. I didn't get much sleep last –' Her eyes widened as her hand flew to cover her errant mouth.

Misconstruing her embarrassment, Hector gave a great roar of laughter as he went out.

Marianne looked at her husband in dismay. 'I'm sorry, Hamish. I don't know why I said that.'

'Probably because it was the truth,' he said, but not unkindly. 'I feel the need of a good night's sleep myself, and so I shall . . .' He paused, eyeing her warily. 'I shall sleep in my own room again.'

'Your own room,' she echoed faintly.

'You know what our arrangement was,' he muttered self-consciously, 'and the chamber maid knows to keep a bedroom ready for me. My mother and father slept in separate rooms for years.'

Marianne felt like saying, 'But not on the second night of their marriage,' only what good would it have done? She had entered into this anything-but-ideal contract in order to have wealth and power, and the gates to that world were to be opened for her a week from tomorrow. Love would be an additional blessing.

Alone in the marriage bed again, Marianne boosted her low spirits by thinking that she would soon be in sole charge of everything and everybody in Castle Lyall, and once she had it running her way, both Hamish and his father would see that she was capable of much more than breeding children. She would provide the two sons they needed in order to be sure of an heir, and then . . .

145

By God, and then! She would make the gentry sit up and take notice of her, fall over themselves to invite her to their homes, be they mansions, castles or palaces. She had the beauty the nobility lacked – horse-faced, most of them. She would be the talk of the glen, the whole of Scotland, even – and England, too.

Chapter Nine

On the first full day of their marriage, Hamish showed his bride the kitchen gardens where all the vegetables were grown, sheltered from frost and winds by the high wall enclosing them, and the flourishing herb patch situated where the kitchenmaid could quickly cut whatever Cook might suddenly decide she needed. Marianne was impressed, although she had never heard of most of the herbs here before.

The flower gardens and lawns also appealed to her – the symmetry of the layouts, the subtle mixing of colours, the more delicate being kept together in patterns around the perimeter, and the shaped beds within graduated up to the most flamboyant. 'I won't remember their proper names,' she whispered to Hamish, after Dargie, the head gardener, reeled off over a dozen, unintelligible as far as she was concerned, before he went off to supervise his undergardeners and left The Master and his wife to carry on alone. 'It sounded Greek to me.'

'It was Latin,' Hamish told her, courtesy forbidding him to laugh.

'We always called *them* red-hot pokers,' she explained, pointing to the tall clump of red and yellow blooms in the centre. 'And that's mappies' mou's,' she went on, indicating the antirrhinums.

'What on earth does that mean?' her husband asked, bemused.

'Surely you ken what . . . ?' She stopped with an embarrassed laugh. 'No, I don't suppose you do. Well, mappies is what we called rabbits at hame, and a mou' is a mouth. To let you see . . .' She took one of the florets between her forefinger and her thumb to show him. 'If you squeeze a wee bit out and in, like this, it's like a rabbit's mouth opening and shutting.'

'So it is!' he exclaimed, trying it for himself.

A large rockery set with alpine plants held her attention next, and when they moved on to where one of the younger gardeners had been trying his hand at topiary, she was fascinated by the shapes he had created. 'That's a duck! And that's a swan! And that's a . . . stork on one leg!' She clapped her hands in delight. 'Oh, I just love this, and he's done animals down the other side. He must be awful clever with his shears.'

Hamish gave a wry smile. 'I doubt if Dargie will be so happy about it. He has spent years training these hedges to be perfect and this boy has hacked into them –'

'No, Hamish, he hasn't hacked into them. He's done it carefully . . . it's a work of art.'

There were apples, pears, plums in the orchard, and even a small orangery built against a south-facing wall, and strawberries, raspberries, gooseberries and blackcurrants in the soft fruits cages. 'I bet Mrs Carnie makes hundreds of jars of jam with that lot,' Marianne remarked, adding without thinking, 'I used to love watching Mam boiling the berries, and she let me sup the scum before she poured the jam into jars. I liked rasps best, then strawberries, then the goosers, but I didna like the rhubarb, for she aye put ginger in, and I canna stand ginger.'

He let her ramble on, not wanting to let her know that he had asked Andrew where she came from originally, and was well aware that she had been in service to a banker's wife in Tipperton. It was the first time she had ever spoken about her first home, and she was using the words of her childhood. She was like a breath of fresh air to him, even when she did remember to talk and act like a lady. If only he could tell her how he really felt about her.

Next day, he took her along well-trodden paths through the woods outside the family's private grounds, and even where there were no paths. 'I suppose we should really call this a forest,' he smiled as they penetrated deeper into a closely packed mass of tall straight conifers, 'but I'd like you to get to know every bit of the estate and love it as much as I do.'

'I love it already,' Marianne sighed, picking up one of the cones that were lying about. 'I love the smell, I love to feel my feet sinking into the pine needles, it's like a thick carpet, isn't it? And it's so dark in here I can imagine wolves circling all round us, waiting to snarl out on us when they're hungry.'

'You wouldn't be scared of wolves?' he grinned.

She chuckled like the child she really was, for she wouldn't be eighteen for four months. 'I'd be terrified, but it's fun to pretend they're there, and I'd have you to protect me, wouldn't I? Any road, the sun sometimes flickers through between the leaves so I know it's a lovely summer's day outside.'

Her bridegroom took her hand. 'Are you happy, Marianne?'

She looked up into his now serious face. 'Of course I am!'

'You don't regret . . . ?'

'I don't regret anything. Mind you, I *am* a bit worried in case your father'll expect too much of me, but I'll do my best to run the house as good as your mother.'

He smiled at the grammatical error; she only made these slips when she was excited or worried, and she would probably grow out of them, yet he hoped she would always retain some of her naïvety and not turn out like all the other girls he knew.

'This really is a big forest,' she observed presently. 'Would you say we're halfway in yet?'

'I'd say we were more likely to be halfway out.' He tried to keep a straight face but it was difficult when hers was so earnest.

'How do you know?' she asked in all innocence. 'What's the halfway mark when you're coming out?' The truth suddenly striking her, she pulled her hand out of his indignantly. 'Ach, you're making fun of me. Halfway in and halfway out's exactly the same.'

'I'm sorry, my dear. I shouldn't have teased you, but I couldn't resist it.'

When they emerged into the open air again, they carried on uphill for some time until they chanced upon a wide flat boulder. 'I think we have come far enough today,' Hamish remarked. 'I don't want to exhaust you, so perhaps we should take a seat here for a few minutes before we turn back.'

While they rested, he pointed out items of interest in the glen below. 'That's the doctor's house. Robert Mowatt is a good friend of mine, and Flora, his wife, is in her middle twenties, I'd say. She is a sensible girl and would be ideal if you needed someone to talk to.' His finger moved a little to the right. 'The manse is next to the church, there, but you can't see it for the trees. I don't know what to make of Duncan Peat. He's quite dour at times although he is a splendid preacher. But you must make up your own mind what you think about him.'

'He was very good about having the funeral and the wedding on the same day,' Marianne reminded him, 'and Miss Edith always used to say we should take people as we find them.'

'That is probably best, and I am sure you will like his wife. When Duncan is with her, Grace behaves as befits the wife of a minister of the Church of Scotland, but she can be great fun if he is not around, which is surprising in view of the fact that her father was also a minister. Robert and Flora are exactly the opposite. She is the quiet one – Robert has more go – yet she and Grace Peat are very close.'

'What about the dominie and his wife?' Marianne could not see the school from where they were sitting, but she knew its approximate position.

'Will Wink is much older, a bit over fifty, and he often comes to talk things over with Father. They sit in the study, with the smoke from their pipes curling out into the hall, and discuss which pupils have the ability to carry on their education. They look on it purely from that angle, not whether or not the parents can afford the fees, because Father takes care of the financial side of it for them. He says that it would be a disgrace if any child could not take full advantage of the brains God blessed him with.'

'That's very kind of him.'

'Well, it usually works out to his benefit in the end. Once they get their degrees, he knows he can get a man he can trust if one of the professional posts here falls vacant. As for Agnes Wink, she keeps herself to herself.'

This surprised Marianne. 'Doesn't she mix with the doctor's wife and the minister's? That's what usually happens in small places – they all stick together.'

'Agnes's father, who sadly passed away last year, was a professor at Aberdeen University before he retired, so she considers herself better than either Flora or Grace – better than her own husband, if it comes to that, because his father was just one of my father's crofters.' Hamish shrugged his shoulders. 'Apparently, when she first came to Glendarril, she was most put out that my mother kept her distance, and for over twenty years she has resented being buried in this backwater of a glen, as she has been heard to describe it. However, if you want to be friendly with her, I shall not object.'

'I'll see how things work out,' Marianne smiled. Even having known Lady Glendarril for only a few weeks, she could visualize her reaction to Agnes Wink if she'd thought the woman was trying to insinuate her way into the castle.

The bleating of sheep made them turn round, and coming towards them Marianne saw a man with a black and white collie keeping the sheep together. The dog hesitated, obviously wondering if he should take a closer look at the strangers, then decided to ignore them, but the man tipped his flat bonnet and called, 'A braw day, Maister!'

Hamish responded in the manner of the glen. 'It is that, Fenton. You've met my wife, of course? Marianne, this is Fenton, one of our shepherds.'

Overcome with shyness, the man whipped off his flat cap. 'I saw you at the . . .' he mumbled, stopping short of mentioning the funeral, and began again. 'I saw you at your wedding, and I'm verra pleased to meet you, m'Leddy.'

Embarrassed at being given the title, but unwilling to make things worse by putting him right, the only thing she could do was to hold out her hand. 'I'm very pleased to meet you, and all, Mr Fenton.'

This served to panic him altogether. His fingers hovered briefly over hers, then he gave a sharp nod and turned, sprinting away from them to catch up with those with whom he felt most comfortable, his dog and his sheep.

'Did I do something wrong, Hamish?' she asked anxiously. 'Should I have told him . . . ? I shouldn't have let him call me m'Lady, should I?'

Her husband smiled patiently. 'What do you want them to call you? Mrs Bruce-Lyall is quite a mouthful, and they want you to be their Lady, even if I'm not the Lord . . . the laird, as they say. There is no Lady Glendarril now . . . Let them call you Lady Marianne if they want to.'

'He was shocked at me for wanting to shake hands with him, though. Did your mother never . . . ?'

'My mother was a stickler for protocol and she considered that our workers and their wives were on this earth for the sole purpose of serving her. She would have died rather than shake hands with any of them.' He paused, realizing the irony of what he had said, then went on,

'They respected her and held her in awe, but I believe we should not set ourselves above them, for we are all the same in the eyes of God. I do think, however, that we will have to be careful not to let them be too familiar with us, Marianne. Not only would they lose their awe of us, we would lose their respect as well. We shall have to walk a very thin line.'

She gave him a nodding smile as if she understood, yet she had not quite grasped his meaning. It was going to be difficult to know the difference between being friendly and being too familiar.

On one of their morning rambles, they came across a small hut in the depths of a dense mass of trees, Marianne was intrigued by its position, almost hidden from view. 'Would this be where the charcoal burners live? I've read about them in history books.'

Hamish gave a gurgling laugh. 'As far as I am aware, there never were any charcoal burners here. This is a still. For distilling whisky,' he explained, seeing her puzzlement. 'My grandfather used to tell us stories about the tricks his workers got up to to save the excisemen from finding their stock of illicit whisky. He always said his men were doing no wrong, for they were not making the spirits to sell, only for their own use – and for his, he always laughed – so they should not have to pay tax or duty on it. It hasn't been used for years.'

'It would be against the law these days, wouldn't it?'

Hamish guffawed this time. 'It was against the law in the old days, too. If they had been found out, the men could have been hanged, or at least dispatched to Botany Bay for ever.'

'Yes, the penal colony,' she agreed. 'I've read about that, too.'

The days passed agreeably, and Marianne found herself if not exactly happy, at least settled.

In spite of his father's professed wish for the next heir to be born before he died, Hamish had still not attempted to make a son, but Marianne was quite content with the way her life was shaping, and she was certainly getting to know Hamish better, his likes and his dislikes.

By the end of that first week, her husband had introduced her to most of the folk in the glen, smilingly accepting the title they bestowed on her. It was as if they had discussed it together and decided to so honour her, although they were bound to know she wasn't a 'Lady' in the true sense. Carnie would have told them how little she'd had when she arrived here, or if not Carnie – Marianne had the feeling that he'd be fiercely loyal to the Bruce-Lyall family – certainly the railway employee at the station. They had probably tumbled to the fact that she didn't speak like gentry and maybe that was why they were so warm towards her. She was one of them.

What pleased her most, was when Hamish began to confide in her about how he would like the mill to be run. 'Father's so old-fashioned he can't see that we need to change things. Our spinning machines and looms must have been there since machinery was invented, and the new models are faster and easier to work, so they would pay for themselves in no time. But he won't listen. "What's the point of getting rid of things that still work perfectly well?" That's his attitude. And I keep telling him we should enlarge the buildings so that we can increase our output, but he can't see that either.'

'Maybe he feels you don't have enough people to cope with the extra work,' Marianne ventured, a little timidly because she knew nothing of the workings of a woollen mill.

'We could build more houses and employ more workers. He is well known all over Scotland for being a fair man, a good master paying decent wages, not like some owners, so there would be dozens of men wanting to be taken on. And their women would help the shepherds' wives with the hand-knitted garments. Plus, if I had my way, I'd install running water in every cottage – not that Father ignores the upkeep of the houses. All the workers, and even the crofters, are encouraged to let the factor know if anything needs to be repaired, but they need to have some sanitation. It can't be very nice not to have an inside WC, and in some cases not even one outside.'

Having been brought up in an old cottage in the last category, Marianne knew that those who were accustomed to it thought nothing of having a dry lavatory, and her thoughts took a different turn. 'You know, Hamish, it might be a good idea to employ somebody to look after the very young children so women who wanted to earn some extra money could work in the mill.'

Hamish shook his head. 'My father would never countenance that.' His sigh was deep and long. 'Anyway, Marianne, I was just being silly, building castles in the air . . .' 'Not castles,' she laughed. 'Just houses to go with the castle.'

He ignored her attempt to cheer him. 'It's no use. He will never agree to that, either, nor any of the other things I want to do.'

The assurance which sprang to her mind that he would be able to do what he liked when *he* was laird remained unsaid, but it hung in the air between them for the rest of that day.

Their 'honeymoon' over, it was time for Hamish to start work again, and once he and his father left for the mill, Marianne thought she had better get to know the layout of the castle as her father-in-law had said, looking at things in more detail. She had been so scared of upsetting Lady Glendarril that she hadn't dared to take more than a cursory glance at any room until now. She decided to start with the ground floor, and went into the entrance hall, but she just had time to notice the row of hooks above the oak chest opposite the front door when the housekeeper came out of the dining room. Miss Glover, whom the new mistress found quite intimidating, was a wraithlike figure dressed entirely in black. She seemed to glide as if she were on casters, silent and unsmiling, terrifyingly forbidding.

'The hooks are for hanging overcoats, ma'am,' she said, her thin mouth forming each word in a way that made her prominent teeth even more prominent. She bent over and lifted the lid of the chest. 'Overshoes and boots are kept in here . . . and the guns, of course, in the grouse season.'

'I see, thank you.' Marianne guessed that the housekeeper had been instructed to show her round and explain things to her, and even if she would have preferred to look at things on her own, it wouldn't be policy to antagonize the woman. 'The kist's the same wood as the door, isn't it?' she asked, for the sake of something to say.

'The *chest* is oak, ma'am, the same as the door . . . which is restricted to his Lordship, his family and their guests,' she added, in a hushed tone, as if she were speaking about God and His angels.

Marianne determined not to be needled, though the woman evidently didn't include her new mistress in the hallowed company by the tone of her voice. 'The white painted walls give a nice welcome to guests, and the sanded floor's so highly polished . . .'

'The floor has never been sanded, ma'am.' There was a ring of pride in what she was saying now. 'It was recorded by his Lordship's grandfather that it had been scraped with broken glass until it took on this fine sheen. Do you see how it reflects the colours from the windows on the staircases, ma'am?'

And so it went on. The secrets of the huge sideboard in the dining room – it took up the whole of one wall – were laid bare to Marianne; the delicate bone-china dinner and tea services and where they had come from; the beautiful silver cutlery in one of the drawers, some with the family crest on the handles, some monogrammed with just a fancy letter L, which, Miss Glover revealed, meant that they had been in the Lyall family even before Marjorie Bruce married into it.

'That was about the middle of the eighteenth century, and she was a direct descendant of King Robert the Bruce, and was named after his daughter, which is why the king of the time granted the family the right to be known as Bruce-Lyall, and the Lord Lyon, King of Arms, approved a new crest.'

Another drawer held silver serving utensils, and a third contained starched damask napkins with the initials

B and L embroidered in white to match the tablecloths in the fourth drawer.

The housekeeper reeled off details of the furniture next, the oval table and ten high-backed chairs with tapestry seats, and the carvers to match, one at either end. 'It took three generations of Bruce-Lyall women to finish all the stitching,' she divulged.

'They're absolutely wonderful, though,' Marianne murmured, hoping that she wouldn't be expected to fill her spare time in the same way. Surprisingly, considering how long she had lived with the Rennie sisters, she hated sewing and had never been any good at it.

'As you can see, ma'am,' Miss Glover continued, 'there are numerous small tables, all darkest mahogany like the rest of the furniture in here, for trays to be set down on, or platters of vegetables to be rested on if the dining table is full.'

While the housekeeper gave details of the portraits on the walls, Marianne, having already studied them while having meals here when Lady Glendarril was alive, turned her attention to the Indian carpet square on the floor. It was almost threadbare in places, the pattern scarcely showing. That would be the first entry she would make in the notebook she was intending to keep, she thought – 'See about new dining room carpet.'

The business room, as Miss Glover said it was originally called, was used by Lord Glendarril as a study. To the right of and very close to the fireplace stood a beautiful desk which had belonged to his father, who had been inclined to feel the cold, and his own desk sat in front of the window to afford him more light. Near the door was a desk with four seats at it, which Miss Glover said was the 'rent' desk, where the tenant farmers came once a year to pay their ten-shilling rents to the factor. The floor here was of pine, deeper in colour than usual because of years, maybe centuries, of beeswax polish applied by perspiring young girls, and had a scattering of small rugs to protect it in the most used areas.

The library fascinated Marianne, two of its walls completely lined with shelves from floor to ceiling, some filled with volumes covered in red leather, some with dark blue covers, some linen covers, all of which looked as if they had seldom, if ever, been read, though not one speck of dust could be seen anywhere. On the shelves on the other two walls, on either side of the fireplace and bay window, were books which had obviously been well-leafed – novels, biographies of the famous and not-so-famous, autobiographies, children's and adults' classics. She had never seen so many books and it dawned on her that here was a wealth of reading that would help her improve her still lamentably poor vocabulary – if she got any time to read, that was. She wasn't too keen on the plaster – or alabaster or whatever – busts, which were placed haphazardly anywhere there was room for them.

'The bronzes are celebrated composers,' her guide supplied, seeing her looking at them, 'and the ivories are famous authors.'

Then they entered the Blue Room, most used of any of the public rooms, where the furnishing fabrics were all in some shade of blue, not really to Marianne's taste because it made the room look cold. The chairs here were upholstered in a rough material which felt like hessian but the housekeeper said was hopsack made in the mill – 'A not altogether successful experiment,' she added. Noting the fading and the neat, but still noticeable, patches over what must be worn parts, Marianne could only agree with this, and make re-covering the chairs another of the early jobs to be done. As they left the room, Miss Glover drew her attention to three miniatures on the wall above a whatnot.

'Lady Glendarril's mother, grandmother and great-grandmother,' she observed, pointing to each one in turn. 'His Lordship did not like them and wanted to take them down, but she held out against him. I am surprised, though, that he has not removed them by this time.'

Marianne had guessed that they were ancestors of Lady Glendarril; they all had the same sour faces and flared nostrils, as if somebody was holding a lump of dog's dirt under them, and if her father-in-law didn't take them down soon, Marianne would do it for him. Luckily, she kept her thoughts to herself. Whatever she did when she started making the alterations she wanted, she was bound to upset somebody, so this was another fine line she'd have to walk. There was also a Red Room – very overpowering with huge paintings of fire-breathing dragons and several luridly coloured urns, so tall that full-grown men could hide in them. Next to that, and probably because there had been too many items to fit into the Red Room, was a Chinese room with disgustingly fat buddhas brooding in every corner, and next to that again, an Indian room with the fire irons set into elephants' feet at the side of the black marble fireplace, and tiger skin rugs on the floor.

All these foreign artefacts, the housekeeper explained with pride, had been brought home by previous generations of Lyalls and Bruce-Lyalls after visits to the east, and Marianne resolved to do something about these rooms at some time in the future.

Throughout this guided tour, conducted at almost breakneck speed and interspersed constantly by the stressed 'ma'am', she had been genuine in the interest she showed, and grateful for the information the housekeeper had imparted, but at long last, to her great relief, the woman said, 'I hope you don't mind . . . Mrs Hamish, but I shall have to leave you now. There are things I should be attending to.'

The change of title told Marianne that the woman was thawing, was accepting her, thank goodness. 'Oh, I'm sorry, Miss Glover. You shouldn't have wasted so much of your time with me.'

'Not entirely wasted, I hope?'

What was surely a hint of laughter appeared in the housekeeper's eyes, and Marianne suspected that she was not so forbidding as she would like to have people believe. 'Definitely not wasted,' she smiled. 'You've learned me . . .' Remembering Andrew's teaching, she stopped to correct herself. 'I've learned an awful lot. It would've taken me years to find out the things you've told me. Thank you very much, Miss Glover. I really enjoyed it.'

'So did I, Mrs Hamish. Now you'll manage to look round upstairs by yourself? Not that there's much to see, mostly bedrooms.'

In Marianne's next letter to the Rennies, she told them that the bedrooms, both in the east and west wings, were

162

reasonably well appointed. 'I just had a quick look in most of them whether they were being used or not,' she wrote, 'but I went through the cupboards in the passages thoroughly, so I would know where everything is, and I made a note of anything that needed mending or replacing. My notebook is full already, but I can leave most things for a few years. I do not want them to resent me as a new broom sweeping clean.'

It was Miss Emily who observed, 'Shouldn't she think of converting one of the rooms into a nursery?'

Miss Edith gave a small frown. 'I would have thought there would be a nursery there already. She must have recognized it, because in these large houses there are usually bars across the nursery windows to prevent any child falling out.'

Miss Esther smiled mischievously. 'Maybe Marianne thought the bars were to stop the Nanny's men friends from getting in.'

A month after she first took over (or gave the appearance of taking over) the supervising of the household, Marianne knew that she was going to enjoy being mistress of the castle.

'I must have been born to be a lady,' she said to Hamish one night when Lord Glendarril had gone to bed. 'All the servants, even the bootboy and the grooms and gardeners, even the Carnies, saluted or curtsied when I spoke to them, and I loved it.'

'That's what they are meant to do,' her husband smiled.

She screwed up her nose. 'It gets a wee bit embarrassing after a while, though. Could I make it a rule that they just do it the first time they see me every day, and not any other times?'

After considering for a moment, Hamish shook his head. 'Not yet, I think. Give them time to get accustomed to their mistress being so young . . . and so beautiful.' As if regretting this compliment, he went on hastily, 'Get them used to doing what you tell them, but you must not order them about like slaves. They will respond much better to kindness and consideration – and you will have to earn their respect before you can relax any of the rules.'

'I can understand that, but I feel awkward with Mrs Carnie; she's old enough to be my granny.'

Grinning at this, Hamish stood up. 'It is time all good people were in bed.' He held his hand out to help her out of her seat. 'Um . . . Marianne, I have not asked before, I was giving you time to settle to your new responsibilities, but . . . will you allow me to come to your room tonight, or are you too tired?'

She could feel her face grow as scarlet as his was. She had often wondered when he would make her carry out this part of their bargain, but surely he didn't need to ask? She was his wife, after all. 'I'm not tired,' she whispered.

Since the day she had agreed to become his wife, she had worried about how she would cope when this moment arrived, yet she felt a little put out when he said, as they went upstairs, 'I'll undress in my room to give you time to . . . get into bed.'

It was a marriage of convenience, she reminded herself, but why did he have to be so . . . distant, about this? Nevertheless, she hastily cast off her clothes and took a clean nightdress out of a drawer. She had been wearing

164

those included in the trousseau bought for her by Lady Glendarril in Edinburgh, but tonight was special, so she carefully chose one of the shifts made and embroidered by Miss Esther, no doubt with the creation of the new generation of Bruce-Lyalls in mind. Knowing that she was wrapped in the love of her beloved friend, Marianne thought, she would, hopefully, be more relaxed and . . . receptive. It should bring her luck!

She had just got into bed when the door opened and she looked up apprehensively, watching Hamish enter and take off his long silk robe. He folded it neatly and draped it over a chair before sitting down beside her. 'Do you normally go to bed with your hair pinned up?' he asked, smiling.

Even recognizing a hint of humour in his eyes, she felt flustered. 'No, I usually . . . my mother used to tell me never to forget to give my hair a hundred strokes with my brush every night, but I thought . . . I didn't have time.'

'Will you allow me to do it for you . . . please?' He rose to fetch a tortoiseshell-backed hairbrush from the dressing table, part of the set which had also been bought for her by his mother, and came back to where she was feverishly removing all her hairpins in readiness.

Neither of them said a word until the required number of strokes had been completed, then Hamish let his hand run lightly down her shimmering coppery tresses. 'You have such beautiful hair, it seems a pity to pin it up.'

She turned to face him now, her face pink with embarrassed pleasure at the compliment. 'Only young girls wear their hair down,' she explained seriously.

'It's a crime to hide it away, especially when it suits you so well like this.' Her deepening colour made him smile.

'But you are right, of course. As lady of the castle, it is only fitting that you look dignified in front of others.'

She gave a nervous giggle. 'Dignified? Me? I don't think I'll ever manage to look dignified, but I'm willing to do my best.'

'Given time, my dear Marianne, you will look every bit as dignified as the highest ladies in the land, although I wish that you could . . .'

'That I could what?' she wanted to know.

'That you could remain as sweet and fresh as you are at this moment.' He turned away abruptly to replace the hairbrush in its designated place, and when he came back, it was to the other side of the bed, where he slipped under the bedcovers beside her.

'You are sure about this?' he asked anxiously.

Nodding, she wished that he would get on with it. This shillyshallying was worse than if he just jumped on her. She knew that was what he was going to do eventually, and it wasn't against her will. His first tender kisses quickly became more urgent, his searching hands more insistent, until her body involuntarily rose to welcome him in.

She had long been dreading it, but it was a wonderful, marvellous, exquisite experience which left her puzzling over why some married women hated it, or so she had heard her mother's friends saying when they thought she couldn't hear. And Hamish had seemed to enjoy it, too, for he had kept kissing her and whispering her name, and . . . Oh, dear God, if this was what it took to make a baby, she wanted to have dozens.

He was sleeping now like a child himself, sleeping as though he was exhausted, and maybe he was. Looking at him, she felt a surge of fondness for him. He was a dear man – he'd been really gentle with her, guiding her over the initial pain so that she knew he hadn't meant to hurt her. It had only been for a few seconds anyway, and he had assured her she would never have any more pain during intercourse. That was the word he'd used. He hadn't said 'making love'. He had never mentioned love, but she hadn't expected him to. He didn't love her, like she didn't love him, though she had the feeling it might be easy for her to change her mind.

When Thomson went in the next morning with a cup of tea for her mistress, Hamish had returned to his own room so that she knew nothing of what had gone on the night before. However, when the little chamber maid went up to make the bed after breakfast, she came charging back brandishing a blood-stained sheet. 'He'd been wi' her last nicht! Look at this!'

Miss Glover frowned, but a scowling Mrs Carnie snatched the bed linen out of the girl's hands. 'It's no' decent to let folk see that, Kitty Bain!' she stormed. 'An' it's nobody's business but theirs, so keep your tongue atween your teeth, an' that goes for the rest o' you, an' all,' she added, letting her eyes take in every last one of the trembling girls, who darted off to carry out their assigned duties.

The cook and the housekeeper sat down one on each side of the big range, looking at each other with knowing smiles. 'He took his time about it, though,' Mrs Carnie said grudgingly.

Marianne's plans for refurbishing certain rooms were turned down by Hector. 'I know you mean well,' he said apologetically, having summoned her to his study one morning, 'but I would rather not have the upheaval, and things are better left as they are. I do not take well to change, especially when it would leave me with hardly any memories of my dear Clarice.'

She was contrite. 'Oh, I'm sorry, I didn't think. I wasn't trying to get rid of the things your wife chose, I was only –'

'I know, my dear,' he soothed. 'But bear with an old man. When I'm gone, you and Hamish can do what you like.'

'But you're not old!' she burst out. In the mornings it was easy to forget how tired he often was in the evening, and how bad his colour could be. 'You'll be here for years and years yet, and we'll be walking on bare floorboards if you don't let me get a new carpet for the dining room soon.'

'My grandfather – or maybe it was my great-grandfather – took that carpet home from Persia.'

She had thought it was Indian, but what did it matter? 'Please, Father?' She had been invited to address him as Hamish did and had been highly complimented by this privilege.

He succumbed to the pleading in her lovely young eyes. 'All right. The mill has no dealings with Persia, I'm afraid, but I have an old friend who captains a merchant ship and trades with some eastern countries, so I shall ask him to get an oriental carpet for me.'

'Thank you, Father!' Marianne had to force the enthusiasm into her voice, because she still was not being allowed to choose. Still, whatever the sea captain took back was bound to be better than the carpet in the dining room at present. But she still had another favour to ask. 'What about the pump for the bathroom? Did you look at the information I sent away for? It would save the poor maids having to hump up pails and pails of water.'

'It is a recognized part of their duties,' he frowned.

The twinkle in his eyes, however, told her that he was testing her, so she went on hopefully, 'We could take a bath at any time, not just when somebody's free to fill it. My mother used to say, "Cleanliness is next to godliness," even when she was bent near double filling the old tin bath we had to use.'

Her father-in-law eyed her quizzically. 'That's the first time I have ever heard you speak of your mother. What happened? Did you quarrel with her or . . . ?'

'She died . . . and when my father married again, the woman didn't like me. That's why I ran away.'

Hector could see by the set of her mouth that she did not want to talk about it. 'I am glad you are a strong person, Marianne . . . you know why. And now I have got on that subject, may I ask . . . how are you finding my son?'

It was an odd way of asking, but she knew what he meant. 'I hope it won't be long till I have good news for you.'

'I am pleased to hear it. Tell Hamish not to leave it too long.' Hector was beaming as she left his study.

She was positive that Hector was wondering if they were trying at all, and she herself couldn't understand why she hadn't conceived, because their couplings seemed to satisfy Hamish, though she did wish that he would do it more often and satisfy her. With time on her hands she began to brood about not yet being pregnant.

Despite Marianne's notebook of lists and the suggestions she had dared to voice, Miss Glover had gradually taken over the entire management of the household again.

It was done in such a way that it was some weeks before Marianne noticed what was happening, and she had to admit that the woman was more competent than she was. The housekeeper had had years of experience, of course, Marianne told herself, guilty at the relief she felt.

With more time to fill, she asked her husband one morning if he would show her round the mill.

Hamish smiled indulgently. There's not really much to see, but if that is what you want . . . Give me time to arrange for someone to explain things . . . get one of the stable lads to take you down in the trap in about an hour.'

Not knowing what to expect, Marianne was quite impressed by what she saw, made all the more interesting when Mr Gillies, one of the overseers, allowed various workers to tell her what he or she was doing. One of the women at the carding machines told her that the process of teasing the fleece out into yarn had all been done by hand when she was a girl. 'Some of the old women still do it at home,' she smiled. 'My ma thinks a machine cannae dae it as good as her.'

'What do *you* think?' Marianne asked.

The woman shot a glance at the man, then said, somewhat defiantly, 'I'd say she was right, but the machines are a lot quicker.'

'Bella Simms is a widow, m'Lady,' Mr Gillies told her. 'His Lordship doesna employ a lot o' women, just them wi' no young bairnies.'

'But is the men's wages enough to keep a family?'

'The wages here are the best in the country, m'Lady, and the shepherds' wives – and any of the other wives that need to – get paid well for the hand-knitting they do.'

'So it's not just cloth, you make, then?'

'Mercy, no! We've got tailors that make the different materials into men's coats and suits . . .' – and here the man's pride in his workplace made him forget his careful mode of speech –'. . . and we sell them a' ower the country. The best o' stuff, mind – nane o' your cheap dirt.'

Marianne looked forward to further amusement when he shepherded her into the next large section, but he was thinking in his best English again. 'This is where the spinners spin the wool into yarn or thread.'

All the machines amazed her, but she was absolutely fascinated by the looms, walking round and asking questions of the men who were deftly making sure that the shuttles were going where they should. She learned from one that the threads going one way were called the warp, and those going the other way were called the weft, and the machines had to be set up to make the shuttle pick up or miss however many threads were needed for that particular cloth.

She discovered also, although she should have realized, that tartan was the most complicated to set up, with the different colours, the different checks, and she couldn't take her eyes off the patterns as they gradually took shape. The foot pedal was only used when the shuttle was in the right position, but the men worked so quickly that there was hardly any delay between each step.

She found that there were several grades of flannel, fine weave, medium and coarse, and the same with the tweeds. She could have remained there all day, but Mr Gillies was anxious to return to his proper duties.

Going more quickly through the place where the wool was spun, put into skeins then dyed, and the smaller room where two men were cutting out at long tables and another two were putting pieces together with meticulous stitching, they came to the huge warehouse where all the finished items, bales of material, hand-made suits, and garments knitted by the shepherds' wives, were stored in readiness for scrutiny by the buyers who came before each new season began.

'We don't deal with the general public,' Mr Gillies told her, 'just retailers, and the orders keep flooding in.' She was glad to hear that. The family's income would be ensured for the future.

He left her at the office, where Hector asked her, 'What d'you think of my domain, then?'

'It's . . . it's . . . I can't think of the right word. Marvellous, clever, everything's going so well . . .'

'So it should be at the wages I pay, and the number of overseers I employ.' His puckish grin belied the menace of his words.

Hamish took her back to the main entrance, saying as they went down the wooden stairs, 'No more visits, Marianne. Father perhaps gave you the impression that he didn't mind, but he does not like any intrusion into his business.'

'I wasn't intruding,' she protested. 'I just wanted to see the inside of the mill, and now I've seen it, I don't need to come again.'

'I'm sorry if I offended you, my dear, but it's best that you know where you stand.'

The stable lad, sitting in the trap waiting for her, jumped down when he saw her coming, but Hamish himself handed her up, which made her feel less upset at him, and

172

by the time she arrived back at the castle, she knew he'd been right to warn her, although she'd had no intention of interfering in the workings of the mill, anyway.

Yet her visit had taught her one fundamental thing. Even if the handful of women workers had been politely forthcoming when she spoke to them, none of them could ever be her friend. The chasm between workers and employers, even employers' wives, was too wide to be bridged. But she missed female company. She missed the Rennies, missed having someone she could talk to, tell her thoughts to, ask advice from. Even if she had lived, Lady Glendarril wouldn't have come anywhere near to filling the bill. The only women – ladies – in the glen who might let her get to know them better would be the wives of the doctor, the minister and the dominie, preferably the first two, after what Hamish had told her, and because they were nearer her own age.

With the intention, therefore, of trying to establish some sort of relationship with at least one of the other two, Marianne set off the following afternoon to call at the manse. The minister's wife had seemed a friendly person when they spoke at the wedding, even telling her not worry what anyone said about them being married immediately after Lady Glendarril's funeral. She obviously understood how the poor young bride was feeling.

Mrs Peat looked a little flustered when she opened the door – Marianne had forgotten that most ministers' stipends didn't run to employing a maid – so she said apologetically, 'I'm sorry if I've come at an inconvenient time.'

'No, no, come in, please. It's just that I wasn't expecting . . .' She led the way into a cosy room where the

173

doctor's wife jumped up from where she was sitting. 'Lady Marianne's come to call, Flora,' she said brightly, as the other woman's mouth dropped open in surprise.

Not altogether sure if she was doing the right thing, Marianne corrected her. 'I'm not really the Lady, you know, so why don't you just call me by my given name?'

Mrs Peat's hesitation was infinitesimal. 'It seems a bit familiar, but if that's what you want, I'm Grace and this is Flora, the doctor's wife.'

They all shook hands before they sat down.

The conversation was a little stiff at first, both Marianne and Flora leaving most of the talking to Grace, who prattled on gaily about anything that came into her head, but at last, Marianne told them of her visit to the mill and how her father-in-law hadn't been too pleased about it, which began a discussion on how much his family had done for the glen over the years. 'Lord Glendarril put both Duncan and Robert through university,' Grace confided. 'They were at school together, the glen school, and the dominie told the laird it was a great pity that two such clever lads couldn't make use of their brains.'

Flora Mowatt interrupted here. 'It started long before Duncan and Robert, though. It was the present Lord Glendarril's father, or maybe his grandfather, who first paid for a local boy's education.'

This led to a discussion on the merits or otherwise of helping a boy from a poor family to get on in the world. 'Duncan says if he hadn't been obligated to his Lordship,' Grace said, at one point, 'he might have been called to a big church in one of the cities, instead of mouldering away here, but, to be quite honest, he hasn't the personality to be in charge of a large congregation.' She looked from one to the other of her companions with a wry grimace. 'You probably think I'm not very loyal to my husband, but he gets on my nerves sometimes, being so bumptious. I often wish he was more like Robert.'

Flora shrugged. 'Robert can be annoying at times, too. He's always getting on at me for not mixing with the other women, helping them out, making sure they're not going short of anything, but I tell him that's not our problem. It's not that I'm not sympathetic, it's just . . . well, I've always been slow at speaking to people I don't know very well.'

'That's why you never get to know them,' Grace said triumphantly. 'It takes a bit of courage to take the first step. Don't you agree, Marianne?'

'I suppose it does,' Marianne said cautiously, not wanting to offend either of them.

'But you did it today,' Grace reminded her. 'You had the courage to call without going through all the rigmarole of leaving a card first.'

Feeling quite at home with them now, Marianne laughed at this. 'I didn't leave a card first because I didn't know that was expected. I wasn't brought up to that kind of thing, you see, but the difference between Flora and me is that she's shy and I'm not. Neither are you, Grace, so it's easy for us to speak.'

When, in about fifteen minutes, Flora stood up to leave, Marianne also jumped to her feet. 'Oh, my goodness, look at the time! Have I overstayed my welcome?'

'You certainly haven't,' declared Grace. 'We've thoroughly enjoyed your company.'

The doctor's wife nodded vehemently. 'Yes, indeed, and Grace and I usually take it turn about once a week, so you must come to our house next Tuesday.'

And so began a new cycle, with Marianne offering to be hostess at the castle every third week.

When they learned of this arrangement, neither Miss Glover nor Mrs Carnie was happy with it. 'Lady Glendarril never asked any of them to tea,' the cook grumbled.

'There was a garden party every summer, of course,' the housekeeper recalled, a little sadly. 'There were marquees set up for the teas, and a beer tent for the men, but nobody was ever allowed inside the castle.'

'Well, I'm not her Ladyship,' Marianne said hotly, 'and if I want to make friends and invite them for afternoon tea, I'll do it!'

Guessing that Hector, too, would not be at all pleased, nor Hamish, she waited somewhat apprehensively for their reaction when she told them and was taken aback when they looked at each other and burst out laughing.

'You said she would take her own way if she wanted anything,' her father-in-law chuckled, 'and I admire her for it.' He wagged his finger at her. 'Just watch, though, my lass. It may not turn out so easy for you every time, but I can see no harm in giving you your head over this.'

Bolstered by her success, Marianne said, 'And I think I'll start going round the cottages to see if any of the wives need anything, something repaired or replaced –' She broke off, noticing that both men were frowning, and unable to say anything to his father, she vented her annoyance at her husband. 'I don't know why you look so disapproving, Hamish. There could be things they don't like to ask the factor to have done.'

Getting no reply, she stood up and gave it one final shot. 'Well, I'm going up to bed. Are you coming to me tonight, or are you waiting another week?'

She practically ran out, but not before she had seen Hamish's face turn dead white, and once in her room she flung herself on the bed. She shouldn't have shamed him like that in front of his father. He didn't deserve it! But why was he always so reluctant when she knew he enjoyed the matings as much as she did? She knew that because . . . well, because of how he did what he did when he did it. Besides, a girl could tell things like that.

She gave a guilty start when there was a knock at her door a few minutes later and Hamish walked in, but before he could start the telling off she was sure he had come to give her, she said defensively, 'I'm sorry, but I couldn't help saying it.' She came to an abrupt halt, for there was not even the slightest sign of anger on his face when he sat down on the edge of her bed.

'There is no need for you to feel sorry – you were right to let me know how you feel, but, as a matter of fact, I *have* been considering asking you if . . . I may . . . share your bed more often, because . . .'

'Because your father told you to hurry up and make a grandson for him?'

'He did, actually, but I had been intending to ask tonight in any case. However, I do not wish to force myself on you if you would rather –'

'You've the right to, as a husband,' she pointed out, not quite so bitterly.

'Ah, yes, in the eyes of the law, but ours was merely a business arrangement, was it not? Still, I had better put more effort into it –' He broke off, his mouth turning up and a smile making his serious face so much more attractive, she thought. He gave an embarrassed cough. 'My turn of phrase was inappropriate, I'm afraid, but I am sure you know what I meant. I am more than willing to become a nightly visitor as long as you don't mind. I will, of course, depend on you to let me know when . . . it is not convenient.'

It took her a little time to understand what he meant by that, then flushing, she whispered, 'I don't mind.'

His eyes now held something she couldn't define. 'Thank you, my dear, and I promise that I will not force my attentions on you once I know . . . well, you know what.' He stood up and, not looking at her again, mumbled, 'I shall not be long. I am just going to undress.'

Left alone, she found her heart was doing all sorts of unusual acrobatics. She had had a vague suspicion for several weeks that she felt more towards him than she had done at first – maybe it wasn't love yet, but not very far from it – and judging by the way his eyes lingered tenderly on her at times, surely he was feeling the same. Was their marriage of convenience going to turn out a real love match after all?

Sadly for Marianne, however, Hamish made no mention of love that night or any of the nights thereafter, although his 'efforts', as he had called them, were really quite loving, and sometimes, at the height of his passion, he kissed her like a lover should, and murmured her name and gripped her tightly as if he never wanted to let her go, but she would be much happier if only he could bring himself to tell her what she wanted to hear. And he made matters worse by going to his own room shortly afterwards.

Hector would probably not have been so pleased about his daughter-in-law's choice of friends if he had heard their conversation one Tuesday a few weeks later.

The ladies had been commenting on how strange it was that the wife of one of the shepherds had just had her first baby after ten years of marriage, while a weaver's wife had taken only nine months from her wedding to produce *her* first, when Marianne suddenly said, 'My father-in-law can't wait for me to give him a grandson.'

'What's stopping you, then?' laughed the minister's wife.

'Grace Peat!' exclaimed the horrified Flora. 'You shouldn't say things like that.'

Marianne shook her head. 'It's all right, I don't mind. Nothing's stopping me, Grace, except my body. I must be like the shepherd's wife, because Hamish and I are trying but we've had no luck yet.'

'Duncan doesn't want any children,' Grace sighed, 'but he's got quite an appetite for . . .' She stopped, colouring slightly, then added, 'I'm on tenterhooks every month because he has a vile temper when he's angry.' She looked pointedly at Flora now, as though demanding that she, too, should lay bare the intimate side of her marriage, and at last, her face a deep crimson, the doctor's wife said, 'Robert and I desperately want a baby, too, and I've been pregnant twice, but I lost them both at three months.'

'I'm sorry,' Marianne murmured, but Grace said accusingly, 'You never told me that, you secretive thing. But you shouldn't be depressed about it. Keep trying. If Robert's managed it twice, he'll manage again.'

'Do you really think so?' Flora's expression had brightened. 'He says the same, that two miscarriages don't mean that I'll never carry to full time, but I thought he was only trying to stop me losing hope.'

'He's the doctor, for goodness' sake,' Grace said firmly, 'so he should know. You and Marianne will have to keep trying, and if I can, I'll stop the douching Duncan insists on to prevent me conceiving. Wouldn't it be fun if we all landed in the family way together?'

Her candour about so delicate a subject, and the very nature of their discussion, forged a firm bond between them, which pleased three husbands and at least one father-in-law, who would all have been absolutely appalled had they known the reason behind the closeness.

Chapter Ten

It was August of the following year before Marianne realized what had happened, by which time she had missed twice, and after she gave Hamish her good news, he completely stopped coming to her room at nights. But there was no doubt that he was proud of himself, strutting about like a cock on a muck midden, with a new spring to his step, and he told his father straight away, though she'd asked him not to say anything yet. She had also been quite put out that Hector had taken it on himself to announce it to all and sundry, for she'd have preferred her condition to be kept secret until it could be hidden no longer.

News of her pregnancy was the talking point in every house in the glen within a day of her telling her husband, mainly because Mima Rattray, shopkeeper and postmistress, had instant access to the ears of all the womenfolk. 'Of course, I never believed yon story that went round about The Master,' she would say after imparting the exciting information. 'There was never nothing peculiar about him.'

One of her customers did dare to justify her own credulity of the rumour. 'Well, right enough, there musta been some mistake there, but you canna deny it was queer he never looked at ony o' the lassies here.'

'But, Lizzie, dinna forget, he's gentry,' Mima pointed out, thus explaining everything, but adding also, 'He'd just been waiting to find the right wife and what's wrong wi' that, tell me?'

Lizzie being suitably cowed, one of the other women in the shop said, 'Aye, there's something to be said for the groom bein' a virgin as weel as the bride.'

This led to a debate on the benefits or otherwise of such a combination, and ended in such a riot of hilarity that Mima had to put her foot down firmly to keep them in order.

Because of the shame they felt at jumping to their wrong conclusions before, the glen folk were extravagant with their congratulation to the laird and the parents-to-be. Marianne responded to their good wishes with shy embarrassment, Hamish accepted them with a smiling murmur of thanks, but Hector acted as if he alone had worked the miracle. He even began carrying a silver flask of whisky with him wherever he went, so that those he met could drink to the fertilization.

Robert Mowatt having passed on the good news in sympathetic confidence to his wife, Flora confidentially told Grace Peat, and so they actually knew before Marianne told them herself, which gave them time to temper their envy. Nevertheless, she could discern more than a touch of wistfulness in each pair of eyes when they affirmed their rapturous joy at her good fortune. 'Your turns are bound to come,' she told them, gently, 'so don't give up.'

Flora grimaced. 'Robert says we should wait a full year from the time I lost the second one, to give my body time to recover. But I don't know . . .'

'At least he's planning for you to conceive again,' Grace sensibly pointed out. 'D'you know what Duncan said when he heard Marianne was expecting? "Thank God it is not you!" What a thing for a man of his calling to say. It's not up to God to stop His ministers putting a bun in their wives' oven.' She looked pensive for a moment, then gave a little giggle. 'There's such a lot of begetting in the Bible, it seems to me He encourages conception, immaculate or otherwise.'

The shocked Flora now burst out, 'I don't know how you can sit there and take God's name in vain like that, and you married to a man of the Church.'

'Not only am I married to one,' Grace nodded, winking mischievously at Marianne who was hard-pressed to keep a straight face, 'I am also the daughter of one – my father was minister of quite a large parish in the wilds of Aberdeenshire – but what I'm saying is, it might be worth my while to pray a lot more, don't you think? To get in His good books, if you see what I mean.'

Rather belatedly, it dawned on the doctor's wife that her friend was joking. 'Grace Peat, I never know when to take you seriously.'

Grace grinned at her. 'You should know me by this time.'

She stood up to fetch the tray she had made ready earlier, and when she went out, Flora leaned across and whispered, 'There's something not quite right about Duncan, I always think. Grace told me once that when he's in one of his black moods, she's scared to speak to him.'

It was Marianne's turn to gasp in shock. 'She's actually *scared* of him?'

'Oh, don't ever tell anybody I said that,' Flora pleaded, 'but I've seen bruises on her arms when she's wearing short sleeves and I'm sure he hits her. She's never admitted it, mind. Says she banged into a door, or knocked against something, but –' She jumped back at the sound of footsteps coming along the little passageway between the sitting room and the kitchen, shaking her head in warning.

Marianne couldn't put it out of her head, and later, on her way home, she tried to remember if she had ever seen bruises on Grace's arms but she didn't think she had. Going inside, she came to the conclusion that Flora had been imagining things. Duncan was a man of God, for goodness' sake. He maybe had moods, all men did, but he wouldn't strike his wife, and there was no sense in mentioning it to Hamish or Hector. It would only lead to trouble where, more than likely, there had been no trouble at all.

Life below stairs in the castle was light-hearted now. 'Mrs Hamish has fair made a big change here,' Mrs Carnie remarked to her husband before they went to bed one night. 'There's no' the fear like there was when Lady Glendarril got on her high horse.' She shook her head and corrected her statement. 'No, to be honest, it wasna fear exactly, but we were aye worried aboot what she'd say, for she'd a wicked tongue on her when she got goin'.'

Carnie drew hard on the pipe he was lighting with one of the tapers the chamber maid supplied him with – from the vase in the master's study. 'She were a good mistress, though,' he observed, snibbing the flame between his thumb and forefinger and laying the taper inside the fender.

'Are you tellin' me Mrs Hamish is no' a good mistress?' his wife demanded, ready to be outraged if he even thought such a thing.

'That's no' what I said. She's no' as strict as Lady Glendarril, an' she's mebbe a wee bit ower friendly wi' the young maids . . .'

'She's tryin' to put them at their ease! Some o' they lassies used to be scared stiff at Lady Glendarril. You get better work oot o' them if you treat them right and dinna shout, that's what I aye say.'

Her husband eyed her with scepticism. 'Is that a fact? I've heard you roarin' at them like a ragin' bull . . . mony's the time.'

'Just when they needed it,' she defended herself, then got back to her original topic. 'Ony road, Mrs Hamish didna come o' the gentry. You can tell by the way she speaks she was workin' class, but my faith, she's learned a lot since she come here.'

'Roberta Glover learned her the maist o' it.'

'Na, na, Miss Glover just learned her some o' it, for she wasna ower proud to ask, and she's took her ain road for a good while now.'

Tired of baiting her, though she should be used to it after near twenty years of marriage, Carnie nodded amicably. 'She's shaped up fine. She's a good heid on her shooders.'

Pleased that he was agreeing with her at last, his wife said, 'You look real tired the nicht, Tarn. I'll put a drappie brandy in your hot milk afore we go to oor bed.'

185

He grinned roguishly. 'I dinna need brandy to kittle me up, as fine you ken.'

She turned a coquettish smile on him. 'Ach you. Behave yoursel'!'

When Marianne went into the dining room one morning in early winter, her husband and father-in-law had finished breakfast, and after Hector went out, Hamish said, 'We were discussing you.'

'And what conclusion did you come to?' The frosty edge to her voice showed her annoyance at being talked about behind her back.

'We think it's time you visited Strawberry Bank. It is almost a year and a half since the wedding, and I am sure the Rennies would be delighted to see you. In fact, Father was astonished that they had not come here again.'

'I've invited them in every letter I write, but Miss Edith says they don't feel easy in the castle.'

'I see, well, all the more reason for you to go to Aberdeen and you had better do it before winter sets in. If you wait much longer, there is a possibility that the journey could endanger your health and the child's, according to Father. You do want to see them?'

Her little spurt of anger evaporated. 'Of course I do! I'll write today and ask which Sunday would be best for them. It has to be a Sunday, you see, it's the only day the shop's shut.'

'In that case,' Hamish said gently, 'you will also see Andrew, will you not?'

There was no sarcasm or jealousy in his voice, so she felt free to answer honestly. 'Yes, so I will. I'm quite pleased about that, for I've always . . . liked him.'

The effusive welcome from Miss Esther and Miss Emily the next Sunday – arms flung round her and lips pressed against her cheek – brought tears to Marianne's eyes, and she was glad of Miss Edith's brusque, 'Come, come, no tears today.' A crushingly firm handclasp, however, revealed that the eldest sister was equally pleased to see her.

After Hamish had been given his share of the greetings, Miss Esther said, 'Sit down, for goodness' sake, otherwise lunch will be ruined, and afterwards, Marianne, you can tell us how you are coping with your new role in life.'

The girl glanced at her husband uncertainly. Since that dreadful day, he had not referred to their quarrel, yet their relationship was no longer what it had been. There was a constraint between them, not enough to make other people wonder, perhaps, but certainly enough to make her feel ashamed of having lost her temper. Unfortunately, she'd had no chance to apologize, there was always somebody else around – an older man and woman had even followed them into the first-class carriage when they joined the London train at Laurencekirk. She hadn't wanted Hamish to come with her, but he had refused to allow her to travel unaccompanied, and how could she talk honestly about *his* home, *his* servants, *his* father, with *him* listening to every word?

But he was smiling and shaking his head. 'Thank you, Miss Esther, for your kind hospitality, but I am sure that you did not count on my being here.'

'It is all right,' she protested. 'I always make more than enough food on Sundays. My sisters will tell you . . .'

'It is true, Hamish,' Miss Edith beamed. 'Even after having a meal on Mondays from the left-overs, we often have to feed the remains to the dog next door.'

'If you are sure . . . ?' He sat down now.

Not only had the long-deceased Mr and Mrs Rennie forbidden their daughters to waste good food, they had also taught them that it was extremely bad manners to talk while they were eating, so little was said during the meal, which gave Marianne further space to think. She had hoped to confide her troubles to Andrew later, in the hope that he could advise her on what she might do – Miss Edith shouldn't think it strange if they went for a walk together as they had been in the habit of doing before – but with Hamish here as well . . . ?

No matter how hard she tried, she could think of no way she could get her old friend alone, and finally accepted that she would just have to make the best of her life with no advice from anybody. In any case, maybe Andrew had stopped coming to Strawberry Bank on Sunday afternoons, which would be a relief in the circumstances.

Miss Esther and Miss Emily refused to allow Marianne to help with the clearing up, which provided her with another short respite before giving an account of her time at Castle Lyall, even making her hope, for one brief moment, that they would forget their curiosity, but she knew perfectly well that they wouldn't – not Miss Esther, anyway; she was like a dog worrying a bone when she wanted to know something.

To Marianne's amazement, just as the two younger sisters sat down, Hamish stood up. 'I am sure you ladies would enjoy your talk much better without a man here, so, if you do not think me rude, I will leave you to it.'

'Why don't you wait till Andrew comes?' Miss Esther suggested. 'He always takes a walk on Sunday afternoons, and I am sure he would be glad of your company. He has had to go alone since . . . since . . .' She came to a faltering halt, looking to her eldest sister for help.

Trying to set her at ease, Hamish smiled, 'Ah yes, I had forgotten about Andrew and I have promised to visit a friend for an hour or two. Please give him my apologies and tell him I shall see him when I come back.'

Then, for Marianne, came the biggest stroke of good luck, a virtual miracle, and from the most unexpected source. 'I do not think Andrew will mind,' Miss Emily said, shyly because it was not often that she took part in any discussion. 'He can take Marianne with him, like he always used to do.'

'What a good idea!' exclaimed Hamish, smiling at his wife, who was regarding him doubtfully but nevertheless with a touch of hope. 'It will be like old times for both of you.'

When he went out, Miss Esther said, 'Doesn't he mind?'

Miss Edith saved Marianne's face. 'Why should he mind? Andrew was her friend long before she met Hamish.'

'Yes, of course.' Miss Esther leaned back, satisfied that all was as it should be. 'Come on, then, Marianne. We want to hear what the mistress of the castle has been doing, before Andrew arrives.'

Once started, she did not find it difficult, and Miss Esther made it easier by asking about the kitchens, which she had never described in her letters.

'When I went to find out what happened below stairs, I got my eyes opened,' she admitted. 'I'd no idea there were so many rooms or so many staff. I thought there would be one chamber maid and one parlour maid, with maybe a couple of young girls to help the cook. I knew there were two footmen, because I'd seen them, and Lord Glendarril has a valet he calls Dick. I thought it was his Christian name, but it turned out to be his last name.'

'And how many staff are there?' Miss Esther prompted.

'There's four chamber maids, three parlour maids, and two still-room maids (who make the tea and coffee and snacks for the servants); they all think they're better than the scullery maids, kitchen maids and laundry maids, two of each, and the poor tweeny who's at everybody's beck and call. Mrs Carnie, the cook, and Dick, the valet, consider themselves above the rest and, of course, Miss Glover, the housekeeper, believes she's superior to the lot of them.'

'You get on all right with her, though?' Miss Esther again.

'We get on fine, in fact, she's been quite a help to me. It was her that told me what all the different rooms down there were for.'

While Miss Esther tried to count the number of servants, with Miss Emily's help when she forgot one, Miss Edith leaned towards Marianne and said softly, 'Are things all right between Hamish and you?'

'What makes you think they're not?'

Her defensive retort confirmed Miss Edith's suspicions, but she did not pry. If the girl wanted to tell her, she would, in time.

Miss Esther asked about the outside staff next, and Marianne told her about the grooms, the stable lads, Carnie, who was Jack of all trades, from driving the family about to doing any odd jobs in the buildings. 'Then there's Dargie, the head gardener,' she went on. He's got three men under him and two young lads.'

192

On being asked how many of the staff lived in, she told them who lived in the servants' quarters or over the stables. 'But a lot of them go home every night. You see, the whole glen belongs to the Bruce-Lyalls, and Lord Glendarril's grandfather or great-grandfather built good solid cottages for the workers on the estate and in the mill, and it's their sons and daughters who get all the jobs that's going.'

She was still holding forth about her dealings with those of the staff she saw every day when Andrew walked in, his somewhat solemn face being transformed by a smile the minute he saw her. 'I didn't know you'd be here today, Marianne,' he gasped. 'Nobody told me last Sunday.'

'Nobody knew last Sunday,' Miss Edith remarked drily.

'I only wrote on Tuesday,' the girl said, embarrassed by the naked love blazing from his eyes.

Realizing himself that he was being indiscreet, Andrew looked away from her and sat down to accept a cup of tea from his Aunt Esther. 'How is Hamish?' he enquired in a moment.

'He's very well, thank you,' Marianne replied. 'He did come with me, but he'd promised to visit a friend. He said to tell you he's sorry and he'll see you when he comes back.'

For the second time that day, Miss Emily took the bit between her teeth. 'He doesn't mind if you take Marianne with you on your walk this afternoon, Andrew, and she has plenty to tell you.'

His guard slipping again, he said, his voice practically begging, 'Are you absolutely sure you want to come with me, Marianne?'

She couldn't tell him that she was desperate to be on her own with him, so she murmured, 'Of course I am, Andrew.'

193

'Don't go too far, then,' cautioned Miss Edith.

Barely able to contain her curiosity, Miss Esther pounced as soon as the young couple left. 'Why did you not want them to go far?'

Her sister smiled enigmatically. 'Don't say you didn't notice?'

'Notice what?' A short pause, then, 'You mean . . . she's . . . ?'

'I am almost sure that she will be a mother in a few months.'

While the Rennie sisters were excitedly discussing this possibility, Marianne and Andrew were walking silently towards the River Dee, he longing to reassure her of his undying love but knowing it was not permissible, and she acutely aware of what he was trying so hard not to say. Although it was into December, it was a bright day and not nearly as cold as it might have been, so Marianne ventured to propose that they find somewhere to sit for a while, and within five minutes they were seated on a fallen tree trunk, sheltered from the strong breeze which had suddenly sprung up.

'Marianne,' Andrew said before she could utter a word, 'I know you want to tell me something, but please . . . nothing personal. I really could not bear to hear –'

'Please, Andrew, you must listen. I don't know what to do.'

He gave a sigh of resignation. No matter how hard he tried, or how much it might hurt him, he could refuse her nothing. 'Go on, then.'

She poured out the sad tale of how seldom Hamish had shared her bed and how, since she had told him she was going to have his child, he had not come to her at all. 'It's awful to feel your husband doesn't love you,' she wailed. 'I didn't love him when I married him, but I think I'm beginning to love him now, and he doesn't want me, except to . . . give him an heir.'

Andrew did his best to be objective. 'You say he has actually . . . made you pregnant? That seems a complete reversal of what you have just told me.' Unable to continue, he came to an abrupt halt, waiting a few moments before muttering, in despair, 'Oh, Marianne, I can't discuss this with you.'

Intent on getting advice, she was insensitive to his feelings. 'I don't see why not. Surely you've come across this sort of situation before? Hamish actually told me he wouldn't mind if I took a lover; he even thinks you *were* my lover at one time.'

A frown crossed her companion's brow. 'Is that what this is all about? Do you want me to *be* your lover . . . a secret lover?' He gave a deep groan. 'I want to be your lover more than anything else in the world, my darling, but not in secret. I would want everyone to know. I would want you to live with me, to prove to the world that the love was not all on my side.' He looked at her keenly, then ended sadly, 'But it is, isn't it?'

'Oh, Andrew dear, I'm sorry. I do love you, but just as a good friend, my best friend. I shouldn't have told you anything. It was cruel of me.'

After a pause that told of deep inner turmoil, he said flatly, 'I did tell you to come to me if you needed help, so . . . I would advise you to wait until your child is born. That could be the spur Hamish needs; perhaps, although

195

he has had a tendency to be reserved he will be overcome by love for you when you lay his son in his arms.'

Her face had brightened considerably. 'D'you really think so? Oh, Andrew, I'm glad I asked you; I knew you could tell me what to do.'

He stood up and pulled her to her feet. 'It is time we went back. It is growing much colder.'

When they returned to Strawberry Bank, Marianne was conscious of Miss Edith looking enquiringly from one to the other of them, and that Miss Esther and Miss Emily seemed to be excited about something, but before any of them spoke, Hamish knocked at the door. It was evident from the easy conversation the two men struck up now that there was no animosity between them, which made Marianne feel rather put out, though she didn't know quite what she had expected.

Shortly after tea, Hamish said they would have to leave, otherwise they would miss the last train home, and Andrew also stood up. 'I'll walk along with you a bit, if you don't mind.'

His Aunt Edith got to her feet. 'And I shall come to Justice Mill Lane with you, to stretch my legs before I go to bed.'

Naturally, Hamish and Andrew went in front, and Marianne waited for the question or questions that Miss Edith was bound to ask.

'Haven't you forgotten to tell me something, dear?'

'What d'you mean?'

'Surely you do not intend to keep so important a secret from us, Marianne? When is your confinement to be?'

The girl gave a wry laugh. 'I might have known *you* would guess. I'm due in March, and I didn't tell you because I was afraid you'd want to give me all the baby clothes in your shop. I don't want that, for Hamish can easily afford to buy everything we need.'

'Yes, I can understand that he will want to provide for his own child, but Esther will want to make as many things for the infant as she can, and you surely cannot deny her that pleasure?'

'No, of course I can't.'

'One last thing, Marianne. I know something is wrong between you and Hamish, so won't you tell me about that, as well?'

'It's nothing. We'd a bit of a quarrel a few days ago, but it'll soon blow over.'

Miss Edith was frowning now. 'It is not good to let it run on for long. My mother used to say, "Never let the sun go down on your wrath." She said it was because she had stuck to that rule that her marriage to Father was so happy, and you would do well to remember it, too. In the meantime, I would advise you to apologize to Hamish tonight, then kiss and make up. You will not regret it.'

Miss Edith bade them goodbye first, and when it was Andrew's turn to leave them, Hamish said, 'You must pay us a visit some weekend, Andrew. We would be glad of some younger company.'

'Thank you, I'd like that very much.'

When they were sitting in a first-class carriage by themselves, it occurred to Marianne that she would probably have no opportunity to carry out Miss Edith's instructions once they went home, and that now would be an ideal time. 'Hamish,' she said gently, 'I'm truly sorry for the things I said the other day.'

197

'No, my dear,' he murmured. 'It was my fault, and you must please accept my apology.'

His kiss was not enough to lift the weight which had been pressing on her, and she came to the conclusion that she would be wise to take Andrew's advice and wait until the baby was born. Surely having his son placed in his arms *would* make Hamish realize that he loved her. Besides, he was probably right to sleep in another room until she recovered from her confinement. She was only six months gone, but she wasn't sure how long into a pregancy a man could . . . do it without causing harm to his wife or the unborn infant.

Chapter Eleven

No winter had ever passed so slowly for Marianne. Even Andrew's visit just before Christmas did not lift her spirits, despite assurances from Thomson that she had hardly begun to show. Nevertheless, she had the distinct impression that her old friend was embarrassed at seeing her, which made her so conscious of her condition that she kept to her room as much as she could. This, of course, infuriated her husband, who accused her of being unsociable.

'He was your friend before he was mine,' he snapped after Andrew had gone, 'and you should have made him feel welcome in our home, instead of which you made him so uncomfortable that I would not be surprised if he does not come back.'

She tried to explain. 'I don't like people seeing me like this. Maybe it doesn't matter to you, but I don't want Andrew to see me looking like the side of a house.'

'Yes, it is always Andrew!' Hamish spat out. 'You care what he thinks of you, but I do not matter.'

Because a woman's emotions always teeter on a razor's edge during pregnancy, Hamish's attitude tipped the balance for Marianne now. 'I'll never stop caring what

Andrew thinks of me,' she shouted, 'though I know he loves me so much he wouldn't bother how I look.'

'You don't want him to see you with another man's child in your belly! That is the whole crux of the matter, isn't it? Possibly you wish it was his?'

'Don't be so damned stupid!' she screamed. 'You canna have a very good opinion o' me when you're sayin' things like that! You tell't me why you wanted to marry me, and I was willin' to produce sons for you, and I'd never have agreed to it if I'd wanted Andrew, would I?'

His eyes narrowed. 'You forget what you are getting out of the arrangement. A castle home, a title some day, and wealth you would never have known if I had not come into your life.'

'I haven't forgotten anything, and I'm grateful to you for what you're providing for me . . .' She paused, gulping, and lowered her voice. 'Hamish, why can't you be grateful to me for what I'm doing for you? I'm carrying your child, but it was conceived through your love for your father and the future of the family, not for me.'

He made as if to move towards her, then checked himself. 'We had a business agreement, Marianne,' he sighed. 'Love played no part in it, if you remember, but I am deeply sorry for upsetting you in your condition. What I said was quite uncalled for. Now, I feel the need of a walk before I go to bed, so shall I call Thomson to – ?'

'I'll manage to go to bed myself.'

He held the door open for her, and as she went upstairs, she was conscious of him watching until she reached the top landing.

On Hogmanay, Hector invited some of his business friends and their wives to see in the new year of 1899 at Castle Lyall, and Marianne had been ordered to be there to greet them. She was almost into the seventh month of her pregnancy, and her hackles had gone up when the three overdressed, bejewelled women had looked at each other knowingly when they saw her. One of them even said, with all the finesse of a bull crashing through a china shop, 'You have put on some weight since you were married.'

Having resolved to be polite to the guests, Marianne smiled. 'Yes, a little.'

A round of puzzled glances followed this unproductive statement, then the same woman, built like a battleship and obviously the leader of the group, coaxed, 'Come now, my dear girl, there is no need to be shy. You can trust us.' Her persistence goaded Marianne into indiscretion. 'Oh, I can, can I?' she said loudly. 'Well, I'm sure you ken already, for Lord Glendarril's likely tell't you, but I'm six month gone and if you count back on your fingers – likely the only way you *can* count and you've maybe done it already – you'll see the bairn wasna made till long after the wedding night.'

Marianne did not welcome the new year along with the guests. In the shocked silence following her outburst, her husband took her firmly by the elbow and shepherded her upstairs. 'I know they are inquisitive old harpies,' he said, 'but they are under my father's roof and we must observe the niceties of being hosts.'

'I'm sorry, Hamish,' she wailed. 'I couldn't help it. That woman was practically asking me outright if I was expecting, and that isn't very polite, is it?'

'That woman,' he said drily, 'is the sister-in-law of Mr William Ewart Gladstone.'

'Him that was Prime Minister?' she faltered. 'Oh, what have I done? Your father'll never forgive me.'

A grin spread over Hamish's face. 'My father cannot stand her and neither can I, so go to sleep and forget about it. Just remember to be more tactful in future.'

When he closed the door behind him, she plumped down on the stool before the mirror on her vanity table and regarded her reflection with distaste. No wonder those women had been curious about her. Her very face had changed! In the first five months, it had been pale and pinched, which is why Miss Edith had guessed how the land lay, but her cheeks were fuller now, with such a deep rosy glow to them folk would think it was the bloom of good health if they didn't see the rest of her. She considered this for a moment and realized that she *was* blooming with health. She'd had none of the morning sickness other mothers-to-be spoke about; no pains except a slight tenderness in her breasts. Her hazel eyes were bright and clear and her auburn hair had its usual sheen.

The aches and pains came in the last month. Her back felt as if it would break with the extra weight, her breasts were uncomfortably heavy and she couldn't see her feet for the great bump at her front. She waddled when she walked, and it wouldn't surprise her if her legs buckled under her one of these days. It was awful to have no control over her body. But the doctor – she had got to know Robert Mowatt quite well on the fortnightly examinations Hector

202

insisted upon – assured her that there were no problems, that she would sail through the confinement.

And sail through it she did! At 3 a.m. on the tenth day of March, after only about two hours of true labour, he delivered her of a baby boy weighing eight pounds twelve ounces and yelling his head off as he was cleaned.

'He's got a fine pair of lungs, at any rate,' the doctor observed, then raised his voice. 'You can come in now, Hamish. It's all over and you have a son.'

The nurse Hector had been adamant about employing handed the tightly wrapped bundle to the father, who asked only one question before he carried it away: 'Is he all right, Robert?'

The doctor nodded. 'Not a thing wrong with him that I could see, and all his parts are there.'

'Why did you tell him that?' Marianne asked when her husband went out. She was hurt that Hamish hadn't asked how she was, but she couldn't say so to a third party.

Robert looked at her sadly. 'He wanted to know if the child could carry on the Bruce-Lyall line. That's all Hector was worrying about, not just an heir to follow Hamish, but an heir to follow that. So do not be upset that your man was only concerned about the infant . . . no,' he grinned, as she opened her mouth to deny this, 'you can't fool me, young lady. I am sure he'll show more interest in you when he comes back, so don't be angry with him.'

Minutes after the doctor left her, Hamish brought back the son she had not been given a chance to see, and her voice was a touch nippy as she said, 'Is your father satisfied with him?'

'He thinks he's perfect, and so do I. Don't you?'

'Since I haven't set eyes on him yet, I can't really say.'

'Marianne, I am sorry . . . I did not realize . . . I should have . . .' A look of horror crossed his face. 'Forgive me, please. The first thing I should have done was ask how you were. Oh, I made a proper mess of it.'

She did not have the energy to argue, and, after all, she thought, in self-pity, the baby had been the most important factor for both Hamish and his father; it was the only reason for the marriage. 'I'm not too bad,' she sighed. 'The last wee while was the worst, but it wasn't as bad as I'd imagined. Maybe your father was right. Maybe I am the best person you could have found to give you sons.' A devil got in her here, a wish to shock him. 'I was the same as a woman at home. When folk asked her why she kept on having babies, she used to say, "Havin' a bairn's nae bother to me. It's just like havin' a stiff shite."'

His shock was greater than she expected. First, he turned white, then the colour rushed back into his cheeks until they were scarlet, and as he stood gaping at her, she had to laugh. 'That wasn't fair of me, Hamish. I wanted to pay you back for neglecting me, but I don't suppose you've ever heard a girl using language like that.'

He closed his mouth and his face gradually returned to its natural shade, but her coarseness had told him how badly he had wounded her by his cavalier behaviour and he attempted to soothe her. 'Father wants to call him Ruairidh.'

He could not have said anything more likely to rouse her to fury. 'Your *father* wants?' she burst out. 'Who had this bairn, me or him?'

'Marianne, that's not –'

'Never mind tryin' to get round me. Just go and tell your father I'm callin' *my* son what *I* want.'

'He meant no harm. He is so used to making all the decisions here that he did not stop to think.'

'What about you? You just agreed with him?'

'I was too overjoyed to think rationally about anything. It is not every day that a man has a son, and that was all that mattered to me. I am afraid that I neither agreed nor disagreed with him, and I am practically sure that, if I explain how you feel, he will allow you to choose any name you want.'

This time her devilment was mild. 'What about Dod, then? Or Tarn? Or Willie?'

After a brief hesitation, Hamish murmured, 'He would not object to any of these. George, Thomas and William are good, strong names.'

'I was only testing you,' Marianne laughed. 'What did your father suggest, did you say?'

'Ruairidh – it's an old family name, but *if* you –'

'Rory?'

'Spelled in the Gaelic way, of course. R-U-A-I-R-I-D-H.'

This appealed to her, but having made a stand, she was not going to climb down. 'Tell your father I'll name this one, but we'll call our second son Ruairidh to please him.'

Hamish had forgotten how well she could stick to her guns, a trait in her that his father admired. 'I will make sure that you get your way, Marianne. What name had you chosen?'

Not having chosen one at all, she picked a name out of the air. 'I thought Ranald would be nice.' She had seen it in a poem when she was at school, and she had always liked it.

While she was resting, it occurred to her that she'd had no chance to test the advice Andrew had given her. It had been the midwife who had handed Hamish his son, and he hadn't given one single thought to his wife till later. After she produced the second son that was wanted, she would likely be left strictly on her own at nights for the rest of her life. She would end up a wizened, unloved old lady unless . . .

Not unloved, though! There was always Andrew.

Marianne came awake slowly and luxuriously. The sun was streaming through the gap she had left in the curtains the night before, the birds were trying to outdo each other with the sweetness of their songs, cows were lowing in the distance . . . yet the small gilt clock by her bed showed only half-past five. June was a lovely month.

Stretching her arms, she decided against rising just yet. Thomson would alarm the whole household if she wasn't in her room when she brought up her morning cup of tea, and she'd have everybody in a proper fankle in no time. Besides, it would be quite nice to have time to consider her life, to set aside the cares of her duties as mistress of the castle. No, her duties didn't actually lie within the castle itself – Roberta Glover took care of the running of the household – but she did look after the needs of, and give advice to, the women of the glen, and they treated her with all the respect she'd ever wanted. They expressed their gratitude in many ways – giving her eggs gathered 'but an hour ago, your Leddyship', a small jacket knitted for her baby, and, from more than one young wife she had counselled, a lovely, soft woollen blanket, edged with blue ribbon for the cot or the perambulator. They looked on her as Lady Bountiful, as someone who could sort out any problem for them, or comfort them in their grief if they had lost a loved one.

She had taken to it like a duck takes to water, like an new-born infant takes to the breast, like a dung beetle takes to cows' sharn. She smiled at her own wit, but it was true, though she'd have to watch not to say 'sharn' in front of anybody here. She'd have to find out what the proper name for it was, because she only knew two other words which were even worse. Her mind went back to what she had been thinking about before: her new-found organizing skills. She had surprised herself by her confident dealing with the minor household problems of the crofters' wives, even with her belly starting to swell and her back giving her gyp. Now her confinement was past, she'd be able to attend to the whole glen with one hand tied behind her back, not that she'd ever try it.

She had been annoyed that Nurse Murchie wouldn't let her breast-feed baby Ranald after the first week. 'It's not dignified to be exposing yourself,' the woman had said. 'None of my ladies ever fed the baby themselves. That's why they employ a nurse.'

It did stop her from being tied to the house all the time, Marianne thought, but having her breasts bound tightly to stop the milk hadn't been pleasant. And she'd have to go through it all again at some time in the not-too-distant future, she supposed. It surprised her that Hamish hadn't come back to her room yet – it was three months since the birth.

A bead of sweat running down her nose made her thoughts veer. It was going to be a hot day again, unbearably hot like yesterday. She had meant to do a few odd little jobs this forenoon and then take a walk through the woods after lunch, but it would be even hotter then. She got out of bed to push open the window a little further, and drew the welcome fresh air deep into her lungs. Oh, she'd have to go out; the perspiration was trickling down between her shoulder blades now, but she couldn't be bothered dressing, nobody would see her at this time of morning.

Creeping along the corridor and down the stairs, she heaved a sigh of relief on reaching the door to the garden without seeing a soul. Her heart was singing as she slipped outside and ran lightly towards the gate at the far end of the rose garden. She had forgotten to put shoes on, but what did that matter? When she was a schoolgirl, she had run barefoot every summer, like all the children in Tipperton. Her feet weren't so hardened to stony ground nowadays though, she reflected wryly, picking her way carefully along the gravel path, but once she was in the wood, the going was a little easier. The thick layer of pine needles wasn't exactly as comfortable as a carpet would have been, but when she came to a stretch of moss, her feet felt almost as if there were springs under them.

Her heart was so light that she skipped along for a while, humming an old song her class had been taught by the dominie's wife, and in another few minutes, her exuberance was such that she could contain herself no longer and burst into song.

'Did you not see my lady go down the garden singing,
Silencing all the songbirds and setting the echoes
    ringing?
Oh, saw you not my lady out in the garden there, Shaming
the rose and lily for she is twice as fair?'

Unable to remember what came next, or even if what she
had already sung were the right words, she pirouetted and
collapsed giggling on the grass verging the small loch she
had reached. It was much hotter now, even in the shade of
the tall pines and, without considering, she jumped up and
waded in. The shock of the icy coldness made her draw a
sharp breath, but it didn't take her long to get accustomed
to it. It felt so good that she laved water all over herself,
soaking her long tresses as well as her thin nightgown.

She cavorted about until she was sufficiently cooled and
then got out, hauling her soggy garment off and spreading it over a branch. There was no sense in risking a chill,
and it should dry quickly in this heat, and so would she.
She sprawled down on the ground, arms and legs spread
wide, and watched the birds flying overhead.

She felt wonderful, as though somebody had wrapped
her in a warm blanket. She could lie here for ever . . .
or anyway, till the sun went down. Her eyes followed a
tiny wren for a moment, then a blue tit which landed
not far from her and hopped around in search of a grub.
A honey bee caught her attention next, buzzing content-
edly from one wild blossom to another. Marianne felt
totally at peace, with nothing to remind her of duties she
should be carrying out. Let them get on with things themselves – they would manage fine without her.

She lifted her breasts so that the skin underneath could have a turn of the warmth – they had returned to their normal size, thank goodness – and then sat up to let her back dry. Some minutes later, she got to her feet and ran her hands down her stomach, as firm as it had been before, then turned round to give the back of her legs a chance to dry. A movement to her right caught her eye. Believing it to be a rabbit or a weasel, she paid little attention until it dawned on her that whatever it was, it was far too big to be either a rabbit or a weasel.

'Who's there?' she called apprehensively.

And rising from where he'd been crouching in the bushes, appeared the most magnificent specimen of a man she had seen in her entire life. His hair was jet-black and curled close to his head and round his ears; his body being bare to the waist, she quickly averted her eyes from the thatch of black curls across his chest. His shoulders were broad, his face lean and tanned to an almost mahogany colour. His eyes were fixed on her, his mouth slightly open . . . as was hers, she realized, snapping it shut and remembering, at the same time, that she was stark naked, which was likely why he was staring at her like that.

'Will you please pass me my shift?' she asked haughtily.

He stepped right out now, placing himself between her and the nightdress she wanted. 'I'd like to look at you a while longer,' he answered, his smile widening into a grin, his eyes twinkling with mischief. 'It's no' often I come across a beautiful damsel wearin' nothin' but her skin, an' by God, you make a right bonnie picture.'

He was so attractive she couldn't help but respond to the compliments he was paying her. 'You make a fine picture yourself,' she smiled.

'Maybe I'd best take off my breeches to make us equal,' he offered, hands going to his top button, but waiting for her to say something before undoing it.

Marianne's reaction to this unpardonable yet fascinating remark surprised her. Her heart had speeded up, deep thrills ran down to her most private place, but, as she took an involuntary step towards him, she came to her senses. 'I'm a married woman,' she declared, with all the dignity she could muster when every fibre of her was aching to be in his arms.

He nodded nonchalantly. 'I noticed your weddin' ring, but it makes no odds to me. Married or single, you're still a bonnie lass.'

'You don't understand!' she burst out, pleading. 'I'm wed on the laird's son.'

'So? I'm pleased to see there's nae difference between a lady an' a workin' lassie when they've naething on, an' your figure's a lot better than mony o' the lassies I've lain wi', the married women an' all.' He undid his top button now, teasing as he said, 'I'm sure you'd like to ken if a tinker's the same as a lord under his breeks?'

'No, no!' she pleaded, somewhat half-heartedly because she *had* wondered about that, although she'd thought he was a gypsy. Then, in her confusion because his eyes were fastened on her bosom, she forgot about being refined and snapped, 'I'm nae a peepshow, so I'll thank you to stop lookin' at me like that.'

Her slip of the tongue made him raise his eyebrows. 'Aye, aye, m'Leddy, I some think you didna start oot as gentry. Was you a skivvy that took the laird's son's eye?'

211

She was outraged at this assumption. 'No, I wasn't! I worked in a shop in Aberdeen before I met Hamish.'

'But you dinna speak like a toon lassie. What did you dae afore you went to Aberdeen?'

Inquisitive though he was, she couldn't help liking him, and what did it matter if he knew the truth? She wouldn't see him again and he'd have no reason to tell anybody. 'I was servant to a banker's wife . . . in Tipperton.'

He gave a triumphant grin. 'So you *was* a skivvy! I ken't you was mair like me than like a laird's son! Now, bein' on the same level, so to speak, you've nae cause to look doon on me.'

'I wasna lookin' doon on you, but a gentleman would've turned his back when he saw –'

'But I never laid claim to bein' a gentleman, noo did I? An' you was getting' ready to gi'e me my marchin' orders though you dinna really want me to leave.'

She bridled. 'Give me my shift!' she ordered, staring him straight in the eye and speaking as firmly as she could.

Continuing to smile, he passed the still damp item over, then said, 'You could mebbe dae something for me . . . if it wouldna be ower much bother? M'name's Jamie MacPhee, an' me an' my brother's lookin' for work . . . well, it's just me that's lookin', for I'm sick o' sharpenin' knives and scythes. We've just got the one grindin' wheel, you see, an' Robbie's been leavin' me to dae near the lot.' He eyed her hopefully. 'You could get me a job at the castle, couldn't you? It'll nae be for lang, for we'll be goin' to pick berries at Blairgowrie in the middle o' July, dependin' on the weather.'

Marianne knew that Dargie would easily find work for another pair of hands, but she also knew that she wouldn't feel easy if Jamie MacPhee were around the castle for any length of time. His eyes, however, were pleading like a young puppy-dog's, and she cast around in her mind for something to offer him. Thankfully, a solution did crop up. 'I just remembered. The minister's wife told me on Sunday they were looking for a man to keep their garden tidy. Duncan, that's her husband, well, he broke his leg and she's not able to keep the weeds down by herself.'

Jamie's eyes had lit up. 'That's just the kind of thing I was lookin' for, an' I'd best go an' see aboot it afore somebody else gets it.'

'Take that first path on the left there, right down to the road and you'll easy find the manse – it's next to the kirk. They've a fair skelp o' ground, mind.'

'That'll nae bother me.' He touched his forelock in mock respect. 'Thank you, your Leddyship, an' I'm sorry for the things I said afore, but I thocht you was just a servant lassie. If you'd been dressed, see, I'd never have said nothin'.'

Marianne smiled uncomfortably. 'Yes, it was my own fault, but I'd be obliged if you'd forget it, and don't say anything to anybody.'

'I'll nae say a word . . .' he paused, his attractive grin tugging at her heartstrings as he added, '. . . but I'll nae forget.'

'Good luck!' she called as she watched him striding away from her.

She walked home slowly, trying to collect her thoughts. What on earth had possessed her to go into the loch? And worse, to take off her nightgown? Nobody, not even Hamish, had ever seen her naked, and God knows what she had looked like, showing herself off to whoever had chanced upon her. No wonder Jamie MacPhee hadn't been able to take his eyes off her. And what if it had been Lord Glendarril? Or Duncan Peat? No, he couldn't walk in the woods with a broken leg. But Hamish? He would likely have disowned her.

Another thing, she thought, turning hot at the memory of it, what had made her take to the tinker like that? Was it because he spoke with a north accent, like the one she was still trying to give up, or was it because he had said those nice things about her? Or was it because Hamish had not been in her bed since Ranald was born?

She was less than halfway to the garden gate when she saw Carnie practically running towards her, but there was nothing she could do to stop her damp shift clinging to her, for he'd seen her. 'My God, Lady Marianne,' he puffed, avoiding looking at her now, 'where've you been? They're going aboot mad back there. Thomson came running down the stair about ten past seven screaming, "Somebody's broke in and abducted the mistress!" and all hell broke loose.'

Marianne hung her head. 'I woke up early and it was so stuffy, I went out for some fresh air.'

He took off his jacket and handed it to her. 'You'd better cover yourself, or The Master'll . . .' He waited until she was as decent as possible, then took her arm and hurried her along the path. When they came to the garden gate, he said, 'You were taking a big chance going out in your goonie, though. Somebody might've seen you.'

'Nobody saw me.'

'You'd come out by the garden door? I'd best get you back in that way, and all, afore his Lordship or the

214

Master sees us and thinks I've been trifling wi' your affections.' Carnie gave a great rumble of laughter which she did her best to join, but the thought persisted in her mind that if she hadn't come to her senses when she did, Jamie MacPhee would have trifled with more than her affections.

When they reached the house, Thomson was highly indignant that she had gone out by herself. 'Not even dressed. What were you thinking about, Mrs Hamish? The men are all out looking for you.'

A range of emotions coming to the surface now, Marianne burst into tears. 'I needed a breath of fresh air, and . . . oh, go away and leave me alone. Surely I can do what I like? I'm not a prisoner here.'

Thomson sniffed and tossed her head as she marched out, but Marianne didn't care that she had offended her maid. All she wanted was some peace. She was tired and hot, and she wished that she could go away with Jamie MacPhee and his brother when they left. It wouldn't bother her that he had no money, and was never likely to . . .

But the lack of money *would* bother her! She had achieved her ambition when she married Hamish, and when he became the Lord, she would have, by right, the title of Lady, which most of the glen folk already bestowed on her. In any case, the period of mourning for Lady Glendarril was long over, though Marianne suspected she would likely be made to wait until she produced a second son, however long that would take, before the day she was waiting for – when she could take her place among the nobility.

Half an hour later, she was awakened from a doze by little Daisy, the chamber maid, calling through the door,

'Thomson told me to get a bath ready for you, m'Leddy, so you'd better take it afore it gets cold.'

'Thank you, Daisy,' Marianne called back. 'And thank Thomson for thinking of it.' She didn't feel guilty any more about this, because no one had to carry the water upstairs since Hector had got men to fit the pump for filling the tank for the bath. They had also installed a gas ring under it, and with the work of laying the pipes for that, Hector had decided that they may as well have gaslights fitted in all rooms. One of her suggestions had led to a vast improvement in the standard of life in the castle.

She took her time over her ablutions and did feel much better for the long soak. Stepping out of the tub, she wrapped herself in the huge white towel laid out for her and opened the bathroom door to find Daisy hovering in the passage. 'Would you like me to help you to dry yourself and dress, m'Leddy?'

'No, thank you, I'll manage.'

She had just gone into her room when she heard heavy feet pounding upstairs, then Hamish flung open the door and took her in his arms.

'Oh, Marianne, where were you?' he cried. 'We searched the gardens high and low, although Thomson was determined you'd been abducted. I thought I had lost you.'

'I wanted some air so I went out for a walk. Then it got so hot, I went into the loch for a wee while to cool down and I'd to wait till I was dry, and my . . .' Appalled at having almost admitted how little she had been wearing, she finished, hastily, '. . . till my clothes were dry, too.'

Hamish stepped back and looked at her accusingly. 'Thomson tells me you had no clothes on, only a nightdress? I hope no one saw you.'

216

'Nobody saw me,' she assured him, her colour rising as she recalled Jamie MacPhee's searching eyes when she stood naked before him, and then, wondering if her husband would react in the same way as the tinker, she let the huge towel slip to the floor.

Hamish said nothing for several moments, but there was no doubt that he was drinking in the sight of her svelte body. She took a step towards him, and because he was her husband, she had no need to break away when his arms went round her again, fiercer than before.

'Dear God, Marianne,' he said hoarsely, 'do you know what holding you like this is doing to me?'

His lips came down hard on her mouth, his knuckles dug into the small of her back, but suddenly, he thrust her from him. 'No, no! I can't! I can't!'

'Why can't you?' she asked, frustration making her unnaturally bold to him.

'If you only knew how much I want to, my sweetheart. I've . . . oh, this is difficult, but I cannot keep it from you any longer. I've loved you ever since I first saw you – standing up to Sybil and her crew during that Hogmanay Ball, but I couldn't tell you before because I was sure that you loved Andrew.'

'Hamish, I told you over and over that I didn't love him in that way, just as a friend.'

His eyes held a trace of sadness now. 'Yet, when I proposed, you said you didn't love me, so what else was I to think?'

'I didn't think I did at first,' she admitted, pausing to kiss his ear before ending, 'but . . . you grew on me.'

He eyed her quizzically. 'Am I to take that as a compliment, or do you mean you got used to me, which isn't the same as loving me?'

'I do love you,' she said, 'but I thought you looked on our marriage as a duty to your father, a duty you didn't really care for.' His gentle but firm push towards the bed made her say, 'What are you doing, Hamish? We can't . . . it can't be long after breakfast time. Somebody might come in.'

He nuzzled her neck. 'Let them all come in. Let them feast their eyes on their master showing his beautiful wife how much he loves her.'

'It's all right for you,' she protested. 'It's me that's naked. You're dressed.'

'I shall soon remedy that,' he smiled, hardly taking time to open buttons as he pulled off jacket, necktie, shirt, trousers, and cast them from him on to the floor.

And now, at long last, came the love-making she had longed for, the caressing, the tender yet meaningful kissing, the exploring hands, the build-up to a height they had never reached before, and she was left in no doubt that he loved her as much as she loved him.

When it was over, she expressed her surprise that no one had come to the door, not even Thomson, and Hamish murmured, smiling at her fondly, 'They are human, my darling. They know what a husband will do to the wife he feared was lost to him.'

'And they likely know you hardly ever slept with me,' she said, embarrassed at reminding him.

He took hold of one of her tresses of coppery hair and twirled it round his finger. 'I wasted a lot of time fretting about you and Andrew.' He put his finger on her mouth as she started to speak. 'Yes, I know that you denied it several times, but a man in love is not always rational.'

'A man in love,' she sighed rapturously. 'Oh, I never thought I'd hear you describing yourself like that.'

'You will hear it over and over again for as long as we live,' he assured her.

This little exchange, of course, only served to keep them in bed, and when they did eventually go downstairs, the two maids in the dining room kept their eyes down. Even Hector didn't look at them, eating his lunch as though he hadn't a minute to spare, but when the servants had withdrawn, he could hold back no longer.

'You might have waited until night-time,' he muttered. 'You know what these lassies are like. It'll be all round the glen in no time that you two spent the whole morning in bed together.'

Stretching out to clasp Marianne's hand, Hamish said, 'We don't care. You maybe will not believe this, Father, but we only discovered today the true extent of our love.'

The suggestion of a twinkle now appeared in Sir Hector's eyes. 'And you couldn't wait?' He gave Marianne a quick glance and then smiled. 'I don't blame you, though. She's a damn fine-looking girl.'

When he, too, went out, Hamish said, 'I'd better go with him, my dear. I don't want to get his back up by staying off work all day, but my heart won't be in it.'

She returned to her room and lay down on the bed to think. So much had happened since she'd woken up and had felt stifled with the heat. She had enjoyed walking barefoot one the carpet of pine needles in the early morning, had enjoyed her cooling dip in the loch, had even, if she was scrupulously honest, enjoyed – revelled in – Jamie MacPhee's flattering remarks.

She wouldn't have been able to look anybody in the face again if she had done what he wanted, especially Hamish. If Duncan Peat ever got to know about it – which he wouldn't for she wouldn't even tell Grace – he would say that God had intervened to stop her from committing adultery. And maybe he'd be right! He was a dedicated minister, she had discovered, having met him in several of the little cottages when someone died or was seriously ill. He had the knack of saying the right thing, of sympathizing as if he truly meant it, of consoling someone who had just lost a husband, a parent, a child, as though that person was the most important thing in the world to him. And they would be, at that moment. It was a great gift to have.

Suddenly recalling what Flora Mowatt had said about him, Marianne shook her head in disgust at the very thought of him hurting his wife. Flora must be mistaken. He wouldn't harm a single living creature!

Anyway, Marianne mused, at least she had done two good turns today. With Duncan having broken his leg – she'd go tomorrow to see how he was – he'd be grateful for help in the garden, and Jamie MacPhee would be glad of the job.

And now, having figured everything out to her own satisfaction, she was free to think about Hamish. It was strange how a misunderstanding on both their parts had caused them to lose two years of real happiness, but they would make up for it. Oh yes, they would make up for it!

Some time later, when she was telling herself that she had better not be too long in dressing for dinner – she wanted to look her best when Hamish came home from the mill – it occurred to Marianne that she owed it to Miss Edith to let her know that their marriage was perfect at last. She had intended inviting them for wee Ranald's christening, but she would write a proper letter instead. Then another, more sobering thought entered her mind. What about Andrew? He was the only other person who knew how things had been between her and Hamish, but would he be more hurt if she told him how things were now? Perhaps it would be better just to say they had improved a little, and tell him the whole truth at some other time.

Chapter Twelve

The summer of 1902 saw preparations for celebrating the coronation in full swing in Glendarril. The dominie and his wife, helped by some of the older children, had freshened up the assembly hall – which also served as a gymnasium, as a sewing room where Mrs Wink showed the older girls how to knit and to stitch, and at other times, where her husband taught the boys woodwork – with two coats of paint, cream from the ceiling to the dado placed well above the reach of even the tallest child, and dark brown from that demarcation line to the floor so that sticky or inky fingermarks would not 'stand out like sore thumbs', as William Wink put it with his usual inability to recognize a pun, although he had made it himself. The same treatment was accorded to the classroom, only one since there were hardly ever more than a dozen pupils on the roll in any one year.

The walls of the hall were then festooned with red, white and blue bunting, and taking pride of place opposite the door were pictures of Edward the Seventh and Queen Alexandra. Trestle tables were to be set up in the playground on 26 June if it was dry, and the whole population of the glen would be sitting down to a repast fit for the Royal couple themselves, which the ladies of the WRI had volunteered to prepare and serve. For weeks, the scholars had rehearsed 'Hearts of Oak' and 'The British Grenadiers' with which to regale the adults between courses, and Mrs Wink was praying that the joyful solemnity of the occasion would rub off on Johnsy Gibb and Davy Marr and make them think twice before tugging any pigtails or, even worse, using them to tie two heads together, which usually resulted in all-out warfare between the sexes.

Still, all in all, it was an exciting time for the country folk, especially for those men who still remembered acting as ghillies at the August shoots Edward had joined as the young and handsome Prince of Wales. One old lady could recall a much more initimate relationship with him but knew that boasting about it, even after forty-odd years, would make some people doubt her son's legitimacy.

Lord Glendarril and family, of course, would be attending the real ceremony in London, and Lady Marianne (as she was still known although not yet entitled to the title) had looked out the robes and coronets – last worn at Victoria's coronation by Hector's parents – and had put them on display in one of the public rooms for a whole day so that anyone who wished could come to see them.

'Marrying into the gentry hasna gone to her head,' the wives told each other, when they were walking back down the long drive, having viewed the robes, 'for there's nae a pick o' side to her.'

Naturally, there were those who disagreed on principle with the decisions made by their employers, as there are in any workforce. Ettie Webster was one such. 'I couldna get ower it when I heard her saying she was putting her laddies to the school here when they're the age,' she sneered the following evening, at a meeting of the Women's Rural Institute in the kirk vestry. 'It just shows she's no' real gentry, for their father and their grandfather, and his father afore him, like enough, was sent to a private school in England some place to be teached, so I thought the laird would've wanted his sons to –'

'The laird did want them to go to his old school,' interrupted Flora Mowatt, 'but their mother wouldn't hear of it. She said she didn't want Ranald and Ruairidh to be brought up thinking they were better than other children in the glen. Mind you, Ranald's just three and Ruairidh's hardly two so she might change her mind when the time comes.'

Grace Peat – president of the WRI – shook her head. 'I don't think she will. In any case, she has been a good friend to me and I do not want to hear anything against her.'

Loud murmurs of agreement to this showed that most of the wives regarded 'Lady Marianne' as a friend. After all, they whispered to each other, didn't she stand and speak to them if she met them on the road any time, even if she'd to come off the bike she'd taken to using for getting around? More to the point, she had started a sort of clothes-exchange for babies and toddlers, even for girls and boys at the school, which was a great help to the mothers with a puckle bairns.

Judging that she had allowed enough time to be wasted, Mrs Peat said, 'Now, we must get down to business . . .'

The meeting proceeded until two committee members rose to make the tea. This was the signal for a hubbub of chattering to break out, discussing the possible consequences of Lady Marianne's boys attending the glen school (a far more important subject to them than the crowning to take place hundreds of miles away), and when they went home, most of the women with daughters under school age were already weaving dreams of being mother-in-law to a Lord one day. Those who had only sons but were still capable of bearing children resolved to produce a girl next time, no matter that they had sworn to their husbands after their last confinement that he need not expect them to have any more.

Grace Peat was no different from her fellow WRI members and was so excited that she didn't stop to think when she went home. 'Oh, I hope it'll be a daughter I have!' The words were scarcely out when her hand flew to her mouth.

Too late! The minister's head jerked up from the sermon he was preparing. 'Are you trying to tell me that you are . . . pregnant?'

His wife flushed, all her dreams for the future disintegrating. 'Yes, Duncan. I . . . I didn't know how to tell you.'

'I am not surprised. Have you forgotten how ill you were when you had pleurisy two years ago? Robert Mowatt as much as said you were not fit enough to have a child. Does he know about this?'

'Y-yes . . . and he has warned me that I may have a difficult time.'

'So! Well, you are taking your life in your own hands and it will not be my fault if anything happens to you.'

Knowing her husband as she did, Grace let him have the last word. It was an awful thing for a man of God to think, never mind say out loud, but at least he hadn't punched her as he so often did when he was angry with her. It was fear of his violence that had kept her from telling him of her condition, made her pull the strings of her corsets so tight she could hardly breathe, and when he found out that she was due in three months . . . Thank goodness the baby seemed small – or at least the bulge around her middle not so very big. If anything bad should happen to her it was more likely to be as a result of what he would do to her than the actual birth.

Marianne was the most excited in the whole of the castle, with the exception of Jean Thomson, who was to be accompanying her mistress to London. Hamish was looking forward to seeing old school friends again, but his father was quite blasé about the whole thing.

'We'll get down there in one day, not like in my parents' time when there was no railway. It took them a week, and I can remember my mother telling me she felt so faint at times they had to stop at the first inn they came to, and some were not fit for decent folk. Of course,' he added with a smile, 'she was always having fits of the vapours. It was fashionable in her day.'

They were to be staying in his house in Piccadilly, which he used any time he was in the capital on business, which was also when he felt obliged to take his place in the House of Lords. The married couple whom he paid to look after the building while he was not in residence had been advised that he and his son and daughter-in-law would be there for about two weeks and, augmented by several temporary maids and boys, the caretakers had made the rooms ready. In spite of all Marianne's pleas, Hector would not allow Hamish to take her on ahead so that she could see a bit more of London. 'You'll not like it,' he told her.

'Maybe *you* don't,' was her spirited reply, 'but I'm sure I will.'

Hector grimaced at Hamish. 'This wife of yours will be the death of me, too saucy for her own good. I sometimes wish we had picked someone else to be the mother of your boys.'

Noticing the twinkle in his eyes, Marianne just grinned. She was proud of her two sons, and so were the glen wives. When they had been at the castle to view the robes and coronets, the sight of the two fair-haired, blue-eyed little boys racing around the lawns had made them smile, they bore such a striking resemblance to their father. Ranald had more than his share of devilment, but also a great deal of charm, which saved him from being punished for the scrapes he got into, whereas Ruairidh was much quieter, and often the butt of his brother's exuberant pranks. None the less, if either one got on Nurse's wrong side, the other manfully defended him. She was going to miss them while she was away, Marianne mused, on the day before she had to make the journey, but this would be more than counterbalanced by her introduction to London society, the realization of all her dreams.

The Bruce-Lyalls arrived in Piccadilly on the evening of 23 June, three days before the coronation, and Hamish forbade Marianne to leave the house the following day. 'You had better take time to recover from the long hours of travelling,' he told her. 'You will want to look your best on the day.'

She was anxious to explore London, but his last sentence made her think. She *did* want to look her best to meet the cream of the nobility, so she had better do as her husband said. She was reclining on a brocaded chaise longue in the drawing room in the late afternoon when Hector burst in and sat down heavily on an uncomfortable-looking chair by the window.

'You'll never guess,' he panted. 'The King . . .' He stopped to wipe his perspiring brow, then began again. 'They are having to postpone the coronation. Right this minute, the King's appendix is being removed.'

'Is that serious?' Marianne asked. 'How long before . . . ?'

'It is fairly serious in a man of his age, and I really do not know how long it will be before he is fit enough to be crowned . . . months rather than weeks, I should think.'

'Does that mean . . . ? Will we have to go home and come back?'

'No, no, it is better that we stay in London, just in case . . .'

Not comprehending what he was hinting at, she felt a surge of excitement go through her. She would have plenty of time now to get to know Hector's titled friends, to do all sort of things she had not expected to do. She would start by exploring this house tomorrow and make friends with the caretaker's wife, who would be able to keep her right on etiquette, etc.

Moll Cheyne had been kept awake all night with Alfie coughing. Deep barks, on and on, till she'd thought he was going to choke, and a cold hand had squeezed at her heart. It was the middle of summer, she mused as she raked out the ashes in the grate, setting aside the cinders which would start the fire today, so it wasn't just a cold he had, and if he died, God forbid, what would she do? He hadn't been fit for the sawmill for a few weeks now, and if he was off much longer, they'd likely be put out of the house, for it went with the job.

Shovelling up the grey dust that was left in the ash-pan, she took it outside to throw on the midden, carefully shielding it from the draught when she opened the door, for she didn't want it blown inside again.

'How is he the day?' asked a voice, as she turned to come back into the house.

She looked up into the concerned face of the foreman sawyer. 'Oh, it's you, Joe. He's nane better. I was up near half the nicht tryin' to ease his cough. I'm right worried.'

'You must be.' Joe Bain was silent for a moment but, realizing that he had no option, he handed her an envelope. 'I'm sorry, Moll, it's nae my doin'. I hope things . . . go a' richt for you.'

He whipped away and she went back inside. She didn't have to open the envelope, she knew what was inside, but she slit the top anyway, and took out the small slip of paper to read the dreaded words.

NOTICE TO QUIT

You are hereby requested to vacate the house you meantime occupy by 26 June. Failure to do so will result in eviction.

She sat down by the flickering coals in despair. What would they do? If Alfie got any worse, she'd have to give up her little cleaning job to look after him, and with nothing coming in, how could they afford to rent a place to live? She had often wished she had some other means of cooking in the summertime when it was too hot with the fire on, but she was glad of it now, for her very bones felt numb with the cold – no, with shock, that's what it was. She'd thought Alec Murchie, the owner of the sawmill, would give them a few months' grace, but the twenty-sixth was less than a week away. She should really keep this bad news from her ailing man, but how could she, when he'd have to be hauled out of his bed in such a short time and made to go God only ken't where?

Mary McKay could likely get him into the poor's house, but it would have to be the last resort, and what about herself? She didn't fancy going back to what she'd been doing before she got wed, though she'd kept her figure, maybe a wee bit more curvy than it was, but most men liked a woman they could get a proper grip of.

While she waited to ask Mary what they could do – the nurse usually called in next door every second day at ten on the dot to see Maggie Burnett's old mother-in-law – she made a start on going through drawers and shelves to see what she would take when she left the house; very little likely, for she'd have no place to put it. She was on the second drawer of the dresser – the furniture all belonged to the mill and would have to be left for the next tenant – when she found a bundle of clippings she had taken from newspapers. She was an incurable hoarder of advertisements she thought might come in handy, corn cures and patent medicines for all kinds of complaints, when a vague memory stirred within her of something else she'd once cut out for future use, something she hadn't wanted Alfie to know she had kept.

Racking her brains, she tried to think what it had been and where she had hidden it, but it was some minutes before she remembered. She gave a satisfied smirk as she removed the lid from the white china hen on the dresser, then lifted out the nest section which could hold one dozen eggs, and nestling underneath, exactly as she had placed it years ago, was the item about his Marion's wedding. It had completely slipped her mind, which showed what a poor housewife she was, for she'd only ever wiped the outside of the white hen, never given it a proper wash.

And then she heard the rattle of Mary's old bicycle and ran out to catch her. 'Will you write a letter for me, Mary?' she asked. 'Once you've done wi' Teenie Burnett?'

'Aye, surely, Moll.' Mary had written many letters for other people in her time as visiting nurse – many of her patients were illiterate, but she knew that Moll Cheyne wasn't. 'Something gey important, is it?'

'Awful important, that's why I asked you, an' it'll need to be posted the day.'

Mary did more than post the letter. After hearing what had happened, she decided to do her best to help the Cheynes. Alfie had slaved all his life at the mill, and it was the saw-dust he'd breathed in over the years that had ruined his lungs, but she knew she'd be as well speaking to the wind as trying to get compensation for him from Alec Murchie, for he was a tight-fisted old devil.

She could recommend that Alfie be given a place in the Institute, but he'd likely refuse to go; his mind was still alert enough to shrink from the idea of 'charity'. There was only one alternative left, and she set off on her bicycle to see Jem Park, local businessman and committee member of the Institute's board. He had bought some near-derelict houses a few years back, and let them to people who couldn't afford to rent better places.

Mr Park was a big, rather awe-inspiring man, but very little, people or events, intimidated Mary McKay. 'I'm here to see about a place for Alfie Cheyne and his wife,' she began, bold as brass. 'He's not fit to work now, and they're being put out of the sawmill house, and I know you've got one empty, for I helped to clear it the day before yesterday, after old Jigger Lome's funeral.'

Jem Park frowned. 'I've got nothing to do with the letting,' he barked. 'You'll have to see my factor, and I would think he's let it by this time. There's a waiting list, you know.'

Mary shook her head in irritation, but went in search of the factor. She had been at school with Greig Lawrie and knew a few little titbits about him that he wouldn't care to reach his wife's ears, so if she had to, she could try a bit of blackmail.

As she had known he would, Greig blustered for a few minutes, swearing that he had already let Jigger's house, then changing, when she said she didn't believe him, to say that she couldn't expect him to let anybody jump their turn. 'There's three after it, and I half promised it to –'

'Then you'll have to take your half-promise back,' Mary said firmly, 'or I'll tell folk about you and Mrs Gill, the doctor's wife.' She had decided to start with his earliest indiscretion and work up to the more recent if the need arose.

His face drained of colour. 'There was nothing atween Mrs Gill an' me! She asked me dae some jobs for her . . . I was only sixteen at the time, for God's sake!'

232

Mary grinned cockily. 'So you were, but a man for a' that, eh?'

The flattery was all that was necessary.

Moll had still heard nothing from Marianne when the day of eviction came and they were forced to move into the cramped place Mary McKay had managed to get for them. Not only that, she had scrounged a few bits and pieces of furniture – a rickety bed, a couple of chairs and a table. It was anything but comfortable, but at least it was a roof over their heads, Moll told herself, and it would only be till Marion – Marianne – came to their rescue. No doubt it would take her a while to get something organized.

Marianne soon discovered that she loved the bustle of the capital, watching, when she ventured out with her maid, the elegant carriages conveying well-dressed matrons and their daughters, even trying to guess who sat in the black hansom cabs.

What pleased her even more when she returned from a window-shopping walk with Thomson, was the sight of several calling cards which had been left while they were out. This was the life she had pictured for herself, on the same footing as the barons and earls, although Hamish told her that barons were a lower rank.

In anticipation of returning the calls, she asked the caretaker's wife where the late Lady Glendarril had shopped for clothes, and on being given directions to a very exclusive salon tucked away in a side street practically just around the corner, she set off on her own.

It was the first time Marianne had bought such expensive clothes for herself, but she kept in mind how Lady Glendarril had dealt with the people who served her in Edinburgh, and when she finished her shopping spree, she was highly satisfied with her selection of day dresses and evening gowns, gossamer shawls and substantial capes. She *had* sensed a condescension in the salesladies' manners at times, even in the models who paraded for her, but she didn't care . . . the owners of all the establishments she patronized had shown enough deference to satisfy her, practically bowing and scraping as each sale was made.

Her husband refusing to go with her on any of the calls she meant to make, Marianne resolved to go alone. 'But it's not done, Mrs Hamish,' wailed Thomson, who had gone with Lady Glendarril on her rounds and knew the tacit rules under which the gentry operated – not more than an hour in any house being one.

'All right then, you can come in the carriage with me,' Marianne sighed. 'I suppose they'll let you wait in the servants' quarters till I'm ready to leave.'

At the first three calls she made, she sensed that the hostesses felt as awkward with her as she felt with them, although none of them said or did anything to prove that. Wondering if she wasn't dressed properly, she chose carefully from amongst her new outfits for her next venture into the revered company, and plumped for a wine-coloured costume with a narrow skirt which just tipped her black kid shoes, and a hip-length jacket with black frogging. This would have been suitably conservative if she hadn't topped it with a bright blue hat trimmed with ostrich feathers dyed in gaudy reds, greens and yellows, which swept over one eye in a provocative style. 'It'll give me a bit of confidence,' she defended herself to Thomson, whose shocked face told her she had gone too far.

The expressions of the ladies in each of the first two houses she visited that day gave further proof of her *faux pas,* and she wished that she had not worn such a frivolous hat. She had the distinct impression that her hostesses and their friends were inwardly laughing at her, but at least their breeding did not let them ridicule her openly like the girls in Aberdeen who had hurt her all those years before.

She was waiting for Thomson in the hallway of her last call in Guildford Street when she realized that her gloves were still on a small table in the drawing room, and with no warning to the young maid who was seeing her out, she turned and walked back. The door was slightly ajar, enough for the muffled hilarity from inside to reach her ears.

'Oh my, wasn't she awful?' someone was laughing. 'And some of the things she said, I didn't know where to look. Verity Chambers says she was only a shop-girl before she married Hamish Bruce-Lyall.'

'That explains it!' giggled another. 'That hat! Did you ever see anything like it? Her taste must be all in her awful mouth.'

'And her accent!' gushed a third. 'I could hardly understand a word she said.'

Cut to the quick and desperate to retaliate, Marianne threw back the door and marched straight to the occasional table to retrieve her gloves, and not until she reached the door again did she deign to look at any of the young women regarding her silently with their mouths agape. Holding the knob, she said, enunciating each word slowly and with staccato precision, 'I hope you can understand what I am saying now. Yes, I was a shop-girl when Hamish met me, and I was just a skivvy before that, but I was taught manners, something you three obviously weren't.'

Speeding up, she went on scathingly, 'I would never, ever, speak about anybody behind her back the way you were speaking about me.' She opened the door wider, but could not resist a parting shot before going into the hall. 'Let me tell you, I hardly understood a word any of you spoke, either, with your marbles in your mouths and your noses in the air. If you're a sample of London society, I'm glad I live in a wee glen in Scotland.'

Slamming the door, she sailed past the goggle-eyed servant and went down the front steps just as Thomson came up from the basement area. The young groom jumped down hastily to help her into the carriage, and Marianne's dark face warned her maid to ask no questions.

When Hamish and his father returned from the business meeting they had been attending, Marianne told them what had happened, keeping a grip on herself to avoid bursting into tears. Hector had a good laugh at how she had dealt with the situation, but her husband tried to soothe her ruffled feelings.

'Never mind them. They have nothing else to do all day but find fault with others. Is that the hat?' He looked at the offending object which had been thrown in rejection on the seat of a chair. 'Maybe the feathers *are* a teeny bit garish, but that was no reason for them . . .'

Catching the gleam of moisture in Marianne's eyes, her father-in-law said, 'Take her upstairs, Hamish, and see she goes to bed. All the excitement of coming to London has been too much for her.'

Overcome with self-pity, anger at herself for ignoring Thomson's silent criticism, and especially with sharp resentment against her tormentors, Marianne allowed Hamish to guide her to her room.

'Shall I get Thomson to come and help . . . ?' He got no further. The burning tears refused to be contained any longer and burst from her in a torrent which alarmed him. 'They are not worth upsetting yourself over, my dear,' he murmured. 'They are not worthy of licking your shoes.'

He drew away when her sobbing eased, and looked sadly into her face. 'I shall have to leave you again, I'm afraid. I promised to go with Father to see a potential new customer in Brighton. Will you be all right, or should I fetch Thomson?'

'No,' she sniffed, 'I don't want her to see I've been crying.'

'We may not be back until tomorrow, and you need someone. She is very discreet. You can trust her not to tell the other servants.'

When she came in, Thomson clicked her tongue solicitously. 'Would you rather I went away for a wee while, Mrs Hamish . . . till you come to yourself?'

Marianne shook her head. 'It's all right. It's just . . . there was a bit of . . . unpleasantness in that last house I called at. Oh, I might as well tell you.'

The older woman listened to the sorry tale with increasing anger and, when it ended, she said, 'The cook told me her mistress and her two sisters spend most of their time criticising other women, and I think they'd been jealous that none of them has such a distinctive hat. Even if they had, I doubt they could carry it off like you.'

Marianne had to smile at Thomson's staunch loyalty.

'No, I could tell when I put it on you thought it was awful and you were right. I'll ask your advice before I buy any more hats . . . not that I'll need any. I'll never come back to London to be made a fool of. Now, you'd better get me out of this costume, and the corset, for it's killing me.'

She stood patiently while her maid undid buttons and unfastened hooks and eyes, turning obediently when instructed to do so, and at last her nightdress was pulled on over her head and she was helped onto the high bed. 'Thank you, Thomson,' she murmured, lying back gratefully.

Left alone again, Marianne's thoughts returned to the glen, and she wondered if her two little darlings were missing her as much as she was missing them. It was the first time she had ever been away from them for any length of time, and the last, if she had any say. Her grass-hopper mind jumped now to something else she would be missing in Glendarril, and she smiled as she recalled the way in which she had learned of the two impending happy events.

It had been Flora's turn for the weekly 'afternoon tea', and immediately she had filled the cups and handed round the plate of home-made scones, she burst out, 'I was afraid to tell anybody till after the dangerous third month, but Robert says it's safe now.'

'Oh, Flora, you're pregnant? I'm so pleased for you!' Marianne had exclaimed.

But she had been in for a second surprise, because Grace gave a little cough and got to her feet, tapping on the table in the manner she used as president of the WRI to get the attention of the members before she made an announcement. 'It falls to me,' she declaimed solemnly, 'to express delight at the statement given by our secretary, and to add some news of my own.' She looked at the other two for a moment and then burst out laughing.

Flora's face had screwed up with perplexity, Marianne remembered, and it had been left to her to say, 'Don't tell me you're expecting, as well, Grace? Wonders will never cease, and when are you due, both of you?'

She had been pleased that both confinements would be in early August, because she should have been home by then, but, as Robert Burns so wisely said, 'The best laid schemes o' mice an' men gang aft a-gley.' Because of King Edward's appendicitis, she was stuck in London. Still, finding out which sex her friends' babies were was a treat for her to go home to, though she would pray every night now that both would be safely delivered.

Robert was cock-a-hoop about becoming a father, but it was difficult to tell with Duncan. He wasn't as forthcoming as Robert, but he was bound to be pleased. Maybe he hadn't cared for the idea of children before – though that might have been another of Grace's jokes – but surely when the infant arrived, he would look on it as a blessing from God.

That was one thing about Hamish. He was a good father, and Marianne did not, and never would, regret marrying him. He loved her as much as she loved him, and as far as the glen folk were concerned, she was a goddess, someone they looked up to and admired for not putting on airs with them. On her first trip to Edinburgh to supplement her wardrobe, as soon as she mentioned that she was the daughter-in-law of the late Lady Glendarril, she had been given honoured treatment, and on the next two occasions she had been recognized immediately she walked in, which had given her a tremendous glow of gratification.

Before she surrendered into the arms of Morpheus, it occurred to her that the only people who had openly not accepted her were the three females (she wouldn't grant them the dignity of thinking of them as ladies) in the house in Guildford Street. She couldn't recall any of their names, except that they were all Honourable Somebodies and probably none of them lived permanently in London. Just the same, they must have known it was her first visit, so what they did was inexcusable.

Let London and all its glories go to the devil, Marianne thought. Hector had been right: she didn't like it, and she would never come back.

Her husband and father-in-law did not return from Brighton until the following day, and she tackled them as soon as they came in. 'I'm going home. I'm not giving anybody else the chance to insult me, and besides, I'm missing my boys.'

Both men were utterly thunderstruck, and it was Hector who rallied enough to say, 'I can understand how you feel, but what about the Coronation? You may never have another chance to see a spectacle like this, and it was the reason you came to London in the first place.'

'Well, I've had enough of it! I just don't want to –'

Hamish interrupted here. 'I know you've been hurt, my dearest, but once you get over it, you'll be all right.'

240

'No, I won't! I'm sick to the teeth of London and all the stuck-up pigs in it. Look, I'm not expecting you to come with me – I'll manage fine by myself as long as I've got Thomson with me.'

'Well, well!' Hector grinned. 'You've lost none of your pluck, I'll grant you that, and if that's what you're determined to do, I'll book seats for you on the last train tonight. You won't need to worry about your baggage, because Hamish will see to it at this end, and I'll send a wire to Carnie so that he will be at Montrose to take it out of the carriage when he picks you up tomorrow.'

The rest of the day was, therefore, taken up with packing, or rather, Thomson did the work while Marianne paced the floor as if she were champing at the bit to be gone. Every piece of luggage ready at last, the exhausted maid sat down heavily and, her conscience smiting her, Marianne said, 'I'm sorry, Thomson. I know I'm not being fair, trailing you away when I'm sure you're dying to see all the people in the streets on the big day, but –'

'No, ma'am, I've had enough commotion to last me the rest of my life, and all, and I'll be glad to be back home again.'

And so Marianne's dreams of making a good impression and being welcomed into the ranks of the nobility came to nothing. The only impression she made had been much less than favourable – had even been, it could be said, downright ridiculous.

After a hot and exhausting overnight journey, Marianne could not help bursting into tears when her two young sons launched themselves at her in exuberant greeting. 'Oh, do be careful,' Nursie warned them, stepping forward to restrain them. 'Mother is far too tired to be bothered with you just now.'

'Let them stay with me for a little while,' Marianne pleaded.

Thomson, knowing exactly how her mistress must feel, said, 'I know you missed them, Mrs Hamish, but you really should have a rest.'

'Ten minutes . . . please?'

Left alone with her boys, she sat down and lifted them on to her lap. Ranald, always more demonstrative, flung his chubby arms round her neck and covered her face with slobbery kisses, while Ruairidh held on to her fingers as if he were afraid she might go away again. Her seven-week absence had seemed a lifetime to them.

By the time the nurse came for them, some twenty minutes later, Marianne was glad to relinquish them, and went up to her room. 'I was just going to lie down on top,' Marianne protested to Thomson when she saw the bed turned down.

'You'll take a proper rest, Mrs Hamish, or you'll be no use for anything. Come on, let me take off your things for you.'

'Oh, yes, that's much better,' Marianne sighed, in five minutes. 'I can't understand why women have to be tightened in so much during the day.'

'It's to give us a decent shape,' Thomson said, frowning at the alternative. 'Now just lie back and shut your eyes, and I'll bring your lunch up . . .'

'Take a rest yourself,' Marianne ordered, so near to sleep that she slurred the words slightly. 'I won't need any lunch . . .'

Thomson was smiling as she pulled the curtains together to stop the sun streaming in. She would wake her mistress in time for 'Mother's Hour', when she spent time in the nursery while Ranald and Ruairidh had tea, then played guessing games before settling them down for bed by reading them fairy tales. Nursie, of course, did not approve of this – she was one of the old brigade who felt that mothers had no business interfering in the upbringing of their children – but Mrs Hamish didn't care.

Barely ten minutes later, Thomson burst into the room and ran straight across to let in some light. When she turned round, her mistress was alarmed to see that her face was chalk white. 'What is it? What's happened?'

'Oh, Mrs Hamish, it's awful! Mrs Peat died ten days ago, and the funeral's past and everything! And they say the minister's near off his head with grief.'

Her hand on her palpitating heart, Marianne exclaimed, 'Poor Grace! What did she . . . ? She never looked very strong . . . I'll have to go and see Duncan, he must wonder why I haven't been to offer my condolences.'

'He'll have known you were away. I'll fasten your stays for you, and it'll not take me a minute to get myself ready . . .'

'No, Thomson, it's best that I go myself. He'll not want anyone else seeing him if he breaks down.'

Pushing away the proffered corset, Marianne pulled on a thin skirt and a lawn blouse, then hurried out. To get there quicker, she decided to cycle, although it wasn't far to the manse and walking would have given her time to think what to say. This was the only one out of all of the duties she had to undertake that she didn't care for and she knew Duncan hadn't cared for it either. It was heartrending to see the sorrow in the eyes of a man who had lost his wife, or a woman who had lost her husband. It was worse when a child died, although women usually bore up better than men.

Grace Peat had been such a lovely person; full of fun and she had never complained about anything. Maybe it would have been better if she had, Marianne mused; maybe the doctor could have cured whatever had ailed her.

As she had expected, when he opened the door, Duncan's face was gaunt, his dark hair dishevelled, his near-black eyes almost lifeless, and as soon as he ushered her into his front room, he held out his arms. Quite taken aback, she held him, letting his shuddering body lie close against hers as great sobs burst from him. She knew not to say anything until he was calmer, but he seemed to take an awful long time, and at last she tried to step back.

'No, don't let me go,' he groaned. 'My parishioners all expressed condolences at the graveside, but Robert Mowatt's the only one who has come to see me since. I need someone to talk to, Marianne, and to hold me! I need you.'

He dropped his head until his chin was resting on her breast, but it wasn't until she realized that his hands were on her buttocks that she felt a tingle of fear. With every second that passed, there came another sign that he was arousing himself by the things he was doing to her, and she wished with all her heart that she had not come out uncorseted.

'Oh, I miss Grace so much,' he moaned, effectively stopping her from trying to wriggle free.

'Of course you will,' she murmured, his words doing a little to reassure her. 'You'd been married for . . . ?'

'For ten and a half years,' he supplied, his fingers caressing her left hip, 'and never once did she refuse me. There are not many men who can say that about their wives. That is why I . . . that is why I . . . I haven't had any release since she told me she was . . . pregnant . . . and she didn't tell me until it was too late.'

'Too late?'

He looked up at her sadly. 'Robert said . . . she was not strong enough . . .' His face crumpling, he burrowed his head into her neck.

His evil intentions soon became crystal clear. His hands were everywhere, one moment pummelling her hips, the next tearing open her blouse and grasping her so roughly that she lashed out with her foot. He had placed his own legs around hers, however, in such a way that she could do him no harm, and in a matter of seconds, he had managed to get her thrashing body down on the sagging leather sofa.

'Duncan!' she pleaded. 'Please stop!'

His only reply was to punch her in the stomach, which proved to her that he didn't know what he was doing. He was past all reason – he had no control over his actions, but, despite knowing it was useless, she continued to fight him. It was an instinctive reaction, but it seemed to make him more violent – he wasn't just touching her in places he shouldn't, he was hurting her, doing his best to make her scream out in agony, and no matter how she tried, she couldn't stop it. But she did stop struggling.

'That's better,' he muttered, his hand less aggressive. Suddenly he said, 'You've only yourself to blame, Marianne. It's your fault.'

245

She couldn't understand what he meant, but she was determined not to say anything to set him off again, for he was absolutely raving mad. 'It's your fault,' he repeated, twisting her nipple until she gave an agonized groan. 'It's your fault and you're going to suffer for it.'

In seconds, he had hauled off her skirt and drawers and was clawing at her most intimate part, but when he changed position to open his trouser buttons, she took advantage of her freedom to lash out at him with her fists and slam her knee into his groin. He merely gave a grunt and landed his knee on her stomach with such force that it nearly knocked all the breath out of her.

'You little bitch!' he snarled. 'You common little bitch!'

When he finally drove into her, the excruciating pain made her lose consciousness, and when she came round, he had obviously satisfied himself, because he was sitting on the chair at the fireside, looking at the cinders and ashes that he had not cleaned out from the night before. She made a little move to see if he would notice, but he appeared to be in a world of his own, and so she made her escape as quietly as she could, each breath laboured, as if she had been running.

Chapter Thirteen

On his way to answer the urgent knocking, Robert Mowatt wondered which of his patients had taken a turn for the worse. Old Willie Cattanach had looked a bit better yesterday; surely he hadn't had a relapse? The doctor's eyes widened in astonishment when he opened the door.

'Good God, Marianne!' he exclaimed. 'What happened?'

He had already guessed, however. Her obvious state of trembling shock, her white face, the long strands of chestnut hair dislodged from their hairpins, the way she was holding her ripped blouse together and the bruises on her arms, told him the whole story without her having to say a word. She flinched when he put an arm at her back to shepherd her inside.

'Who was it?' he asked gently. 'Who did this to you?'

Unwilling, or unable, to talk, she shook her head, and Flora, whose mouth had fallen open at the sight of her, came forward. 'Marianne, you must tell us.' She turned to her husband to whisper, 'Go and get a blanket for her,' and when he was out of the room, she bent over the distressed victim again. 'Who was it, my dear? For what he did to you, he must be punished.'

She was still waiting for a reply when Robert returned with the blanket. 'Go and make a cup of tea,' she ordered him. 'I'm sure she'll tell me if you leave us alone for a while.'

With the closing of the door, Marianne looked up at the woman who had come to be as close a friend as she could afford to have amongst her father-in-law's tenants. 'Promise you won't tell him?'

'I can't promise that, Marianne. He has to know.'

'But I don't want it reported to the police . . . Duncan's been through enough already . . .'

Flora Mowatt looked as if she'd been felled with an axe. 'Duncan?' she gasped. 'Duncan Peat? Don't tell me it was *him*? Grace always said he was a violent man, but . . .'

'I only heard about Grace this morning . . . so I went to tell him how sorry I was, and . . . he looked so pathetic . . . and he wanted me to hold him . . .' She paused, then went on, 'I was so hot I'd taken off my corset . . . and I didn't put it on to come out . . . so he . . . so he . . .' Her babbling came to a stammering halt.

Flora's sympathy for her changed to fury at her attacker. 'Losing his wife is no excuse for raping you!'

At last the tears came, noisy ragged sobs seemingly dredged up from the very innermost part of her, and Flora stood back and let her cry. It would help to wash out the shame she must feel, though it wouldn't banish it altogether.

The doctor, who had waited until the storm was over, came in with a tray when Marianne quietened. He looked quizzically at his wife, who said, 'Yes, she's told me.'

'Who was it, then?' he asked, somewhat tetchily, not accustomed to people holding anything back from him.

She lifted the teapot and started pouring. 'She doesn't want me to tell you.'

'Godammit, Flora, I have to report it to the police.'

'Calm yourself, Robert,' she soothed, handing a cup to Marianne. 'It's going to be hard enough for her to face him again without the whole glen knowing what he's done.'

He swallowed, trying hard to contain his irritation at the feminine logic. 'She wouldn't have to face him again. The police would lock him up. At the very least, when Lord Glendarril comes back he will send him away.'

Her face working in agitation, Marianne burst out, 'You can't put the police on him, not when he's newly lost his wife!'

Robert seized on what she had inadvertently revealed. 'Duncan? But good God –'

'He didn't actually . . . I managed to get away before he . . .'

'That's not the point, though! The intention was there!'

'But he didn't! He didn't, Robert!' She looked imploringly at Flora now, but before his wife could say anything, Robert cried, 'You're not doing him any good by shielding him, you know! He could –'

'I'm not shielding him! Please, Robert, just leave the matter there!'

'I can easily find out. I only need to examine you.'

'Don't touch me, Robert Mowatt!' she screamed, her eyes frantic with apprehension. 'Don't you dare touch me!'

'I only want to know the truth!'

'I'll tell you the truth,' Flora put in quietly. 'Yes, Duncan did rape her but she doesn't want anybody else to know. Finish your tea, then you had better take her home. We can discuss what's to be done when you come back.'

While the doctor went to harness his pony, Flora got a coat for Marianne. 'Cover yourself with this, my dear, and nobody will be any the wiser. I can understand why you don't want the police involved, but think about it when you're calmer. He shouldn't get away with what he's done to you.'

Marianne gave a long uneven sigh. 'I don't want them to know.'

She said nothing to the doctor on the short journey to the castle, but when he helped her out of the trap, she murmured, 'Please don't report him, Robert. He didn't know what he was doing . . .'

She managed to creep upstairs without anyone seeing her, and had put on another blouse and skirt and tidied her hair before Thomson came in. 'I wondered if you were back,' the maid observed. 'How's the minister bearing up?'

It was all Marianne could do to keep her voice steady. 'He's very . . . low . . . as you'd expect.'

'Yes, yes, of course. Will I tell Cook you're ready for lunch?'

'No, I don't feel like eating.'

'You'll still be upset about Mrs Peat. Well, just ring if you feel like having something later on.'

Having seen Marianne safely inside, Robert took matters into his own hands by going to the manse before he went home. Ever since Grace died, he had felt that the minister was balancing on the fine line between sanity and insanity, and Marianne's visit, well meant though it was, must have tipped the balance the wrong way. Anyway, he wanted to know what the man had to say for himself. He had never cared much for Duncan Peat, not even when they were boys together. Being two years older, Duncan had bullied Robert and threatened him with all kinds of weird punishment if he told anyone. That was why he had believed Grace about a year ago when he had been attending her for blinding headaches and she had confessed that it was fear of her husband that caused them. He had calmed her then, given her powders to help her to sleep at nights, had even had a word with Duncan, but he'd had the feeling that his little talk with the man had only made things worse.

The doctor knew that his hands were tied as far as police were concerned, but he'd have to pass on word of the rape to Lord Glendarril and, more urgently, issue a warning to the offender. He would tell the pervert that it was only Marianne's pleading that had saved him from being reported to the police, and that nothing would save him from jail if he interfered with any other woman in the glen.

When Robert arrived at the manse, he was not really surprised to see the outside door standing wide open – probably just as Marianne had left it when she ran out. Dreading what he might find, he was reluctant to enter the house, but it was a duty he could not avoid. He was relieved to find the man sitting by his fireside, muttering to himself. He did not appear to be conscious of another presence until he was tapped on the shoulder, and when he raised his head, Robert gave a grunt of satisfaction. His suspicions were correct – there was no recognition in the man's wild eyes, he was dribbling from the mouth, he was sitting in a pool of urine. He was absolutely mad!

There was further trauma for Robert Mowatt the following day when he called at Hillside Mental Hospital to ask if the newest inmate was showing any sign of returning to normal.

The superintendent, biting his lip nervously, led the way into his private office. 'Peat strangled himself with the bed-sheet sometime in the night. It was only discovered when an attendant went to give him his breakfast this morning, and I cannot tell you how badly it has affected all the staff. It is the only suicide in my five years' service here, but there is nothing I could have done. I visited him last evening in the room we keep for very disturbed persons, and he seemed much calmer, so I decided that he could safely be left alone. In my experience, a good night's sleep quite often helps to clear the brain but . . .' The man shrugged his shoulders.

Robert's first reaction was guilt that he had abandoned Duncan at his lowest ebb. If he had spent the night with him, made sure that he did nothing desperate, he might have pulled through.

'Do not blame yourself,' the superintendent said gently. 'I, too, feel guilty. I should have had someone sit with him, but, frankly, I doubt if he would ever have recovered. It is better this way.'

Not convinced of this, the doctor shook the superintendent's hand and went home to tell Flora, who said, 'Of course it's better he killed himself, though it's a terrible thing to say. Once word got round of what he did to Marianne, his life wouldn't have been worth living. His parishioners thought the world of him, but they'd have turned against him, I'm sure. His Lordship would have put him away. God knows what poor Grace had to put up with. You know, Robert, I really miss her – she was a lovely person, wasn't she?'

Robert sighed. 'Yes, she was. Far too good for him.'

It was a nine days' wonder! The good folk of the glen had gossip aplenty to turn over, rumours abounded, speculations ran wild – the minister had tried to hang himself in the manse, that was why he'd been committed to the madhouse, but his head had been taken out of the gas oven just in time; there was even a faction who suspected that some woman had been involved, but the consensus of opinion was: 'Poor man, it was losing his wife and bairn that turned his brain, and them that try suicide and fail usually make a right job of it the next time they try.'

Only two people had any idea of what had actually taken place and they were not saying anything, not even to each other. Robert was nearly sure that it was Duncan Peat's ill treatment of his pregnant wife that had killed her, while Flora thought that the minister had been verging on mad lustfulness for some time. His hands had brushed her breasts once when she'd been arranging flowers in the kirk, and touched her hip another time, accidentally she had believed, but now she wasn't so sure. Maybe she had got off lightly, and she must do something to cheer her friend who had not been so lucky.

Flora went to the castle the day after Duncan's suicide, leaving the large perambulator outside and proudly carrying its tiny occupant inside. 'I thought I'd give you a wee while to get over things,' she announced, when the young parlourmaid showed her in. 'But I thought you'd like to see my daughter.'

Her eyes widening, Marianne gasped, 'Oh, Flora, I'm so sorry! I was in such a state . . . I should have asked . . .'

'It's all right, Marianne, I understood.'

'But I should have asked . . . I'm truly glad it went all right for you this time. Third time lucky, they say. A daughter . . . how nice!'

'She was born two weeks ago.' Flora pulled down the shawl. 'Isn't she adorable?'

'She's absolutely gorgeous!' Marianne gazed entranced at the tiny infant with black hair and dark blue eyes that seemed to have a touch of mischief in them. 'What's her name?'

Flora was beaming with pleasure. 'Esmerelda. Melda for short. Robert let me choose and I've loved that name since I read *The Hunchback of Notre-Dame* when I was just a girl.'

'But Esmerelda was a gypsy.' Andrew had recommended this novel as a favourite of his mother's.

'I know, but it's still a lovely name.'

Thomson came in then with a daintily set tea-tray and, of course, begged for permission to take the tiny babe below stairs, and when the two young women were left alone, Marianne said, 'She's more like Robert than you, but babies change so quickly, don't they?'

'I hope you're none the worse for what happened,' Flora murmured, awkwardly. 'It'll take time to get over it, but at least you won't have to see him ever again.'

'Thank goodness, and I'll have to forget what he did . . . or try to.'

The funeral was over – quite a good turn-out considering – but despite the darkness in the one-roomed house, Moll Cheyne couldn't bring herself to open the curtain. She had missed Alfie since the very second he drew his last struggling breath, and this mark of respect was all she had to remind her of how quickly he had gone.

When she'd had to tell him they'd to move out of the cottage, she had pleaded with him to let her write to Marion – she'd had no reply to the letter Mary McKay had written for her – but he was, had been, a thrawn, independent man, and above all else, as far as his daughter was concerned any road, unforgiving. 'I don't . . . want her . . . charity,' he'd managed to get out.

'She can well afford it.' Moll had wanted to shake him for being so stupid. 'The sawmill's stopped payin' you, so we'll nae be able to rent a decent hoose, an' we've nae money laid by.'

She could still remember how agitated he'd got at that, which was why she hadn't suggested taking another cleaning job although Alfie needed her constant nursing, anything to get a few bawbees. He'd have said she was wanting to show folk he couldn't support his own wife, when, poor soul, he'd put himself in an early grave with being so determined. They hadn't got a decent house, of course, just one garret room two stairs up that Mary McKay had found for them, so damp that if she hung her coat up on the hook on the back of the door after being out to buy what little food she could afford, it had green mould on it before she needed to put it on again.

But there wasn't a soul in Tipperton could say she had neglected Alfie. She'd gone hungry herself so she could give him something he liked – though he hardly ate anything at all – and she'd picked up all the lumps of coal she saw lying on the road, fallen off the cart. She hadn't cared that folk might speak about her, hadn't cared about anything except looking after Alfie, until . . .

Moll let out a hopeless sigh. She had gone begging to the council to help with the shilling rent she couldn't pay at the end of their third week there, and had been told, 'We do not pay rent for anybody. If your landlord evicts you, it will be the Institute for you.'

The Institute, Moll thought angrily. She would have sold her soul to the devil to keep this from her dying man, but while she was out, the factor had called, given Alfie their notice to get out and told him it was the poor's house for them. That was what had killed her husband! He was still alive when she went home, and had managed to tell her, in laboured breaths and with deep shame in his eyes, about his visitor, but had stopped breathing almost as soon as the two dreaded words 'poor's house' had passed his lips.

Her hands came up to her head in anguish. If only she had ignored his pride and written to Marion again . . . but it was too late now. There was no sense in telling her that her father had died. She wouldn't want to know, not after all this time. And the fine lady needn't feel any responsibility for her stepmother, either. Moll Cheyne had a good pair of hands on her, and a sister in Glasgow who wanted her to go and live there, so she didn't need anybody's help . . . especially not Madam High-and-Mighty Marion's.

But, by God, the girl shouldn't get away with ignoring her father's plight. She hadn't done anything for him while he was ill, but she could damn well pay for a gravestone.

It was the least she could do.

Marianne's wish to put the rape behind her was doomed to failure. Two days after Duncan Peat's funeral, Robert Mowatt went to Laurencekirk station to collect a parcel from the London train. Seeing Hamish getting off, he thought this chance of a private talk with him was too good to miss. As the future Lord Glendarril, Hamish had the right to know, and his wife certainly wouldn't tell him.

While Carnie was stowing the luggage on to the high-slung carriage, the doctor moved forward. 'I'd like a word with you, Hamish. It's . . . um . . . a bit delicate, so if you tell Carnie to pick you up at my house, you can ride along with me.'

The arrangement made, Hamish got up on the small trap and listened as Robert's story unfolded. 'Grace Peat dead?' he said sadly, when he received the first piece of information. 'Oh, poor Duncan! I had better go and see him before I go home.'

'No, no, Hamish, you can't do that! Wait and hear me out!'

Hamish had been registering sorrow up to this point, but his nose wrinkled in puzzlement at the vehemence in his friend's words, and a look of total incredulity flooded his face in a few moments. 'That can't be true!' he exclaimed. 'For

257

goodness' sake, he's a minister of the Church! He wouldn't lay a finger on the lowest maidservant, let alone –'

'He was a monster at the end,' Robert stressed firmly, 'and there is no blame whatsoever attached to Marianne, I can assure you. She called at the manse with the best of intentions and he flung himself on her. She did try to fight him off, but I very much doubt if any woman could have. The deranged have the strength of the devil, you know. It took three men to carry him out when . . .' Breaking off, he looked at Hamish in appeal. 'I had to certify him.'

'I can't believe that Marianne . . . that he . . . *raped* her.'

Picking up a trace of suspicion in these last words, Robert said hastily, 'Speaking as her doctor, Hamish, I advise you not to let her know I have told you. Perhaps I was wrong in doing so. She feels deeply ashamed although she has no need to be, and the sooner she can erase the attack from her memory the better.'

At the gate of the doctor's house, Hamish professed to be grateful for being acquainted with the facts, however unpalatable, but the thought of his wife being raped by a mad Duncan Peat gnawed at his innards as he transferred to the carriage to make the last leg of his journey. By the time he reached the castle, his mouth was bone dry, his head was pounding, his stomach churned and he staggered slightly when he set foot on the driveway.

Carnie eyed him anxiously. 'Was the doctor saying something to upset you, Master? There's been that many stories goin' round, you'd be best no' to heed any o' them . . . an' if I was you, I wouldna say anything to Lady Marianne. I ken for a fact she'd been to see Duncan Peat the day he

258

was taken away, for she left her bicycle and the doctor got Peter Wink to take it back to the castle, and I've the feeling he did something, the minister, I mean . . .' The old man pulled himself up. 'Ach, I'm just a bletherin' skate, as bad as the rest o' them.'

Marianne jumped to her feet when her husband entered what had been the Blue Room but which was now a delicate shade of cream. The nervous tic at her cheek and the way her hands opened and shut convulsively told him that what Robert had told him was true, and he had to force himself to kiss her cheek. 'I left as soon as I could after the Coronation. Father is still down there, but I was worried about you.'

'I got home all right,' she said stiffly.

The restraint between them was practically tangible; neither could smile at the other and it was as if they were strangers, looking away in embarrassment each time their eyes met.

At last, Marianne said, 'Why don't you sit down, Hamish? You must be tired after your journey. I'll ring for a pot of tea.'

Her mundane manner in the face of what he had learned nudged him out of control. 'I don't know how you can stand there so calmly!' he spat out. 'As if nothing has happened!'

Her face blanched. She had known that the rumours would eventually reach his ears, but she hadn't expected him to have heard before he even crossed the threshold. 'Who's been telling tales?' she asked, her sarcasm a screen for her fear of the consequences.

'So it's true?'

'I don't know what you're speaking about.'

'I'm speaking about Duncan Peat. How could you let him . . . ?'

Shaking her head, she wrung her hands in anguish. 'Hamish, I did *not* let him!'

'No? That's not what I've been told.'

This snapped her self-control now. 'All right, believe what you like and who you like, but I swear I did not *let* him do anything.'

'But it's him! A man of God! It would be against all he ever stood for to . . . fornicate with another man's wife when he had just lost his own.' Giving a gasp as an unwelcome thought struck him, he took a step towards her and stuck his outraged face close to hers. 'I must have been blind. You had been carrying on with him even before Grace died! Perhaps Ruairidh is *his* child?'

Without stopping to think, Marianne gave him a resounding slap on the cheek. 'How dare you speak to me like that? I've never let any man touch me except you.' She couldn't say more. The insult was too great to bear, and putting her hands to her eyes, she burst into a flood of tears.

Love for her overcoming all else, Hamish put his arms around her, and the stiffening of her body did more to convince him that she had been taken by force than further denials would have done. 'I should not have said that, Marianne,' he mumbled, 'and I am deeply sorry.'

Marianne had been fearing Hector's return, fearing the anger he would direct at her; he was bound to blame her. He wouldn't take the word of a shop-girl, even though that shop-girl was the mother of his two grandsons. On the morning of the day he was due to arrive, she asked

Hamish to tell his father about Duncan Peat before he brought him back to the castle. 'He might have cooled down by the time he reaches here,' she explained, thinking that it was highly unlikely.

She worried when they took so long to arrive back from the station, and she trembled with dread at what her father-in-law would say to her when they did turn up, but she never dreamed how he would be brought home.

Lord Glendarril had died of a seizure on the station platform. Robert Mowatt helped Hamish and Carnie to carry him in, laying him out on top of his father's desk in the study rather than in his bed upstairs.

Then Carnie turned to Hamish and astonished them all by saying, 'Will I go to Brechin for the undertaker, your Lordship?' He was the only one who had realized the import of the death.

Hamish looked in horror at Robert. 'Oh, my God!' he moaned, then, gulping back a noisy sob, he hurried out of the room.

The doctor put a hand on Marianne's arm to prevent her following him. 'Leave him just now, your Ladyship.'

'Don't call me that. I'll always be Marianne to you and Flora.'

'Thank you, my dear. Hamish has had a terrible shock, and –'

'Were you there when it happened?'

'No, Carnie came for me, but I was too late.'

'Do you know if Hamish had time to tell him about . . . ?'

'If you think he died because of you, forget it. I've been telling him for months that his heart wasn't up to all the rushing about he was doing, but he wouldn't listen.'

'But if Hamish had told him about Duncan, wouldn't that have been bad for his heart, and all?'

'My dear Marianne, stop torturing yourself. I was expecting it to give out at any time. In any case, I have just remembered. Carnie said Hector hadn't even set foot on the platform when he clutched his chest, and he and Hamish had both rushed to help him down. Then he collapsed altogether and Carnie came for me. Rest assured, my dear, your father-in-law died knowing nothing of what happened.'

Hector looked so peaceful after the undertakers had done their job. Hamish ordered the funeral for a week later, and so began seven days of what Marianne could only think of as the 'lying in state'. What seemed like millions of people – glen folk, relatives, men with whom he had done business, lords and ladies, dukes and duchesses, earls and countesses – milled around the castle before and after the burial service, and if it hadn't been for the self-effacing Miss Glover, Marianne wouldn't have coped. Because a new minister had not yet been appointed to the parish, Hamish had asked Mr Munro from Arbroath, a great friend of his father's, to take the service, a task which the elderly man was only too honoured to shoulder.

Marianne's deep sorrow for the loss of the man who meant more to her than her own father had ever done was made much worse on the day of the funeral by the shaking that assailed her when she neared the church, and when she was passing the manse, it was all she could do to keep moving, for Duncan Peat's lust-distorted face kept swimming before her eyes. Hamish, of course, was too immersed in his own grief to pay any heed to her, and it fell to Robert Mowatt to help her into the kirkyard, between the lines of people from near and far who had known and liked Hector Bruce-Lyall.

Her old horror of graveyards returned at that moment, and she clung to the doctor's arm as a ghostly Hector floated past her, looking at her accusingly and shaking his head. She was practically paralysed with terror before the service ended, and Robert had to whisper, 'Bear up, Marianne, it's all over now,' before she could put one foot past the other.

The glen folk had always accorded her the courtesy of referring to her as Lady Marianne, but when the mourners returned to the castle and she heard someone calling Hamish 'your Lordship', the realization of her entitlement to the title did much to restore her equilibrium, and to boost her confidence amongst the high-born guests in her home.

She had been pleased to see Andrew Rennie and his aunts in the kirk, but when she invited them to the funeral tea, Miss Edith had said, 'Thank you, your Ladyship, but we must go home,' and Andrew had said, *sotto voce,* 'Well, you've got your wish, Lady Glendarril.'

The line of people had moved on and she hadn't had another chance to speak to them, to tell them that she was still just Marianne, the same as she had always been.

Most of the women, not worthy of the title they held, had talked more to Miss Glover than to her, and even when they did address her directly, their manner was condescending. Only one had singled her out and had a conversation with her.

'I saw them all giving you the cold shoulder,' she had begun, 'but don't you worry your pretty young head about it. I got much the same treatment when I married Clarice's cousin and I've survived. In fact most of them have forgotten by now that I ever was a shopkeeper's daughter and had no right to mix with the likes of them. I'm Lady Matthewson, by the way, Barbara to you, and my daughter's Hamish's age. He used to come to Maxton House sometimes to play tennis with Pam – before he met you – but why don't you get him to bring you over to see us some time? Once the mourning period is past?'

Marianne hadn't known what to say. She was pleased to be invited, but was afraid that, if she did pluck up the courage to go, Lady Matthewson might change her mind about welcoming a shop assistant to her home. 'Is your daughter not with you today?' she enquired.

'Pam's touring Europe at present. She thought a lot of Hector, though, so she'll be very disappointed at not being here for his funeral.' Barbara Matthewson's eyes were caught then by someone she knew and, excusing herself, she walked away.

The parlour maid seemed ill at ease the day after the funeral when she knocked and opened the morning-room door. 'There's a . . . woman at the door asking to see you, m'Lady.'

Marianne raised her eyebrows. 'Didn't you ask who she was?'

'I did ask, m'Lady, but she wouldn't tell me.'

Marianne frowned and began, 'Tell her I do not wish to see anyone at –' but before she could finish, a figure appeared in the doorway, a figure from her past – a past, moreover, that she did not want to be reminded of, especially now.

264

'Oh, m'Lady, I told her to wait outside,' the maid was excusing herself, but the woman came right into the room saying, 'I think *her Ladyship* will see me.'

If the maid noticed the sneering emphasis, she gave no sign, but scuttled out so quickly that the door swung shut with a thud.

Marianne regarded her visitor coldly. 'What do you want?'

Sitting down as if she were well accustomed to being in such opulent surroundings, Moll said, 'I wouldna have needed to come if you'd ta'en some notice o' the letter I sent a while back.'

Marianne was genuinely puzzled. 'I received no letter from you.'

'Oh, so that's the wey o' it, is it? You're sayin' you never *received* it, are you? Well, let me tell you, *m'Lady,* it was Mary McKay that wrote it for me, an' it was her that posted it, so I ken fine you *received* it, unless you're cryin' Mary a liar?'

Marianne could feel her self-confidence draining away with each sarcastic word. Moll had made her feel like a child again, a silly child who had run away after stealing five sovereigns . . . but surely her father's wife wasn't here because of that? 'When . . . was . . . the letter sent?'

'I can tell you that easy enough,' Moll sneered. 'It was the twenty-second day of June, that's when, just days afore we was put oot o' the hoose.'

'Put out? But why . . . ?'

'Your father had to stop workin' wi' his chest, and we got a notice to quit or we'd be evicted, an' I got Mary to write an' ask you if you could send us some money so we could rent a decent place. A fat lot you cared, for you never answered, but Mary got us a room in Bridge Street.'

She had stopped for breath, but Marianne said nothing. She had never thought of her father since she left, had never even wondered if he was well or otherwise.

'Aye, my fine leddy,' Moll went on in a few moments, 'that's made you think. Here's you in your castle, wi' every blessed thing you need an' servants to run after you, and there was me and your father in one room wi' the damp runnin' doon the wa's.'

Marianne was caught on the raw. 'And little you cared about me when I was at hame,' she snapped. 'Him nor you, you were that ta'en up wi' each other you hadna time for me.' She did not notice that, in her anger, she had reverted to her old tongue. 'I bet you were glad to be on your own wi' him, and it didna bother me. I managed to better mysel'.'

'You did that, a' richt,' Moll spat out, 'but what would your servants think, an' your fine friends, if they ken't you'd once been a skivvy and stole money fae your mistress?'

Marianne was even more infuriated by this. 'Are you threatening me? If I don't give you money, you'll tell them, is that it?'

Losing her temper now, Moll shouted, 'I dinna want your money . . . nae for mysel', ony road. I'll manage to work for what I need, but I think it's only richt that Alfie gets a gravestone, an' you can weel afford it. Mair to the point, it would let folk see his only lassie hadna forgot him.'

Marianne's chest was heaving now. She'd had enough to cope with before Moll turned up, and if the only way to get rid of her was to erect a headstone to mark her father's grave, so be it! 'I'll get my solicitor to arrange it,' she said loftily. 'And I'll get to the bottom of this letter you say you sent. I can assure you, that if I *had* received it, I would not have let my father die in a hovel.'

'Aye, weel, then, just you mind.' Obviously at a loss as to what to say now, Moll decided against saying anything and stalked out, leaving Marianne leaning against the back of her chair with her heart palpitating.

Once she recovered, she went to Hamish's study and took out a sheet of crested notepaper, thankful that he'd been called to London on urgent business – some query about a price which had been quoted and not stuck to, that was all he'd told her except that he would not be home for at least a week – because she didn't want him to know about this. He believed that she had run away from home because she was being ill treated, but neither her father nor her stepmother had ever been physically cruel to her. It was more that she'd resented being ousted from her father's affections by a person she thought was common . . . but Moll had apparently been a good wife, looked after him right to the end.

The tear which plopped on to her hand now made her more ashamed of herself than ever. She *should* have contacted him, found out how he was, if they needed help. He had worked hard for her when she was small, and looked after her single-handedly after her mother died – until he married again. She had never wanted for anything . . . and he had died in poverty.

Then she remembered the letter Moll had said she sent. What had happened to it? Stretching out her hand, she pulled the bell rope at the fireplace and in less than a minute, the little parlour maid appeared at the door. 'Yes, m'Lady?'

'Rosie,' Marianne said, uncertain as to how to word her question because she didn't want to blame the girl if it wasn't her fault, 'I have just found out that a letter came for me while I was in London, which seems to have got lost. Would you know what became of it?'

The girl had been smilingly waiting to hear what was required of her, but at the mention of the letter her face lost every vestige of colour and she looked as if she were about to faint.

'Are you all right, Rosie?' Marianne enquired anxiously.

'Oh, m'Lady, I'm sorry! I can't tell you how sorry I am. I forgot all about it. You see,' she hurried on, desperate to explain, 'Cook asked me to go and get the veggies Dargie had promised her, and I just went out the door when Postie handed me that letter, so I stuffed it in my pocket and carried on. I stopped a wee while to speak to Davey Black, he's assistant gardener since Ben Rogie left and we'd been . . . keeping company . . . still are,' she confided, blushing a little. Then the haunted look returned to her eyes and a tear trickled out. 'Oh, m'Lady, I know I shouldn't have wasted my time like that, and that's why I forgot about the letter. I'm that sorry. I hope it was nothing important?'

Marianne's smile was rueful. 'It was very important, as it happens.'

'Oh, m'Lady, you're not going to sack me, are you? I didn't mean it . . .'

Marianne hesitated. Her first instinct was to send the girl packing, but she liked little Rosie, who always spoke in her best English and always did what she was told willingly and efficiently. Besides, the poor thing hadn't meant it, yet . . . 'Tell me, Rosie,' she said, as something occurred to her, 'why didn't you find the letter if it was in the pocket of your apron? Surely you would have noticed it when you carried on with your own work.'

'It was pouring rain that day, m'Lady, and I'd put on my coat, and I've never had it on since.'

Her eyes brightened a little. 'It'll still be there! Do you want me to get it?

'Yes, I *would* like to see what it said.'

While she waited for the parlour maid to return, Marianne dipped the pen into the crystal inkwell, but she had only written 'Dear Andrew' when the girl came hurrying in, holding out a rather crumpled envelope which her mistress grabbed and tore open. It was written in a beautiful script, which astonished Marianne until she remembered that it was Mary McKay who had actually done the writing, likely interpreting what Moll wanted to say.

Marion,

I wish to let you know that your father is very ill. He has not been able to work for some time now, so the mill is putting us out of the house. He needs constant attention, so I can not take a job myself. We will have nothing coming in and I am forced to ask you if you will help us. If you can let us have enough to give him a decent roof over his head and the nourishing food he needs to give him strength to recover, that is all I want from you.

Moll Cheyne

Marianne heaved a somewhat ragged sigh, then realized that the girl was still waiting. 'It's all right, Rosie. I'm not going to sack you, but please be more careful in future.'

The girl did not take the intended dismissal. She had told Cook about the awful-looking woman who was in with the mistress, and knew that Mrs Carnie would expect her to find out who it had been. It was not in Rosie's nature to be bold, or to poke her nose into other people's business, but she was well aware that her life wouldn't be worth living downstairs if she didn't. And so, her face as red as a cock-turkey, she stammered, 'Had the l-letter to do with the w-woman that was here? I know there was a row, for I heard you both shouting.'

Taking a moment to decide how to answer this, Marianne said, 'She wrote it and she couldn't understand why I hadn't replied. But it's all sorted out now, so get back to your duties and we'll say no more about it.'

'Thank you, m'Lady.'

Before knuckling down to writing to Andrew, Marianne couldn't help wondering if it would have made any difference if Moll's letter had been sent to London along with the rest of their mail, and came to the shaming conclusion that it probably wouldn't have, especially if it had followed the afternoon tea fiasco. At that time, she hadn't had even a drop of the milk of human kindness left in her, and she'd had no compassion for anyone else. She would most certainly have torn the letter up. She had never liked her stepmother and she'd have thought it was just a begging letter.

Since coming home, she'd had an even worse trauma to face, one she could never have come through without help . . . from Flora and Robert . . . and Hamish. He was still getting over it himself, and his father's death, which was why she couldn't let him know how callous she had been towards her father and it was time she got this letter written. She meant to do what little she could for her father now, but she needed Andrew's help.

Chapter Fourteen

Andrew had been surprised, and very pleased, by Marianne's letter. Having the Lord and Lady Glendarril as clients would be good for business. She had been married for over five years now, and he had only seen her for a few hours at a time, yet his heart still beat a full drum roll every time he saw her. While the train sped south, he decided that he should manage to cope with seeing her and her husband together for a whole weekend.

Carnie was waiting for him at Laurencekirk, but sadly for Andrew, he was in a talkative mood. 'His Lordship's no' back yet,' he said, as he laid the young man's valise on the seat. 'He's still away in London, but her Ladyship's expecting you.'

This information had the same impact on Andrew as if he had been slapped in the face with a wet fish. Marianne must have known when she wrote that she would be alone. What was she up to? Her indifference to him at Hector's funeral had worried him. He had got the distinct impression that he was intruding on a very deep private grief, but even when he reminded her of his promise to be there for her when she needed him, she swore that nothing was wrong. Perhaps, however, she had been too upset to talk about it then, and she may be ready to confide in him now.

Carnie broke into his thoughts. 'Master Ruairidh was a bit down all day yesterday, but he's brighter the day.'

This did much to ease Andrew's anxiety. He had forgotten about the two boys – they would be around during the day, which would make things easier. 'I have heard that children can be quite ill one day and back to normal the next.'

'That's what Nursie said when her Ladyship wanted to get in the doctor. The bairn's just three yet, of course, so it's little wonder she frets. Master Ranald, now, he's a sturdy wee man, never nothing wrong wi' him, an' it's just as well, for it's him that'll come into the title.' Carnie's weatherbeaten face sobered. 'I sometimes get a queer feelin', though. Old Lord Glendarril had a twin brother, you see, Randolph his name was, and being a couple of hours older, he was the heir, but he caught a terrible chill the winter he would've been twenty-one, and he never saw his birthday.'

The elderly man shook his head mournfully. 'And Master Hamish, the present Lord, was the second son by about an hour, but young Randolph, after their uncle, he picked up some germ and died when he was fourteen.'

'Neither death was caused by a hereditary disease,' Andrew pointed out quietly, 'and if Ranald is as healthy as you say, I should not think there is any chance of Ruairidh ever inheriting.'

'It's the name that bothers me, Mr Andrew. That was two Randolphs that died young, and Ranald's no' that much different from Randolph, is it? I'm sure there must be a curse on the elder sons –' He broke off, then added darkly, 'Things like that comes in threes.'

273

Andrew had to laugh at this. 'I would not have thought that you were so superstitious, Carnie, and surely you do not believe there are curses in this day and age. We are almost three years into the twentieth century. Ranald will grow to be a fine young man, and with his mother's genes in him, he will be one of the best lairds this glen has ever seen.'

Marianne was waiting outside with the two small boys as Carnie drew the carriage to a halt at the steps. 'Oh, Andrew, it's good to see you again!' she exclaimed, coming forward as if to hug him.

Evading this, and hoping to discourage her from trying again, he bent down to her sons with a smile. 'My, you two have grown!'

'I'm as big as Rannie,' Ruairidh said confidentially.

'You are not!' his brother protested.

'Say hello to Uncle Andrew properly,' Marianne prompted, 'or else he'll think you're always arguing.'

Gravely, they both held out their hands and said in unison, 'Hello, Uncle Andrew.'

'Hello there,' he responded heartily. 'I wish I'd had a brother to argue with when I was young.'

Four large blue eyes regarding him curiously. 'Had you nobody to play with, either?'

'I had a dog . . .' His voice tailed away. He could still recall the awful wrench when he had said goodbye to Duke – far worse than losing his father.

'I'm as clever as Rannie now,' Ruairidh announced.

'No, you're not. I know more than you,' Ranald boasted. 'I can say my catechism, and I can say the alphabet backwards as well as . . .'

'That's enough,' Marianne said sharply, putting her arm through the visitor's to walk up the steps. 'Stop pestering Uncle Andrew. He's tired after his journey and needs a wee rest. You'll see him later on.'

'Oh, good!' Ranald grinned. 'Is he staying for a while?'

'He goes home on Sunday. Off you go, and don't let Nursie forget to give you your syrup of figs tonight . . . remind her it's Friday.'

Both boys pulled faces but scampered off obediently. 'They're not so bad,' Marianne smiled, as she opened the door of the ex-Blue Room, the most comfortable in the house and consequently, the most used.

'They're very well-behaved,' Andrew observed, taking a seat on the couch as his hostess had indicated. 'Carnie was saying that Hamish is down in London.'

'Yes, he did ask me to go with him, but he'd expect me to make the rounds of his friends' wives, and I can't stand any of them. How are your aunts, Andrew? I hope Miss Edith got over her bout of flu?'

'She only stayed off work for two days, but, unfortunately, Esther went down with it, in a much more severe form. Their doctor seemed quite concerned for her but she said last Sunday that she had begun to feel better.'

'I'm glad to hear it. And Miss Emily?'

Andrew smiled fondly. 'She soldiers on. I keep telling her and Edith that they should retire from the shop – they are both over sixty now – but they just laugh at me.'

'The shop's their life. Don't force them into giving it up.'

'I wouldn't dare try,' he laughed.

It was halfway through the afternoon when he said, 'We had better get down to business and have it out of the way. What was it you wanted to see me about?'

'Can I speak about something . . . personal first?'

The pain in her eyes alarmed him. 'Is anything wrong?'

'Not exactly . . . well, you could say there was, but . . . oh, Andrew, I didn't want to let anyone know, but I'll have to tell you.'

She sank down on the couch beside him but before telling him anything, she held one hand out to him and, presuming that she wanted him to hold it to bolster her courage, he clasped it to his chest. 'What is it, my dear?' he asked huskily.

She started with the lost letter and her shame at not having kept in touch with her father, waiting for him to absolve her of all blame, but he looked at her with his head on one side. 'I was afraid that this might happen. In fact, I am surprised that it didn't happen sooner, if this Moll was the kind of woman who ill treated a young girl.'

'Oh, Andrew, I'm sorry,' she wailed. 'I told you that story so you wouldn't think so badly of me for running away. She never touched me, not in anger, at any rate.'

'But you said you ran away because you stole some money,' he reminded her. 'Why in heaven's name did you tell me that and not tell me the truth about your step-mother?'

Her nerves at breaking point, Marianne cried, 'I don't know. It just came out and I can't think about –' She broke off, biting her lip, then blurted out, 'It's all piling on top of me, Andrew!'

The concern in his face changed to uncertainty. 'Is there more that you have not told me?'

'Not about that,' she muttered, averting her head. It's just happened so quick after –'

Her abrupt, agitated stop made him say, 'Go on, Marianne. What else happened? Tell me!'

'I was raped,' she stated baldly, 'and don't ask me to tell you anything about that, for I haven't told anybody . . . I can't. Not yet. Not ever.'

Pity for her surged up in him as he took her in his arms, biting back the questions he wanted to ask: who, where, why, and how had the opportunity arisen? 'Please don't upset yourself like this, my dear. I know it must have been traumatic for you, but it was not your fault.'

'But *he* said it was,' she moaned. *'He* said it was my fault. When he was . . . Oh God, Andrew, you've no idea what it was like. He was like an animal. Oh God! Oh God!' She buried her face in her hands in anguish.

He crooned soothing words to her, patting her gently on the back whilst silently cursing her unknown assailant. At last, when he thought that she was over the worst, he said, 'Does Hamish know about this?'

She nodded, then raised her eyes to him. 'He . . . he doesn't know what to do . . . he's never had to cope with anything like this, and I didn't mean to tell you, Andrew, but you've got the knack of worming my secrets out of me.'

'I am glad of that, my dear.' He smiled. 'I would hate to think that there were any secrets between us now. Believe me, Marianne, as I told you long ago, no matter what you have done, or do in the future, I will stand by you.

I have not stopped loving you and never will, so bear that in mind. All I ask of you is that you will be scrupulously honest with me at all times.'

'I will, Andrew, I promise.'

He drew in a deep breath. 'Now, shall we continue? It will help to take your mind off things. What was it you wanted to see me about? Do you want to divorce Hamish? Is that it?' She had mentioned no such thing when she wrote, but it was the first thing that had occurred to him, perhaps a hope which had lain latent in him since the day of her marriage, although he was not aware of it. Her astonished gasp, however, told him that he was mistaken in his premise.

'No, of course I don't want to divorce Hamish! I love him! I really do, and he loves me.'

'I'm sorry, Marianne. Tell me what it *is* you require of me and I shall do my best to –'

'I . . . need some fresh air. Come on.'

He followed her along the hallway and down to the basement kitchen where she introduced him to Mrs Carnie as the weekend guest. 'We're going to take the dogs out a walk,' she went on, 'but I thought we might have a cup of tea first.'

'In here?' asked the cook, incredulously. She was not accustomed to her domain being invaded in an afternoon, especially by the mistress. Lady Marianne, Lady Glendarril as they should call her now but old habits die hard, usually left everything to Roberta Glover, menus included, and seldom put in an appearance herself at any time of day.

'It'll save you preparing a tray and sending it up.'

'Aye, there's that to it,' the woman smiled, 'and every-thing's ready, anyway.' She produced a plate of small sandwiches while the young kitchenmaid went to the dresser. 'We won't bother with plates or saucers, Kate,' Marianne told her. 'Just a cup in our hands.'

Andrew made a friend for life of the cook by helping himself to one of the triangles and popping it into his mouth whole. 'Mmmm! This is absolutely delicious.'

Colouring with pleasure, Mrs Carnie beamed at him. 'Eat the lot, I'll easy make some more. There's still half a jar of that plum chutney I made last October. The longer it's kept, the better it gets.'

'There's plenty here,' Andrew said, and while he set about emptying the plate, Marianne smilingly calmed the dogs, who had heard the magic word 'walk' and could hardly contain their excitement.

When they went outside, the two red setters bounding on ahead, Andrew realized that she had been very sensible in taking him to the kitchen first. Talking to the cook, even for so short a time, had cleared the tension which had grown between them, and made it possible for them to behave naturally towards each other. She showed him the circle of stones known to the glen folk as the 'Fairies' Ring', where legend had it that the little people danced at twelve o'clock every Midsummer's Night. About half a mile further on, still climbing the hill, they came across a long mound that she explained was a barrow, a burial ground from Roman times. Being a city person – Edinburgh born and brought up, and now domiciled in Aberdeen – he was fascinated by the extent of her knowledge of, and obvious love of, country lore.

When he spotted a wooden shack half hidden behind two massive firs, he asked, 'The woodcutters aren't going to start cutting here, are they? What a shame, they're such beautiful trees.'

Her gurgling laugh reminded him of those times past when, young and carefree, they had walked along the banks of the River Dee, and he had to stifle the urge to tell her. She had promised not to say anything out of place, and he must not do so, either.

'It's not for woodcutters,' she told him. 'This is a still, where men of the glen made whisky in the olden days, and had to hide from the Revenue men, the Excise men. Hamish says somebody's started it up again . . .' She turned to him, her eyes dancing. 'Will we go in and take a look, Andrew?'

He caught her frivolous mood. 'Why not?' He went ahead of her and shifted a weighty chopper which had obviously been placed there to camouflage the real purpose of the hut, then eased the door open. The large distilling vat with its tapering filter was so shiny and looked so well cared for that they exchanged knowing glances, and Marianne looked around for any sign of recent activity.

Tumbling to what she was searching for, Andrew removed one of the wide flat sticks propped against one wall. 'Look at this!'

'This' turned out to be a collection of bottles containing a clear liquid. 'That's not whisky, though?' he asked.

'I think it is,' she grinned. 'Hamish told me last year they'd given him a taste of their latest batch. He said it looked like water but took the roof off his mouth and the lining off his stomach. I thought he was joking, but maybe he wasn't.' Suddenly remembering her companion's profession, she said, 'I know what they're doing's against the law, Andrew, but you won't report them, will you?'

He flung his head back and his laughter bounced off the rude walls and the empty metal vat. 'I'll not tell, Marianne. I've enjoyed this walk more than anything I've done for years. You're so good for me . . .' He caught himself. 'I shouldn't have said that.'

'Yes, you should. It lets me know you've forgiven me for what I said earlier. We're back to being best friends, aren't we?'

'For ever and ever,' he assured her, 'but I think we'd better go back before Mrs Carnie sends out a search party for us.'

While he closed the door and replaced the axe as he had found it, Marianne called to the dogs, who were poking their noses down rabbit holes, their tails swishing feverishly from side to side. 'Romulus! Remus! Here, boys! We're going home now.'

'What was that you called them?' Andrew asked as he joined her.

She explained that it was how Hamish had referred to them in fun not long after they were born, and the names had stuck.

To make the walking easier, they followed the course of the burn which used the path a glacier had gouged out in its descent from the mountains at the end of the Ice Age. At this point, the water swept over any obstacles in its way in a raging torrent, but by the time it left the glen it had lost its impetus and slowed down, uniting with another stream to

281

make a river which meandered sedately towards the North Sea. 'I love coming this way,' Marianne remarked, 'even though it's just me and the dogs. It's too far for the boys.'

When they arrived back at the house, Marianne said, 'Half an hour till dinner, just time to have a quick wash and change of clothes.'

'Oh, are men expected to change into dinner jackets?'

His concerned expression made her laugh. 'Hector always did, but it depends on how Hamish feels, and since he's not here, you don't need to bother. Put on something you're comfortable in.'

On his way downstairs to join her in the dining room, wearing one of the pullovers his Aunt Esther had knitted for him each Christmas, he hoped that Marianne, too, had put on something comfortable, and was glad to see her in a baggy jumper and equally out-of-shape skirt. She looked up at him and smiled. 'Well, this is nice. I never feel happy when I'm dressed formally, but that's one of the penalties I have to pay for marrying into . . .' She glanced apologetically at him. 'I'm sorry, Andrew. I'd made up my mind not to say anything personal while we had dinner.'

Andrew had also been thinking while he washed and changed. If she wasn't contemplating divorce, she must be thinking of making a will. Probably Hamish had already made his with the family solicitor, but Marianne, being Marianne, would want to let Andrew do it for her. Thinking about their own death was quite upsetting for some people, and that would be why she had been putting it off. But it couldn't be put off for ever.

'I think we should get your business out of the way tonight, though,' he said. 'That'll give you time to think

282

it over, and if there's anything you want to change, I can alter it before I leave tomorrow.'

'Tomorrow?' she exclaimed, in obvious disappointment. 'I thought you were staying till Sunday. Are you scared of being alone with me in the evenings?'

'I feel it is not proper for me to be sleeping in the castle while your husband is away.' There was a slight pause before he murmured, 'It is not you I am afraid of, my dear, it is myself.'

She coloured, but he could tell that she was pleased by the flattery. 'I suppose we *should* get things over with tonight. We'll get down to it as soon as we finish dinner.'

Over the meal he told her how well the legal firm in which he was junior partner was doing now, paving the way for her to put her faith in his ability, and she recounted stories about the glen folk and the droll things they said when she went amongst them, but, at last, they were wiping their mouths with the starched napkins – embroidered, Andrew noticed, with the Bruce-Lyall coat of arms.

'We'll have coffee in the study,' Marianne instructed the maid, and Andrew jumped to his feet to pull back her chair for her. 'I brought some paper with me to write down what you want to say, so I'll just run up and get some.'

'There's paper in the top drawer there,' she told him, pointing to the massive leather-topped desk which had originally belonged to Hector's father but which he had never used himself. Hamish, however, had taken it as his.

Walking across to it, Andrew cast a covetous eye on the exquisite carving on the burnished mahogany legs and heaved a sigh. 'What a beauty! I wish I could afford a desk even half as good as this.'

'You will, some day.'

The top drawer held a large selection of different sizes and thicknesses of paper, from which Andrew selected a few sheets which did not have the identity of the owner embossed on them, and laying them in a neat pile in front of him, he picked up a pen from the crystal container and dipped it in the matching inkwell. 'Now, what were you thinking of putting in your will?'

Marion seemed taken aback by this, but she answered readily enough. 'Of course, I didn't think of asking you before, but you'll be able to tell me about the jewellery Hector left me. His wife's will had said it had to go to the girl Hamish married.' Her eyes took on a concerned look now. 'It *is* legally mine, isn't it, though the will was made long before Hamish even met me?'

'Oh yes, it's legally yours. Had she lived, Lady Glendarril would no doubt have instructed her solicitor to insert your name.'

'I expect she would,' Marianne said, rather uncertainly. 'Anyway, when I die I suppose it'll go half each to whoever Ranald and Ruairidh marry?'

'Yes, that would be feasible,' Andrew murmured, making a note of it. 'Now, shall I give you a moment to think about what else you want to do?'

'No, I know exactly what I want to do. First, I want you to order a stone for my father's grave.'

Hamish's head jerked up. 'A gravestone? Is that why you asked me . . . ? You do not want to make a will?'

She shook her head impatiently. 'I wasn't pleased when Moll asked me to do it, but the more I've thought about it, the more I want to. A good decent-sized granite stone, not

284

marble, but he wouldn't like an angel or anything like that over his head, so maybe just a wee bit of decoration round the sides. At the top, get them to put "CHEYNE", then underneath that, "Anne Lawrie, dearly beloved wife of Alfred Cheyne, born 24 February 1862, died 12 April 1892".'

'She was only thirty? How tragic.'

'It was, wasn't it? Then below that, I'd like: "Also the above Alfred Cheyne . . ." I'm not sure when he was born, but Moll will have his death certificate and it'll be on there.'

Andrew raised his head again. 'Is that all?'

'Not yet. Down at the bottom, in fancy letters, I want: "Together in love again." And that's all.'

'Your stepmother will probably not be pleased about this, especially the last part. Don't you think it is rather . . . rubbing her nose in it?'

'I'll put what I like, I'm paying for it with my own money. Hector left me a fairly decent legacy, and I'll instruct the bank to let you draw on it.' She was pensive for a moment and then said with a smile, 'I was remembering a gravestone in the cemetery at home – not that I went in there very often, but this one made everybody laugh. I don't remember any of the names, so I'll make them up as I go along. "Annabel Duncan, with her dates of birth and death, dearly beloved wife of William Smith." Then underneath that, "Margaret Ross, also dearly beloved wife of William Smith," and underneath that again, "Matilda Jackson, also dearly beloved wife of William Smith." Then, of course, underneath them all, "Also the above named William Smith." But the funniest thing was what he'd had put on the gravestone, maybe after his first wife died. "Behold, I live for ever-more." That was what was inscribed on the pedestal bit. I know it was referring to Jesus or God, but it looked as if he was saying, he'd buried all three of his wives and he would never die. But he did . . .' Andrew's still solemn expression made her break off. 'It's not really funny, though?'

Andrew obliged with a smile. 'Yes, it is. It is just that I am rather perturbed about what you have asked me to do. You are quite sure about it?'

'Certain.' Watching him put away the unused sheets of paper, she said, 'You know, Andrew, you saying you thought I wanted to make a will has made me think. Maybe we *should* get it done while you're here.'

He turned round to face her now. 'Don't you think that you should talk that over with Hamish first? He may prefer you to use whoever was his father's man of business.'

'I think he'll want you to do it for us, seeing you're a good friend, but maybe I *should* wait.'

'It is entirely up to you.'

'There's one thing I've been worrying about. Hector's twin brother died young and so did Hamish's, that's why they inherited the title, so can you tell me . . . if anything ever happens to Ranald *and* Ruairidh, God forbid, who would inherit when their father dies? Would everything go to the Crown?'

'You are worrying needlessly, Marianne. I made inquiries into this while I was still a student, just out of interest, and when the title "Viscount Glendarril" was created, it was stipulated that it must pass to the nearest male relative. This, fortunately, can go through the distaff side – in other words, to the son of a daughter or sister – but not to the woman herself. In the absence of nearer relatives, a search would be made for cousins or second cousins, and should that be unfruitful, the title would lapse. Where the estate is concerned, of course, it would depend on the will made by the deceased peer, and where no will has been made, if a search does not turn up a claimant, then the estate goes to the Crown. But since the last two generations of Bruce-Lyalls have produced only sons, I think both title and estate are safe for many years to come. Does that satisfy you?'

'Yes, thank you very much, Andrew. I knew I could depend on you.'

'And you always will, my dear.' He came over to sit beside her now, taking her hand as he said, 'I know that I should not say this, Marianne, but you mean more to me than –'

'You mean a lot to me, too,' she broke in, 'but I can't . . .'

'I know,' he sighed, 'you can't love me in the way that I love you.' He looked into her eyes, his heart speeding up as it always did when she regarded him with that sad little smile, and he had to force himself not to take her in his arms and kiss her into submission. She would never be his and he must be content with the closeness of their friendship.

She dropped her eyes suddenly. 'Andrew, why don't you try to find another girl? Maybe I'd feel a wee bit jealous if you did, but I'd be happy for you . . .'

The noise of voices outside brought her to a halt, and in the next minute, Hamish strode in, looking surprised to find that his wife was not alone.

287

'I thought you wouldn't be home till Tuesday!' Marianne exclaimed, a trifle guiltily.

'I finished my business yesterday, but I decided to catch the first train this morning. It's good to see you again, Andrew. If I had known you were to be here, I'd have travelled overnight.'

Andrew gathered from this that Marianne had not told her husband she had invited him, and she broke in now, clearly ashamed of the subterfuge she had employed to get him there, but, just as clearly, determined to brazen it out. 'Hamish, do you remember us discussing making our wills – some time ago?'

'Ah . . . yes.' Hamish's response was only a fraction slow, but enough to let Andrew know that there had been no such discussion.

'Well,' Marianne continued, 'I wrote to Andrew before I knew you were to be away, asking him to come and give us some advice. I thought it would be nice to have a friend as our solicitor.'

The ensuing silence made Andrew wish that he was any-where but at Castle Lyall. 'You must be tired, Hamish,' he said, getting to his feet, 'so I'll make myself scarce to give you peace to talk it over. I'll see you both in the morning.' He looked at neither of them as they wished him good night and, going upstairs, he was thankful that Hamish had the decency to wait until he was out of earshot before hauling his wife over the coals for putting him in such an embarrassing position.

Marianne sat apprehensively until the sound of a door closing noisily released her husband's tongue. 'So?' he

288

began. 'I am supposed to believe that you invited Andrew here not knowing that you were to be alone? Do not deny it – I am not an imbecile!'

'Oh, Hamish, I never thought you were! I wanted someone to talk to, that was all, and I've always been able to tell my troubles to Andrew. You know that.'

The dark frown eased. 'As you can see, I still have a touch of jealousy where he is concerned, but I should not have doubted you. I am sorry, Marianne. My only excuse is that I am practically dead on my feet. There was some problem with the train, and we were stuck outside Edinburgh for at least a couple of hours.'

'Do want something to eat before we go to bed?'

'No, thank you. I had a meal in the dining car.'

She let him take her hand and lead her up the stairs, wishing that he could see sense about Andrew. He must know by now that there was not, and never had been, anything more than a deep affection between her and her old friend.

On Saturday morning, Hamish, rested now and trying to make reparation for his boorishness of the night before, suggested that they all go on a picnic since it was such a lovely day. 'Ask Cook to make up a basket,' he instructed his wife, 'and get Nurse to make sure that the boys are wearing suitable clothes. We'll go and see Carnie about a carriage, shall we, Andrew?'

Andrew said no more about returning home now Hamish was back, and was glad of the holiday spirit.

Hamish chose to take them further up the glen, to a large clearing where he spread a tartan travelling rug on the mossy grass for the ladies to sit on, and the forenoon went extremely well, the men playing all sorts of games with the two little boys while Marianne and Nurse just enjoyed the sunshine.

After lunch – and Mrs Carnie had done well in the feast she provided – Nurse said, 'Ranald and Ruairidh usually have a wee nap about now, so if the rest of you want to take a stroll, I'll stay with them.'

It was during this stroll that Hamish voiced his decision. 'I was thinking, early this morning, Andrew, and I believe we *should* have a change of solicitor. Old Bowie is getting on, must be about seventy, and it seems to me that having a friend to look after our business is just what the doctor ordered. What do you say, Marianne?'

'Yes,' she smiled, 'I'd say we couldn't do better.'

'Right, then, Andrew, we can get down to brass tacks after dinner tonight – that is, if my sons haven't exhausted us both by then.'

When the three retired to bed that night, the wills had been made, papers had been drafted for the transfer from Mr Bowie to Andrew Rennie, and Marianne was very glad that the matter of Moll's visit and the headstone had not been brought up. She knew it was worse to keep secrets from her husband than keeping them from a friend, but she didn't want Hamish to know how she had neglected her father, nor what she was prepared to do as atonement.

Chapter Fifteen

It came as quite a shock to Marianne when Flora Mowatt came one Monday afternoon in the early summer of the following year and told her that Robert was thinking of buying into a practice in Dundee.

'But . . . you're the only true friend I have in the glen since Grace died,' Marianne wailed. 'I used to think some of the women who come to the WRI knew what happened . . .' breaking off, she looked helplessly at Flora and muttered, '. . . in the manse that day.'

'It had been your imagination, Marianne. Nobody else knows except the four of us.'

'I still need you, though. Tell Robert he can't take you away! I'll get Hamish to have a bathroom put in for you. I'll –'

Flora smiled as she laid down the coffee cup she had been holding in her hand. 'Oh, Marianne, he won't take any bribes. He was born and brought up in the glen and he doesn't want to leave. There's still a lot of folk who remember his father.'

Marianne nodded. 'Yes, Hector used to speak about him. "Old Bob Mowatt didn't often get paid in real money," he told me, one night he was reminiscing, "but his patients gave him vegetables and eggs, and pork when any of the farmers killed a pig, and dozens of other things. He lived like a lord, did old Bob . . . better than I did at times.'"

Flora laughed along with her for a moment, then her face straightened. 'I'd made up my mind to tell you . . . Robert doesn't think I should . . . but I couldn't have left . . . I don't like keeping it secret from you.'

Marianne eyed her apprehensively. 'That sounds very serious.'

'It is serious. Robert doesn't think he can go on with the deception, that's why he decided to move.'

'Look, Flora, I don't want you to go, no matter what you tell me, but you'd better get it over before I die of curiosity.'

The doctor's wife took a deep breath. 'Well . . .' Shaking her head, she stopped briefly, then lowering her eyes, she whispered, 'It's about Melda.'

'If you think we're annoyed at her being brought here so often, we're not. Everyone likes her, even Miss Glover.'

'That's not . . . oh God, Marianne, I can't tell you! You'll never be able to forgive me for . . . living such a lie all this time . . .'

A smile crossed Marianne's face. 'Don't tell me you and Robert aren't married? I don't care about things like that, but we'd better not let anybody else know. Hamish might –'

Her hands almost white with being gripped together, Flora cried, 'It isn't that! We've been married for thirteen years, but Melda's not our child! She's Grace Peat's.'

A shocked Marianne gave a loud gasp. 'Her baby lived?'

'Are you all right? Shall I ring for one of the maids to bring you a glass of brandy?'

Flora stood up to pull the sash at the fireside wall, but Marianne said, 'In the tantalus . . . over there . . .'

Following the pointing finger, Flora hurried across and poured a good measure of the spirits into a brandy goblet. 'Drink that!' she ordered, handing it to her stricken friend.

In only a few minutes, a touch of colour appeared in Marianne's ashen cheeks. 'You were telling me about . . . the baby,' she prompted shakily.

'I'd better leave it for another day.'

'No, sit down and tell me now.'

Flora sat back in her seat and let out a long sigh. 'Poor wee mite, no mother and no father. Of course, Duncan's parents died some years ago – they were very proud when their son was ordained minister in their kirk – and Robert did everything he could to find out if Grace had any living relatives, but their solicitor said her mother and father had gone to India and they'd both died of some tropical fever.'

'So the poor infant . . . ?'

'She'd have been put in a home and I couldn't stand aside and let that happen. The only thing was for us to adopt her. Robert didn't want to distress you, Marianne, that was why he meant to leave without telling you, but I had to be honest with you.'

Marianne took a small fluttery breath. 'I'm glad you were, Flora, but I wish you'd told me at the time.'

'If you remember . . .' Flora bit her lip,'. . . you were in London and the day you came back . . . you were in an awful state when you came to us, and we thought you knew . . . that Duncan had told . . .'

'He didn't mention the baby, and I never had time to ask what happened. I just took it for granted that it had died, too, and later on, when I started going out again, I heard two of the women agreeing with each other that seeing the tiny coffin being buried with the other one had torn at their heartstrings.' Her mind, which had tensed at Flora's first revelation, was filling now with hateful things she didn't want to remember, preventing her from thinking clearly, but one thing still had to be cleared up. There had been a tiny coffin . . . and if Grace's baby hadn't died . . . She had to ask, otherwise it would nag at her very being for evermore. 'So whose baby was . . . ?' Before she finished her question, the answer hit her. 'It was yours, wasn't it?'

'We shouldn't have done it, I know, but oh, Marianne, it seemed the right thing to do. You see, my baby was stillborn about three hours before Duncan sent young Peter Wink to ask Robert to go to the manse, and when Grace died, in spite of all he did to save her, he could see Duncan wasn't fit to look after the infant, so he took her to me. When he laid the poor little mite in my arms, I lost my heart to her straight away, and when she snuggled round to my breast, I suckled her without thinking. We only meant to keep her till Duncan came to his senses, but . . . well, you know what happened.'

Marianne knew very well what had happened, but her mind refused to think about it. 'I don't know what to say, Flora,' she faltered.

'I'll give you time to think it over. Tell Hamish everything if you want to, and let him know we are prepared to leave Glendarril, that Robert has the chance of a practice in Dundee.'

Marianne let her friend go without ringing for a maid to see her out. Her brain had been taken over by one thing, and one thing only. Melda, the girl she had looked forward to having as a daughter-in-law at some time in the future, was Duncan Peat's child! Duncan Peat!

She sat on by herself for over an hour, wondering what on earth she could do, brooding about the man who had caused her so much misery. If she told Hamish what Flora had said it would be bound to remind him of that terrible day, and possibly rekindle the doubts he'd had that she had let the minister do what he wanted. God, if he only knew how she had fought against the maniac! How she had screamed, and bitten, and kicked . . . and all to no avail.

He had taken her by force, ruthlessly, uncaringly, hurting her as much as he could. How could anyone understand the bitter shame she felt at being treated like an animal by another animal crazed with lust?

Crazed! That was it exactly! Mad! Crazy! Insane! He'd hanged himself in a madhouse, what could be madder than that? A person couldn't go off his head overnight, not even over a week, or a month, or a year. He must have been like that when . . . he made his wife pregnant, and his daughter had the same genes, the same dark hair and dark eyes . . . the same latent madness. Oh yes, it was definitely latent, hiding under the surface until something triggered it off.

Dwelling on this, Marianne's own mind was perilously near to breaking point, but at last, drained, she got to her feet, resolving not to divulge Flora's secret to Hamish. She would tell him that Robert was thinking of moving to Dundee, and, ignorant of all the facts, he would probably try to persuade the doctor not to leave. If he was successful, she would have to steel herself each time she saw Duncan Peat's daughter.

Robert had already agreed to remain in the glen by the time Flora went back to the castle. 'Robert and I are very grateful to you for not telling Hamish,' she said. 'Neither of us wanted to go to Dundee, and I honestly don't think the truth can ever come out.'

'What about Ina Berry? She must have known what happened.' Marianne had only remembered that morning about the woman who usually helped at births, sometimes officiating alone if the doctor was not available.

Flora reddened. 'She wasn't there. She'd been looking after her own mother in Luthermuir on the Friday and Saturday – she'd had a seizure, you see – and Robert told her before she went that she needn't come back till Monday. He thought it would be Tuesday at least before he needed her, but Grace and I were both early. So it all worked out perfectly, as though it was meant.'

'Y – yes,' Marianne said, uncertainly. She had a nasty feeling that Robert Mowatt had engineered the whole thing, though she knew it was ridiculous.

For the next thirty minutes, they discussed glen gossip, then, when she was taking her leave, Flora said hesitantly, 'This will be the last time I say anything about it, but . . . I hope you won't treat Melda any differently now you know who her –'

'Of course I won't,' Marianne assured her.

Flora went away convinced that she had no further need to worry, but once again, Marianne sat thinking for some time afterwards. How could she treat that child the same as before now she knew Duncan Peat had fathered her? Perhaps she should have told Hamish that the girl did not come of a decent family, as they had thought; that she was the seed a deranged fiend had implanted in his delicate wife. A new thought arose now. What if Grace hadn't been as delicate as she had seemed in that last year of her life? Perhaps she liked her husband's sexual assaults, even enjoyed them? The daughter they spawned could have the same genes, and what if she sat her cap at Ranald . . . or Ruairidh? What kind of blood was that to inject into the Bruce-Lyall line?'

At last, Marianne decided that it was not only too late to tell Hamish about the baby nobody knew had survived, it would be like opening an old wound to make sure it wasn't infected. Hamish might not have forgotten what happened that day, but he hadn't mentioned it for a long time, and there was no sense in reminding him.

All she could do was to remove their sons from any temptation before they were old enough to recognize that they were tempted.

Part Two

1917–1947

Chapter Sixteen

The war, now in its fourth year, had ruptured the slow way of life in Glendarril. Most of the single men – anxious in case they missed all the excitement and adventure if they tarried – had volunteered within a week of it beginning and, tragically, some were killed before its sixth month was over. Instead of deterring others, however, this had fired even married men with families with the desire to settle the score with the murdering b———s. So now, the only males around were either under eighteen or over forty, and a few who could still be safely at home had cheated their ages and gone off blithely to fight the enemy.

With the rapid depletion of the mill workforce, Hamish Bruce-Lyall, Lord Glendarril, had thought he would have to close it down until the men came home, but fate was on his side. In March of 1915, when the foreman was making sure that no one was taking longer than the allowed half-hour to eat his 'dinner piece', he overheard something that made him prick up his ears. Two of the apprentices were discussing what could be done to prevent the rumoured closure.

'The laird should gi'e the wives the jobs,' said one. 'My mother says she could work as good as ony man.'

The other shrugged his shoulders. 'I bet we could work as good as the men, an' all, if he let us.'

Thinking that their repartee would make his boss smile, Hughie Black duly recounted it and was disappointed that not even the flicker of a smile crossed the man's face. It wasn't like him to be so drear, but of course he had a lot of worries on his mind.

Late in the afternoon, Hamish called the foreman into the office. 'You know, Black, that might not be a bad idea of yours.'

About to say, 'What idea?' the foreman remembered. 'Hiring women?' he asked incredulously. 'But that wasn't my idea, just young laddies blethering. A wife could never do her man's job.'

Nevertheless, when a poster was hung outside the post office the next day, it brought a queue of women to the mill, and Hamish employed the lot. Thus all the adult females became involved, for grannies and widowed neighbours, even those in their seventies and eighties who had never had any children of their own, volunteered to mind the infants and under-fives. With her own two safely away at boarding school, Marianne had made a round of the houses each weekday on a bicycle, in case there were any problems, but there never were, and even if there had been, the elderly women would never have told her. They looked up to her, respected her, offered her tea and home-made girdle scones and pancakes, because they wanted her to see how well they were coping.

The old men, who had worked in the mill since before they left school at twelve or so, were none too pleased at having to waste time showing the newcomers the 'ropes', but the women – glad to be doing something to take their minds off sons, husbands or lovers at the front – learned quickly and soon earned their admiration.

It did not take long, unfortunately, for admiration to deepen into attraction in some cases. Men of fifty were not too old to get a thrill from seeing a shapely ankle or having an unaccustomed view down a blouse when its wearer had opened the top buttons because of the heat. Illicit liaisons were nothing new, of course, for folk in a glen got to know each other better than those in a town, but with husbands out of the way for months at a time, they became a flourishing night-time sideline.

Not yet sixteen, Esmerelda Mowatt – known as Melda – was generally acknowledged to be the prettiest girl in Stonehaven's Mackie Academy. Even the other girls grudgingly admitted it, although some were inclined to be jealous of her long black hair and creamy skin, and the way her black lashes curled away from her dark blue eyes. She accepted the adulation calmly, giving no indication of how she felt, yet she was not a vain person, nor a cold fish. She joined in the other students' pranks and laughed as heartily as any; she bore the other girls' cattiness without losing her temper; she was not above carrying on a mild flirtation but drew the line at going the least bit beyond that. Eventually, apart from those whose skins were so thick that they did not recognize a rebuff unless it was accompanied by a slap in the face or a knee in the groin, they stopped trying to make her forget her principles.

If they had but known, it wasn't just her principles which kept her from taking the biggest step a young girl ever takes

– the surrendering of her virginity – but the thought of the two boys who had been her closest companions until they'd been sent to boarding school almost nine years earlier. As soon as she was old enough to think of such things, she had decided to marry Ranald Bruce-Lyall . . . or maybe Ruairidh. She couldn't quite make up her mind which, for they were both so fair and handsome, though Ranald's blue eyes usually held more than a touch of mischievous devilment, while Ruairidh's had become more serious as he grew older.

Last time she had seen them, Ranald had the suggestion of a moustache on his upper lip and had teased Ruairidh because his whiskers hadn't started growing yet. That was the one thing about Rannie she didn't much care for: he was inclined to make fun of his brother, though he jumped to Ruairidh's defence if anyone else dared to criticize him. But she only saw them now when they came home on vacation, as they called their holidays.

They still seemed to enjoy her company, though she was so much younger than either of them. Unfortunately, last time they'd been home, Rannie's seeming need to do things which led to trouble for himself and his brother had involved her, too . . .

They were in the woods, not playing the childish games they had done before, not cycling like mad things until one or other fell off, but sitting on a mossy bank just talking, when Rannie said, 'They've started up the still again. When we were home at Easter, I heard Carnie warning Jimmy Black to watch himself. He said if they were caught, it would mean jail for them, and they did stop for a while, but I took a look last Thursday afternoon and they're at it again.'

'What's a still?' Melda asked.

He jumped to his feet and pulled her up. 'I'll show you. Coming, Ruairidh?'

His brother unwound his long legs. 'Might as well.'

The showing, worse luck, led to the tasting, but what Melda thought was water in the huge container burned her mouth and she spat it out. Rannie, however, was determined to show that he was a man, and Ruairidh struggled hard to keep up with him. After about twenty minutes, the boys began to act strangely, their limbs not behaving properly, their words slurring a little, and in another half-hour, they reminded her of the time she had seen Jimmy Black and two of the old shepherds falling about as they tried to walk along the road, singing at full pitch, and when she told her father, he had said they were drunk.

That was when she realized what was wrong with her two companions. She managed to get them on their feet, and going between them with their arms round her shoulders and hers round their waists, she got them outside, but had to wait several minutes until they stopped being sick before she could take them towards the castle. She couldn't think what to do other than take them home, though she knew that their mother would be very angry when she saw the state they were in . . . and with her, too, probably.

They hadn't quite reached the gate into the rose garden when Rannie's legs gave way, and the three of them landed on the stony path, and this time, no matter how hard she tried, she just could not get them back on their feet.

'I'll have to go and get Carnie,' she told them, aware as she ran off that neither had understood a word.

The coachman collared one of the stable lads and between the three of them they got the miscreants to their feet and more or less trailed them to the stables, where Carnie ducked their heads into the water trough, over and over again, calling them every name he could think of, rough words not meant for female ears. After almost an hour, he gave up and let them sprawl on the cobbled yard, coughing and retching, but miraculously conscious of what was going on. Thankfully, it was a warm April day and the sun soon dried their hair and the necks of their thin cotton shirts. When they went inside the house, they were almost back to normal, apart from somewhat pasty faces, which Rannie excused by saying they had eaten some berries which must have been poisonous.

Melda's mind returned to the present. She'd had hardly any time with them recently. Every time they came home, their mother either had visitors to stay or had accepted invitations on their behalf to the homes of rich families where there were marriageable daughters. Lady Glendarril seemed to be doing her best to introduce her sons to prospective wives. Not that they took it seriously; they just laughed and said they had no intention of marrying anybody just to please their mother, and besides, they were far too young to worry about it.

Melda was counting the days until the start of the Christmas holidays when she was given some bad news.

'You won't see the Bruce-Lyall boys this time.' Becky Drummond, daughter of the minister, took a delight in saying things to hurt the girl she envied more than any other. 'Oh, goodness! Did you not know they're in the army?' she went on, her sneer deepening.

Melda hadn't known, but was angry at herself for rising to Becky's baiting by showing her surprise. Trying to cover up, she grinned. 'Oh, that! Last time they were home they said they were going to enlist, but they thought they wouldn't be taken till summer.'

She waited until the crestfallen Becky had moved away before she let herself mull over what she'd been told. She knew they had been in the cadets at their college since war was declared. Rannie had said they were training to be officers, but he hadn't said anything about actually joining up and she felt quite put out, for they had never kept anything secret from her before. But maybe Becky had made it up to annoy her.

Unhappily, Melda discovered when she went home that the information was genuine. Her father had been called to the castle to attend to Lady Glendarril that forenoon.

'Her blood pressure was sky high,' Robert Mowatt told his wife. 'It was Ranald's idea, but she's spitting mad at Hamish for buying them into the Royal Scots Fusiliers without discussing it with her first. I can't understand her. She should be proud that her sons are so patriotic.'

'Her boys mean everything to her,' Flora pointed out. 'She's bound to be terrified they'll be killed. I know I would, if it was me.'

The doctor took another helping of mashed potatoes. 'I suppose so.' He turned to his daughter now. 'I bet you're proud of them? They'll soon be off to France to fight for their country.'

Melda fought to banish the fears her mother had aroused in her, and losing the battle, she burst into noisy sobs and ran out of the room. Her father raised his eyebrows. 'What's wrong with her?'

Flora shook her head sadly. 'She's grown too fond of them. I think that's why their mother sent them to boarding school originally.'

'Why? It was a cruel thing to do when they were always together, like two brothers and a sister.'

'Oh, Robert,' Flora sighed, 'don't bury your head in the sand. When they were younger they were like brothers and sister, but it was obvious when Ranald was only about ten that there was going to be trouble.'

'Trouble? Because two boys and a girl liked each other?'

'Because the two boys loved the same girl, because the girl loved both the boys.'

'Melda will choose when she is ready, and whichever one she picks, the other will have to accept it.'

'You're not thinking clearly, Robert. Marianne will want her sons to marry within their own class.'

'*She* was only working class when Hamish married her. The old laird told me at the time he was glad his remaining son had taken a wife who would put some life into the Bruce-Lyall blood.'

Flora laid her hand gently over his. 'That's just it, dear. Have you forgotten whose blood runs through Melda's veins?'

Clearly deeply disturbed, his eyes slid away. 'Surely Marianne would never hold that against her?'

'I wouldn't be too sure. Remember what Duncan did to her?'

The doctor ran his free hand through his thatch of wiry greying hair. 'Does it really matter now?'

After a moment's reflection, Flora said, 'I don't suppose it does.'

Ranald wished now that he had not pressed his father into buying him and his brother commissions in the Fusiliers, in which his grandfather, Hector, had been an officer when his twin brother died. Then he'd been ordered home by *his* father to be trained to run the estate.

But this wasn't the adventure Ranald had thought it would be. He and Ruairidh were both stationed in Inverness yet saw little of each other. The initial zeal, the spirit which had spurred him to train as an officer in the first place, was somewhat blunted now, and, as he wrote to his mother, he was bored stiff up here and wished he had been posted directly to France to see some action.

His boredom was considerably brightened on meeting a very attractive seventeen-year-old at one of the officers' dances. She was a vivacious girl who fixed her sights on the tall, blonde second lieutenant as soon as she was introduced to him. While they recovered from an eightsome reel, she told him her name was Catriona MacLennan and he gave his as Ronald Lyall. He and his brother had both decided that life would be simpler if no one knew that their father was a lord.

At the beginning of the last dance, 'Ronald' suggested going outside for some air, and was flattered at how eagerly she agreed. Her unhidden admiration went to his head, and without having planned it, he steered her towards a dark corner.

It was the first time he had ever been alone with a girl, and his stomach knotted with excitement as Catriona opened her lips to his kisses. Inexperienced, he copied the moves his fellow officers bragged about, and when she arched her back, he knew she was his for the taking.

So he took her, and liked it so much that he took her again.

The following day, he sought out Ruairidh to boast about his conquest, and was deflated when his brother's face broke into a wide smile. 'Oh, great! Now you've got a girl, I'll be free to tell Melda I love her.'

This was not how Ranald saw things. Ruairidh had no right to take it for granted that he wouldn't want Melda now; he wanted her more than ever, really wanted her. Catriona was only a stopgap. Wisely, he kept these thoughts to himself and resolved to arrange his furlough as soon as he could . . . before his brother's, that was imperative.

Melda was astonished but delighted to see Ranald Bruce-Lyall waiting for her when she came out of the Academy one afternoon at the end of May, so pleased that she hitched up her skirts and raced to the kilted figure as fast as she could. Grinning, he lifted her off her feet and kissed her in front of everyone, sensuous kisses that took her breath away and had the schoolboys hooting.

Letting her go at last, he whispered, 'It's good to see you, Melda.'

She tried to still her fluttering heart. 'It's good to see you, too, Rannie, but where's Ruairidh? Didn't he come home with you?'

The tiny frown which flitted across his face at this was gone in an instant. 'We don't all get leave at the same time. He'll likely get his when I go back. Now, how do you get home from here?'

'I take the train to Laurencekirk to collect my bike.'

'I thought that would be it, so I left my bike there, as well.'

He put his arm round her waist and they ambled along until Melda said, 'We'd better put a step in. The train won't be long.'

On the fifteen miles' journey, she listened to his humorous accounts of being a raw young officer when the sergeants had ten or twenty years' service behind them. 'They don't think much of us "wet-behind-the-ears-jumped-up gentry", so it's best not to put a foot wrong. They don't know I'm the heir to a title, and I try to learn from them and not to get their backs up by pretending I know better than them, but it's bloody hard going.'

'What about the ordinary soldiers?' Melda asked, guessing that it was from them he had picked up the swearword she had never heard him use before. 'Do they object to having young officers? Do they cast up that you're gentry?'

'Not to our faces, though I bet they resent us. Mind you, there's a few of them came from boarding and public schools themselves. They're the ones who wanted no privileges because of that, whereas I'm happy to have a decent bed at nights and a batman to look after me.' He winked to show that he was joking.

At Laurencekirk, they collected their cycles from the station yard, but before they set off for the glen, Ranald said, 'I've got to see you alone, Melda. We haven't had a chance to talk properly yet.'

Her heart sank. 'If it had been the school holidays, I could have met you any evening, Rannie, but my examinations begin in a week, and I've hours of studying to do. My father'll be really disappointed if I don't pass, for he's set on me studying Medicine at university, and taking over from him one day.'

'Couldn't you say one of your school friends in Laurencekirk has asked you to tea, and she says you'd better stay all night so you don't have to cycle up the glen in the dark?'

Melda saw a big flaw in this. 'Where would I sleep if I said that?'

Rannie didn't meet her eyes. 'I could book a room for us. I'm sure the Western must be used to officers spending the night with one of the local girls.'

Melda shook her head. 'I don't think Father would let me be away for a whole night, and, in any case, I couldn't face a hotel clerk.'

'Don't you want to . . . be with me?'

His wounded look made her say hastily, 'You know I want to be with you, but not like that, Rannie. It's . . . sordid, cheap.'

'Yes, I suppose you're right.' Ranald comforted himself by thinking that Catriona would jump at such an offer if it were made to her. He might try it when he went back. Piqued, however, at being refused by a girl he could have sworn had always loved him, he attempted to punish her. 'I might go and ask Becky Drummond out again. She can give a man an exciting night.'

Having known him for so long, Melda was sure that there was no truth in either of these statements, and decided to ignore them. 'I could get out for a while on Sunday afternoon,' she ventured.

'That means I'd just see you once. I go back on Tuesday.'

A little devil got into Melda now. 'You'll always have Becky to give you some excitement,' she said sarcastically, and putting her foot on the pedal, she hoisted herself onto the saddle and cycled off.

Ranald came racing after her, but he waited until they were well into the glen before he took hold of her rear mudflap and pulled her to a stop. 'I'm sorry, Melda,' he panted, as he cast first his bicycle and then hers down at the roadside. 'I don't know anything about Becky, I've hardly ever spoken to her, never mind anything else.'

'Then why . . . ?'

'To make you jealous.' He grinned at her mischievously. 'You're the only girl for me, Esmerelda Mowatt.'

Her heart flipped over. He had never said anything like this to her before, but . . . she couldn't encourage him; Ruairidh's face, leaner and a little paler than his brother's, had come to the forefront of her mind and was hovering there as if to warn her.

'Come on, Melda,' Ranald coaxed. 'We'll find a place to sit down and have a proper talk.'

'I can't,' she murmured. 'If I'm late home . . .' She raised her eyes to his. 'I *will* meet you at the old hut on Sunday afternoon, though, I promise.' Even as she said it, she wondered if she was being foolhardy. Rannie wasn't a boy any longer, to roll around with on the ground as the three of them had done when they were younger, innocent fun that could never be repeated. He was a grown man now, an officer in the army, so handsome in his dark green kilt and khaki barathea jacket that a pain was gnawing at her insides.

'You're sure you'll be there?' he asked, his eyes, a slightly lighter shade of greyish blue than Ruairidh's, quite serious now, as if her answer was a matter of life or death to him.

313

'I'll be there.' She lifted her bike and saying, 'Three o'clock,' she cycled off, waving to him airily and feeling cheated that he didn't follow her.

When she reached her home and dismounted, she looked back hopefully, but there was still no sign of him, and she propped the bicycle against the gable end and went inside, wondering where he'd gone. She stayed inside the porch for five full minutes, pretending to brush the dust off her boots, but really watching for Rannie going past, and when she gave up, she tortured herself by imagining that he must have gone looking for Becky Drummond.

She thought about Ranald at every opportunity over the next few days, and felt bitterly let down when he didn't turn up outside the Academy again. An awful feeling had risen inside her that he knew Becky better than he professed, and to settle her doubts one way or the other, she sought out the girl at the midday break.

'Have you seen Master Ranald since he's been home?' she asked, trying to sound casual.

The question was a dead giveaway, as even a girl less perspicacious than Becky would have realized, and the minister's daughter wasn't going to pass up the chance to take Melda Mowatt down a peg or two. 'Every day. He's so manly in his uniform, isn't he? He told me his mother got it made by a tailor in Aberdeen, and it's far smarter than the ordinary soldiers get.' She widened her green eyes to feign surprise. 'Why did you ask? Haven't you seen him since he came here to meet me that day?'

Melda's heart cramped. 'He was waiting for you?'

'Of course he was. He apologized later and said we shouldn't blame you for jumping to the wrong conclusion.

314

After all, you always hung round him and his brother before they went away, didn't you?'

Never having come in contact with such an accomplished liar before, Melda took every word as gospel. The colour had drained from her face but she had enough grip on herself to say, 'I'm sorry if I spoiled it for you that day, Becky. Like you said, I used to hang round them and I naturally thought –'

'Oh, it doesn't matter now,' Becky interrupted with a gracious smile. 'And I know you're seeing him on Sunday afternoon, but he'll be with me on Sunday night. He's been with me every night.' She met the other girl's eyes shamelessly for a moment before walking away.

Between then and Sunday, Melda's mind was in deep confusion over what she should do. Should she leave Ranald waiting? Or should she meet him and let him know how sorry she was for butting in when it was Becky he had been there to meet? Yet, every now and then, she suspected that Becky hadn't been telling the truth. Melda would eagerly linger over that until it came to her that Becky knew things that only Rannie could have told her: where he'd had his uniform made, for instance, and the meeting that had been arranged for Sunday. They must have been alone together some time, speaking confidentially, or how would she know?

On Sunday afternoon, she decided to keep her promise. She owed it to Rannie to explain, to tell him that she knew about Becky, to accept his apology for leading her on (if he made one), or to accuse him outright of philandering if he tried to bluster it out.

When she reached the old hut, the still long since gone, he was already seated inside, and patted the soft floor of golden pine needles to show she was to sit beside him. The scene brought back memories of rainy days during long-ago school holidays, the three of them playing guessing games to pass the time, squabbling if one tried to cheat, laughing hilariously if one made a comic error. She did sit down though, but not as close as he had indicated, and she wasted no time in getting to the point. 'Becky told me.'

Ranald screwed up his nose. 'Told you what?'

'About you and her.'

'There isn't any me and her,' he said, somewhat shortly. 'I only said there was to –'

'To make me jealous,' Melda finished for him. 'I wouldn't have been, you know. I'd have been glad for you, I'd have wished you well, but you lied to me. That's what I can't get over.'

'I didn't lie,' he protested, edging nearer and putting an arm round her waist. 'I really don't know anything about her, but I did meet her once on the road since I saw you, and we spoke for a few minutes, that's all.'

Melda shrugged off his arm. 'Did you tell her where you got your uniform made?'

After thinking about this for a moment, he smiled. 'Yes, I did, now you come to mention it. I didn't know what to say to her, and I was just making conversation.'

'It had been a long conversation,' Melda said sarcastically. 'You'd time to tell her you were meeting me this afternoon, and likely a whole lot of other things.'

'I don't like you in this mood,' he observed.

'Oh? I won't bother you any longer, then.' She made to stand up but he grabbed her arm.

'Melda, what's got into you? I told you you're the only girl for me, so be sensible. If I wanted Becky, why would I tell her about you? I'd the feeling she hoped I'd ask her out, so I told her I was serious about you. I didn't mean to let anyone know that yet, but it's true. I love you, Melda Mowatt, and I'm going to marry you when the war's over.'

Before her astonished brain could form any words to answer this, his arms were round her, his lips travelling slowly from her ear round to her mouth, and when the long tender kisses began, all she could do was give herself up to the pleasure of them.

But when the mild caressing became forceful fondling, the kisses more demanding, Melda knew that she had to stop him before he went too far. 'No, Rannie,' she gasped, as his hands strayed towards an intimate part of her. 'Please don't!'

'You must let me, Melda,' he begged. 'I wasn't going to tell you in case you got upset, but we're being sent to France when I go back.'

She drew in a ragged breath. 'To France? Oh, Rannie, no!'

'I didn't think we'd have to go so soon,' he admitted, 'but I've got to do what I'm told. I don't want to scare you, my dearest, but . . . well, to put it bluntly, I . . . might be killed, so you have to let me . . .'

She struggled against his insistent hand. 'No, Rannie, I can't.'

He looked at her accusingly. 'You don't love me?'

'I do! I do! But . . . decent girls don't . . . let men . . .'

'They do if they love them.'

She was thankful when he leaned back from her. If he'd kept on, she might have forgotten her principles, or at

317

least pushed them aside. As it was, she wouldn't have to despise herself for being weak. It was better this way.

To take his mind off his biological needs, Ranald began to talk about their childhood, about their schoolfellows in the glen, about those men and women they had thought of as ancient when they were young but some of whom could only have been in their thirties or forties, about those who had passed on. 'There's hardly any what I call "characters" left,' he remarked at one point, and they laughingly recalled the eccentrics of bygone days, the men who had made whisky in the still – Rannie looking sheepish as he recalled his own experience of the raw spirit – the women who, when their husbands were occupied elsewhere, had kept open house – and open legs – for the itinerant tinkers who came to the glen looking for casual work before they went to the Blairgowrie area to pick strawberries and raspberries for Keiller's jam factory in Dundee.

'D'you remember Pattie Raeburn?' Melda giggled, all restraint between them forgotten already. 'She used to hang a pair of red bloomers on her washing line to let that big Highlander know the coast was clear.'

'I remember that,' Ranald gurgled, 'and we bairns timed how long he took to get there and how long he stayed with her. Ruairidh and I once saw him running out at the back when her man was going in at the front.'

Mention of Ruairidh made awareness creep back to Melda. How would she face him when he came home on leave, after what she and Rannie had been doing? How could she tell him it was his brother she loved?

'I think it's time I went home,' she said, her voice a fraction unsteady.

'Must you?' Ranald groaned. I'm sorry for what I did earlier, but I'm glad we've had time to get back to a normal footing.'

She looked away. 'I'm sorry I couldn't –' She broke off.

'No, you were quite right, but don't forget, Melda, I do love you, and I will marry you when the war's finished . . . if you haven't fallen in love with somebody else before that.'

'I won't,' she assured him.

'Not even Ruairidh?' he murmured, then immediately cried, 'No, that's not fair of me.' He held out his hand to help her to her feet.

She couldn't have answered his question truthfully, she was well aware of that. It had always been Rannie *and* Ruairidh, together not singly, that she had played with, laughed with, thought of, and she had the feeling that, if Ruairidh were to kiss and fondle her when he came home, as his brother had done, she might tell him she loved *him,* too.

She didn't protest when Ranald took her hand as they walked towards the path, there was nothing binding in that, and when they came within sight of the road, she let him draw her behind a tree and kiss her. It was a friend's kiss, nothing more, before he took her face in his hands and looked earnestly at her.

'Melda, I shouldn't have tried to make you commit yourself, so don't say anything until after Ruairidh's been home, and if you'd rather spend the rest of your life with him, I'll understand.'

'Maybe he wouldn't want that,' she whispered.

'He told me he loved you, and we agreed to let you decide which of us you wanted without putting any pressure on you.'

She swallowed a lump which had risen in her throat. 'What if I can't decide?' she wailed. 'I feel awful about it, Rannie, but I honestly don't think I'll be able to choose between you.'

'Don't feel badly about it, Melda. We knew it would be hard for you since the three of us were always together, but we've agreed to abide by your decision and the loser will take himself out of your life.' He gave a lopsided grin. 'I'd better warn you, though – I'm not a very good sportsman.'

His eyes darkened again. 'Melda, won't you please let me . . . ? I could be killed, remember.'

Struggling against his tightening arms, she managed to gasp, 'I could easily give in, Rannie, but I mustn't. I don't want to spoil . . . my wedding night.'

The words 'whoever it's with' hovered in the air between them, and he heaved a long sigh. 'I know you're right, my dearest girl, but I did hope you'd send me off to battle a happy man.' He let her go abruptly, almost pushing her from him. 'I'm not being fair, to you or Ruairidh, so you're at liberty to tell him when he comes home that his brother's not to be trusted.'

Melda felt the tears spring to her eyes. She knew why he was acting like this, and who could blame him? It must be difficult for him to be natural when he knew he'd soon be facing the Huns.

'Please don't cry, Melda,' he said. 'I'm making an unseemly fuss, and I promise I'll dance at your wedding. Come on, I'd better get you home.'

The sun disappeared behind the distant Cairngorms as they walked, and the sky was shot with red, long streaky patterns that changed with every minute that passed. 'I love the sunset,' she said shakily.

'Then I'll think of you each sunset from now on,' he smiled.

Chapter Seventeen

With Ranald in France, Ruairidh Bruce-Lyall was champing at the bit to be in the heart of the fighting, too, and wishing fervently that his furlough at the end of July would be embarkation leave. Never a great letter writer, he sent no word to his mother of when he would be home and was counting off the days until he could surprise her and Melda by just turning up. With only a week to go, he was called to the CO's office, and sure that this was it, he hurried there with a spring in his step, his blood racing with an excitement which held just a trace of apprehension at what might lie in store for him once he was across the Channel.

A mere ten minutes later, he retreated to his billet to be alone, dismissing his batman with a curt, 'I won't need you today!'

He sat down awkwardly, even his bones rebelling at being forced to support him in such circumstances. But it couldn't be true. There must be some mistake. Rannie . . . oh no! Not Rannie!

'Nobby' Clark, a veteran of the Boer war, had seen the same blank eyes, the same stony face, in other men he had served, men whose father or mother had died, or whose sweetheart had just thrown them over, but the mail hadn't arrived that day, so Lyall couldn't have had a letter telling him anything like that; besides, he had never mentioned having a sweetheart. Certain that some dire trouble had befallen the normally cheery young man who had always treated him as a friend, the batman did not move away from the door, and in just seconds, the sound of anguished sobs reached his ears. He steeled himself not to intrude on what must be a truly private grief, but he was a compassionate man who couldn't bear to hear anyone suffering.

Giving a light tap, he walked in, his throat constricting when he saw the huddled figure sitting, head on arms, at the table, a picture of abject misery. 'Go away . . . please?' came the muffled voice.

Nobby came to attention. 'Sir!'

'Please leave. There's nothing you can do.'

Ignoring this, the older man moved nearer and laid his veined hand on Ruairidh's shoulder. 'No, sir, you're wrong there. Whatever's wrong, you need somebody to help you through . . .'

'Nobody can help me through this.' Ruairidh lifted his ashen face and regarded his batman sadly. 'The CO just told me . . . my . . . brother's been killed in France.'

'Oh, sir, I can't tell you how sorry I am.'

Ruairidh's bottom lip quivered again and his next words were most unsteady. 'He's only been over there . . . less than a month.'

Nobby was almost as shocked as his officer. There was a small framed photograph of the brothers propped on top of the military chest in the corner, proud of the new uniforms they were wearing, probably why the picture had

323

been taken, and he had often thought how alike and full of life they looked . . . and now, one of them was lying dead in a rough grave in some French field.

He pulled himself together. 'Do you want me to pour you a spot of brandy, sir?'

'All right . . . please.' Ruairidh didn't think it would do any good, but he did feel glad of the other man's presence after all.

In a minute, Nobby handed him a half-filled glass. 'Get that inside you, sir, and you'll feel better.' He stood holding the bottle as he watched the young man forcing the spirits between his frozen lips, and then murmured, 'Another, sir?'

Ruairidh shook his head. 'No, thanks, Nobby. Oh God, I don't know how my mother . . . She's not one of those flappy women who can't cope in an emergency, but she thought the world of Rannie . . . I'm glad he got home before he . . . she'll be grateful to have seen him so recently.'

Thinking that it would do him good, Nobby let him talk about his glen, about his parents, but it was only when he began to reminisce about what he and his brother did in their childhood that the name Melda cropped up. Melda? Nobby thought. It was a funny name, and it could be anything – a dog, a beloved horse – but it soon transpired that Melda was a girl. He gathered that she had been regarded almost as a sister years ago, the only playmate they'd allowed to join their childish games, but they'd both come to care deeply for her, to love her, most likely. He wondered when it would cross the lieutenant's mind that he'd have a clear field to court her now, but after toying with the idea of offering that as a sort of consolation, he thought better of it. It would be insensitive at this time.

When Ruairidh stopped talking, he eyed his batman mournfully. 'I'm sorry, Nobby. I'm ashamed of myself, babbling on like a child.'

'That's all right, sir. It usually helps to talk about it, and I didn't mind. How d'you feel now, sir? There's a bit more colour in your face.'

'Yes, I do feel slightly better. I should have told you when you came in first, but I . . .' Ruairidh paused, looking away briefly to compose himself. 'The CO's given me permission to go home tomorrow. I'll be leaving first thing in the morning.'

'I'll have everything packed ready, sir. I'm sure your mother will be glad to see you.'

'Possibly, but I'm dreading it. How can she forget him when he was the one with the charm, the one who had only to smile at her to make her overlook all his naughtiness?'

'I don't suppose she wants to forget him,' Nobby ventured shrewdly, hastily adding the forgotten 'sir'.

Ruairidh shot him a grateful glance. 'I don't suppose she does . . . and neither do I.'

Encouraged, Nobby said, 'And the young lady, sir? Melda?'

'Ah, yes! I didn't mean to bring her into it, but . . . well . . . Melda's two years younger than me, three years younger then Rannie.' He heaved a shivering sigh. 'We spent a lot of time with her when we were at the glen school, then we . . . Rannie and I . . . were sent south to boarding school and only saw her during vacations, always

325

the three of us together. We both fell in love with her, and last time I saw Rannie, he said we'd have to let her choose between us. He was home before he was sent to . . . and he must have seen her, but I don't know . . . maybe he didn't say anything to her.'

'She won't have to make a choice now,' Nobby said softly.

Ruairidh either didn't hear, or didn't understand. 'She might have made her mind up already and if it was Rannie, she'll be . . . God, I'll be afraid to ask.'

'You shouldn't say anything, sir,' the batman advised. 'Not yet. It's too soon for you and her to be sensible about it.'

'Should I tell her I'm going to France, too?'

'That's up to you, sir, but I think she'd want to know. For one thing, maybe it's you she –'

'Maybe it's me she likes best?' Ruairidh's mouth twisted wryly. 'I doubt it, but you're right – she will want to know.'

Even crouching over the roaring fire, Marianne could feel no heat. She didn't think she would ever feel warm again. Ranald was dead! Her dearest Rannie! She had always loved him more than Ruairidh, though she had tried not to show it. He'd been just that wee bit more mischievous, more affectionate, more outgoing. She had always been glad that he was the elder, that he would inherit the title from his father. His father! Oh, when in heaven's name would Hamish come home to her? He was never here when she needed him.

The woman sitting at the back of the room had been watching her mistress for any signs of distress, and thinking that she could detect a slight change in the stony expression, she leaned forward ready to offer more comfort. But the tears didn't come again.

Marianne's thoughts were still on her errant husband – errant in the sense of not fulfilling his duty as supporter or comforter; he had even been away when his second son was born. Ruairidh's birth had been the worst, two whole days of sporadic pains that escalated in strength and left her drenched with perspiration. Thomson had only allowed the hired nurse to take her temperature and assess the stage of the labour, and had taken upon herself the task of sponging her mistress, changing her nightdress and gripping her hands while her body was bucking in agony.

As if that hadn't been bad enough, Marianne mused, it had been followed by four solid hours of pain so excruciating that she had longed to die, and at its height, Robert Mowatt, summoned by the nurse at the onset of this last stage, had to shove Thomson out of the way to extract the infant. With Rannie, she'd had twenty minutes of discomfort, slight enough to let her have a degree of rest, and hardly any real pain before he slid out with no help from anybody. It was no wonder that she had always felt more drawn towards him, not that Ruairidh could help what he had put her through . . . nor could he help what she was going through now, even if he did get home.

Her barely audible catch of breath was heard by Thomson, who said, 'Do you want anything, m'Lady? A cup of tea?'

Marianne sighed. 'If I drink any more tea, my skin'll turn brown. Are you sure you sent that telegram to the right address, Thomson? His Lordship should have been here by now.'

327

'He hasn't had time yet, m'Lady. He'd only have got the wire about dinnertime, and he'll catch the overnight express, so it'll be . . .'

'. . . tomorrow morning before he gets here? But that's so long . . .'

The sound of a horse's hoofs and the swish of carriage wheels made Marianne sit up straighter. 'This'll be him, thank God. He's caught an earlier train.'

Thomson pulled back the edge of the heavy curtain. 'It's not his Lordship, m'Lady. It's Master Ruairidh.'

Marianne rose shakily, and was holding both hands out when her son strode in. 'Oh, Ruairidh!' she moaned, sagging against him as he swept her into his arms.

Satisfied that she was leaving her mistress in safe hands, Thomson went down to the basement, to let the cook and the housekeeper know the young Master was home. Mrs Carnie had retired at the same time as her husband, three years ago now, and had gone to live in Perth to be near her sister. Miss Glover had left not long afterwards to look after her mother, who was over eighty and not in the best of health. The new holders of these posts were nice enough women, Jean Thomson reflected, but they weren't the same as the two she had worked with for over twenty years and who had become good friends.

'I'm right glad for her Ladyship,' Mrs Ross observed when she heard the news. 'She was needing one of her own to be there with her. Oh, I know she's had you, Jean,' she added quickly, 'and you've looked after her as well as anybody could, but it's not the same as family, is it?'

'I suppose no'.'

In the drawing room, Ruairidh was feeling inadequate. The only family death he could remember, vaguely, had been his grandfather's, and he had been an old man, so it wasn't such a tragedy for any of them. And his arm was getting cramp with holding the weeping woman, the woman who had never been in his arms before, nor he in hers since he was a very small boy.

'Why don't you sit down, Mother?' he murmured.

Drawing comfort from the feel of his arms, the strong young bones, she said, 'I've been sitting all day, ever since the telegram came.'

They were her first coherent words to him, and believing that her quiet weeping had eased her grief, he took hold of her by the elbow and guided her back to her seat. 'When did the telegram come? I heard late last night.'

'The boy delivered it first thing this morning, as soon as he started work, I suppose. Knowing what was in it, he was ill at ease with me and said the postmistress had told him to make sure I had someone with me before I opened it.'

'Father's not here, I take it?'

'He's in London, but Thomson took care of me.' Marianne gulped suddenly, and held a damp handkerchief to her eyes. 'Like she took care of you when I was giving all my attention to your brother. I did love you, too, Ruairidh, but I couldn't show it . . . I'm sorry. My only excuse is that Ranald was a name I chose, and Ruairidh was what your grandfather wanted . . . though that shouldn't have made any –'

'It's all right, Mother. I understood. Rannie was the bright one, he always got on better with people than I did.'

This was too much for her. 'Oh God, Ruairidh. I can't bear it! I can't! You don't know how I . . . !'

Alarmed by her sudden eerily wailing screeches, he kneeled at the side of her chair and put one arm round her waist. 'You're bound to feel that way just now, Mother. I feel exactly the same, but we'll come to terms with it . . . some day.'

She burrowed her head into his shoulder, her tears running down his neck and under his collar, and he felt an upsurge of love for her that made tears come to his own eyes. It was several moments before she sat up and said, 'I don't know why you weren't jealous of Rannie. You must have known I loved him best.'

'I loved him, too,' Ruairidh said simply.

'I feel ashamed of myself,' she muttered. 'It wasn't right of me to make more of one than the other. I did love you, you know.'

'I know, Mother, so don't be ashamed. A woman often feels more for one of her children, so I've heard. And likely a father, as well, though I don't think ours had any great love for either of us.'

She looked outraged. 'Oh, don't think that! Your father's a man who can't show his love properly, not even to me, but I swear he loved both of *you* very dearly.'

'Do you mean . . . he doesn't love you?' Ruairidh asked wonderingly.

'No, I don't mean that. He does love me, but I wish he would tell me sometimes. And he's never here when I need him.'

Mother and son sat silently until Thomson tapped at the door and carried in a tray laden with home-baked scones and cakes. 'Excuse me, m'Lady,' she announced, 'but Cook says you and Master Ruairidh must eat something.

330

"Tell them a full belly keeps the back up", was the way she put it.'

The suspicion of a smile crossed both white faces, and when Marianne shook her head, her son lifted the teapot purposefully. 'You must eat, Mother, to maintain your strength.'

At that moment, there was the sound of another arrival, and before Ruairidh reached the window to look out, his father was inside the room.

Too distraught to notice anyone else, Hamish went straight to his wife, who had tottered to her feet. 'Marianne,' he moaned, taking her gently into his arms and stroking her hair. 'Marianne, I'm so sorry I wasn't here for you . . .' Overcome, he broke off, but not before a large teardrop spilled down his haggard cheek.

Clearly embarrassed by this, he would have drawn back, but Marianne wouldn't let him. 'Hold me, Hamish!' she pleaded. 'I've been waiting for you to hold me.'

At this point, Thomson crept out, but Ruairidh was fascinated by the sight of his normally erect father caving in and kissing his wife as if he had been in London for years instead of days.

'I love you, Marianne,' Hamish whispered hoarsely. 'The trouble was, I was brought up not to show my feelings – Mother said it was unmanly – and I wish I'd let my sons know I loved them, too.'

His heart full, Ruairidh tiptoed out, leaving his father and mother in a passionate embrace.

Chapter Eighteen

It hadn't taken long for the bad news to wing its way round the glen; in fact, most of the inhabitants had known about Ranald Bruce-Lyall's death before his mother did. Mima Rattray – wife of Dougal in whose small general store the post office had a counter – was not by nature a gossipy woman, but by dint of her occupation she had first-hand information on things she felt should be public knowledge; not *aired* in public, of course, but divulged on a one-to-one basis with the stricture that nobody be told that it was she who had passed it on. Although she also warned her eager listeners that it was to be kept secret, Mima knew that, human nature being what it was, the titbit would be told in whispers whenever two or more women got together. But she considered that her under-cover tactics in no way broke the confidentiality of her position as a trusted civil servant. She was only keeping the community abreast with local news, after all.

'You'll never believe this,' she had begun every time on this tragic day, leaning towards each woman and murmuring the words in her best English as befit-ted her position, 'but the young Master's been killed in France.'

And each reaction had been the same. 'Ranald? Oh, no!'

'It's true, as sure as I'm standing here. The word came this morning and Ruairidh's home and his Lordship, though they didn't arrive till long after the telegram was delivered.'

'Poor Lady Marianne.'

'Yes, it's her I'm sorry for. She's not like old Lady Glendarril, she wasn't brought up to face up to death and things like that. She was just a shop-girl before she married, if you remember?'

Her listener on one occasion, however, was a former maid at the castle, known as little Rosie then but now a hefty lump of womanhood. She had information to divulge to the postmistress that she certainly wouldn't have heard before, so she, too, leaned across the counter until their two heads almost touched. 'She wasna aye in a shop, though. She was once a skivvy!'

'A skivvy?' Mima's eyes were as big as soup plates. 'Surely not!'

'God's honest truth! She stole some money an' ran awa'.' Rosie stopped to savour the bemused, practically agonized, expression on the other woman's face. It wasn't often anybody could tell Mima Rattray something she didn't know already, but this . . . !

The eyes narrowed. 'Who tell't you that?' The refined voice was forgotten in her disbelief.

'I'm tellin' you. I was there when her stepmother come to say her father was deid.'

'An' what had her father's death to dae wi' her bein' a skivvy an' stealin' money?'

'It jist come up, like.' Rosie went on to relay all she had heard at the time of Moll Cheyne's visit, but ended, 'I

333

dinna ken if she *did* put a stane on his grave, though, for she wasna pleased aboot the wumman bein' there.'

'Whit wey did you never tell me this afore?' Mima said angrily.

'Mrs Burr said she would sack the lot o' us if we as much as said a word to onybody.'

'I wish I'd ken't.' Mima was relishing the idea of turning this titbit over, and over, and over.

'No, no! You must promise never to say onything. My God, I wouldna like to think what would happen if you did. We'd get thrown oot o' our hoose, but you'd be worse. You'd lose your fine job, an' all.'

This reminder was enough for Mima, and Rosie, satisfied that she had got the better of the postmistress for once, went happily on her way.

It was fortunate for Esmerelda Mowatt, who had gone to Arbroath for the day since Mackie Academy was on holiday for the summer, that she met no one on her way back from Laurencekirk station; to have learned on the road that Rannie had been killed would have been unbearable. As it was, when she arrived home at half-past six and was told by her mother, she had to temper her horror and shock. For well over a year now, she'd had the feeling that her friendship with the Bruce-Lyall boys was frowned on by her father as well as Lady Glendarril – it was almost as if her Ladyship had said something to him, goodness knows why . . . or what.

Nevertheless, Melda could not hide her sorrow for her old playmate altogether. 'Poor Rannie!' she gulped. 'And the poor laird and his wife. And what must Ruairidh be feeling? They were always so close.'

Flora could not help giving a sigh of relief; she had dreaded her daughter's reaction, yet she had used practically the same words herself when Robert told her. 'Yes, it's very sad, and I'm not surprised that Marianne has made it known that she wants no callers. Mind you, as her friend, I'd have liked to let her know that we're all thinking of her. His Lordship wasn't back, the last I heard, and I doubt if Ruairidh will get home. There must be a lot of brothers . . . soldiers . . . oh, you know what I mean.'

'Yes, I know what you mean, but surely . . . ?' Her voice breaking, Melda came to an agonized stop. 'I'm going for a walk.' She had to get away before she lost control of her grief.

'I kept your tea hot for you.'

'I'm not hungry.' She dashed out, knowing and not caring, that her mother would see how deeply she had cared for Rannie.

She ran into the woods, stumbling over stones and rotting old tree stumps in her haste to get to the ramshackle hut, the scene of their last meeting, when she had refused to give in to his pleas.

Feeling unwanted, as he had so often felt before, Ruairidh took the old track through the trees, thinking idly that these silver birches, tall and almost straight, had been there long before he was born. How many of his ancestors, he wondered, had also trodden this path in the throes of sorrow or guilt? People would say his sorrow was natural, that any man would mourn the sudden death of his brother, but what would they think if they knew the truth? His was not a natural sorrow. Oh, there was sorrow there, a gut-twisting sorrow for the boy who had come from the same womb, the boy who had been his constant companion until they went into the army, but there was also overwhelming guilt at how quickly he had realized that with Rannie gone, there was no rival for Melda. He hadn't been thinking clearly when Nobby hinted at it, but it had come to him on the train home from Inverness that he no longer had cause to be jealous.

The combination of emotions was so potent that Ruairidh stopped to give himself the consolation of a cigarette. He hadn't smoked before being in the Fusiliers, but finding himself the odd man out in the officers' mess, he had succumbed to the pressure. Leaning against a tree trunk, he inhaled deeply, his mind forming a picture from the past: two very young, fair-haired boys playing cricket with a dark-haired, chubby-faced girl who never demanded a turn of the bat. The scene changed again: the boys, a little older, were playing tennis, the girl quite content to retrieve the ball for them.

Then had come the split, Ruairidh recalled. Rannie and he had been sent to boarding school, and that was when things started to change between the three of them. As a child, Melda had only shown the promise of being a real beauty, but it was soon plain that Rannie was attracted to her as much as he was. The metamorphosis was gradual; they probably wouldn't have noticed if they had still been seeing her every day, but on each vacation, they saw a different stage of her development. First, her cheeks lost their chubbiness, and her facial bones formed into a perfect oval. Next, her eyes grew a more pronounced blue, her eyelashes lengthened until they swept her cheeks when she blinked. Highlights appeared in her wavy black hair, so long now that it reached past her waist.

Her body lost its childish flatness and her hips broadened just a little, giving curves enough to make any man's heart-beats quicken. But it was on their last visit home together that they'd seen the greatest change, the change which set brother against brother to a certain extent. Her chest had swelled into an upturned bosom, and they could tell by her rounded stomach that she wore no corsets yet. He had felt shy with her, Ruairidh recalled, and even Rannie had been taken aback, but being Rannie, he'd soon got over it.

'My, my, Miss Melda!' he'd grinned. 'Aren't you the young lady?' His tone was light, but Ruairidh had seen that his eyes were fixed on her breasts.

She had coloured becomingly. 'Stop teasing, Rannie,' she'd smiled, but she'd clearly been pleased at the compliment. Then she'd turned to him. 'What about you, Ruairidh? Do you think I'm grown up?'

He'd felt tongue-tied. There were so many things he'd wanted to say to her, but not in front of his brother. 'You're really p-pretty, M-Melda,' he'd stammered.

Now, stamping on the stub of his cigarette with the heel of his highly polished boot, Ruairidh made sure it was properly out before walking on. There had been a long dry spell and the slightest spark amongst the old pine needles, yellowed moss and bracken could start a raging inferno. He caught sight of the old shack after a few moments, the site of so much of their play, when the three of them would act out the stories they'd read, Rannie always taking the hero's role. Was that the onset of his jealousy? Rannie rescuing the fair maiden who rewarded him with a kiss? Not a loving kiss, of course, for she'd only have been around twelve at the time, though they'd been about fourteen and fifteen, old enough to feel the stirrings of manhood.

He couldn't remember properly, Ruairidh mused. He hadn't really recognized the pangs in his heart as jealousy until he was sixteen. He could recall that day very well. It had been during a summer vacation, and fourteen-year-old Melda had met them at the old hut as usual, her long legs bare, her thin dress rather skimpy in length, the bodice, obviously too tight, opened halfway down.

Rannie had suggested that they act out the story of Robin Hood and Maid Marian, and surprised Ruairidh by graciously allowing him to be Robin. He'd had an ulterior motive, of course. 'I'm Will Scarlet,' he had laughed before disappearing.

Melda had looked at Ruairidh. 'What are we supposed to do?'

'I don't know, but didn't Robin make Marian his wife?'

'I can't remember, but we can easily pretend to be married.'

That was when love had hit him, straight between the eyes. Until then, he'd liked her, had wanted to be with her, had even thought he loved her, but it had been nothing compared to what he felt in that instant. That was a love that would have made him lay down his life for her if necessary, or jump to his death from the top of one of the surrounding mountains, if she asked him to. It had also been a love that he was too young to show, and when she told him to put his arm round her like a husband, he had the devil's own job to keep from trembling. 'No, just link arms,' he mumbled. 'That should do.'

He had ambled along with her for a few minutes, his brain so fogged by the touch of her arm that he'd forgotten what they were actually doing, so he got a proper shock when Rannie stepped out from behind a tree, and grabbed Melda. 'Come to me, my Lady Marian,' he boomed.

'You're not supposed to do that,' she exclaimed, struggling.

Taken unawares, Ruairidh could only watch them grappling.

'I want you for my own,' declaimed Will Scarlet. 'It is my right as –'

He came to an abrupt halt, his face scarlet. 'I'm sorry, Melda,' he mumbled. 'I didn't mean to do that.'

'I know you didn't.' But she whirled away from him and ran off.

Rannie had turned to his brother then. 'I didn't mean it, truly.' He looked apprehensive, as if waiting to be castigated.

Puzzled, Ruairidh said, 'What did you do? I didn't see.'

'Just as well.'

This roused further curiosity in Ruairidh. 'Tell me!' he demanded.

'I touched her . . . it was an accident!'

'Where did you touch her?'

'A button must have come off her frock with us wrestling, and I took hold of one of her tits by mistake.' Rannie grinned suddenly. 'I wouldn't mind doing it again, though. It gave me . . . you know . . .'

He had wished Rannie dead at that moment, Ruairidh recalled. Not that his brother had actually made love to any girl at that age; it was just the thought that he might be . . . first with Melda. That had worried him, still worried him. When Rannie was home last time, he'd been alone with her, and he could easily have charmed her into . . .

Almost at the shack, Ruairidh heard someone inside weeping quietly. It could only be Melda, but was she just crying for an old playmate, or breaking her heart over the death of a recent lover? He stood for a second, trying to make up his mind whether to go in to comfort her or to leave her to mourn in private, but the need to share his own mixed feelings decided him.

'I hope you don't mind me intruding . . . ?' he began.

'Oh, Ruairidh!' She jumped up, tears streaming down her face and hurled herself at him in her misery. 'I'm so glad to see you!'

Wrapping his arms around her, he shushed her, patted her, kissed her hair, and when his own tears started, he squeezed her against his chest, wishing that he could build some sort of barrier to protect her from the bufferings of fate. 'Oh Melda,' he groaned, 'I loved him, too, you know.'

'But you don't know . . .' she sobbed. 'You don't understand . . .'

'I think I do. You loved him, and you let him –'

Her head jerked up. 'No, Ruairidh, that's just it, that's what's so awful. He pleaded and pleaded with me, and I wouldn't! I knew he was going to France and could be killed, but I couldn't let . . . decent girls don't do that . . . but I wish I had!'

340

With her lovely eyes looking sorrowfully into his, tear-drops still dangling from her lower eyelids, all he could do was bend to kiss her quivering lips, a kiss that opened the floodgates and made them forget everything but the craving for the ultimate solace. No words were needed as they lay down on the cushion of old pine needles the winds had blown in through the broken door, and their passion, generated by the conflicting emotions in each young breast, was a revelation which had to be repeated several times before they separated, exhausted, and reality reared its ugly head.

Chapter Nineteen

At daybreak, Melda was still wide awake, unable to sleep because of the questions in her mind.

Why had God let Rannie be killed?

Why had she sent him off to war without proving she loved him?

Why hadn't she stopped Ruairidh?

But that last wasn't fair. It wasn't Ruairidh's fault. It wasn't anybody's fault. They had been locked in each other's arms, seeking desperately for the strength to accept the death of someone they both loved, and what followed had been a natural progression.

But should she, *could* she, excuse it so easily? How could they have thought that it would ease what was champing at the very core of their hearts? Of course, they hadn't been capable of logical thought at the time; they couldn't foresee the weight of the guilt that would descend on them later, crushing them like ants under a tackety boot – for Ruairidh must be feeling the same.

Was it Rannie she truly loved? He had been most fun, an extrovert whose charm could have persuaded any girl to do whatever he wanted . . . yet she had withstood him. Ruairidh, on the other hand, whilst not exactly an introvert, had a quiet appeal about him, an appeal which had succeeded in rupturing more than her morals.

Melda shuddered at the oversimplification, a crude explanation for what had been a wonderful, heavenly experience, although afterwards – after the seeming eternity of the two hours they had been together – when they were drained of all feeling, they had avoided looking at each other and walked silently back to the road. It was as if anything further would have shattered the spell.

And now? She came to the conclusion that her love for the brothers had been equally divided. Life without Rannie would possibly be less exciting, but also less of a strain, because he himself had raised doubts in her as to his trustworthiness. He had teased her about Becky Drummond, or pretended that he'd been teasing, but there had been a touch of mischievous wickedness in his eyes which suggested that it might have been true, or that he wished that it had been. She could not begin to imagine him taking a wife – he would have baulked at the confines marriage would impose – whereas she could see Ruairidh as a perfect husband.

Ruairidh lit another cigarette, grimacing at the overflowing ashtray by his bed. It had been one hell of a night! After seeing Melda home, he had roamed through the woods for hours, agonizing over what he had done. He had taken advantage of her, there was no other word for it. She'd been crying her heart out for Rannie, and had admitted wishing she'd given in to him before he was sent to France, so didn't that prove it was Rannie she loved? And bumbling great fool that he was, Ruairidh Bruce-Lyall had taken what should by rights have been his brother's.

Now, even if she swore that she loved him, he would never be sure that he wasn't second best. Could he be happy with that, or would it cause a rift between them? If he ever dared to ask her to marry him and she accepted, wouldn't he keep thinking that she'd have been his sister-in-law if Rannie had lived, not his wife?

Ruairidh eyed his cigarette with loathing; he had smoked far too many of the blasted things since he was given the God-awful news, and this one tasted absolutely foul. Snibbing the glowing tip carefully so as not to knock any of the old butts or ash on to the floor, and putting the stub behind his ear in the way his batman always did, he lay back to think things over for the umpteenth time.

'We shouldn't have been so selfish last night,' Marianne murmured.

Hamish wound a tendril of her tousled auburn hair round his finger. 'What do you mean . . . selfish?'

'We only thought of ourselves losing a son –' She broke off to steady the tremble in her voice. 'Poor Ruairidh lost the brother he was always so close to, and I ignored him after you came in.'

'You needed me,' Hamish reminded her, 'and I don't think I'd have got through last night if it hadn't been for you, my darling.'

She looked at him gratefully. Last night, after their tears were spent, he made love to her and told her how much he loved her as he hadn't done in years.

'My darling,' he said again, looking at her as if begging her to understand, 'I have been all sorts of a fool. I knew, deep down, that you were not to blame for what Duncan

Peat did, but I could not bear to think of him . . . It tore me apart to think . . . Every time I looked at you, I could picture him touching you . . .'

'I know, I know,' she murmured, although, at the time, she had been unable to consider how he had felt, and even yet she could hardly bear to let her mind dwell on that terrible day.

'So many years wasted,' he said softly, kissing her brow, 'and all because I was too obstinate to admit . . . to accept. . .' He heaved a great sigh. 'It had happened, and nothing could change that, and I should have comforted you and helped you to get over it, instead of which, I thought only of how it affected me. Can you ever forgive me, my dearest?'

Her heart full, she whispered, 'Of course I forgive you, Hamish, my dear, but I should have tried to see it from your point of view. I couldn't understand why you turned from me . . .' She broke off tearfully.

'Oh, my dearest dear, I should not have brought it up . . . not now . . . at this time . . .'

He also tailed off, clasping her to him until she thought he would crush her bones to powder, which did a little to counteract the burning grief that had been slowly consuming her since the telegram was delivered. Gradually, however, his grip relaxed and shortly after that, his breathing became steady and deeper, and she knew that he had fallen asleep again. It didn't matter. Most likely none of the maids would dare to intrude on them today. They would be left to console each other, to get up when they felt like it, to eat only if they wanted to.

Her thoughts began to wander now. Their marriage hadn't been altogether an ideal one, though they'd been happy together, up to a point. For many years they had missed out on . . . the deep fulfilment that comes with true, openly expressed, love. If only she had realized why Hamish had closed the door on that. If only she had realized that a man's outlook on things was completely different from a woman's. If only he had been less restricted in his view of what had happened to her. It wasn't her fault. She'd gone to the manse with the purest of intentions, and that vile brute, that – she delved into her memory for a stronger expression and came up with one she had once heard in Tipperton – bugger o' hell! Yes, that's what he was, and she hoped against hope that he would rot there till the end of time. But she shouldn't even think about him.

She drew a shuddering breath. What should she think about? Not about Ranald. Not yet. Not until the searing pain in her heart had subsided. Get back to Hamish, she told herself. They'd have to make the most of whatever time they had left to be together, and at nearly thirty-nine, she surely wasn't too old to give him another heir . . . just in case Ruairidh . . .

Sheering off the unthinkable, she was conscious that Hamish was awake again, and said the first thing that came into her head. 'Like you said a while ago, we had each other to help us through the night, but Ruairidh had nobody. He went out not long after you got home, remember, and I didn't hear him coming in again. Did you?'

'Yes, long after the hall clock struck two.'

'As late as that? I wonder where he'd been.'

'Would he have gone to see Melda? They used to be a threesome with Ranald when they were children.'

Marianne's eyes filled with tears once more, but she didn't voice the objection she had to any liaison between Ruairidh and Melda. It was better not to tell Hamish who the girl's biological father was – she didn't want to remind him of the man, and besides, it was Flora and Robert's secret. 'I never had the chance to ask you, dear. How did you manage to get home so quickly? The telegram I sent wouldn't have arrived until . . .'

He clasped her hand now. 'I probably knew before you, my dearest. A friend in the War Office came to tell me about midnight, so I took the early morning train, but I wish . . . oh, I never want to leave you again.'

'I'd better call at the castle this morning.' Robert Mowatt pushed his chair back and stood up from the breakfast table.

'They don't want any visitors,' his wife reminded him.

'I'm not going as a visitor. I should really have gone as soon as I heard yesterday to see how Marianne was bearing up, but wee Lexie Murison had a bad attack of croup, and by the time I'd drained all the muck from her throat somebody said Ruairidh was home, and it wasn't long before somebody else told me that Hamish was back as well, so I knew she'd be all right.'

Flora's nose had screwed up at the mention of what he'd had to do for the little girl, but she was glad when he went out, giving her the chance to speak to her daughter in private. 'You didn't tell me Ruairidh was home,' she accused her. 'Was that why you raced off yesterday without any supper?'

Melda shook her head. 'I didn't know he was home till . . . I met him accidentally later on.'

'It was after eleven before you came in. You couldn't have been with him till that time of night?'

'Yes I was. He'd just lost his brother, remember, and we were . . . going over old times, when we were bairns running wild in the school holidays.'

'You thought a lot of Ranald, didn't you?'

'I thought a lot of both of them.'

Her mother eyed her calculatingly. 'I think you liked Ranald best, though, but don't forget . . . Ruairidh's the heir now.'

Melda's cheeks flamed. 'I'm not going to chase after Ruairidh to please you. Anyway, you know fine Father wouldn't like it, goodness knows why.'

Fully aware that her husband was afraid of what Marianne would do if he allowed her son to court Duncan Peat's daughter – she was obsessed with the idea of insanity – Flora gave a tight smile. 'I could probably manage to talk your father round.'

She was not going to sit idly by and let something that had happened sixteen years ago spoil her chances of becoming mother-in-law to the future Lord Glendarril.

Not wanting to fuel the hope her mother seemed to have for her, Melda kept away from the old hut all that week, and when she saw Ruairidh helping his mother from their carriage at the church gate on Sunday, she was so taken aback at them for showing themselves in public at such a time that she didn't know what to say. It turned out that, at the laird's request, the minister was holding a memorial service for Ranald. With his body lying in some foreign field there could be no funeral as such, but

348

the Reverend Stephen Drummond's emotional words brought tears to the eyes of every person there and did much to ease the grief of all the men and women who had lost sons in the war.

As was the custom, the rest of the congregation kept seated until the laird and his family left, and when everyone was outside, they stood in small knots discussing the service and the terrible toll that had been taken on the young manhood of the area. Feeling sad enough without listening to so many gloom-laden conversations, Melda walked on when her parents stopped to talk to friends, and was glad she had when she saw Ruairidh waiting for her at the gate.

As she neared him, he doffed his peaked hat and twirled it in his hands. 'Will you meet me in the hut tonight?' he asked shyly. 'I want to tell you something.'

'Yes . . . all right,' she mumbled, all she could manage with her mouth so dry.

'Half-past seven?'

At her nod, he moved away to join a man she hadn't noticed before, an older man, probably one of his father's friends though she didn't care who he was. All that concerned her was what Ruairidh was going to tell her.

Andrew Rennie had been shocked to learn of Ranald Bruce-Lyall's death and honoured to be asked to attend the memorial service for him. It had proved a truly moving experience, more so as he had sat behind Marianne and Hamish, both painfully erect in an effort to hide the depth of their suffering. That was the penalty they had to pay for being nobility, he had thought – the duty of maintaining dignity even in the face of heartbreak – watching the woman's hand searching for her husband's, noticing the throbbing vein at the man's temple.

His heart had gone out, too, to the young man next to Hamish, a soldier like the brother whose life was being celebrated. He knew how close the boys had been and could practically feel, himself, the anguish that Ruairidh was enduring at still being alive when Ranald was dead.

When they emerged into the sunlight again, Ruairidh said, 'I won't come in the carriage, Mother. I need a walk to clear my head.'

Also feeling the need of some fresh air before tackling the lunch he had been invited to stay for, Andrew said, 'Would you mind if I came with you?'

'I'd enjoy it, Uncle Andrew.' When the carriage drew away, he added, 'I hope you don't mind, but I want to talk to a girl I know.'

'You should have said. I wouldn't have foisted myself on you.'

'I won't be a second, if you'll just walk on a bit.'

Amused by the boy's subterfuge, Andrew walked on, and it wasn't long until his companion joined him again, his step somewhat lighter. 'Everything all right?' Andrew queried.

'Yes, she's going to meet me in the evening, and . . .' Ruairidh's eyes begged the man to understand, '. . . I'd be grateful if you didn't offer to come with me again.'

'Will this be common knowledge, or should I keep it to myself?'

Ruairidh gave an embarrassed smile. 'I'd be obliged if you'd keep it to yourself, Uncle Andrew . . . please.'

'Yes, of course, and you need not have worried about me butting in again. I am going home in the afternoon.'

At the castle, Ruairidh said, 'I'm going to my room. There's bound to be a lot of people here, and I can't . . .'

As it happened, only Marianne was in the drawing room when Andrew went in. 'Hamish has gone up to change,' she told her old friend.

'Ruairidh thought there would be a lot of people here.'

'I can't face anybody yet,' she said, somewhat shame-facedly.

'You shouldn't have invited me back either. I'd have understood.'

'That's why I asked you; I knew you'd understand. Oh, Andrew, it feels like a part of me has died.'

Longing to show how much he felt for her, he drew a chair up next to her and took her hand. 'I am so very, very sorry about Ranald, my dear, and I wish I could have been here to support you when you . . . got the telegram. You must have been devastated since neither Hamish nor Ruairidh was at home.'

She sandwiched his hand between hers. 'It was like I was turned to stone, at first. I couldn't feel anything, and I didn't really take it in till Ruairidh arrived – his CO brought his furlough forward a week – and we were still comforting each other when his father turned up. Hamish has been a rock to me, though he was heartbroken himself . . . and d'you know, Andrew, sharing our sorrow brought us closer than we'd been for years.'

351

Conscious that she was looking at him warily, as if unsure what his reaction would be, he said, 'I am truly glad for you, Marianne.'

As he confided to his Aunt Edith in a few hours, when he went to tell her how the memorial service had gone, 'I *am* glad for her, though I had hoped to be the one to provide the comfort she needed.'

'Andrew,' Edith said sadly, 'I know you have worshipped Marianne ever since you met her, and I have the feeling that she loved you in her own way, but she knew what she wanted. She had set her mind on being rich, and Mammon is a hard taskmaster.'

'If she had waited, I could have given her everything she wanted.'

'You could not have given her a castle, Andrew, nor a title. I am afraid she wanted to get as much as she could out of life, and if she missed out on love, she has only herself to blame.'

Andrew had to admit the truth of this, but when his aunt hinted that Marianne's wealth and her position in the glen community had possibly gone to her head, he said, staunchly, 'She does not put on any airs. I could see for myself that everyone in the church looked up to her, and she treats them all the same, from the lowest maid in the castle to the doctor and the schoolmaster. Hamish's workers and tenant farmers and their wives all showed respect when they told her how sorry they were about her son, yet no one appeared at all awkward with her.'

Edith nodded her snow-white head and smiled. 'She has the knack of getting on well with people, whatever their station in life. I can see you resent me criticizing her,

352

Andrew, but I can assure you that I still care for her, very much. She was like a daughter to us when she was here . . . as you have always been like a son.'

Getting to his feet, he went across and lifted her wasted hand to his lips. 'And I was extremely fortunate in having three such dear ladies to mother me through university and see me through the ordeal of being best man at the wedding of the only girl I shall ever love.'

Tears sprang to the old woman's eyes. 'My dear, dear Andrew.'

He straightened up resolutely. 'No more sentimentality. I have had quite a harrowing day, and it is time I went home to bed, but I shall see you again next Sunday.' He bent to kiss her cheek and then went out, his eyes suspiciously moist.

Aunt Esther had been the first to go, from a heart attack a little over three years ago. That was when the other two sold up the shop and retired, and only a month or two later, Emily had died under the surgeon's knife during an operation to remove gallstones. It was probably fortunate that Edith had outlived her two younger sisters, however, because she had always been the strongest and had made all decisions.

All afternoon, Melda fluctuated between wanting to meet Ruairidh and dreading it. What was he going to say? If he wanted her to commit herself to him publicly, she couldn't. She was newly sixteen and her father would not agree to any engagement, particularly not to Lady Marianne's only surviving son. But maybe Ruairidh wasn't going to propose. This meeting could just be a ruse to get her alone, to take his pleasure with her again.

When the time came, therefore, she set off apprehensively, but when she entered the old shack and saw him sitting with his back against the rickety wall, his face serious, his eyes looking straight ahead, she knew that he would never trick her into anything.

He jumped but made no move towards her. 'I should have told you this last time I saw you, Melda, but we were both so upset . . .' He halted, looking down at his feet as if ashamed to remind her of their last meeting. 'You don't know how sorry I am for –'

'What should you have told me?' she interrupted. It was dangerous to speak of that other evening.

'I go back to camp tomorrow and . . . this was embarkation leave as well as compassionate. We're being sent overseas very soon.'

Giving a horrified gasp, and forgetting the promise she had made to herself, she was in his arms and they were murmuring the endearments all lovers make to each other. But it was not long before Ruairidh broke away. 'No, Melda,' he muttered shakily, 'I didn't plan this. I don't want to . . . take advantage of you again. It's not fair when you haven't had time to get over Rannie.'

'I'll never forget him,' she whispered, 'but I've been thinking . . . I've always loved you as two halves of one whole, and I honestly don't know what I'd have done if I'd had to choose between you.'

'You'd have chosen him,' Ruairidh said, but there was no evidence of bitterness. 'He was the one who could make people laugh, he was the one with personality.'

'Oh yes, but I *had* realized that he was turning out to be a bit of a heartbreaker, that he could make any girl think she was the only girl in the world for him,' Melda pointed out. 'You're different, Ruairidh. You wouldn't say anything like that unless you meant it.'

He clasped her hand. 'You *are* the only girl in the world for me, Melda, but it's too soon . . . I don't feel happy about saying it myself yet. It's . . . oh, I don't know, the world's in such a state. Maybe when we're at peace again . . .' He heaved a long, doleful sigh. 'I can't make plans for a future I may not have.'

Raising his hand to her cheek, she burst out, 'Don't say that! Of course we'll have a future, so there's no need to grasp at happiness, is there? Just remember when you're over there that I love you and I'll be waiting for you.'

Determined not to let their emotions overtake them again, they reminisced once more about their childhood; about their fellow pupils at the glen school, some of whom, like Ranald, had been killed, though Melda didn't mention that; about Rannie himself, whose name was not the bogey it had been last time. Well aware of how easy it would be to slip, they kept their kisses as light as they could, reserving their passion for the time when there would be no war, when they would be free to love each other without having a sickening dread looming over them afterwards.

Chapter Twenty

After six weeks, Marianne still had not come to terms with what had happened, but Hamish was being exceedingly patient with her. She knew she was like a fragile piece of china waiting to be knocked down again and smashed beyond repair, yet the way Thomson fussed over her, ready to step between her and anything the least bit threatening, only irritated her.

Why couldn't people see that she was still mourning her son? And how could they carry on with their unimportant lives so soon after Ranald's death, as if it meant nothing to them? Even Flora Mowatt seemed more inclined to tell her how grateful she should be for having one son left alive than to commiserate with her about the one she had lost. It was all right for her – she had no sons.

For as much as Melda had been worrying about Ruairidh's safety, she had a far greater worry on her mind now. When she missed once, she had prayed that it wasn't true, but another month had gone past and she would have to face up to it. She was carrying Ruairidh's child!

She was shivering with cold, yet it was a glorious Indian summer outside, quite a common occurrence in September.

The trouble was, she couldn't cope with this predicament on her own, but she couldn't tell her parents.

Her father, an old Victorian patriarch, was loud in condemnation to his wife and daughter of the glen girls who had illegitimate babies. 'It serves them right!' he always said. 'Surely to God they could stop their lad before it gets that far,' and she, in her innocence, had agreed with him . . . until lately. Even if she'd wanted to, she didn't think she could have stopped Ruairidh, and it hadn't entered her mind, in any case. If that had been all, if it had been any other boy, she might have braced herself to tell her father of her condition, but because it was Ruairidh, he'd be doubly mad. For years now it was as though he had something truly bad against the laird's sons, which had been reflected in their mother's aloof attitude to her, which had started about the same time. She hadn't been invited inside the castle any more, but it hadn't stopped the boys from letting her join them in their play.

As for her own mother, she was a Victorian-style wife, never daring to disagree with her husband, though she wouldn't do that in this case anyway, because she, too, was dead against unmarried girls landing in the family way. She wouldn't excuse her daughter's plight, no matter who the boy was, so there was no point in asking her for help.

There was no one to turn to. She had no address for Ruairidh – they had never written to each other – and she wondered if his mother would tell her how to contact him if she went and asked.

The next morning being a Sunday, she went to church knowing that no amount of prayers or singing praise to the Lord would help her now. First, she had to find out if Lord Glendarril was at home, for she could never say anything in front of the laird. She was thankful that only his wife and Jean Thomson were seated in the Bruce-Lyall stall. At the close of the service, her shame at what she would soon have to confess made her hold her head down as Lady Marianne went past on her way out, her usual ornate hats replaced by a plain black toque.

Trailing her way home, Melda decided that she had better go to the castle today. This was the first time his Lordship had been away from home since . . . and he might not be away again for months, and by that time the whole of the glen would know she was 'in the family way', and what a scandal there would be.

Fortified by a bite of lunch, she went out for the walk she usually took while her father was having a nap, some-times not more than forty winks if he was called out, and he needed all the rest he could get. As she walked up the curved drive, she tried to plan what to say; she would have to tell the truth, for she was useless at telling lies. And she'd been heartened by what her mother had said before she came out.

To her dismay, her father had been holding forth about the number of girls who had been 'wronged' by a soldier they'd met at one of the dances being laid on for servicemen in towns and villages for miles around. 'It's a damned disgrace!' he had declaimed. 'But they're as bad as the boys, if you ask me. They must know what they're doing, and who do they think will look after their love children? Their mothers?'

His wife had shaken her head. 'Marianne's always very sympathetic to the girls who shame their families.

She finds second- or third-hand prams and cradles for them, and gives them enough money to buy the other essentials, and she never condemns them.'

Robert had snorted. 'It would be different if the blame lay at her own door, though. She wouldn't be so sympathetic.'

Flora had eyed him slyly. 'I know at least one mother who was certain it was Ranald Bruce-Lyall who fathered her daughter's child.'

'Ach! Women's gossip!'

The rest of that story came back to Melda now. The 'shamed' girl had told her, months later, that the laird's wife had paid for the confinement in a small nursing home miles away from the glen, and had found employment for her where she could keep her child. Besides that, long afterwards a farm labourer from somewhere near Brechin had admitted to being the father. Melda had been relieved at the time that it wasn't Rannie, but she had doubts about that now. The Bruce-Lyalls could have paid the farmhand to make his confession to save their faces.

Climbing the nearest set of steps, Melda steeled herself for the confrontation to come and gave two loud raps on the oaken door.

'It's the kitchen door you should've come to,' the little maid told her when she asked to see Lady Glendarril. 'And her Ladyship never sees nobody without an appointment.'

'She'll see me, Jessie.' The sight of her old school friend had given Melda some extra courage.

Jessie shoved her lace cap up off her brow. 'She'll gi'e me a row if I show onybody in the now, for she's havin' a rest.'

'Go in and tell her I have to speak to her – it's important.'

Marianne was sitting in a chair by the fire wearing a silk peignoir over her underclothes when the light tap came at her door. 'Come in,' she called, frowning, because she did not feel like seeing anyone. 'Yes?' she asked, when the maid opened the door. The girl looked scared, but since it was her first week as parlour maid – she had previously been kitchen maid – her mistress could understand how she felt. 'What is it, Jessie?'

'There's somebody asking to see you, m'Lady. I said you wasn't at home to folk, but she says it's important.'

'She? Did she give you her name?'

'She didna need to, m'Lady. It's Melda Mowatt, and we was at the school at the same time.'

'Show her in.' A chill of presentiment made the woman draw her négligée closer around her. Why on earth would the doctor's daughter want to speak to her? When the visitor appeared, she looked every bit as scared as the maid had been, and Marianne, forcing a smile to her lips, prepared for an unpleasant surprise. 'I believe you have something important to tell me, Melda?'

'Yes, your Ladyship,' Melda murmured timidly, wondering if her nerve would hold until she got it out.

Marianne gestured to a chair. 'Sit there and tell me.' The girl sat down, but it seemed that she was unable to come out with whatever had brought her to the castle. 'I won't eat you, my dear. Tell me.'

'I've come . . . I thought I'd better . . . you see . . . I'm expecting.'

The last two words, bursting out like the cork from a champagne bottle, were so unexpected that Marianne did not understand at first. 'But why come to me? What can . . . ?' With comprehension came a violent lurch of nausea that had her gripping herself together in case she was actually sick. Then she felt as if her body was floating away, that she was looking down on a scene which had nothing to do with her. After a few moments, reality returned and, noticing that the girl was looking anxious, she managed to say, 'It is my son's child?'

'Yes, m'Lady, but it wasn't just his fault . . .'

'No?' Marianne was desperately trying to think how to cope with this situation, so similar to many she had dealt with over the past few years, yet so different, the boy concerned being of her own flesh and blood. 'It might be best not to apportion blame,' she quavered.

'But I want you to understand,' Melda said beseechingly. 'It was the night he came home on leave, and we hadn't arranged to meet, but we'd both gone to the old hut in the woods, and . . .'

Marianne was scarcely taking anything in, she felt so angry at her son for putting her in this position, and she said nothing as the girl continued.

'. . . and we were both crying, and trying to comfort each other, and we got to kissing, and then –'

Marianne sat up in astonishment. 'You were trying to comfort each other? You and Ranald? What on earth for?'

It was Melda who looked astonished now. 'Not Ranald, m'Lady. It was Ruairidh.'

'Ruairidh? But Ruairidh wouldn't . . .' Her head swimming, Marianne had to stop. Much as she had hated to think ill of Ranald, she could easily see him as the culprit, whereas her younger son could never . . . 'I suppose you are going to say he raped you?'

'No! Ruairidh would never harm me, he loves me, and I love him.'

A warning bell started ringing in Marianne's head. Was this talk of love a prelude to a forced wedding? She could not allow Ruairidh to marry the daughter of that madman! It must be all of sixteen years since the minister had made that attack on her, yet she could still see his deranged eyes, still feel his clawing fingers, his hot breath. Oh no! She would have to do something to prevent . . .

She drew a steadying breath and smiled sugar-sweetly to take the edge off what she was about to say. 'You can't have this child, of course. You can't disgrace the Bruce-Lyall name like that. I will have to arrange for an abortion.'

'But it's your grandchild!' Melda gasped, shocked both at the very idea, and that it should come from this respectable pillar of the community.

'I am well aware of that, but with Ranald . . . gone, Ruairidh is heir to the title, and he can not have an illegitimate child hanging over him, possibly dividing the family in future generations and causing embarrassment in this one.'

'But he'll marry me when he comes home,' Melda said firmly. 'I'm sure he will, when I tell him . . .'

Marianne's manner changed completely, her face hardening, her eyes narrowing as she barked, 'You will *not* tell him about this! I will arrange for you to have an abortion, and . . .'

This was too much for Melda. 'I will *not* have an abortion!' she said, firmly but quietly in case Jessie heard. 'It's my baby, and you can't make me! I know you're the laird's wife, and you likely think you own the whole glen, but you don't own me! I won't let you kill my baby!' She glared defiantly at the woman.

Marianne's hand itched to slap her across the cheek, but she would lose control of the situation if she did. Making up her mind that appearing to climb down might be the best policy, she changed tactics again. 'I'm sorry, my dear,' she said softly, 'I was trying to think what would be best for you, but I can understand you wanting to keep the child. The trouble is, I haven't had time to think properly, so I want you to go home now and come back in the evening. Ruairidh's father will not be back until tomorrow, so come round the side of this wing, and I'll let you in by the french window. We don't want the servants to start wondering why you are here a second time, and if Jessie asks you why you wanted to see me, tell her you brought a message from your father.'

When Melda left, Marianne went upstairs to dress for dinner, as she usually did at this time. She must do nothing to rouse the slightest suspicion that something was wrong. The hour she normally spent in answering letters could be used to think how to get rid of Melda or her expected child . . . preferably both.

Her hour of concentrated thought was almost up when a plan occurred to her; a scheme to out-scheme all schemes. It would take a lot of arranging, probably much greasing of palms, but it could be done . . . as long as Andrew Rennie played along with it.

Chapter Twenty-one

Melda Bruce opened her eyes slowly, hardly believing that the birth was over. For hours there had been brief respites between the labour pains, and then they had accelerated into the excruciating agony that had made her scream and scream until she was sure that her lungs would burst. She had been praying for God to take her, to release her into that heaven where no pain existed, when she was given morphine to help her through the final stage, and the last thing she clearly remembered was feeling ice-cold though she was drenched in perspiration. But she felt better now. Someone had sponged her then told her she had a son, but she couldn't remember anything after that.

'How do you feel now?'

The young nurse who had held her hand and stroked her brow during her labour was by her bed again, and Melda gave her as bright a smile as she could to show how much she appreciated the kindness. 'Still a bit tired, but not too bad.'

'You'll soon get over it.' The girl seemed to be on the point of saying more when the ringing of a bell made her hurry out.

Melda lay back lazily, suddenly realizing that she hadn't asked if her son was all right. That must have been what the nurse had been going to tell her if she hadn't been called away, but she'd tell her next time she came in. Lady Glendarril had said she wouldn't be allowed to see it, but at least she knew which sex it was.

She took a good look around her – she had been in no state to notice anything when she was taken through from the labour ward. Like the rest of the maternity hospital it was disinfectantly clean, but there was a more homely look to this private room. It was furnished with a matching walnut chest of drawers and cabinet, two padded armchairs and a small circular table standing on one beautifully carved leg that ended in three clawed feet. The walnut bed ends supported a firm spring under the mattress, so the bed was quite comfortable, with a plump feather pillow for her head and several fluffy white blankets. She snuggled down into the soft eiderdown that lay on top, and closed her eyes again.

It had all been so unexpected. At first, when she had refused to agree to an abortion, she'd thought that Ruairidh's mother was going to strike her, but only for a moment. She was bound to have been angry, of course, being defied by a sixteen-year-old girl whose condition would cause the glen folk to think that one or both of the laird's sons had seduced her. But later, when the woman had had time to think, she came up with what she'd said was an infinitely better solution. For the hundredth time, Melda wondered how she had ever let herself be talked into it, but it had been the only option open to her. Her mind went back.

Although she had bravely refused to entertain the thought of having her child's pre-life terminated, she had felt anything but brave when she made her second visit to the castle. Her stomach churned, her legs shook, her breath came in harsh gasps, but she kept saying, 'No!'

Suddenly, Lady Glendarril's expression had softened. 'You know, my dear, I can understand how you feel. If I loved somebody, I wouldn't want to dispose of his child either, but there is another way to save all our faces. I could arrange to have it adopted.'

Not caring a fig about saving anyone's face, least of all her own, Melda clung to the back of the nearest chair. 'I told you! I want to keep it! It's mine . . . and Ruairidh's, and when I tell him the things you've been saying, he'll never want to see you again.'

The woman's face turned grey. 'So you would have me lose both my sons? I did not think you could be so cruel.'

'I'm sorry, your Ladyship, it's just . . . you're getting me so muddled, I don't know what I'm saying.'

'Sit down, my dear, and we'll discuss it.'

Melda kept standing. 'There's nothing to discuss. I'm not getting it aborted, and I'm not letting it be adopted . . . '

'Please sit down . . . Melda, you're overwrought, too upset to think clearly. I was not thinking clearly either when I spoke of abortion, but I cannot . . . I can *not* allow you to flaunt my son's bastard –'

'Oh!' Melda gasped, sitting down because her legs gave way. 'What an awful thing to say!'

'It's the truth. A bastard, that's what it will be, and I will not allow Ruairidh to admit being the father, nor take any responsibility for it.' Marianne's eyes hardened. 'If you refuse to do as I say, I shall tell him – and his father – that you do not know whose child it is, that it could be any one of the soldiers billeted in the old hall. That would put an end to any hope you may have of marrying my son.'

'But you can't do that!' Melda wailed. 'A lady in your position? You can't tell a downright lie!'

'I will, if you force me to. I am fighting for my family's good name, remember, and that means more to me than anything. I dislike making threats, but I am prepared to go to any lengths to . . .' Taking in a deep breath, Marianne hesitated before going on. 'On the other hand, if you will only be reasonable, we can work out something to your advantage.'

Melda stared at her. She had gathered earlier that the laird's wife could be devious, so what had she hatched up now? 'What do you mean?'

'Well, you may not have heard, but Jean Thomson is leaving me at the end of next week. She has been my personal maid since I was married, and I have worried that I may not find another one so dependable.'

'You're offering me her job?' Melda was astounded. 'But wouldn't that . . . ? When they notice I'm expecting . . . it would look like you're admitting it's Ruairidh's.'

'No one will notice your condition. I have told my husband, ever since we heard about Ranald, that I need a decent holiday to help me accept it, but he is always too busy to spare the time. He suggested taking me to London next time he goes, but there are reasons I do not want to go there, and in any case, his trips last for only a few weeks, and we need longer than that.'

Wondering what was coming, Melda decided that nothing Lady Marianne said or did would surprise her – but she was wrong!

'How far on are you?'

'Nearly three months now.'

'Good! I will book a holiday for myself and my companion . . .'

Mystified, Melda murmured, 'Companion?'

'Have you not understood? If I employ you to replace Thomson, it will explain why you have visited me twice in one day, but it will also let me take you away from all prying eyes. We will leave as soon as possible – Thomson will instruct you in your duties first – and no one we know will see you again until after the birth, which, of course, will be in a reputable maternity home or small hospital. Until nearer the time, we can take lodgings somewhere as mother and daughter, and to save tongues wagging, we can say the boy you were going to marry was killed in the war. I'll pay all expenses.'

Almost struck dumb by the thoroughness of this plan, Melda managed to say, 'And the conditions . . . ?'

Shrugging, Marianne smiled. 'You let me arrange for the adoption of the child. You don't ask to see it.' She paused with her eyebrows raised. 'You have not been writing to Ruairidh, have you?'

Melda's head-shake encouraged her to go on. 'Good, but part of the bargain is that you will never tell anyone about this, ever! Your father does not know, I hope?'

'Oh, no, I couldn't tell him – he'd have thrown me out.'

'I doubt it, but it is good that he doesn't know, *and* Ruairidh must never know, either,' she stressed. 'You will stick by that, otherwise . . . ' She left the sentence unfinished.

The veiled threat had been the deciding factor, Melda recalled, and in just over three weeks, she had travelled to Aberdeen on the train with her employer. They had been met at the station by the man she had seen with Ruairidh after the memorial service for Ranald, introduced by Lady Glendarril as Andrew Rennie, the family solicitor, who was to pay all expenses incurred by them while they were away. He it was who had organized everything – the booking of their rail tickets to York, the finding of the cottage just outside the city, the booking of the Brightfield Maternity Home for Unmarried Mothers somewhere nearby, even the hiring of a woman to cook and clean for them for as long as they needed her.

'Why York?' she had asked, when they were on their way south.

'I've always wanted to go there,' Lady Glendarril had replied, and Melda had had to be satisfied with that.

She had enjoyed their stay, though. The little house was perfect for their purpose, being set in the lovely Yorkshire countryside and just a short bus ride from York itself. Until Melda became too large to feel comfortable travelling, they took days out here and there; to Ripon to see the lovely old cathedral and, a bonus, the street market which was in full swing the day they went; to Robin Hood's Bay, where they took a walk along the stretch of golden sands before they lay down in the late autumn sun to rest; to Scarborough, much busier, but not so quaint. They also took numerous separate days to explore York itself, taking the bus right into the centre of the city each time. They made for the minster on their first visit, being overawed by the beauty of its architecture as they stood outside, and after walking around inspecting the interior, they sat down for almost an hour, marvelling at the peace which descended on them.

It was when they came out into the sunlight again that Melda said, 'I still don't know if I'm doing right, but this is like a holiday to me and I'm glad I came.'

Marianne patted her arm a little self-consciously. 'I know how much you've been suffering over the decision you made, but believe me, it's best. We have got to know each other better, and I hope you do not think so badly of me now?'

Melda certainly didn't feel so antagonistic towards her, but there was still a bitterness there.

For the rest of their visits to York, to see the castle, to walk the walls, to search out all the ancient buildings, they felt easier with each other, and by the time spring came and Melda was only able to waddle along some of the lanes around the cottage, she was looking on Marianne as a benefactor she was indebted to.

And indeed, when her pains began, the older woman had taken her to hospital in a hired car and the young nurse had told her that her 'mother' would wait outside the labour room until the birth was over. Of course, she had been too drugged to notice whether or not Lady Glendarril was there when she was taken out.

'Now, you understand everything you have to do?' Marianne asked. 'Or do you want me to go over it again?'

The elderly matron bridled a little at this. Never in her life had she needed to be told anything twice. 'Yes, of course I understand, Mrs Bruce,' she said, in a voice as starchy as her uniform. 'But I do not understand why –'

'You are not being paid to understand.' Marianne retorted. 'Just do as I have told you. It really is best for everyone concerned.'

She had no fears that the woman would break her promise. She had seen the greed that lit up her eyes at the first mention of money, and she wasn't being asked to do anything illegal. If it had been against the law, Andrew would have had nothing to do with it.

'We always like to see the couple who are adopting,' the matron said nervously, still unsure.

'I have talked to them,' Marianne said firmly, but untruthfully, 'and the solicitor who arranged the adoption has known them for some considerable time, so you have no need to worry. They will be ideal parents.'

The matron still looked doubtful, but her hand shot out to accept the envelope Marianne handed her. 'Thank you, Mrs Bruce, but I would like to point out that I would not have entertained your plan if I had not needed the money. I am due to retire in just over a month, and my mother is getting to the stage where she will need a lot of medical attention. I was worried that I might not manage to pay the doctor's bills . . . nor for the medication she may need.'

Marianne watched her tucking the envelope into her handbag. Two hundred pounds would keep the mother in medicines for a long time. 'Now that we have settled everything, I will take a peek into the nursery and then I'll have a word with Melda before I leave. When will she be fit to come home? I don't want to risk her seeing any of the other babies and getting upset, and I can have her collected by car.'

'In that case, and since it is a week since her delivery, you can take her away tomorrow, provided you keep her in bed for another seven days. We usually insist on a fortnight's stay, but these are rather different circumstances.'

Going into the corridor, Marianne drew in a deep, shivery breath. That was the worst part over, and the rest was up to Andrew. In the nursery, she stood between the two cots looking down at the sleeping infants with mixed feelings. Neither she nor Melda had thought of the possibility of two babies although there was a long history of twins in Hamish's family – both Hector and Hamish himself being twins – and they were so lovely, so feminine, so tiny, so complete . . . but she must harden her heart. They must be sent away, so that even if Melda had an urge to try to find out what had happened to them, she wouldn't know where to look.

Marianne turned to leave but her eye was caught by a bundle of pillows lying on a cabinet, and what came into her mind then was so awful that she felt faint, and yet. . . and yet . . . Heaving a sigh, she turned and went out. It would have been the best way, but she couldn't do it.

'I still can't believe it!' Melda sobbed. 'Nobody said a word about my baby being ill . . . '

'They hadn't wanted to worry you,' Marianne soothed, trying to ignore the pang of unease that stabbed at her. She had thought that with Melda never having seen her baby – she hadn't been told there were two – she wouldn't be so distressed, but she had been weeping sporadically ever since she'd been told 'it' had died.

'I want to go home,' Melda hiccupped suddenly. 'I want my mother!'

'No, no, my dear. We'll have to wait a week or two, you're not fit to travel yet.' Neither could she be taken home from a supposed holiday in this state, Marianne warned herself. As a doctor, Robert Mowatt would know something was wrong. She had landed in a proper mess with her lies, but that's what she got for manoeuvring other people's lives, and she'd have done anything to save her family's line from contamination.

For the next few days, all Melda could speak about was her dead child. 'If I could only have seen him,' she wailed one afternoon. 'It's awful to think I gave birth to him and never saw him. You should have let me see him, m'Lady. Nobody would have known . . . even if he had lived.'

Marianne swallowed the lump of whatever was choking her, repentance, grief, guilt, shame, she couldn't quite tell which . . . maybe all four . . . and fear? But nobody could find out. Nobody . . . ever!

Melda excused her pallor when she eventually went home by saying she'd had a high fever from something she had eaten while she was away, and her father innocently compounded the lie. 'It must have been botulism,' he nodded. 'That's food poisoning, and it can leave you wabbit for a long, long time.'

Melda searched in vain for an equivalent of the Scots word but she needed more than one to come anywhere near it – pale, sickly, run-down, exhausted. Yes, wabbit was exactly how she felt, and she was thankful for her father's timely remark. She would also remain forever grateful for the speed at which Lady Glendarril had spirited her away. Nobody, not even her father, would ever guess why.

The only person she would have wanted to know, she thought wistfully, was Ruairidh, but if she told him, his mother would spin him that awful lie. She had been cut to the quick by that threat, wondering what her Ladyship had against her, but had realized that she was desperately trying to protect her son. If Ruairidh had found out about the baby, he would have insisted on giving it his name, and marrying her would have been an open admission that he was the father of her child. However loyal to the laird's family the local folk were, they would take it for granted that The Master had raped her, although they might not think any the less of him for it. The gentry did that sort of thing, didn't they? That was their attitude, but it was to avoid this that she had promised Lady Glendarril she would never tell him.

But the infant hadn't lived! So why shouldn't she tell Ruairidh when he came home? It would draw them closer to have made a son together and lost him. If he confronted his mother, though, wanting to know why she had kept it secret, she might still swear blind that the father was an unknown soldier. No, Melda decided, it was probably safer to leave things the way they were.

She was snapped out of her reverie by her mother saying, 'What's up with you, Melda? You're away in a dream.'

Given the afternoon off this first day back to tell her parents about her holiday, she was glad to have plenty to talk about, and described the sight-seeing in great detail. When she ended, however, rather lamely at the point where she had been 'taken ill', her mother looked shrewdly at her but said nothing until the doctor was called away.

'I can't understand why Marianne would want to stay in a little cottage in Yorkshire away from her husband and friends. Not that I've ever heard about many of *her* friends going to the castle, just that man who's supposed to be her solicitor.'

'He *is* her solicitor,' Melda pointed out. 'She'd got him to arrange everything for her, and he'd taken in hand to pay all the bills for the trip, though she didn't run up a lot. I think . . . I know she hadn't got over Ranald's death, and then with Jean Thomson leaving, it was too much for her. That's why I agreed to go with her. She maybe looks a strong woman with nerves of steel, but she's not really. She knows what she wants and makes sure she gets it, but she has a soft side. I couldn't have wished for a kinder person to look after me when I came out of hospital.'

Her mother pounced on this. 'You were in hospital? She should have let us know if you were as bad as need hospital treatment.'

Her face scarlet at revealing part of her secret, Melda tried to laugh it off. 'It wasn't nearly as bad as that. I shouldn't have been in a hospital at all, but she said she was responsible for me and she'd never forgive herself if . . . '

Flora gave a satisfied sigh. 'She'll still be all on edge, of course. After losing one son, she must be worried about the other one, still over there in what was enemy territory.'

Her teeth clenched because she, too, was worried about that one, Melda could only nod at this.

'Is she keeping you on as private maid, or whatever she calls it?' her mother wanted to know now. 'You should never have taken the job on, not when you'd been

375

accepted for Aberdeen University. You know your father always wanted you to follow in his footsteps as a doctor.'

'She hasn't said,' Melda admitted, only realizing it at that moment. She had always dreamed of being a doctor, but what was the point of launching into a long degree course at this time? The war had been over for months now, and surely Ruairidh would soon be home and they could be married. His Lordship had boasted to her that his son was one of the Army of Occupation left in Germany to make sure the Armistice wasn't broken, but Lloyd George couldn't keep them there for ever?

She was so sure that it would work out for Ruairidh and her that it didn't cross her mind to have any doubts.

At the castle, Marianne's mind was also on Ruairidh's return home. With the war over, he was in no real danger now, so she hoped that he would not be demobilized for some time yet . . . long enough for her to persuade Melda to take up the chance of a career as a doctor. Once at Medical School, she might fall in love with someone else, and a battle between Ruairidh and his mother would be averted.

Laying down his newspaper, Hamish observed, 'It'll be good to have Ruairidh home again.'

'Yes,' she agreed. She could sense his unspoken wish that Ranald, too, could have come home, but she couldn't bear to have him say it.

Her husband, if she had but known, was just as unable to mention their dead son as she was, and it took him a few moments to stifle the great sorrow he felt. 'You haven't told me much about your holiday,' he said at last. 'I hope you found the peace you sought? And how did you get on with Melda?'

'It was very peaceful,' Marianne smiled, 'a tiny cottage in Yorkshire, and Melda was an ideal companion. She had lost . . . a boy she was fond of, so she had some idea of how I felt.'

'She's a nice lass,' Hamish nodded. 'You know, maybe it's too soon to say this, but I would quite like Ruairidh to marry a girl like her.'

His words cut through his wife's senses like a knife. 'A girl *like* Melda,' she said hastily, 'but *not* her.'

Hamish looked at her sadly. 'Why not? She comes of a good family –'

'She does not!' Marianne shouted. 'She –' She broke off and her voice dropped to a whisper. 'I should have told you long ago, only I thought it wouldn't be necessary, but she's not Robert and Flora's child.' She stopped to lick her dry lips. 'Oh, Hamish, I can't speak about it.'

'You can't leave me in the dark now,' he said sharply. 'If she's not the Mowatts' child, whose child is she?'

Unable to look him in the eye, she muttered, very quickly so as to get it over with, 'She's Duncan Peat's child, the baby everybody thought had died with Grace, but Robert gave her to Flora because she had just lost theirs, and nobody was any the wiser.'

Looking mystified, Hamish stroked his chin. 'But Grace and Duncan were both decent people, too, so why . . . ?'

Seeing remembrance dawning darkly in his eyes, Marianne whispered, 'Now do you understand?'

Aware that the memory of the minister's attack on her had upset him again, Marianne let the matter drop.

He would likely recall how the man had taken his life in Hillside Mental Hospital and proved himself to be insane. Surely Hamish couldn't think Melda was a suitable wife for Ruairidh now?

Chapter Twenty-two

Melda could not fathom Lady Glendarril's logic. She would have thought that she would want to keep her maid-cum-companion rather than have her leave after less than a year, but it wouldn't make the slightest difference to the decision she herself had made. She was *not* going to begin a medical degree course even if her employer had promised to finance her throughout her years of study, not now that Ruairidh was coming home. If he had stopped loving her and didn't want to marry her, she might consider a career, but otherwise, no.

There had been an air of excited expectancy in the castle, in the whole glen, since word got out that the 8th Battalion of the Royal Scots Fusiliers was being relieved of its peace-keeping duties on the Black Sea, where it had been posted from the Rhineland some months after the armistice, and the men should be home within the next week or two. Melda lingered over the thought of seeing Ruairidh so soon, her happiness so intense that her heart ached.

She wished she knew exactly when he would arrive – she wanted to look her best for him – but he'd likely be so glad to see her again he wouldn't care how she looked. A softly ecstatic sigh escaped her as she pictured how he would sweep her into his arms and kiss her in full view of whoever else was there . . . even his mother? She wasn't too sure about that, but surely to goodness, when Lady Glendarril saw how much they loved each other, she would understand why her personal maid had turned down 'the chance of a lifetime', as she had called it, but it wasn't that as far as *she* was concerned, Melda told herself. The only 'chance of a lifetime' she wanted was to become Ruairidh's wife.

A soft tap at the door of her room at the castle made her sit up. 'Yes?'

'Her Ladyship wants you.'

'Thanks, Ruby. I'll be right down.'

Her heart had speeded up almost out of control. The only reason she'd be summoned at this time in an evening would be if Ruairidh had arrived, so she took a hasty glance in the mirror to make sure that her hair was tidy before running downstairs. She knocked on the drawing room door as she always did and waited until she was asked to come in, but her spirits sank as her eyes swept the room and found only Lady Marianne there, grim and clearly uneasy.

'M'Lady?'

'Sit down, Melda. I do not relish what I am about to do, but do it I must. You have refused the opportunity I gave you – thrown my goodwill back in my face – so . . . I will have to ask you to leave.'

'Leave?'

'I admit I have no fault to find with the way you carried out your duties, but there are other things to consider. My son will be here shortly, and bearing in mind what happened last time he was home, I think it would be best if you were not in the house to lead him into temptation again.'

Melda was outraged at this. 'Oh, m'Lady, that's a horrible thing to say. I told you before, I didn't lead him –'

'Perhaps you didn't, but the temptation will always be there, and will magnify if he sees you every day.'

'But he's going to marry me.'

A peculiar sound, almost a sneering snort, escaped Marianne. 'You cannot for one moment imagine that I will let my son marry the daughter of a madman?'

Melda gasped. 'How dare you say that? My father is a doctor, a well-liked member of this community. It's you that's mad!'

'Robert Mowatt is not . . .' Marianne hesitated, bracing herself before going on, 'Your father was minister in the glen at one time. He was never a stable man, too easily aroused . . . in more ways than one, and when his wife died giving birth to you it was enough to tip him over the edge into insanity. I had been away and didn't hear about your mother's death until I came back, and when I went to tell . . . Duncan how sorry I was, he . . . attacked me. I did not mean to tell you this, but he was committed to a mental institution where he . . . hanged himself a day or so later.'

Melda's round eyes regarded her in disbelief. 'You've invented these lies to keep me away from Ruairidh, but it's no use. He loves me, and he'll marry me whatever you say.'

'Not when I tell him you were pregnant to one of the Seaforths and didn't even know which, you'd been with so many.'

Her stomach churning with disgusted horror, Melda cried, 'But you made that story up as well, and Ruairidh'll believe me before he –'

Marianne gave an unpleasant smile. 'He will not believe that his mother wanted you to have *his* child adopted, because I will deny it emphatically, and if you persist with your nonsense, I'll tell him you begged me to pay for an abortion. You are breaking the promise you made me, so why shouldn't I break my part of the bargain? As for the facts of your birth, ask Robert Mowatt. He will confirm what I've said.'

Tottering to her feet, Melda made for the door, making no sign that she heard Marianne saying that her wages would be ready in the morning. Nevertheless, when she reached her room on the second floor, she did not, as might be expected, throw herself down on the bed to cry. She was beyond weeping. To have been so near achieving her heart's desire and then have the woman she had thought was her friend tell her something that couldn't, couldn't possibly, be true . . . The other thing, the threat about the Seaforth Highlanders, that wasn't so bad; Ruairidh would have seen it for the lie it was, but she had a strong suspicion that he would be appalled if she really was the daughter of a mentally defective man. However much he loved her, he wouldn't risk the taint of insanity in any children he may have.

She sat for some minutes, torturing herself, unable to lay the blame for her troubles on any one person. She could fully understand now why Lady Glendarril had suggested aborting the baby, why she was so against a marriage, why she was willing to tell lies to prevent it . . . if her story was true. Melda's head jerked up. As the woman had said, there was one sure way to prove it, or preferably, disprove it. She would pack and go home right away – she couldn't stay here any longer – and she would demand to be told the truth.

In less than fifteen minutes, she was carrying her case down the back stairs on her way to tell the other servants – who usually congregated in the kitchen in the evenings – that she was leaving. 'Don't tell her ladyship till morning,' she warned Ruby and rushed out before the astonished women could ask any questions.

Robert Mowatt was sitting alone by the fire. He quite liked when Flora was out at one of her WRI meetings; it gave him peace to think, because he was growing increasingly uneasy. Ruairidh Bruce-Lyall would be home any day now and Robert had a sneaking feeling that the boy would ask him for his daughter's hand in marriage. The thing was, while *he* would be happy to give his consent, Marianne, knowing the truth of Melda's birth and having that unhealthy obsession about Duncan Peat, would do her best to talk her son out of it.

The doctor heaved a noisy sigh. It was such a delicate situation. On one hand, he could easily convince Ruairidh that Peat's madness was not hereditary, just a consequence of losing his wife and . . . as he thought, his child. On the other hand, if he encouraged young Bruce-Lyall to defy his mother, he would be putting his own job in danger. Marianne would not stand idly by and let him make a fool of her. She would get Hamish to send him away from the glen and in all probability ruin his career for ever. Was Melda's happiness worth such a sacrifice? She was a beautiful girl, she would find another man to love . . . but how would she meet any other men when she was tied to the castle? Should he try to persuade her to make use of her education and work for a degree in Medicine? It would likely take some doing to prise her away from Ruairidh, but it would be the best thing all round.

Getting to his feet, Robert took a glass and a bottle of whisky from the sideboard to toast his decision, which he knew would anger most of the people concerned. Flora was pleased at the idea of her ' daughter' being wed to the laird's son, so she would go mad at her husband for inter-fering, and the boy and girl themselves would feel hard done by . . . but they were young, resilient. They wouldn't take long to get over it. The only person who would thank him, mentally at any rate, would be Marianne.

He was enjoying his third whisky when Melda burst in, her drawn face grey. He jumped up in alarm when he saw her suitcase. 'What's wrong?'

Flinging the case from her, she ran into his arms. 'Oh, Dad, Lady Glendarril says my real father was a mad minister,' she cried, the tears she had been holding back flooding out.

Wishing that he had full control of his senses, Robert stroked her back, kissed her hair and searched frantically for an answer which would pacify her, yet let her see what the consequences to him might be if she and Ruairidh took their own way.

When he said nothing, she looked at him hopelessly, tears still coursing down her cheeks. 'Obviously, since you haven't denied it, the minister *was* my father. Why did you never tell me?'

Her misery tore at his heart. 'Melda, my darling girl –'

'You won't get round me that way!' she cried derisively. 'Tell me! Was my father mad?'

Gathering that she was resigned to being the minister's daughter, Robert felt able to make a definite statement. 'No, Duncan Peat was not mad.'

'How do you know? How can you be so sure?'

'Sit down, my dear, and I'll tell you what happened.'

Sitting warily on the edge of a seat, she listened as he told her of the infant left motherless by Grace Peat's death, of Duncan's total disinterest in the child, of his own wife's inability to bear live children.

'Flora was devastated by losing her third baby,' Robert continued, 'and no one knew the Peat baby was still alive, and . . . oh, I know it was wrong, but I didn't think there would be any harm in it. In fact, at the time I thought it was the only thing to do. I carried it here and told Flora she might have to give it back if Duncan . . .'

'But he didn't want it back?'

It was as if they were talking about a doll, not a living child, the doctor thought before he went on to explain why he had committed the man to Hillside – not naming the girl he had raped.

Melda gasped at this. '*You* committed him . . . and yet you still say he wasn't mad?'

'I was sure he'd recover once he got over . . . He was crazed with grief over his wife's death.'

'But he didn't?'

'He hanged himself.'

385

After a short meditative silence, Melda asked quietly, 'If he hadn't . . . taken his own life, if he'd got back his senses, would you have told him his child was still alive?'

'That's an academic question.'

'Would you?' she persisted.

'I don't know,' he admitted. 'He killed himself . . .'

'Because he couldn't get over losing his wife . . .' The girl paused and looked at him with her eyebrows raised '. . . and his child?'

Robert looked away. 'Possibly. I've tormented myself about that ever since.'

After a moment, Melda said, 'If everybody thought the baby had died, who told Ruairidh's mother?'

'Flora felt guilty about it, too, so she told Marianne. That's why –'

Melda straightened up. 'I see now! That's why she tried to keep them from seeing me in their school holidays?'

'Yes, I'm afraid so.' Robert leaned over to pat the girl's hand. 'I'll try to make Ruairidh understand. I'll tell him everything and maybe it'll turn out all right in the end, my dear.'

In view of what she knew of Lady Glendarril, Melda wasn't at all sure of that, and not really having come to terms with what she had just been told, she went to bed even before Flora returned from her WRI meeting.

Ruairidh arrived in the middle of Saturday forenoon, throwing down his kitbag to hug his mother, then shaking hands with his father.

'The first thing I'm going to do is to ask Melda to marry me,' he grinned, not even unbuttoning his greatcoat.

Realizing that he had not seen the girl since he came back from Edinburgh the previous morning, Hamish demanded, 'Where is she? What have you done, Marianne?'

His wife's face turned scarlet, but her voice was quite steady. 'She left on Thursday night.'

'Left? But why?'

'She wasn't really suitable as a lady's maid-cum-companion.'

Hamish frowned. 'Not suitable? Ridiculous! She was the most suitable you were ever likely to find.'

Marianne couldn't hide her agitation, and Ruairidh regarded her quizzically. 'You never said in any of your letters that she was your lady's maid, Mother, but you'll have to find a new one in any case. Like I said, I'm going to marry her as soon as I can.'

His father beamed. 'You couldn't do better, son.'

'He couldn't do any worse!' Marianne screamed.

The two bewildered men glanced at each other, but with no further explanation, she went on, 'I won't allow you to marry her, Ruairidh, and that's that!'

'I'm going to marry her whatever you say, whatever you think you have against her!' His voice had risen, and turning, he strode out.

Hamish rounded on his wife. 'What is all this? What has she done that's so bad?'

'It's not what she's done, it's who she is!'

'Who she is? She is Duncan Peat's daughter, isn't she? She had a good background – father a minister of this parish, mother also the daughter of a minister.'

'Her father may have been minister of this parish, but that didn't make him good. He was as mad as they come.'

387

'But that was his wife's death –'

'That's what brought it to the surface, but it must have been there . . . since he was born. And when I remember your father's insistence on good blood in the family, I can't believe you'd be willing to let Duncan Peat's blood contaminate your son's children.'

With a sinking of his heart, Hamish realized that Marianne was unusually desperate. Her obsession with Peat's lapse, although understandable to a certain degree, was getting beyond what was acceptable, and it would have to be stamped out, faced up to, head on. 'You are being unreasonable,' he said, quietly but firmly.

Before he could say what he had intended to say, however, she burst out, angrily, 'I wish you'd try to understand, Hamish! He *was* mad, raving mad. Robert had to have him certified –'

'Granted, but Robert was also under the impression that Duncan would return to normal once he got over Grace's death, and I say we should bow to his superior knowledge. You must banish all your mistaken, unhealthy certainties from your mind, Marianne, because I am going to agree to our son marrying his daughter.' With that, he turned and walked out.

His wife realized that, for once, her husband was not going to stand for any argument, but wished she could make him understand how she felt. Every time she went to church, or even passed the manse, her stomach churned wildly, her heart beat faster, her mouth went dry, for it wasn't only Peat she hated, but all ministers, everywhere. They were all the same – hypocrites who thought only of their own pleasure. Look at that boy in Aberdeen – he'd been studying for the ministry. Even Mr Drummond, the present incumbent of the glen kirk, looked at all the young girls' legs as they went past. What was worse, as far as she was concerned, was his habit of squeezing past her when it was her turn to arrange the church flowers, and no doubt he did the same to other members of the 'Rural' when their turns came. He possibly got a thrill out of it, but it sickened her, and proved her point.

Melda blanched when she opened the door to Ruairidh, and recoiled when he tried to take her in his arms.

'What on earth's happened?' he asked. 'My mother says I shouldn't marry you . . .'

'Neither you should,' she muttered.

His eyes showed the hurt he felt. 'I don't understand, but we can't talk here.'

Although she was doubtful as to whether or not she could hold out against him if they were alone together, she put on her coat and followed him outside. They had to thresh this out.

Once they reached the woods and she realized where he was heading, she muttered, 'Not the hut, Ruairidh.'

'Why not? That's where we –'

She couldn't tell him the result of their previous visit. She couldn't risk breaking the promise she had made to his mother. 'Not the hut,' she said again.

'I thought you loved me as much as I love you.'

'Things change,' she prevaricated. 'You've been away for such a long time.'

He took her elbow in a vicelike grip and propelled her forward. 'I wish I knew what's going on, but I know you can't have stopped loving me.'

He pushed her through the doorway and, with his hands on her shoulders, turned her to face him. 'You haven't stopped, have you?'

With his blue eyes entreating her, she could only shake her head, and he said exultantly, 'I knew it! Oh, my darling, please tell me what's wrong. If it's something you've done to offend my mother it doesn't matter to me.'

'I didn't do anything,' she gulped, 'it's . . .'

His kiss stopped her, and the love for him that flooded from her eyes, from her mouth, from the closeness of her body, told him all he wanted to know. 'Oh, my darling, darling, Melda,' he whispered, 'I knew you hadn't changed. I knew you still loved me.'

'Yes, I still love you,' she admitted, 'but I can't marry you.' She jerked away from him and ran through the open door, but, pounding after her, he soon caught up and yanked her to a halt.

'You'd better tell me why,' he said harshly.

Unable to stop the tears, she sobbed, 'Ask your mother. She'll be pleased to tell you.'

'I want you to tell me.'

'Let me go! I can't marry you! I can't!'

Letting her go, he watched her speeding away from him.

Chapter Twenty-three

Tempers were frayed in the castle during dinner, the dark moods of the laird's wife and son passing below stairs via those who came in contact with them.

'God kens what's going on,' Ruby sighed, having had to climb up and down to the kitchen several times for unusual items requested. 'The only pleasant face is the laird himsel', and I think it's his smile that's annoyin' *her*.'

The cook, Mrs Burr, red-faced and sweating with the heat from the vast range, tutted in disgust. 'Fancy her getting angry at him for smiling . . . of course, we need to mind she wasna born into the gentry like him.'

'True enough,' agreed one of the chamber maids. 'I'd forgot about that, for she's aye so . . .'

Mrs Burr had already regretted the reminder. 'She's no' a bad mistress, though – a bittie short in the trot sometimes, but aye fair. She never raged a soul that wasna needing to be put in their place.'

'She sacked Melda for nothing,' Ruby reminded her.

'Aye, that was a funny business. In fact, if you ask me, there's been a lot mair funny business lately, and I was tell't on good authority, no names mind, that Master Ruairidh was seen in the woods wi' Melda on Saturday . . .'

This was another eye-opener for Mrs Burr's underlings, who were drinking in her every word. Nodding knowingly, she went on, '. . . so that could be the reason she got the sack. Her Ladyship couldna let her son take' up wi' the lass that was her maid.'

Ruby felt obliged to stick up for the girl who had been her friend, 'You ken, I never understood why Melda took on being a lady's maid, for she was well educated, bein' the doctor's daughter.'

'That's another thing,' Mrs Burr said triumphantly. 'I've the idea there was more to *that* than met the eye.'

The scullery maid, a fair-haired thirteen-year-old normally as timid as a rabbit, could contain her curiosity no longer. 'What d'you mean, Cook?' she burst out, then turned crimson at having been so bold.

Mrs Burr was too taken up with what she was thinking to give more than a cursory glance of reprimand at this lowliest member of the household. 'Of course I might be wrong,' she began, her set face denying even the possibility of such an event, 'but –' She halted, shaking her head. 'No! It's no' my place to say onything, and I'm saying no more.'

In spite of the chorus of voices begging, 'Oh please, Cook,' she was true to her word, and would only remind them that they had duties to carry out.

Robert Mowatt was rather wary of speaking to Marianne when he called three days later, but unless he made her see sense, as Hamish had requested him to do, there was bound to be trouble of some kind.

He was relieved at her welcome, however. 'I suppose you've been called in to talk me round.'

He nodded. 'You'll have to accept things, my dear. I can assure you that Duncan Peat only suffered from temporary insanity. I know how you must feel about him, but . . .' He stopped and started again. 'There is no tainted blood in Melda's veins. You must believe that, because your prejudice is breaking two young hearts, and you could lose Ruairidh if you don't give in.'

She turned her head away, and he couldn't help thinking, not for the first time, what a handsome woman she had become. Her hair, still a lustrous copper, was piled high on her head in loose waves, her nose was as straight as any of the Greek statues in her rose garden, giving her a strong profile. She had kept her figure, too, her corset nipping in her waist and pushing up her bosom and her hips still boyishly slim, even at the age of . . . she must be forty if she was a day. His eyes travelled down to the shapely ankles which were all he could see below the narrow skirt. She looked every inch the true aristocrat, though she could lay no claim to being of noble birth.

'Robert.'

The soft voice stopping his appraisal of her, he lifted his head and met the full power of her lovely brown eyes. 'Robert,' she murmured again, 'I can't help admiring your nerve, coming to tell me I'm a wicked mother.'

'That's not what . . .' He inhaled deeply, then said quietly, 'I'm going to tell you something I never meant to tell anyone, but I hope it will help you to understand why I took the infant from the manse that night. Duncan said he wasn't her father, and I was afraid he would try to harm her in some way.'

Marianne was taken aback by this information. 'If he wasn't her father, then who . . . ?'

'He thought it was the gardener – you know, the tinker. The man came back for a few years on his way to and from the fruit-picking, to tend the manse garden after that first summer when Duncan had a broken leg.'

Even more shocked at this, Marianne exclaimed, 'But Grace would never have –'

'It was just in his imagination,' Robert pointed out.

Something she had forgotten for many years now made its way to the surface of Marianne's mind. 'Oh, God! That's what he meant! He said it was my fault, and I thought he was blaming me for leading him on, which I never did, but he'd meant –' She broke off, looking at the doctor imploringly. 'Don't you see, Robert? I was the one who told Jamie MacPhee they were needing a gardener at the manse. That's what he'd been blaming me for.'

'More than likely, but don't forget that he was not responsible for his thoughts at that time. I can only assure you, however, as I have done before, that his condition would have been purely temporary.' He regarded her now with his eyebrows raised.

She smiled wryly. 'You haven't changed my mind about the man, Robert, but you *have* made me realize I'm fighting a losing battle. I've done all I could to prevent his daughter from being the mother of the son Ruairidh needs as the next heir, yet why should I bother when Hamish doesn't seem to care about decent breeding any more? So I'm going to climb down. They can be married in St Giles and I'll take her to Edinburgh before then to let her choose her trousseau, like Hamish's mother did with me.'

She gave a dry laugh. 'I only hope I don't die before the wedding, like she did.'

Robert stood up now. 'You won't die,' he grinned. 'You've a constitution like a horse. I'd better go, though. There could be urgent calls waiting for me.'

She rose to her feet and clasped his hand for a moment. 'Thank you for coming, Robert.'

'Thank you for not being too proud to give in. You'll not regret it, Marianne.'

'I hope not. I do like Melda, you know, as a person.'

'I'm glad to hear it. I was a bit worried you would –'

'Take my spite out on her? No, no, I'd never do that.' He saw himself out and had a new spring in his step as he walked smartly down the avenue. He felt like sprinting as fast as he could to tell Melda the good news and watch the sadness leave her eyes, but he was too easily puffed these days. He'd have to tell Flora to stop making suet puddings, otherwise he'd soon be as round as a ball.

Marianne sat staring into the fire for some time after her visitor left. She felt drained and little wonder. For over a year she'd had a deep fear in her, a fear that she had tried to banish in the only way she knew, yet she had just made it possible for it to flourish and become reality. Plus . . . a new fear had reared its ugly head, a smidgen of fear that could grow into something big if she didn't face it now and stamp it out.

Grace had been quite a delicate woman, shy with strangers despite her outgoing manner, genteel as befitted one who was the daughter of one minister and wife of another, so it was impossible to imagine her breaking any of the ten commandments. So why had Duncan said that? He must have had some reason for . . . but he was beyond all reason that day. Possibly he'd been jealous of the tinker because of his good looks, and that jealousy could have been building up every time Jamie MacPhee was there. He had been left on his own after the funeral, brooding about it, and finally gone over the edge and taken it out on her, the first woman who'd gone into the manse. Whatever Robert Mowatt said, the man had definitely been insane, and that kind of insanity wasn't temporary. It *had* been there from the day he was born, lying in wait for something to trigger it off.

Marianne gave her head a small shake of resignation. No one, not Robert nor Hamish nor anyone else, would ever convince her otherwise, yet she had committed herself to agreeing to a union that was absolutely abhorrent to her, and she would have to abide by that.

When Hamish came home, he strode straight across to her. 'You look worn out, Marianne. Why don't you go to bed, and I shall arrange for your meal to be sent up?' Getting no answer, he said, 'Robert's been to see you, hasn't he? I asked him to call to –'

'To get me to climb down about the wedding?'

'To try to make you see sense. I am sorry to have to say it, my darling, but you were being most unreasonable, and I thought that perhaps he could –'

'He didn't get me to change my mind about Duncan Peat – I'll never do that – but I said I would agree to Ruairidh marrying Melda.'

Hamish bent and kissed her cheek. 'I am so pleased to hear it, and I am sure that you will never regret it.'

'I'm glad your mother gave in,' Melda sighed.

Ruairidh ran his finger gently down her cheek. 'I'd have married you even if she hadn't.'

'I couldn't have gone against her. I'd never have felt easy in the house with her.'

'I'd have taken you away, my darling. I still could, if you wanted me to. We'd be happier on our own somewhere.'

'I know we would, but you're the heir. You can't just go away when you feel like it. Your father would probably disown you and cut you off without a shilling.'

He grinned. 'I'd give it all up for you.' His face sobered. 'I mean that, you know.'

'I wouldn't let you. You've a duty, a role to fulfil and you can't let your father down.'

'I suppose not. He's desperate for us to give him a grandson.'

'Must it be a grandson? Wouldn't a granddaughter please him?'

'A female can't inherit.'

With a twinkle in her eyes, Melda murmured, 'Well, we'll have to see what we can do.'

Forced to succumb to pressure, Marianne was now planning a lavish wedding. Unfortunately for her, both bride and groom were adamant that they would rather be married in the glen kirk than in the big cathedral in Edinburgh. Furthermore, Melda insisted that she wanted a plain, inexpensive gown and that her mother would help her to make one, which did not go down at all well.

Adding fuel to the fire, Hamish laughed off his wife's moans that people would think they were short of money giving the future laird a tuppenny-ha'penny do. 'If you're speaking about all those horsy-faced uppity old frumps who used to be friends of my mother's,' he grinned, 'or the huntin', shootin' and fishin' pals of my father's, let them think what they like. Our son's taking a daughter of the glen for a wife and it's glen folk we want to celebrate with us.'

Marianne's pained sigh made him slide his arm round her waist. 'Why can't you be happy for them, my dear? Surely you can see how much they love each other?'

'I do see, Hamish, and I am happy for them, it's just . . . well, we were married in the glen, as well, and . . .' She stopped, drawing back from the memory of the man who had joined them in holy matrimony.

Her husband swung her round and kissed her tenderly. 'I had not forgotten, my darling, and the only thing I regret is that it took me so long to tell you I love you.'

She looked at his dear face and summoned a smile. 'I'm sure Ruairidh and Melda won't regret it, either.' She felt the coldness coming back into her heart, the coldness she had been trying to dispel for days because she truly did not want to hold the girl's parentage against her.

The wedding was everything that Ruairidh and Melda had wanted. The Reverend Stephen Drummond – the incumbent there for seventeen years now – conducted an impressive ceremony, and it was not only the two mothers who were moved to tears. When the lovely young bride lifted her veil to let her handsome groom kiss her, the 'Oohs' and 'Ahs' echoing from every corner of the kirk were followed by sniffs and the flourish of handkerchiefs, men's as well as women's.

Then the whole congregation was transported to the castle in the Bruce-Lyalls' carriages adorned with the family crest, and though several journeys had to be made, those who were left until last did not complain; they didn't mind waiting.

Extra staff had been engaged to ensure the smooth operation of providing and serving the banquet, all the best china and silver cutlery were on show, and once the guests had eaten as much as they possibly could, the tables were cleared and placed round the walls of the dining room to be set out with the bottles of spirits. All the inhabitants of Glendarril took full advantage of the filled glasses handed round, and with whisky available almost on tap, it was not surprising that many a man thought he was kissing his own wife in the ballroom when it was somebody else's he was dancing with; an honest mistake . . . or so he professed. The women didn't seem to mind, not even Marianne. It had taken one brave soul to give her a swift kiss during a waltz, then she had a steady stream of partners, most of whom gave her a proper smacker on the lips.

'I'm glad she's entering into the spirit of things,' Robert Mowatt murmured to Hamish. 'I was a wee bit afraid she'd –'

'She's got over all that,' Hamish said, watching his wife fondly. 'Your little lecture did the trick, thank goodness.'

The doctor deemed it best not to say that he hadn't convinced her of anything. She had promised that she wouldn't take her spite out on Melda, but even if she fully meant to keep that promise, there was always the possibility that something the girl would say or do might trigger off the paranoia again.

Marianne's thoughts at that moment, however, as she sat down and let her eyes follow the radiant pair, were not on Duncan Peat; she was recalling the two sweet infants she had thought of suffocating. She thanked God that she hadn't, but she didn't regret instructing Andrew Rennie to put them up for adoption. She had safeguarded herself by telling him to keep her identity secret – to prevent them turning up at some time in the future to claim their inheritance. She had also forbidden him to tell her where they had been placed or anything about them, but to salve her conscience had ordered him to send a size-able allowance to the adoptive parents each month until they came of age – to provide for the twins' maintenance and education.

She glanced at Andrew, standing on the other side of the room, and catching her eye, he came across to ask her to dance. When they got into the rhythm of the Scottish waltz, he said, 'You're looking very serious, Marianne. I hope nothing's wrong.'

'Nothing you can do anything about, Andrew. It's all in the past.'

The slight squeeze he gave her let her know he understood, so she rewarded him with an affectionate smile. 'I don't know what I'd have done without you, Andrew. You've always been there for me.'

'And I always shall be, my dear.'

'But I shouldn't have asked you to . . . I don't know what you must have thought of me.'

His love for her was evident as he regarded her earnestly. 'You know what I think of you, Marianne, what I've always thought of you. Nothing will ever change that.'

A lump came in her throat – he was such a good man. She sometimes wondered . . . To cover the embarrassment of her thoughts, she said, 'Why don't you find yourself a wife? I'm sure you must meet some eligible young women in the course of your work.'

He shrugged wryly. 'I seldom meet young women. My female clients are generally widows – middle-aged matrons or ancient matriarchs who control their families by threatening to disinherit them. Besides, I'm happy the way I am. What about you? Are you happy with Hamish?'

'Yes, Andrew, I am. He's a loving husband.' Even now, after all this time, she saw the pain surfacing in Andrew's eyes, but it was too late to unsay it.

She wished that Miss Edith had been here for him, but his last aunt had passed away some time before, protesting right up to the last moment, according to the nurse he had paid to check on her every day, that she didn't need a doctor. Poor old dear, Marianne reflected, she was always so independent.

Because the glen folk had not had a celebration like this in the memories of many, they made the most of it, not only the men who clamoured for a dance with the laird's wife or the wife of the future laird, but the women who, their courage also bolstered by the free alcohol – claimed the young Master for a dance, and even the laird himself.

Not until the beer and whisky had almost run out did they show any sign of leaving, and the Bruce-Lyall family, now extended by one, stood outside to wave them off. When they went inside, Ruairidh, with his arm still round his bride, said, somewhat bashfully, 'If you'll excuse us, we'll go up to bed now. It's been a long day.'

Andrew, who had been asked to stay the night, got to his feet a little unsteadily when Marianne and her husband entered the sitting room. 'I had better get to bed, too.'

Hamish grabbed his sleeve. 'No, no, you'll take one last dram with me, surely?'

Marianne left them to their nightcap.

Chapter Twenty-four

When the young couple returned from their three-month honeymoon in France, Ruairidh joyfully announced that Melda was pregnant and, the Mowatts having been asked to the castle to welcome them home, there followed a round of cheek-kissing and back-slapping in which Marianne had to steel herself to take part. Fortunately for her, with so much commotion going on, no one noticed her hesitation . . . except Melda, who concluded that her mother-in-law, like herself, was remembering the boy infant who had died.

To banish this from both their minds, she said, turning rather pink, 'The doctor in Paris said my *accouchement* was due in six months.'

Showing none of her embarrassment, Ruairidh boasted, 'He said I must have planted the *enfant* on our wedding night.'

The two fathers glanced at their wives to see how they had reacted to this indiscretion, a breach of good manners especially in mixed company, then caught each other's eye and bellowed with laughter.

'Good for you, son!' boomed Hamish, and Robert added, 'Well done!'

Marianne tried not to show how nauseated she felt, and when Flora leaned over and murmured, 'Well, it was only to be expected, wasn't it?' she nodded stonily.

When Ruairidh attempted to take Melda in his arms that night, she pleaded exhaustion from the travelling and turned away. If he had been too blind to notice that his mother wasn't pleased about the baby, it wasn't up to her to tell him. Not that the woman had said anything, it was a look in her eyes at one point, as if she hated her son's wife. But why? She couldn't still believe that the minister had been afflicted with an insanity which could skip a generation and be passed on to his grand-children? Yet it had taken her, Melda, some time to believe her father – she would always look on Robert Mowatt as her father – when he swore to her that the man would have recovered from his temporary madness if he hadn't killed himself.

What else could Ruairidh's mother have against her? The boot should really be on the other foot. It was *her* fault that the other baby, her first grandchild, hadn't lived. If she'd just let it be born where it should have been born, everything would have been all right. But maybe it wouldn't, Melda conceded sadly. Maybe it had been meant to die all along. If it hadn't, she would have always been wondering where it was, what had become of it . . . and remembering that it had been conceived on the day she had learned of Rannie's death, which wasn't exactly a pleasant thought. She *had* been grateful to Lady Marianne for seeing her through that pregnancy and saving her from being the butt of gossip in the glen, but she'd only done that for her own sake, to preserve the good name of her family, and its pure blood line.

But she had better not start her marriage off on a sour note by tackling the woman about her present attitude, Melda mused. Ruairidh wouldn't want friction between his wife and his mother, but she wouldn't knuckle under to the woman if she started ordering her about. She was the next Lady Glendarril, wasn't she? With a sob in her throat, she turned to her husband.

When it came to the last month, with Melda's belly appearing to be almost at bursting point, Hamish excused Ruairidh from all duties at the mill to let him be with his wife as much as possible. 'She's just a young slip of a thing,' he explained to his wife. 'She has no idea what childbirth means, and she needs him here with her.'

Marianne couldn't help thinking that she had been little older when she produced Ranald, and that Melda *did* know what childbirth meant, but she didn't feel like arguing with him. She had her old worry on her mind again. She couldn't possibly allow Melda to keep her child if it turned out to be a boy, bringing the possibility of madness into the Bruce-Lyall blood. The problem was, she'd only had Hamish to contend with last time, unobservant and gullible. It had been easy to pull the wool over his eyes and whip the girl out of sight, but Ruairidh was different. He'd been furious, and had refused when his father had told him to book Melda into an extortionately expensive maternity home in Edinburgh rather than trust the local 'howdie' to bring this special child into the world, because he couldn't bear the thought of her being taken away from him.

Robert Mowatt, of course, as the man the whole glen thought was Melda's father, was out of the question, they were all agreed on that, which relieved both Marianne and the young mother-to-be, for the doctor would know as soon as he examined the girl that this was not her first pregnancy. It was he, however, who gave Hamish the name of a highly recommended trained midwife.

A solution to the problem of what to do with the baby occurred to her which made her draw a deep shuddery breath. Could she possibly ask Robert . . . ? Would he do for her what Andrew Rennie had done before? It would be worth trying, and it would only be necessary if Melda produced a boy.

Before the arrival of the trained midwife from Edinburgh, everyone in the castle was affected by the tense nervousness that seemed to pervade the place, but Nurse Crombie, as starchy as her voluminous apron and the cap sitting squarely on her straight greying hair, had an efficient manner that inspired confidence. She organized a special room for the confinement, and when Melda's first pains began, she shepherded the girl there and banned Ruairidh from even opening the door.

'The father can not be present at the birth,' she lectured when he protested vehemently at being excluded. 'It is just not done, and I will look after your wife. Nothing will go wrong, I assure you.'

Marianne, however, categorically refused to be kept out, but was such a nuisance that Melda asked her to go down and keep Ruairidh company.

Having timed the contractions for hours, Nurse Crombie rang for a maid when it was clear that there was some complication, and asked her to send someone for the doctor.

Luckily, Robert was on his way and arrived five minutes later, his face grim as he took the stairs two at a time. The tension was building to a climax now, in the room upstairs, in the sitting room, even in the kitchens, where Mrs Burr boiled endless kettles of water to make tea.

Ruairidh's walking up and down irritated his mother, also in a highly emotional state, and she barked, 'For goodness' sake, sit down. You're not helping anything by tramping about like a raging bull. And put out that cigarette. You've done nothing but smoke since I came in.'

'A cigarette might help you, too, Mother,' he snapped. 'You're like a hen on a hot girdle, hodging about on that chair.'

Both realizing that they might say something unforgivable in their agitation, they kept quiet until Robert came in. Holding his hand up to stop the double flow of questions, he sat down wearily. 'It's a girl, a real whopper – 9 pounds 4 ounces, but they're both well. Let Ruairidh go up to see them first, Marianne. You'll get your turn.'

When the door closed behind the young man, the doctor said, 'It's a pity it's not a boy. She had a rough time and I've told her she shouldn't have any more. I'll leave you to tell Ruairidh.'

Marianne felt as though she had just been set free from a dank prison cell. It was a girl! It would be an only child! She had been worrying for nothing!

Dorothea was the axis round which the world of Castle Lyall revolved. From the laird himself down to the little scullery maid, they were besotted by her. In the nursery, her every move was watched by Nurse Shepherd, who had been employed after Nurse Crombie moved away to attend her next confinement, and when the perambulator was put outside in the sunshine, her slightest squeak had someone running to pick her up. And the tiny red-faced bundle soon became a podgy, golden-haired, blue-eyed beauty who could smile when it suited her but found she got more attention if she went into a tantrum.

'She's got a right wee temper, that one,' Mrs Burr observed one day when the child was barely a year old.

'Aye, Cook,' Ruby smiled, 'but she's such a bonnie wee toot you canna help but like her.'

'They're going to spoil her, though, running after her like that.' She gestured towards the nurse, who was haring across the lawn to lift her charge. 'Still, if I'm right, she'll no' have things all her own way for much longer.'

'Oh, my!' Ruby said in dismay. 'Melda's no' expecting' again, is she? The doctor said she wasna to have another ane.'

'I'd say she was in her third month, by the look o' her.'

'Well, we'll be in for it now. The mistress'll no' be pleased.'

Marianne was definitely not pleased when Melda at last plucked up courage to tell her. 'You stupid girl!' she burst out. 'You know you shouldn't –'

Melda, however, was subservient no longer. 'It was Ruairidh's idea as much as mine,' she interrupted. 'Dorrie's being made too much of, and the only way to stop that is to give her a brother.'

'A brother?' Marianne echoed faintly. 'How can you be so sure it'll be a boy?'

'I can't be sure, of course, but Ruairidh wants a son.'

'But you'll be endangering your life, didn't you remind him of that?'

'No, I deliberately made light of any problems. I want a son as much as he does – a son and a daughter, the perfect gentleman's family.'

'I think you should talk to your father. Um . . . how far on are you?'

'Four months.'

Marianne bristled. 'Why didn't you tell me before?'

'Because I knew what you and my father would say, and neither of you can do anything about it now.'

Their eyes locked, each knowing what the other was thinking, yet bound by old promises not to speak of it.

As Marianne had foreseen, Robert was truly angry when Melda did acquaint him of her condition. 'I told you!' he shouted. 'Your womb . . . oh, I can't explain it to you, but you're going to have to look after yourself. No lifting Dorothea, no running, even hurrying, and you'll have to lie flat for at least the last two months.'

'Is it as bad as that?' Melda faltered.

'I wouldn't have advised you against a second child otherwise. I'd better speak to Ruairidh.' He looked at the pale girl sadly. 'You won't have to let him . . .'

'I can't expect him not to.' She paused, her eyes filling with tears. 'He might look for somebody else.'

'He'd have me to reckon with if he did!' Robert declared hotly.

'Father, don't say anything to him, please. I'll be very careful till the baby's born and I'm sure I'll be all right.'

'As long as you remember then.'

For the next three months, Marianne and Melda were on the defensive when they spoke to each other, but when the young mother-to-be was ordered to lie flat in bed, her mother-in-law surprised her by being very attentive. Marianne had more or less resigned herself to Fate. What she actually told herself was that there was many a slip 'twixt cup and lip, as she had heard Miss Edith say more than once.

As it happened, the old saying was truly prophetic. Melda lost the baby near the end of the seventh month, and her father pulled no punches when he tackled his son-in-law. 'God knows what you think you're doing, Ruairidh. I advised Melda last time that she should not have any more, but I am going to order it this time. If you make her pregnant again, you will be as good as passing a death sentence on her.'

'Oh, no!' Ruairidh was appalled. 'I'd never do anything to hurt her, Robert, you know that.'

'But you are young and virile, and passion is no respecter of intentions, however sincerely meant, and even if you practise birth control, which is used all over nowadays, there would always be a chance that you'd forget, or something would go wrong, and . . . where would you be? You could possibly get the son I know perfectly well you want, but you would probably lose your wife. I would advise a hysterectomy as soon as possible.'

'A hysterectomy? What does that involve?'

'It is an operation to remove a woman's reproductive organs.'

Ruairidh looked utterly shocked at this. 'Is this a . . . dangerous operation?'

'There is always danger when an operation is performed, but methods are improving all the time, and I would say there is little chance of anything going wrong. A few weeks in hospital, possibly a month or two of being careful not to do anything strenuous, and then she should be as right as rain.' He hesitated before stating what should have been obvious but which had clearly not occurred to Ruairidh. 'It means, of course, that she can have no more children.'

'I see.' His face blanching, the younger man fell silent, obviously turning it over in his mind, but at last he murmured, 'I'd rather have Melda fit and well than have a son and heir, if that's what you're worrying about. Will it be up to her to decide whether or not . . . ?'

'I will give her the choice, and you must persuade her that if she does not agree to it, her health will deteriorate . . .'

Marianne's relief on hearing this news made her feel as if she would be at peace for ever, though she wished that she had known from the outset that Ruairidh and Melda had been destined not to have a son; she could have saved herself years of fretting. She revelled in the thought that only the purest of blood would run through the veins of future Glendarrils, whoever inherited the title.

It was not altogether surprising that Marianne overlooked the possibility that her granddaughter – also granddaughter of Duncan Peat – could eventually produce a son, who would be heir after Ruairidh, could be the next but one Lord. It had been so long since Andrew Rennie had told her that the title could be passed through the distaff side, and so much had happened in the years between, that she had blotted it from her memory. As far as she was concerned, the danger of contamination was finally over.

The folk of the glen, of course, ignorant of Melda's real parentage and believing the title had to be passed directly to a male, were bitterly disappointed that the Bruce-Lyall line would stop with the present Master. Mima Rattray, as usual, held forth to all who entered the post office. 'It's an awful pity Master Ranald was killed. He'd have made a string of sons to carry on his name.'

One brave soul had the temerity to put her right on one point. 'Only one would have inherited the title, though.'

The postmistress gave her head an irritated shake. 'I know *that*! What I meant was he'd have made sure there was aye a son to follow on. Like, if there was another war.'

'There can never be another war, Mima. The Great War, as they're calling it, was the war to end all wars, wasn't it?'

Feeling that she was coming off worst in the discussion, Mima tutted loudly. 'You never know, Maggie. Nothing on this earth's ever certain, and if there *was* another war, Master Rannie would have had plenty stand-bys.'

Maggie thought it wise to climb down now, but she couldn't resist one last barb. 'Aye, well, you're maybe richt, but Master Rannie's no' here now, is he?'

She had left virtually nothing for the postmistress to take as surrender. 'No,' she admitted, truculently, 'I was just saying . . .'

The entry of another customer brought this difference of opinion to a close, and Maggie went out quite pleased at having beaten Mima for once. The postmistress, however, immediately started up the same subject again, knowing that little Lizzie Black was easily browbeaten.

Dorothea took full advantage of being the centre of attention in the castle, screaming her head off when she didn't get what she wanted, and by her second birthday, she was beginning to get out of hand altogether. Her father, therefore, issued instructions that she must be disciplined, that she would have to learn to control her temper.

Ruby, of course, was loud in protest at this . . . in the kitchen. 'Poor wee Dorrie, she's only two, for goodness' sake. What does he expect?'

Mrs Burr shook her head. 'She'll have to learn. She's that spoiled she thinks the whole place revolves round her.'

'So it should, she's such a bonnie wee thing with her fair curly head and rosy cheeks. She's that like her father, with the same blue eyes and all, but she's got her mother's spirit, if you ask me.'

'Melda had aye plenty spirit,' chimed in Jessie Black. 'I was at the school wi' her, and she was awful clever. We could never understand why she didna go to the university in Aberdeen, for we was sure her father wanted her to be a doctor like him. Of course, she was aye close to the laird's boys, an' maybe that's when she made up her mind on being mistress here some day.'

Mrs Burr, a native of the glen who had married a Glaswegian and only returned to her place of birth when he died, now said, 'Mima Rattray tell't me once there was mair atween her an' Master Ranald than folk kent. Becky Drummond once tell't her that Ranald tell't *her he* was meetin' Melda in the woods – an' that was on the last nicht o' his last leave, poor soul.'

Jessie frowned. 'But a'body kens Becky Drummond tell't lies. I never believed a word she said, though she *was* the minister's lassie.'

Ruby, as Melda's personal maid – although she was more often doing a housekeeper's work – was closer to her than any of them. 'Ranald was a bit o' a rogue though, an' I think she saw through him. Any road, you canna deny she loves the Master.'

'Aye, you're right there,' Mrs Burr sighed. 'And he loves her, and all. They'll make a fine laird and his lady when the time comes.'

With her daughter taken over by the nursemaid, Melda felt time weighing heavily on her hands, and decided one day in the autumn of 1922 to cycle down to the mill to see what exactly went on there. Unlike his father, Hamish welcomed his son's wife's interest in the family business and took her through every process himself. She was intent on seeing everything, but he did notice that she spent more time in the design department than anywhere else. Joking, he said, 'Would you like to try your hand at creating a new patterned cloth?'

'Would I like?' she exclaimed, clapping her hands, 'I'd be delighted.'

Although most of the men in the department had known Melda as a child, and had heard then that she was clever, they were still amazed at the technicality of the drawings she produced and the suggestions she made as to the colours which should be used in the checks. Hamish was absolutely stunned, and said she could come in as often as she liked to give him some more ideas.

The only person who was not pleased about her newly discovered talent was her mother-in-law. 'Your father wasn't happy about me going round the place,' she reminded Hamish.

'I am not my father,' he smiled, 'and things are different now. We have quite a few women workers – some of the men did not come back from the war, remember.'

They both fell silent at that, remembering the tall fair-haired boy with the twinkling eyes and ready charm who had not returned either.

Before Melda took up her appointment, as she thought of it, even if her father-in-law had not meant it as such, she decided to take a day in Edinburgh to see the kind of materials that were most popular in the shops, for ladies' and gents' wear.

'Are you sure about this?' Ruairidh asked. 'You surely don't want to tie yourself down to a job, do you?'

'I'd love to tie myself down,' she laughed, 'especially to a job I'd really love doing. I feel useless at home, you know, spending most of my time out with the dogs, or chatting to one of the gardeners. Your mother does her bit, looking after the needs of the glen folk, so why shouldn't I do something, too? Nursie hardly ever lets me spend any time alone with Dorrie, so . . .'

'I see your point. Well, if you like, I can come with you and we'll make it a little holiday – say a long week-end? What d'you think? Or we could make it London, if you like?'

'I think Edinburgh'll do for a start.'

Somewhat taken aback at first by their proposal, Hamish suddenly became very enthusiastic, sending off telegrams to the managers of several stores asking for their co-operation.

'Looks like Melda's going into the mill,' Mima Rattray observed to the first customer after he had left the post office. 'Her and the Master are having a trip to Edinburgh to look round the big shops to see what sells best.'

Chapter Twenty-five

In late spring of 1925, Melda decided that she would like to try something new. She had introduced many variations of designs for the different kinds of cloth the mill produced, and she needed another challenge.

'I was thinking of finding out about Fair Isle patterns,' she told Ruairidh one day. 'Jean Lambie's cousin's here on holiday from Shetland, and I began copying from her scarf, but there must be other patterns and combinations of colours. So if I go there and –'

Her husband frowned. 'I can't go traipsing up to Shetland with you just now. I've to supervise the worsteds and tweeds we'll offer the buyers for next winter, and Father's trying to set up a better range of light-weight flannels for ladies' costumes.'

'I wanted to go on my own anyway. Fiona goes home next week, so I if I travelled on the boat with her, we could discuss –'

'Can't you discuss whatever you want to discuss with her before she leaves?'

Irritated that he couldn't understand how much better it would be if she saw things for herself Melda said sharply, 'She can't keep dozens of patterns in her head. It took me ages to write down one, and she told me she has a whole set of charts on graph paper at home. She says that's the proper way to knit Fair Isle, not written in words like in the leaflets wool shops sell – two brown, one natural, three white, and so on – and she's willing to let me copy them.'

'Why don't you ask her to do it for you? Or ask her to post them on and you can return them when you've copied them? I'm not keen on the idea of you going so far away by yourself.'

She had to laugh at this. 'I'm not a child now, Ruairidh. I'll be twenty-three soon, and what harm could I come to in Shetland?'

After a moment's reflection, he said, 'I'd be happier if someone was with you. What about Ruby?'

'Oh, you know Ruby. She'd always want to show she's a lady's maid, and I don't want anyone to say I think I'm any different from them.'

'Jean Lambie, then? If I'm any judge, she'd jump at the chance of a free holiday with her cousin.'

'Wouldn't that leave you short of a knitter?'

'Yes, but we'd manage, somehow.'

Ruairidh was not put to the test, however. When Hamish heard of Melda's plan, he pronounced it a dashed good idea. 'And you don't need a guard dog,' he smiled, patting her shoulder. 'No doubt there will be other women on the boat home.' He turned to his son. 'She's a big girl now, Ruairidh. You'll have to let go of her, and there's no need for her to hurry back. She can take the whole summer if she likes. That nurse can keep Dorothea under control.'

Ruairidh gave in, but told his wife later, 'It's all very well for Father, but I can't do without you all summer, my darling.'

Not sure whether to be annoyed that he thought of her as a chattel or to treat it as a compliment, Melda opted for the latter and gave a soft laugh. 'It shouldn't take long to copy down Fiona's charts, but I'd like to ask her friends as well, to get as many designs as I can while I'm there. I'm sure all the shepherds' wives'll be itching to start knitting when they see them, and I won't be more than three or four weeks away.'

'Four weeks?' he groaned. 'That's a lifetime.'

Marianne's air of suppressed excitement puzzled Hamish, but he asked nothing until Ruairidh had left in his new Singer with Melda and her luggage – Jean Lambie was to be collected on the way.

'What's going on?' he demanded, eyeing her suspiciously as they closed the big oaken door and returned to the dining room to finish breakfast. 'You're up to something.'

After a brief hesitation, she said, 'I'm in the process of creating a grandson for us.'

He tutted his displeasure at what he took to be levity. 'I can't see Melda even looking at another man, and besides, as you know full well, she can't have any more children, sons or otherwise.'

Her finger tapped the side of her nose secretively. 'Not Melda.'

'Good God! You're surely not going to encourage Ruairidh to –'

'I'm just giving him the opportunity. If I can get him to fall for one of the girls I'm going to invite on Sunday afternoons –'

'But, Marianne, even if he makes a son with another girl, it would be illegitimate, and think of the scandal there would be.'

'I thought Andrew could arrange for an annulment of his marriage.'

Hamish snorted. 'On what grounds, may I ask? Ruairidh can't claim non-consummation, not when Melda's already given him a daughter.'

'A divorce, then.' Marianne's sharpness betrayed her irritation. 'Then a son would be legitimate, otherwise there won't be an heir to follow him, unless you're hiding some relatives up your sleeve.'

He shrugged. 'I don't know of any still alive, not even forty-second cousins, and I don't think even Andrew could dig any up.'

On Sunday, the Hon. Patricia Matthewson roared up the drive to Castle Lyall just before three o'clock in a red two-seater sports car with her grandmother looking apprehensive at her side. Marianne, who hadn't seen Lady Matthewson since Hector's funeral twenty-three years earlier, was dismayed to find that Patricia was not what anyone could call a beauty – having what could only be described as buck teeth, and a neighing laugh to match.

Ruairidh did as he had been instructed by his mother and asked the girl to have a game of tennis, but he could not understand why his mother had made contact with the Matthewsons at all. By the time a dainty afternoon tea was served, he'd had enough, and so, pleading a mountain of paper work to clear, he disappeared into the library.

At dinner that night, he turned on Marianne angrily. 'Don't ask me to be nice to that monster again! She couldn't say anything without braying and it went right through my head.'

The following Sunday went much better. Lord and Lady Furness had brought their whole family with them – two sons who had been at boarding school with Ruairidh, and a daughter he and Ranald had both enjoyed seeing when they were in their early teens. Kitty was even more attractive now, and was obviously attracted to him, lying close beside him when he flopped down on the lawn after the exertion of the doubles match. The two mothers were chatting in the shade facing towards them, the fathers were smoking pipes on a bench near the library window but also watching them, and when Edwin and Sydney, both mad about cars, disappeared to the garage to inspect Hamish's new Lagonda, their sister put her lips to Ruairidh's ear.

'Can't we go somewhere a bit more secluded?' she whispered. 'This is like sitting in a goldfish bowl.'

Her perfume had started a flicker of desire in him, her breath fanned it to a glowing ember, and jumping up, he guided her towards the path to the woods. He knew he shouldn't, but he was missing a woman's company. He steered her past the old hut where he and Melda had first made love, and remembering that evening made him realize the risk he was taking now. 'We'd better turn back, Kitty.'

'Oh, Ruairidh,' she pouted, 'don't you like being alone with me?'

'I do, Kit, but . . . it's playing with fire.'

421

She slid her pointed tongue seductively over her lips. 'And you're scared of being burned? We used to have fun together in the old days and I quite fancy getting a bit singed, myself.'

He was beginning to fancy more than a slight singeing, but he said, 'No, Kit. We're older now, and I've an adult need in me.'

'So have I,' she murmured, turning to press her body against his, 'and it's best to give in to your feelings.'

Her kiss, long and searching, rekindled his inner fire so that his mouth sought hers again, his hands went involuntarily to the small of her back then parted to follow the swells of her buttocks. He would have been lost if Kitty had left him to continue at his own pace, but in trying to hurry him on, she guided one of his hands to where she had opened the buttons of her thin dress. His fingers sank into one breast for only a second before he jumped away from her – alarmed by his reaction to the stimulus. 'We can't . . . I'm a married man.'

'So were nearly all the others I've had,' she murmured huskily. 'I get a bigger thrill knowing the man's another woman's husband, and they say it's more exciting for them, too.'

The knowledge that he was just another married man she wanted to add to her list of conquests sickened him, and although it did cross his mind that he wouldn't be taking advantage of a naïve virgin if he did take her, he pushed her roughly away. 'No,' he said firmly, 'I love my wife and I'd never even dream of being unfaithful to her.'

He walked her back to the castle without saying another word, left her on the lawn, then marched straight past both sets of parents and upstairs to his room. Stretching out on his bed, he wondered if he'd been a fool. Nobody would have known – except himself, and that was what had stopped him. He would never have lived easily if he'd done what he wanted. He couldn't have faced Melda without remembering and feeling ashamed and guilty. A deep remorse flooded through him as he recognized the passion building up in his loins at just the memory of Kitty's softly curved body and the sweetness of her kisses.

Damn it all! he told himself furiously. Melda's every bit as sweet and curvaceous. He had been tempted because he was missing her, and he should be thankful that he'd had the willpower to withstand that temptation. Vowing that he would never again get into a situation like that, whoever the girl was, he wondered why his mother had begun to invite people to the house, something she very rarely did. Worse still, why were they families with marriageable daughters?

'I'm certain something happened,' Marianne said triumphantly. 'He's ashamed of himself, that's why he hasn't come down to dinner.'

'It's nothing to be pleased about,' Hamish frowned, 'and please do not speak about it in front of the servants.'

It took a great effort of will on her part to wait, and as soon as they were alone in the drawing room, she started. 'I could read the signs, you know.'

'You think they'd been fornicating?'

'There's no need to be so crude,' she objected.

'That's the only word for it, the only decent word, that is.'

423

Marianne scowled at him. 'I can't invite her every week, that would be too obvious, but I'm sure they've started something and we'll have to hope it develops naturally.'

At that moment their son walked in, and without thinking, Marianne said archly, 'Kitty'll make a good wife to some man, won't she?'

Ruairidh's expression was icy. 'I hadn't given it a thought. Melda's the only wife I'll ever want.'

Marianne's face warning him not to say anything, Hamish muttered, 'I'd better take the dogs out.' The two red setters, grandsons of Romulus and Remus, sprang from the hearthrug and dashed through the door as soon as he opened it.

'I just came down to say good night, Mother,' Ruairidh mumbled, 'but before I go up again . . .' His face turning scarlet, he averted his head for a moment and then burst out, 'You're so transparent, so devious, it'd be laughable if it weren't so pathetic.'

She did not seem one whit abashed that he had caught her out. 'You need a wife who can give you a son, and Melda can't now she's been rendered useless. Your father would like to see you with an heir before he dies.'

The slur on his wife made him see red. 'If Father's so desperate for a bloody heir to follow me, why doesn't *he* do the needful? I've seen him eyeing Nursie, so he must still be capable.'

Outraged, Marianne cried, 'How dare you speak of your father like that? He'd never dream of being unfaithful to me.'

'And I'll never be unfaithful to Melda, though I came damned near it today before I saw sense.'

Marianne pounced. 'So I was right! You and Kitty *had* been –'

Hanging his head, Ruairidh whispered, 'That's what you planned, was it? Well, she tried her best, but I did *not* give in to her. All the same, I went further than I should, and if you knew how badly I feel, you'd have some pity for me.'

After a moment's reflective silence, Marianne said softly, 'Shall we let it be our secret, then?'

No more girls were offered as sacrificial lambs, and although Kitty Furness turned up the following Sunday, Ruairidh kept to his room and left his mother to excuse his absence. He was pleased to receive a letter from Melda the following day, asking him to collect her from the North Boat at Aberdeen on Wednesday – pleased, yet apprehensive.

Describing her stay in Lerwick, Melda could sense her mother-in-law's antagonism; Marianne's jealousy of her son's wife was almost tangible. Not only had Melda returned with a huge selection of Fair Isle designs and instructions for knitting them into scarves, ladies' jumpers, men's pullovers, gloves, children's outdoor sets consisting of patterned tops and plain pantaloons, but she had also been told how the various dyes were obtained for the Shetland floss, the two-ply wool in which all true Fair Isle work is carried out.

Having shown her husband and his parents her range of graphs, she produced samples of the fine wool. 'The older women just use white, natural, grey and moorat – this mossy brown – that was traditional, but the younger ones are using other colours as well, not garishly bright like some national shops do under the pretence of them being real Fair Isle, but muted shades of rose, rust, lemon, blue, green, all dyed from woodland plants – lichens, grasses and natural sources.'

She glanced around her three listeners. Hamish was studying the skeins of wool as if trying to visualize the transformation from the dirty fleeces of the mountain sheep to this fascinating rainbow. Marianne had the hint of a sneer on her face as she contemplated the graphs with their explanatory keys at the side. Ruairidh was the only one to meet Melda's eyes, and instead of lingering on her with the love she had expected, he turned his head immediately away.

'They're not all the same,' Marianne observed abruptly. 'Look, a cross on this one stands for natural, but on this one, natural's a blank square, and it's the same with all the colours . . . different on every sheet of paper.'

Melda did her best to stifle her impatience. 'That's because I got them from different women. Each one writes them down in the way her mother taught her. They hardly need to look at the patterns now, in any case, they've knitted them so often. They stand outside their doors, their hands working back and forth like shuttles, you'd hardly credit the speed they can go, and everything – from the largest man's pullover to gloves and scarves – is done on four needles . . . wires, as they call them.'

Marianne's eyebrows rose in disbelief. 'They can't knit standing up . . . not when they're using a lot of colours at a time. The balls of wool would get all tangled up.'

'If you had taken time to look properly,' Melda began, an edge to her voice, 'you'd have seen it's seldom more than two colours at a time, and they break off each colour at the end of the last row it is used, and join it in when it's needed again. I know that sounds as if there'll be an awful lot of ends, but they darn them all in so you'd never notice, and it means there's no long stretches of wool to snag on rings or fingernails when they're being worn or washed. And the wrong side of the work is as neat as the right side.'

'Stop criticizing, Marianne,' Hamish snapped, as his wife opened her mouth again, 'and give credit where it's due. Meida has done a marvellous job, and we'd better have a selection of Fair Isle goods ready for the buyers coming to get their winter stock. Nothing big, of course, maybe gloves and scarves, enough to whet their appetites.'

That night, bitterly disappointed that her husband was lying like a stone beside her instead of loving her as she had hoped, Melda tried to bring him round. 'I can't understand why your mother's annoyed at me. I was just trying to get more interesting work for our knitters and extra business for the mill.'

Having brooded about his own misdemeanour since Sunday, Ruairidh decided he would have to get it off his chest before he could resume relations with his wife. He had not, however, had time to think how to confess without hurting her. 'That's not why she's annoyed at you,' he began. 'She blames you for there not being an heir to come after me.'

Her heart sank. 'We've always known that, so why are you telling me now? Have you done something that needs that as an excuse?'

'I've done nothing . . . not really.' It was the first lie he had ever told her, and he could not keep it up. 'Oh,

427

Melda, I've got to tell you. Mother invited the Furness family for afternoon tea one of the Sundays you were away, and Kitty . . . I took her for a walk after we'd had a game of tennis.'

'Kitty Furness? Wasn't she one of the girls your mother tried to get you or Ranald to marry at one time? You must have known she was up to something, inviting them here.' Only then did she understand what her mother-in-law had wanted to happen. 'Are you trying to tell me . . . you made love to Kitty Furness?' Her eyes brimmed with tears at the thought of how quickly he had betrayed her.

'No, Melda! It's what she wanted, yes, and I nearly did.'

'Nearly did?' Her voice was heavily sarcastic. 'How nearly? Did you kiss her and fondle her, and . . . and . . . oh, how could you, Ruairidh? I know you can't stop once you're roused.'

'I can't deny I was roused, but I thought of you, my darling, and shoved her away.' He turned towards her in appeal. 'Melda, I could say it was all down to her, but it was as much my fault. I wish you could understand how ashamed I am, though I wouldn't blame you if you can't forgive me . . . but . . . please try, please!'

Her mouth was trembling. 'You're sure you didn't . . . ?'

'I just kissed her, I swear it, but it's been eating at my innards ever since. I'm so sorry, my dearest! I don't even like her and I've hurt the only woman I'll ever love.'

She *was* hurt, so much that her first instinct was to retaliate by hurting him, but what was the point?

Neither Ruairidh nor Melda tumbled to what was going on that summer. He was pleased to be trusted to deal with so much of the business of the mill on his own, and she was delighted to be allowed to promote the Fair Isle side single-handedly. The fact that they were never away at the same time, that she was sent off perhaps a week after her husband returned, and vice versa, escaped them in the satisfaction of their work, and they spent what little time they had in each other's company discussing plans.

Ruairidh did think it strange that he bumped into Kitty Furness in Edinburgh on one trip, Newcastle on another, but because she appeared to be just as surprised by the meetings as he was, he accepted them as coincidences and didn't mention them to his wife. There was no sense in making her think things that weren't true, because he had learned his lesson and had refused Kitty's invitations in both cities to have a drink at her hotel, nor had he taken up her barely veiled hints that he should take her to his.

When, however, she appeared one Sunday afternoon in September at Castle Lyall while Melda was in Glasgow, he could see his mother's hand in it and determined to call her bluff. He asked Kitty to have a game of tennis, and afterwards, flopped down with her at the edge of the lawn. When, as he had known she would, Kitty suggested going for a walk, he said, in a loud stage whisper, 'Why don't we go up to my room instead?'

His mother's intake of breath satisfied him that she had heard and he prayed that she would be so outraged that she would stop him there and then. She did nothing, however, so he helped Kitty to her feet, put an arm round her waist and let his hand rest on her hip as he steered her past the deckchair.

That was when Marianne's parasol came sharply down on the back of his legs, and never was he more glad of any pain. 'You will not take that girl to your bed!' she said sharply. 'This is not a brothel! Surely you didn't expect me to turn a blind eye to your . . .' She paused briefly, searching for a suitable word, and recalling what Hamish had said earlier, she ended,' . . . to you fornicating under my roof.'

He turned to face her. 'I thought you wanted me to put Kit in such a position that I'd have to marry her?'

Kitty jumped in at this. 'Here, wait a minute! Who said anything about marriage? I'm only out for a good time. I don't want to end up with no waist, varicose veins and a noisy baby tying me down.'

'I know you don't. It was my mother's idea . . .'

'And I thought you'd fallen for my charms,' she murmured, doing her best to look crestfallen.

'Kit, I'm truly sorry for subjecting you to –'

She giggled now. 'Don't be sorry, Ruairidh. I knew you wouldn't say that in front of your mother if you meant it, so I guessed what you were up to. It's a pity, though. I'd have enjoyed finding out how good a lover you are.' She turned to look scornfully at the older woman. 'You obviously don't know how much your son loves his wife, Lady Glendarril, and I wish I knew why you've been trying to use me as a wedge between them.'

'Melda can't have any more children,' Ruairidh explained, 'so there won't be any heir to the title when I die.'

'She could only give him a daughter,' Marianne said bitterly.

Triumph replaced the puzzlement on Kitty's face. 'Well, there you are!' she beamed. 'Dorrie will marry eventually, and she'll surely have a son. Hey presto, there's the next heir.'

'She's right, Mother,' Ruairidh said eagerly. 'And you'd better keep your fingers in your own pies after this. Come on, Kitty, I'll see you to your car.'

Teasing him, she backed away, looking afraid. 'I don't know if I can trust you. You might throw me into the back seat and rape me.' She winked saucily at Marianne as she turned away.

When Ruairidh joined his mother again, she said angrily, 'That exhibition was all for my benefit, was it? I thought you meant what you said. I thought –'

'Mother, we all know what thought did. I knew you wouldn't let me take Kit to bed.'

'I see. You depended on me to stop you? What if I hadn't?'

A boyish grin curved his mouth. 'Kit wouldn't have taken another refusal from me, so I'd have been on top of her right now and you'd maybe have got your wish.'

'You're being very indelicate,' she frowned.

He locked eyes with her. 'You've been far worse than indelicate. I've told Melda about Kitty and luckily for you, she doesn't want any unpleasantness, otherwise I'd have taken her and our daughter away from here altogether. I might yet, if you try any more of your tricks.'

The incident put an effective end to Kitty's pursuit of Ruairidh, and to Marianne's attempt at getting him to provide an heir for the title. Unfortunately, it did nothing to stop her jealousy of her daughter-in-law, who was building up a very profitable Fair Isle department at the mill, and to whom Hamish was referring more and more for advice on current trends in woollen fabrics.

Melda was content with her life and was careful, in her differences with her mother-in-law, not to let them escalate into full-blown rows; she no longer held Marianne in awe, but she didn't fancy making a mortal enemy of her. She did, however, stand up to Marianne if she deemed it necessary, blocking her from getting her own way.

'I used to think Melda was a quiet wee mouse,' Hamish confided to his son while they were having a glass of port and a cigar after dinner one night. 'But she's developed quite a shrewd brain, and she commands a lot of respect from the workers, and the buyers from even the largest of stores. The trouble is, your mother's been cock of the walk for so long I think she's just a teeny bit jealous.'

The understatement of the century, Ruairidh thought, yet oddly enough, it didn't worry him now. His wife could hold off herself, she wouldn't let anyone ride roughshod over her, not even his mother. And that was as it should be.

Chapter Twenty-six

Just as Marianne had done so many years before, Melda had sent her child to the glen school, but Dorothea didn't fit in as well as her father and mother had done. She was quite bright and outgoing, but her arrogance kept the local children from being friends with her. Nevertheless, with her keen willingness to learn, she soon outstripped others of her own age.

The dominie – forty-six-year-old Philip Stewart, not a product of the glen but the best candidate who had applied on Willie Wink's retirement some years before – even went to the mill one day to talk to her father. 'Dorothea could go to university in time, so I hope you will allow her to go on to Mackie after the holidays. She will be given every bit as good an education there as in any public school for girls that you care to name.'

'Oh, I know that, and her mother would slaughter me if I suggested sending her away,' Ruairidh smiled. 'My wife was a product of Mackie herself, so I am sure she will want Dorothea to follow in her footsteps.'

He made to turn away, then realizing that the other man looked as though he had something else to say, he waited, having a fairly good idea that it would be about

Dorrie not behaving properly, and after opening and shutting his mouth a couple of times, Mr Stewart said, very apologetically, 'I do not relish having to say anything like this, but . . .'

'Yes?' Ruairidh encouraged. 'Whatever you have to say, spit it out. What has she done?'

The dominie looked more uncomfortable than ever. 'I am afraid . . . she is developing rather rapidly . . .'

'She's only eleven, for heaven's sake, man. She has hardly started to develop yet.'

'That is perhaps true physically, but –' Mr Stewart broke off, wringing his hands.

This annoyed Ruairidh greatly. Whatever the girl had got up to, it surely couldn't be as bad as . . . but Philip Stewart was from a little village somewhere on the west coast, and he was likely easily shocked. 'Has she been swearing, or what?'

'Oh no, her manner of speech in class is exemplary, although she is inclined to use rather colourful language in the playground. It is a different . . . oh, this is most difficult, Mr Bruce-Lyall.' He hesitated, but catching signs of impatience in his listener's face, he hurried on, 'She is taking a great deal too much interest in boys.' He paused again for a moment. 'I have caught her myself teasing them.'

'What d'you mean, "teasing them"?' Ruairidh's voice was dangerously calm if the other man could have recognized it.

'She was . . . lifting her skirts and showing them her . . . thigh.' He stopped altogether now, his face beetroot red, his eyes sliding away.

'I am sure there had been a perfectly simple explanation for it. She could have fallen and skinned her leg or . . . or something like that. Was that the only incident, or have there been others?'

'That was the only one I saw.'

'I must assume that you are too ready to jump to conclusions.'

'Mr Bruce-Lyall, I am dreadfully sorry I brought the subject up. You are most likely right in what you said, and I was making a mountain out of a molehill. Please, I can assure you that nothing like this will happen again.'

Thinking that the whole situation was somewhat ridiculous, Ruairidh gave a snorting laugh. 'What did you think she was doing? Letting them put their hands up her knickers? At eleven?'

A subdued impression of a smile crossed the dominie's face. 'Yes, it does sound far-fetched, doesn't it?'

Positive that it was exactly what the man had thought, Ruairidh said sharply, 'Too far-fetched for my liking, and I want to hear no more of this kind of thing.'

He did not tell Melda what had been said – he knew it would just upset her – and he did not approach Dorothea when he went home because he didn't want to put ideas into her head. The dominie was a narrow-minded, dirty-minded fool, and had been making something out of nothing, possibly to titillate himself, and even though he was a good teacher, he would be out on his ear if he ever said anything like that again.

As it happened, it was Kirsty, one of the large clan of Blacks, who reprimanded the girl. 'You shouldn't carry on with the boys like you do, Dorrie,' she told her one afternoon on their way home from school.

'I wasn't carrying on with them!' protested Dorothea.

'Oh, you little fibber! I seen you! You and our Billy and Tommy Rattray!'

'We were only having a laugh. They wanted to see my legs.'

'Well, don't let them see them again.' Just months older in actual age but five years older in worldly wisdom, Kirsty knew what her brother and Tommy Rattray had been after. One of the older boys had tried to get his hand up the leg of *her* knickers last year – she'd kicked his shins – but Dorrie was maybe too much of a lady to do that, though it didn't stop her from swearing like a trooper.

Dorothea had been quite peeved at Kirsty Black. What right had she to tell anybody off for something she likely did herself? Besides, Billy Black and Tommy Rattray had only been kids and she *had* only been having a bit of fun with them, but now, a year later, it was *Jakey* Black she was interested in, he was so tall and good-looking. He wasn't very clever, he'd left the glen school as soon as he was fourteen, but that made him all the more interesting. He was a gardener's boy at the castle now, so he was *hers*, wasn't he – to do with what she liked . . . and even to let him do what he liked to her, as long as he didn't punch her or anything like that.

It was quite easy to get him alone. She waited till she knew he'd be inside the stables and then went in after him, making sure nobody saw her because she knew she would be in trouble if she was caught. He had looked up in

436

surprise the first time, and she felt so shy all of a sudden that she couldn't tell him she wanted him to kiss her, just to see what it was like. She'd been alone with him several times after that, and it had finally dawned on the big galoot that she was making up to him.

That was when he grabbed her and pushed her against the wooden wall. It wasn't as nice as she had hoped. His mouth was all slobbery and his breath smelled, and she couldn't get away from him no matter how hard she struggled. To make it worse, his horrible great hand had touched her chest, and his knee was trying to prise her legs open.

Dargie, almost retiring age now, had seen Miss Dorrie coming out of the stable once or twice before, looking a wee bit guilty, and he'd wondered what she'd been up to, but he'd never dreamed . . . ! 'You filthy bugger!' he shouted, yanking the lanky boy away from the girl by the scruff of his neck. 'God Almighty! What the hell d'you think you're playin' at? Get oot o' here this minute, and it's the last I want to see o' you.'

Crimson-faced, the youth scampered off, and the old gardener turned to the girl now. 'As for you, Miss Dorrie, I some think you were askin' for it, but maybe you're no' auld enough to realize . . .' He had to stop, for a sickness was flooding up in him at the thought of what could have happened if he hadn't stopped it when he did. Jakey Black was just fifteen, but he could easily father a bairn, and the lass was twelve or thereabouts, so she'd be capable of conceiving.

She drew herself to her full height and looked him straight in the eye. 'You won't say anything, Dargie!'

He felt quite shocked, for it was an order not a request . . . the brazen little madam! 'I'll no' say anything, Miss Dorrie, but no' for your sake. I wouldna like to think on the hurt it would cause your mother and father if they ken't their lassie had been lettin' a stable laddie paw at her like yon. But if this kind o' thing happens again, wi' ony o' my men, I'll go straight to your father and tell him. D'you hear me, now? You'll regret it if you dinna heed what I say, for you could easy land in the family way.'

Walking away from him with her head in the air, Dorrie suddenly recalled a conversation she'd heard about a year ago between the two young parlour maids.

'Ooh, Jenny, you never let him?' one of them had asked in a shocked voice.

'Well, I never meant to let him,' Jenny had said, 'but he . . . well, Vi'let, you ken.'

'No, I dinna ken. What did he dae?'

'You ken! My mother aye tell't me no' to let a lad inside my bloomers, but he was kissin' me and strokin' the top o' my leg an' afore I kent what he was daein' he was inside me, never mind my bloomers.'

Violet had given a gasp at that, and then, spotting the girl nearby, had hissed, 'Watch what your sayin', Jenny.'

So that was all she had heard, Dorrie recalled, but a few months later, Jenny left suddenly, and she'd heard the other maids saying she was in the family way. But she could hardly believe what Dargie had said. That couldn't be the way to make babies. There must be more to it than what Jakey had done, but she wouldn't give anybody else the chance to do it.

Chapter Twenty-seven

As the years passed, Dorothea matured more in body than in mind, and she took no interest in the discussions going on around her, mostly concerning Hitler and the trouble he was causing in Europe. She still sulked if she didn't get her own way. At seventeen, having gained the qualifications necessary for entering university, she was determined to take up the opportunity, but she met with opposition from all quarters. The only person who encouraged her was her grandfather, who said it would do her good to knuckle down to the discipline needed in studying.

'Your mother didn't go to university,' Marianne scolded one day at Sunday lunch, 'even though she passed the entrance examinations.'

'That was different!' Melda snapped. 'There were reasons, as well you know.'

On another occasion, another attempt to make him change his mind, Ruairidh told her, 'As my daughter, you do not have to earn your living, and I do not want you to go.'

'What about thinking of what I want for a change?' Dorrie retorted. 'I can't sit around here all day looking decorative.' Giving a laugh at the very idea, she went on, 'Anyway, I'm not a very decorative person, am I?

I want to be doing something, something useful, and the only way –'

He shook his head. 'Being a wife and mother is the most useful thing a woman –'

'Why did you send me to the Academy, then, if you didn't want me to use my education? I don't feel ready to settle down and raise kids. I don't think I ever will.'

'You'll feel differently when you meet the right man,' Ruairidh soothed, out of his depth and wishing that his wife hadn't gone to Aberdeen for the day.

'*If* I ever meet the right man,' she said scathingly, 'it wouldn't make an ounce of difference. What's the point of having kids and then rejecting them . . . like you did?'

Her father gasped at this. 'You were never rejected, Dorrie! You got everything you ever wanted, far more than you needed . . .'

'But that's not love! You and Mum were always so busy with the mill, you hardly paid any attention to me.'

'Oh, come now. That's a bit too much, Dorrie. Your mother and I loved you in spite of the spoiled brat you were when you were younger.'

'Thank *you*!' she said sarcastically. 'It's nice to know what you think of me.'

At this, Ruairidh lost his temper. 'All right!' he said loudly. 'Go to university if you want to. You may learn how to behave when you are subjected to proper discipline, but do not expect to come running home here if you do not like it.'

It was while she was home for Christmas at the end of her first term as a medical student, that Dorrie met

Archie Grassie. She had gone to the midnight service on her own – her mother and father said they were too tired, and her grandparents had gone to bed early – so she made for the Bruce-Lyall pew. She enjoyed all the old carols she remembered from her childhood, and while the collection was being taken, she had a quick glance round to see who else was there, or rather, who wasn't there, because the little church was quite full. The Black tribe were out in full, she noticed, even Jakey, who had almost given her her first taste of sex. Studying him now, so rough and bucolic-looking, she wondered how she could have borne to let him touch her. Her eyes travelled on again, until she came to where the minister's wife was sitting at the other side of the aisle. The Drummonds had moved to another parish and the popular Mr Mathieson had been called to the glen. Mrs Mathieson wasn't alone today. She had a very personable young man sitting beside her – a very, *very* personable young man.

Dorrie could scarcely keep her eyes off him, and when the service ended, she kept sitting until Mrs Mathieson and her companion rose to leave. He wasn't really all that handsome, but he was well over six feet tall, with dark curly hair, and very smartly dressed. She got to her feet now and joined the moving line of people which had reduced to a mere trickle.

'Nice to see you, Dorrie, dear,' Mrs Mathieson said, as they made their way outside. 'Archie, let me introduce you to Dorothea Bruce-Lyall. Archie's my baby brother, Dorrie.'

'Not so much of the baby,' he laughed. 'I am delighted to meet you Miss Bruce-Lyall.'

'Dorrie, please,' she said breathlessly, wishing that she could sound more sophisticated.

441

'Then I am delighted to meet you, Miss Dorrie.'

'Oh, damn!' Phyllis Mathieson exclaimed, then covered her mouth in embarrassment. 'It's a good thing that only you were near enough to hear me, Dorrie, but I just remembered that Gil asked me to tell old Mrs Black something. Just carry on, Archie, I'll catch you up.'

He looked questioningly at the girl as they emerged into the crisp winter air. 'May I escort you home, Miss Dorrie? I take it you are going back to the castle?'

She couldn't help giggling. 'I don't usually wander round the glen at this time of night, but I'd be glad of an escort.'

He was extremely easy to talk to, she discovered, and even when he said that he was studying for the ministry, she still felt drawn to him, although, like her grandmother, she didn't much care for men of the cloth. Not that she had ever understood why her grandma was like that, for she was never intimidated by anybody. Still, Archie Grassie didn't look like a minister, didn't speak with the drone of a minister, and, above all, didn't make her tongue-tied like Mr Mathieson did.

Walking steadily along, careful not to step on any of the iced-over puddles glistening at the sides of the road, they told each other their hopes for the future, discussed life in their different areas of study and arrived at the door of the castle much too soon for her liking. 'Thank you for seeing me home . . . Archie,' she said, shy now that they were standing alone in the darkness with just a quick flash of moonlight as the clouds scurried across the sky.

'It was a pleasure, Miss Dorrie,' he smiled.

Going inside, she wished that he had asked to see her again, or arranged to meet her in Aberdeen, but contented herself with the hope of seeing him during their next vacation.

Dorothea's Easter visit home – so eagerly looked forward to in the hope of seeing Archie – was a sad occasion. Hamish had been suffering for days with a flu-like sore throat and a racking cough, which Marianne had been treating with a linctus, but his condition worsened on the day after his granddaughter arrived. Robert Mowatt, the girl's other grandfather, was called in, but when he came downstairs after examining his patient, his face was grave.

'I should have been called in earlier,' he said. 'His heart, which was never very strong, as you know, Ruairidh, has been under a great deal of strain from the coughing, and . . .' He looked down at his feet as if unwilling to meet his son-in-law's eyes any longer. 'I honestly can't see him pulling through this.'

Melda drew in her breath sharply. 'Oh, no! Is there nothing you can do, Father?'

'I have done all I can to make it easier for him, but . . .' He raised his head again. 'I think someone should relieve your mother, Ruairidh. She tells me she hasn't left his side for more than a few minutes since he took to his bed, and strong as she is, she can not stand up to that.'

Dorothea jumped up. 'I'll go.'

She went out before anyone could argue with her and ran upstairs anxiously. Of all her grandparents, she loved her father's father best. Both her grandmothers kept so busy that she often felt she should make an appointment to talk to them, and Grandfather Robert, being the only doctor in the glen, was often called out in the middle of a conversation with her, but Grandfather Hamish, no matter what he was doing, had always taken time to answer her questions, to allay any fears she had.

She didn't know what to expect when she went into his room, but his drawn face with the cheekbones jutting out like those of a skeleton, and the effort he was having to make to breathe, tore at her heart. If it hadn't been for the laboured movement of his chest, she might have thought he had already passed over.

'It's me, Grandfather,' she said as brightly as she could with such a heaviness in her. 'I've come to sit with you a while, if you don't mind? To give Grandma a rest.'

Marianne, a gaunt shadow of her usual self, shook her head. 'I'd rather stay here with him.'

The girl forced a smile. 'Doctor's orders, I'm afraid. Off you go, now. We'll get on fine, we always do, don't we, Grandfather?'

A ray of agreement showed in his eyes for a second, then the pain returned once more, and the coughing began. Marianne waited until it was over before she walked to the door. 'I'll have a cup of tea, then, and come right back.'

The girl sat on the chair she had vacated, still warm from her presence, and leaned forward to take the man's scrawny hand. She talked to him as if he were able to answer, although she left no awkward pauses. She told him what she did at university. She described the tutors, the large room lined with tiers of seats, where the medical students watched experiments, or scribbled in their note-books, scribbles that they would have to spend time later in deciphering and recording legibly. She also gave him little descriptions of her fellow students, how they spoke, how they dressed, how they teased each other, and was rewarded, once or twice, by a hint of a smile at his lips. But every so often she had to wait until a fresh bout of heaving coughs subsided before she could carry on.

At last, stuck for something else to say, she told him about Archie Grassie. 'I met him at the Christmas Eve service,' she explained. 'He's Mrs Mathieson's young brother, and he's at the university, too, though he's a bit older than me. He's just got another year to go before he gets his divinity degree, and I don't know where he'll be going after that. I suppose he'll have to wait till he's called to a church.'

A faint pressure on her fingers let her know that the old man had understood why she was telling him this. 'I don't know if he's the one for me, Grandfather,' she murmured, 'but I wouldn't mind if he was. I like him, and I'm sure you'll like him too.' Her mouth dried up as she realized that the two would probably never meet.

As she fumbled for the handkerchief in the pocket of her cardigan, she was surprised by a rasping, 'Don't . . . cry . . . Dorrie.' There was a long pause, the silence shattered by the whistling of his lungs, and then he said, I'm . . . happy . . . to go.'

She jumped up and kissed the wrinkly cheek, tears streaming down hers as she said, 'D'you remember taking me to see the whisky still? And telling me about my father and his brother getting drunk, and my mother having to take them home? D'you remember the time I fell in the burn when we were out walking the dogs? I could only have been about four, but I'll never forget how you waded in to pull me out. Your shoes and socks were soaking, remember?'

Another squeeze, scarcely noticeable now, made her swallow convulsively. 'You always took my side, didn't you? You always stuck up for me. Who'll I have if you leave me?'

At that moment, Marianne returned, hurrying over to assess her husband's condition. 'Go downstairs and tell your father and mother to come up,' she ordered the weeping girl.

Marianne went all to pieces when her husband was pronounced dead, and Ruairidh, at a loss as to how to deal with her, did the only thing he could think of – he telephoned Andrew Rennie, who dropped all commitments and rushed to be with Marianne at this dreadful time. He was a pillar of strength to her, enabling her to voice her feelings, as she could not do to her family.

'Oh, Andrew,' she wept, when her son and daughter-in-law left them alone, 'how am I going to live without Hamish? I admit I didn't marry him for love, but love did blossom for us and he was the best husband a woman could ever have had.'

'I know, my dear,' Andrew murmured, gripping her hand as they sat by the fire.

'I feel awful, saying that to you when I know how you must feel . . .'

'I only feel great sadness for you, Marianne. I came to think very highly, and very fondly, of Hamish, and I can fully understand the depth of your sorrow. I wish that there was some way I could eradicate it, or alleviate it, but I feel helpless . . .'

'You *are* helping me, though, Andrew. I mean, nobody can eradicate it, but you're making it easier for me to bear.'

They sat there for hours on end, neither saying much when Melda or Ruairidh came in, or when Ruby brought them a tray at lunchtime, only a perfunctory, 'Thank you', yet Marianne could actually feel the flow of affection and sympathy emanating from her old friend.

During the funeral service, unmindful of what other people would think, Andrew sat with one arm round her shoulders and his free hand grasping hers, giving her strength enough not to break down in front of the glen folk.

It was not until after the last of the visiting mourners departed – Hamish's business friends, men and women with whom he had come in contact during the latter years of his life – that Marianne said, horrified at the thought, 'You must have had to cancel an awful lot of appointments to be here for three whole days. Are you not afraid you'll lose your clients?'

Her concern touched him. 'Do not worry, my dear. The young assistant I took on some years ago has turned out so capable that when the senior partner retired last year and I stepped into his shoes, I gave Graham the chance to come in as the fourth member of the firm. He has a good manner with people, especially the old ladies – he would most likely make quite an impression on you.'

She managed to summon a smile. 'Yes, I'm an old lady now, of course.'

'I didn't mean it that way. You are not . . . you never will be . . . old to me.'

In the midst of the maelstrom that followed on the day of Hamish's death, Dorrie, with no one paying any heed to her, felt a desperate need to be alone, yet it seemed quite natural that she should meet Archie Grassie in the walk she took.

He held her hand in his as he said, 'I didn't like to intrude, but I was hoping I might meet you.' He said nothing that might upset her, just tucking her arm through his and strolling along beside her, stopping every now and then when she began recalling times past with her beloved grandfather.

'I know what it is like to be the only young person in a bereaved house,' he told her when she stopped talking. 'Everybody is too busy to consider your feelings. It was the same when my mother died.'

Coming to a prickle-free mossy patch, he made her sit down with him, and put his arm round her shoulders. 'Let it out,' he advised, 'the anger that a loved one has been taken, the resentment at being left to mourn alone, the sadness of the memories of him that should be happy. But, Dorrie, I promise that they will be happy again, once you have accepted his death.'

'How do you know all these things?' she whispered, bewildered that he was describing her feelings so accurately. 'Was it the same for you?'

'It is the same for most people, my dear.'

After that first meeting, he arranged to see her every afternoon, neither of them saying very much, but his mere presence comforted the poor girl as nothing else would have done. He sat next to her through the ordeal of the kirk service, and stood at her side during the interment. They continued to meet every afternoon, sometimes also in the evening, getting to know each other in a way that they would never have done under different circumstances, and when it was time for them to return to Aberdeen, they travelled together.

Much closer now, they saw each other every weekend, sometimes in Glendarril but mostly in the city, and one night after a particularly tender leave-taking, she told her grandfather – she often spoke to him when she was alone – that Archie Grassie *was* the man for her. 'And I'm sure he feels the same about me,' she whispered into the darkness of her room. 'He often knows exactly what I'm thinking, and not many men can do that with a girl.'

Something, however, kept her from telling her grandmother about Archie. She couldn't say what it was, just a feeling that the old lady wouldn't approve, but there was plenty of time to think about that when their studies were over.

With war looming ever more certainly, Dorrie was planning for the actuality of it. It was all very well for her father to say she should keep on with her studies, but, if war did come, she wanted to be doing something to help, not just taking screeds and screeds of notes that she might never have occasion to use.

Her father had been horrified when she told him. 'What do you propose to do?' he had asked, his eyes steely.

'I was thinking . . . well, I know I haven't got my degree yet, but I could offer my services to one of the forces as a first-aider, or something like that.'

His scowl told her what his answer would be, and she was ready for it. 'Yes, I'm under age, and I know I'd need parental –'

'Exactly, and I will not give my permission. You know nothing of what a war entails, the horrors, the . . . killings . . .' He stopped, clearly remembering his own experience of armed conflict, then added, sadly, 'The dead bodies didn't bother me so much as seeing the injured, sometimes left to lie where they fell . . .'

She had been astonished at the change in him. She had never heard him speak like that before, nor seen him so distraught. 'But that was twenty years ago,' she pointed out. 'Things are different now, modern equipment . . . there wouldn't be any hand-to-hand fighting, I shouldn't think. The seriously wounded would be transferred to hospitals, and the slightly wounded would get first aid there and then.'

'Dorothea,' his icy calmness and the use of her full name alarmed her, 'you are so childish you cannot, or will not, understand the meaning of war, and if you do not put this ridiculous idea out of your head, I shall be forced to remove you from university altogether, and have you home here where we can keep an eye on you.'

She thought better of arguing any more. What was the point? There might never be another war, and if it did come, she would take her own way whatever he said.

Over the next few months, Dorrie took more interest in the newspapers and the wireless news bulletins than she had ever done before, discussing with Archie the inroads that Hitler was making into other countries in Europe, agreeing with him that war was becoming more and more of a certainty. He told her that, if it did come, he intended offering his services as a chaplain to one of the armed forces, but she didn't tell him what she had planned. It was only right that she should do something, too, but she knew that he, like her father, would not be pleased about it.

Like the rest of Britain, the people of the glen heaved deeply relieved sighs when Neville Chamberlain returned from his talks with the Führer in Berlin in September with his assurance that there would be 'peace in our time', especially in the homes where a son, husband or lover was of the age to be called up or, worse still, volunteer.

'My Gordon was dyin' to get a excuse to get awa',' complained the wife of one of the younger of the Black family.

'Him and a lot more like him,' nodded Mima Rattray, who had been hearing the same from nearly all her customers that day. 'War always gives men itchy feet.'

'I suppose it's the thocht o' bein' free o' their wives that does it, the idea o' takin' up wi' the young lassies that hang aboot army camps.' Babsie Black shook her head at the perfidy of men and then added, with great satisfaction, 'But they'll ha'e to bide at hame noo.'

The men concerned – the young blood, the hotheads, the henpecked husbands and the youths whose mothers had a stranglehold on them – spent several nights in the Western or Royal or Crown Hotels in Laurencekirk – sometimes all three – drowning their disappointment. They had the sense to travel there by horse and cart, because Pat Black's Betsy knew her way blindfolded, and they'd get home safely, however drunk they were by closing time. Of course, this couldn't carry on for long; for, apart from heads and stomachs rebelling after several nights of it, money ran out, and the glen got back to normal.

But not for very long.

Chapter Twenty-eight

War was declared in September 1939, but it was into 1940 before its impact was felt in the glen. Many young hotheads had volunteered within the first six weeks, but soon conscription came for the twenty to twenty-seven-year-olds. Ruairidh did not argue when Melda pressed Dorrie to give up her studies and learn how to work a loom; at least it kept her safe, and he was glad when even wives with young children came to offer their services. Melda organized a creche, but Ruairidh pessimistically said, 'I don't know why you're bothering. It probably won't be long before there's no work for anybody. There'll be no orders coming in.'

She had, however, thought of a way to safeguard the mill. Delegating Marianne to supervise the creche, and much against her husband's wishes, Melda took herself off to London in the early spring of 1941, bulldozing her way into an office in Whitehall with barely time to expound her plan before the Ministry of War was moved out of the capital. As it happened, by sheer good luck the officer who saw her had been at boarding school with Hector, Ruairidh's grandfather, and being a Scot himself, he promised to do everything he could to help.

Like the mills of God, the wheels of any ministry in war or peace work exceeding slow, so Ruairidh had doubts about Melda's version of her mission when the orders finally arrived. 'Ach!' he groaned. 'A dozen bolts of khaki, and the same of air-force blue. That'll not keep us going for long.'

'If they like what we send them, they'll double it, maybe treble or more. It's just a pity we can't make up the uniforms, too.'

'If we can run full out making the cloth, I'll be happy,' sighed Ruairidh.

On the first Wednesday in June 1941, Archie Grassie telephoned Dorrie to say he would come to see her on the Sunday, because he was leaving Aberdeen on Monday.

Over the next few days, she was glad she was kept so busy. She had no time to brood during the day, and even when she went to bed, she was so tired that she fell asleep without even wondering where Archie might be sent.

They met in their usual place in the woods on Sunday afternoon, and as soon as she joined him, Archie said, 'I think I'm being sent to North Africa, and I'm glad to be going where I'm needed.'

Dorrie didn't feel at all glad. He would be in the heart of the fighting. What if he didn't come back? She couldn't voice her fear for him, she didn't want to instil fear in him, but she couldn't let him go without telling him how she felt. She waited until they came to the small glade where they had often tossed their thoughts and ideas to each other. Without a word, they stopped and sat down side by side and she turned to look at him. He wasn't what anyone would call truly handsome, but she loved the way his dark hair curled, and his fair skin made his brown eyes look almost black. His nose was inclined to be sharp, though, his mouth . . .

She gulped. She didn't want him to go to North Africa. She didn't want him to go anywhere, but was it safe to tell him that? 'I'll miss you,' she whispered.

His hand caught hers, and she looked up into his eyes, losing herself in the depth of them. 'Will you?' he murmured. 'Not as much as I'll miss you.'

They gazed at each other for several long moments, and then he sighed, 'Why did it take me this long to find out I love you?'

'I'm the same,' she burst out rapturously. 'I've just realized.'

With the realization came the need to kiss, to touch, to get to know each other in the fullest way, but not in haste. They made the most of every second of the time they had left, and somewhere in the midst of the passion, a proposal was made and accepted.

Some time later, they had to force themselves to break the spell and make their way back through the trees. 'I'd better come in with you, my darling,' Archie said, as they neared a side door. 'I expect your father would like me to ask him properly for your hand.'

'I suppose so,' she grinned, 'and we'd better not tell him I'm all yours already.'

'And every part of me is yours,' he assured her, giving her one last kiss.

Marianne was furious. If it wasn't bad enough that Dorrie's blood was one-quarter inherited from an insane minister, the headstrong girl was determined to marry the minister son of another minister, which meant that any children they had would be . . . what was a half plus a quarter? – three-quarters? That couldn't be right, could it? – whatever it was, there had better be no children of this marriage. It was unthinkable that the heir to the Glendarril title would be three-quarters a man of God . . . even more than that if you took Melda's real mother into account, for Grace had also been the daughter of a minister.

Marianne's obsession about Duncan Peat had deepened over the years into a phobia which included all ministers, a paranoia with neither reason nor rhyme behind it, which ridicule from her husband had forced her to keep hidden. No matter how hard she had tried to make Ruairidh understand that he shouldn't, he had given the two young people his blessing. No one paid any attention to her nowadays, she fumed. Gone were the days when everyone in the glen looked up to her and asked her advice when they were in any sort of trouble. Of course, with so many of the men called up or going off to fight of their own free will, most of the women were heads of their households and had learned to be strong.

What hurt her most, Marianne decided, was the way her own family treated her. She had been relegated to looking after the creche while Melda had taken complete charge of the mill, to let Ruairidh direct his full attention to the running of the estate . . . she said. It was true that the factor who had collected the rents from the tenant farmers and crofters, and the estate manager who used to arrange for any repairs necessary to the cottages, had both been called up, so Ruairidh did have everything to do himself, but they could let her have responsibility for something. She was capable of so much, and any elderly woman would manage to control a bunch of skirling under-school-age brats.

Her mind returned to the problem of Archie Grassie. He would have left Aberdeen by this time, and seemed to think he was bound for North Africa, where the war was not going too well for Britain, so maybe she was worrying for nothing. According to Lord Haw-Haw, the Germans and the Italians had the British in full retreat, so Archie might be killed – or would God not permit that to happen to a minister, a padre, as Archie called himself? There were rumours that some troops of the Highland Division were to be sent to Glendarril for mountain training. She hadn't liked the idea of hundreds of soldiers of all ranks milling around, but if one young officer managed to take Dorrie's fancy . . . she could send one of those 'Dear John' letters to Archie.

After all, he hadn't had time to buy her a ring, so they weren't really engaged. Not officially.

When it came, some three months later, the Invasion of Glendarril, as Ruairidh dubbed it, was not as big an upheaval as they had imagined, and his mother was quite pleased that only officers were billeted in the castle itself. This meant that Dorothea saw them every day, which would take her mind off Archie Grassie . . . hopefully. The lower ranks were distributed throughout the glen, in all houses large enough to sleep at least two, and with so many husbands and boyfriends away, everyone could foresee trouble – a proliferation of trouble. The school hall, which had formerly staged only concerts put on by the pupils at Christmas,

456

was appropriated to provide weekly entertainment for the troops, and, because of the closeness of the original small community and the relatively small number of soldiers foisted upon them, no difference was made between officers and other ranks at the dances and various other amusements arranged by the Entertainments Officer.

The females in the glen soon adapted to the change. From fifteen to fifty, they welcomed the attention paid to them by these uniformed strangers, who did not remain strangers for long; who, in fact, soon got to know some of the women just as intimately as their absent husbands. Not to be outdone, the young girls, ignoring their mothers' warnings, relinquished their maidenhood at the first asking. It was all very exciting for both sexes – days spent working hard, and nights, to put it plainly, spent in every bit as physically demanding a manner, but so much more enjoyable.

As one young soldier sighed ecstatically to the boy who shared his room, 'If this is war, Lachie, I hope it goes on for ever.'

His friend, however, a tubby lad from the island of Islay, was finding the pace just a little too hectic. 'I chust hope I can keep going, Chamie,' he muttered. 'That Chanet would neffer let me stop if she got her way.'

Jamie gave a loud guffaw. 'And you're complaining? Make the most of it, Lachie boy, and pray the powers that be have forgotten about us. If they haven't, we'll likely be posted to somewhere in the jungle or some other God-forsaken hole with no dames!'

The powers that be had their sights on all regiments, all battalions, of course, wherever they were, even in the most remote outpost, and with no prior notification – except a coded message to Lord Glendarril, telling him that the training had been completed – evacuation of the first batch of soldiers was speedily effected, and great was the consternation – the weeping and wailing and gnashing of teeth – of their hostesses when it was discovered that the men had virtually disappeared overnight. Five young girls, one barely fifteen, had been left pregnant, and fathers were vowing vengeance on the 'horny buggers' who had done the dirty deeds. The trouble was, they learned to their greater disgust, that their daughters didn't even know their names in most cases. Three mothers of girls who had been seduced, willingly or otherwise, were keeping their own secrets – two whose husbands had been overseas for more than a year, and one whose spouse thought he must have been drunk when he fathered the child his wife was carrying, because he couldn't remember a blessed thing about it.

Most of the pregnancies were kept hidden for as long as possible, only four anxious mothers booking the services of the 'howdie' as soon as they recognized the symptoms their teenage daughters were displaying and got the truth out of them.

Soon, as more soldiers came and went, even the most timid of the maids in the castle was telling lies in order to meet a soldier. 'Please, Cook,' little Evie pleaded on the day following her usual afternoon off, 'Ma wasna lookin' good yesterday an' I wanted to see what like she is the day.'

Mrs Burr's eyes held compassion that first time and the girl was allowed an hour off, but on the request being repeated just two days later, she tumbled to what was

458

going on. 'So your mother's no better, is she?' she asked sarcastically. 'That's funny, for Ruby saw her last night goin' to the Rural meetin'. But maybe you've got a different mother these days? Wi' a khaki uniform?'

Evie's face turned crimson, and remembering the girl's age, Mrs Burr said, 'You're only fourteen, lass, ower young to be goin' wi' lads. Wait till you're sixteen, that's time enough.'

The thought of the handsome youth she had met, the memory of his kiss, gave Evie the courage to protest indignantly. 'But he'll likely be sent awa' afore I'm sixteen, an' I promised to meet him. Please, Cook, even just half an hour?'

'Ach, I'm a right auld fool,' observed the woman, nodding her permission, 'but just this once, and you be careful, mind. Dinna let him tak' advantage o' you.'

Although this was exactly what the maid hoped he would do, she shook her head vigorously. 'Oh no, Cook! I'll no' let him touch me.'

At eight o'clock, therefore, Evie was hurrying through the rose garden to the side gate, her heart beating twenty to the dozen, her mind set on one thing. 'I've only got half an hour,' she told the young soldier when she reached their trysting place.

Bobby McIver needed no second telling and wasted no time in getting down to business, as Evie related to Jessie, her bed-mate, later that night. 'He started in kissin' right away, an' we didna even tak' a walk, for he had me doon on the grass in aboot twa seconds.'

'Ooh, Evie!' Jessie was not a great conversationalist, but the two words were enough to show how eager she was to hear more.

'So then he was kissin' me some mair, an' openin' my buttons at the same time, an' he says, "That's fine big tits you've got, Evie," an' I was fine pleased aboot that, for I used to think they were ower big, made me top heavy, like.'

'Go on, then. Once he had your buttons open . . . ?'

'Oh, I canna tell you what it felt like, Jessie. He was kissin' me there, an' all, and I went a' shaky an' there was thrills goin' richt doon me, so when he put his hand up my skirt I didna stop him . . .' She stopped to look appealingly at her friend. 'He said he was showin' me how much he loves me, an' oh, it was good.'

'But you havena tell't me . . .'

Evie told her, in her own explicit words, because she didn't know the polite way to describe what she and the boy had done, but she would have been less than happy if she had heard what Bobby McIver was telling *his* friend.

'She's a walk-ower, Gibby. She only got a half-hour off, an' she was as desperate for it as me. A coupla minutes an' we was lying down, another coupla minutes an' I had her tits out, another coupla minutes an' she was letting me do the needful.'

'Lucky bugger!' muttered Gibby. 'You should've asked her if she'd a chum for me.'

'She's no' off again till Friday, but I'll see what I can do.'

Thus it came about that Jessie was enlisted, very willingly, into the deception that followed. In order to see the boys as often as they could, the two maids sneaked out every night after they were supposed to have gone to bed, splitting into pairs as soon as they met their lads. For Gibby, it was his first time with a girl, yet that didn't stop him from 'doing the needful' as Bobby had described it, and besides Jessie was an 'older woman' and soon showed him the ropes, and all four participants went to bed after their meetings thoroughly satisfied in every way.

This happy, carefree situation carried on for several weeks, until, one night on their way back to the cottage where they were billeted, Gibby asked about something that was puzzling him. 'I hardly like to say this, Bobby, but has Evie tell't you something?'

'Tell't me what?'

'Well, me an' Jessie was four nights withoot it 'cos she'd the curse, but you and Evie . . .'

Realization came with the impact of a punch in the face, and Bobby's eyes widened in apprehension. 'She hasna said onything, but, my God, Gibby, you're right enough. She hasna had the curse. Oh Christ, man, what'll I dae?'

His friend looked at him with deep pity. 'You should have used a French letter like me, but it's ower late now. There's no sense in shutting the stable door after the horse has bolted, as my granda used to say.'

'Never mind your bloody granda! What can I dae?'

'There's nothing you *can* dae, as far as I can see. She's just newly fifteen, so you canna wed her, an' I think it's against the law to . . .' He paused, then said, 'You say she hasna said onything yet? Maybe she doesna ken what it means? Maybe we'll be oot o' here afore it dawns on her?'

'You'd better no' say onything to Jessie. She surely doesna ken, either.'

'I'll no' say a word, but you'd better hope it's no' lang till we're posted.'

If Evie noticed a slight cooling off in her lover's ardour, she said nothing to him nor to Jessie, putting it down to

461

the rumour that was going round that the boys' unit would soon be leaving the glen, and it was not until they had actually gone, without either boy promising to keep in touch, that it came to her that she and Jessie had just been used. What did not occur to her, however, was that she was carrying Bobby McIver's child, at least not until Ruby happened to pass a comment on how fat she was getting, and even then, it was Jessie who put two and two together.

'Hey, Evie, you're no' . . . that Bobby didna land you in the family way, did he?'

'What?' Evie's face blanched, then the colour flooded back. 'I dinna ken. How dae you . . . ?'

'Has your monthlies stopped?'

'I havena had them for a few month noo, but that suited me fine. Bobby wouldna have been . . .'

'Oh, God, Evie, you're expectin'! Did you no' ken the signs?'

Mrs Burr was not at all pleased, and cursed herself for being so stupid. Evie was easy meat for the likes of them soldiers; one kiss and she'd likely have been opening her legs. But however sorry she felt for the maid, she could do little to help, except promise to go with her when she confessed her sin to Lady Marianne. 'We can wait another month maybe, but her Ladyship's aye been real understanding to other lassies in the same predicament.'

As it happened, she did not have to carry out this task. Two mornings later, an agitated Jessie came running into the kitchen. 'Evie's no' in her bed, an' I never heard her goin' oot.'

The poor girl was found floating in the pond in the rose garden, but Jessie, good friend that she was, only said when questioned by the laird and the doctor, that Evie had been upset because the lad she'd been in love with had been sent away. Mrs Burr drew her own conclusion, also Robert Mowatt, and probably half the women in the glen, but her death had come as such a shock that not one person passed any comments on it.

As the months passed, Robert Mowatt became angrily aware that the population of the glen was to be greatly increased thanks to the activities of the young soldiers, and likely of the officers, too, who should have set a good example. In fact, the doctor reflected one day when he saw Meggie Park waddling along to the shop – her stomach grossly fat although her husband had been a prisoner of war in Germany for almost two years – he wouldn't be surprised if one or two of the married men in the glen who had not been called up had jumped on the bandwagon. If they happened to fill a belly or two in the process, the women concerned could always blame the army.

A compassionate man, Robert could sympathize with the poor souls who'd had little or no loving since their men went off to war, so he let it be known that he would attend such confinements free of any charge, be they the result of a liaison with a soldier or with a neighbour's husband.

'How can we expect people to behave decently?' he asked Ruairidh when the laird went round for a chat one night. 'The whole world's been turned upside down by war, and peace-time ethics and rules have gone out through the window.'

'You know,' Ruairidh observed, his eyes twinkling, 'I sometimes wish I'd been a lot younger so I could have had a fling, too.'

'You're not that old.'

'I'm over forty, and what would my mother have said if I'd put some girl in the family way?'

Robert grinned roguishly. 'She'd have been delighted if it had been a boy.'

'Aye,' Ruairidh sighed, 'she's still going on about there not being an heir to follow me.' He paused, considering the wisdom of saying more, then decided to get it off his chest. 'And she's still got that old obsession about ministers. She even let slip the other day that she's pleased Melda never had a son to inherit Duncan Peat's insanity.'

It was the doctor's turn to hesitate. 'I wish she could see sense. I've told her over and over again that Duncan Peat was not mad, just temporarily off balance, and I can vouch for Melda being as sane as any of us – saner maybe, for she has a good sensible head on her shoulders, which is more than I can say for Marianne, at times.'

Ruairidh sighed again. 'It's just that one thing she has a blockage about. She even worries about Dorrie being tainted and passing the madness on to any son she has – not that there's any chance of that till the war's over.' He straightened his back and concentrated on this new topic. 'Things are looking a bit brighter for us at the moment.'

'Yes, but Monty was the man for the job. I don't know why Ike was made over-all commander.'

'Um . . . I shouldn't be telling you this, but I know you won't let it go any further. I've heard on the grapevine that we're gearing up for the big push.'

Robert gave a derisive snort. 'That rumour's been going round for ages now.'

464

'We'll just have to wait and see, then, but it can't come soon enough for me. I haven't anyone close in the forces, but the past four years have seemed like four centuries.'

'It's the parents and sweethearts of the boys who are away fighting . . . it must be hell for them.'

'I can vouch for that,' the laird said morosely. I had a brother in the last war, remember, and he didn't come back.'

'Oh Lord, I'm sorry, Ruairidh! I didn't meant to upset –'

'I know you didn't, but it's the kind of grief that never leaves you. Mother has never been the same since that telegram was delivered, although losing Ranald brought her and Father closer together.'

Seeing the pain in his friend's eyes, Robert wished fervently that he had not opened his big mouth.

Melda felt compelled to talk about her daughter, although her mother-in-law would not have been her first choice as confidante. 'I don't know what to say to Dorrie. She hasn't heard from Archie for weeks now, and neither has his sister. Phyllis keeps saying he can't have been killed otherwise she'd have heard, but Dorrie never speaks about him. It's not good for her to keep it bottled up, is it?'

Marianne clicked her tongue. 'No, she'd be better if she got it out.' She hesitated for a second, then said, 'I don't think he was the right one for her, anyway.'

Melda was outraged. 'Yes, I know you've had an ill will against him all along, just because he's a minister, but poor Dorrie really loves him.' She turned away before she told the old woman what she thought of her and her obsession.

There was nothing for Dorrie to do but wait, and Phyllis Mathieson had promised to let them know the minute she heard anything.

Only two days later, when the minister's wife came to the castle, Melda knew it was bad news before Phyllis even opened her mouth. 'Archie hasn't been killed, has he?' she asked anxiously.

The woman nodded tearfully. 'I promised to let Dorrie know if . . . I heard anything. I won't stop . . . You'll understand I can't talk . . .' She whipped round and walked away.

Melda was left feeling completely at a loss. She hadn't had a chance to say how sorry she was, to try to give comfort . . . and how could she break it to Dorrie? What should she say? She could remember how she had felt when she'd learned about Rannie, and she hadn't really known whether she loved him or not. She looked up as Marianne came into the room, and in her despair, let fly at her. 'Well, you'll be pleased to know Archie Grassie's been killed!'

'Oh!' Marianne's hand flew to her heart. 'That's a cruel thing to say. I admit I didn't care for the idea of Dorrie marrying him, but I would never have wished him dead. Poor girl!'

'I don't know how to tell her.'

'Do you want me to . . . ?'

Melda shook her head. 'It's up to me, but I am not relishing the thought of it.'

The girl took it better than any of them had thought, weeping for only a very short time and then saying she wanted to be on her own and going up to her room. None of them was surprised, however, that she did not appear the following day, and it was the day after that

466

before she came down for something to eat. Her eyes were red-rimmed, her face was puffed, her movements were slow and unsteady, but her voice was firm. 'I'm going to London.'

'What?' her mother, father and grandmother exclaimed almost in unison.

'I'm going to London,' she repeated. 'You'll manage fine without me at the mill, and I want to make use of what I learned at University, so I'm going to volunteer for the ambulance service.'

'You don't need to go to London for that,' Ruairidh pointed out. 'You could be somewhere much nearer home.'

'I want to be in the thick of it,' she said, looking round at them defiantly, although tears were glistening in her eyes. 'I have to do something to . . . keep my mind off . . .' Her voice broke.

Her father would have argued, but her mother laid a restraining hand on his arm. 'Are you sure that is what you want to do?'

'Positive!' She looked directly at Ruairidh. 'I'm old enough now not to need your permission.'

He nodded sadly. 'Yes, of course you are, and I will not stand in your way. I shall have the house in Piccadilly made ready for you to use any time you need it.'

'Thanks, Dad.'

Only two days later, Dorothea Bruce-Lyall was in London, volunteering as an ambulance driver, and Melda's life revolved around her daughter's letters.

The Allies had eventually gained a proper toehold in Normandy when the last of the 'war-babes' was delivered.

As Campbell Scott, the dominie, remarked, 'This school is going to burst at the seams in five years.'

Contrary to what Marianne had feared, there had been very little scandal, because almost every girl had been involved in some way with the ever-changing series of lusty fresh-faced youths who had invaded the glen. In some cases, the boys had done the initiating, but in just as many, the girls had made the running. The women – except those who were too old and withered to be interested – had gone for the more mature men, the NCOs and officers, who were every bit as avid for sex as the rank and file. So it would have been the pot calling the kettle black if any snide remarks had been passed. They were all in the same boat – with the exception of the wives of the dominie, the doctor, the minister and the laird, who, although they may have been tempted, had foregone the pleasure – and many of them were dreading the day when their husbands or boyfriends would come home.

'The end of the war's going to be the telling time,' Marianne remarked to Flora Mowatt.

'The telling time?'

'The day of reckoning. Quite a few men will be coming home to find their wives have had children by somebody else. There'll be hell to pay.'

'So there should be,' Flora said grimly. 'When a woman marries, she pledges herself to her husband for life.'

'And he pledges himself to her,' Marianne retorted drily, 'and I bet most of them have been having a high old time with the *mademoiselles* and *Fräuleins,* yet they'll hit the roof about their wives being unfaithful to them.'

468

'What would you have done if you thought Hamish had been unfaithful to you?'

Marianne shrugged. 'I wouldn't have been too happy, but if he'd made another son, I'd have forgiven him.'

The doctor's wife shook her head. 'I couldn't be like that. If I thought Robert had made love to another woman, I'd want to kill him . . . then I'd kill myself.'

'To be honest,' Marianne admitted, 'I'd have been pleased in one way and angry in another. It must be terrible to know you've been betrayed. Still, there's not much fear of Ruairidh going off the straight and narrow. Nor Robert,' she added hastily.

Melda's fears were to be realized more quickly than she had imagined. Only seven short weeks and five short letters after Dorrie's departure, they received the official notification of her death. The officer in charge, the man who must have written a number of similar communications, praised her sterling work, her bravery and dedication in even the most horrendous of air raids, but there really was no easy way for him to tell them. Dorrie had apparently been helping to rescue some children in a building next door to one which had received a direct hit, when a wall caved in on top of her. It had taken several hours for them to get her out, but mercifully, the letter went on, she had not suffered. She had died instantly.

Melda did not believe this, but, as she pointed out to her husband, it was kind of the man to try to shield them from the truth. Once again, as at the time of Ranald's death, they clung to each other for comfort, and although their inevitable coupling was perhaps not so ardent as it had been then, it still afforded them some solace.

Feeling somewhat excluded, Marianne went to talk to Flora Mowatt. 'They've no time for me,' she complained. 'I miss Dorrie just as much as they do.'

Flora patted her hand. 'Of course you do, Marianne, dear, but she *was* their daughter.'

After a moment's thought, Marianne said, 'Yes, I can see the point you're making. When we lost Ranald, Hamish and I were like young lovers again. I wouldn't have come through that if it hadn't been for him . . . and now I've nobody.'

'Don't get maudlin, my dear, it doesn't suit you.' Flora knew how to treat her old friend. 'You have Robert and me, and all the people in Glendarril know how you are feeling and sympathize.'

'Yes, I suppose so. You're right. I shouldn't feel sorry for myself, when so many of the people in the glen have lost somebody, too.'

'I know it's little comfort, but time does heal, and until it does, we must carry on as usual.'

Time did eventually not heal, exactly, but blunt the edge of the Bruce-Lyalls' grief, and life went on, though not quite the same as before.

The people of Glendarril did not bring 1945 in with their usual vigour. All reports from the war fronts grew more encouraging by the day, and what Marianne had called the 'telling time' – the day of reckoning – was looming ever closer for those women who had taken their pleasure where they could, which is how she thought of them, although

Robert Mowatt regarded them as poor unfortunates. But, whichever way they judged themselves, the women understood that Nemesis was about to catch up with them, and the doctor was kept busy prescribing pills and powders for ailments brought on by nerves.

At precisely six o'clock on 8 May, the day on which Churchill had announced the end of hostilities, Robert took an unprecedented step. Having heard the steady tramp of feet going round to the side door, he thought dismally that he'd be lucky if he finished consulting by bedtime, and when he entered the waiting room to summon his first patient, he could have screamed. The place was filled to capacity! A second glance, however, told him that there was not one man there, and a marvellous idea struck him. They were all suffering from the same guilt and anxiety because their sins would soon be laid bare, so why shouldn't he attempt mass treatment?

'Good evening, ladies!' he boomed, smiling to hide his nervousness. 'We all know why so many of you are here tonight, and it seems to me that, rather than see each of you individually, it would be much quicker if I just talked to you here to let you see how futile it is to worry about something which nothing can change.'

A sign of unrest, accompanied by a low murmur, made him hasten on. 'Yes, I do realize that your men will be back shortly, and some of you have good reason to fear your husband's reaction to what you did, but I am practically sure that every man will be so glad to be home that he'll . . . if not exactly excuse you, at least accept the child he knew nothing about. Of course, he is bound to be angry at first, and it's up to you to make it up to him, to

471

show him such love as you have never shown him before. Tell him how sorry you are, and that it happened because you missed him so much, and if he is still angry and threatens to leave you, assure him, through your tears, that you can not live without him any longer. Turning on the waterworks usually works – I know.'

He was relieved to see them looking hopefully at each other. 'You are wondering if my advice will work, and it may not in all cases, but surely you must be willing to try anything to keep your man? You must think calmly over what to say, no counteraccusations no matter what you suspect, and I feel certain the situation will ease. One word of warning, however. Do not, whatever the provocation, hint that he is not as good a lover as the child's father was. That would be fatal! Now, I'll leave you to talk about it, but I will be in the surgery for another half-hour if any of you want to see me privately. My advice would still be the same, and for those who say they can't sleep for worrying, a couple of aspirins is all you need.'

He had almost left the room when he hesitated and turned. 'They won't be demobilized straight away, you know, and it will be time enough to worry when you hear when your man will be home. Good night, ladies. I hope everything works out for you, but if it gets sticky, remind him that you weren't the only one to make a mistake. There must be hundreds, even thousands all over the world.'

The homecomings were spread over some months, and it was almost 1947 before the last stragglers arrived home, those who had been prisoners of war, those who had been in the fight against the Japanese. Oddly, they were the least upset about their womenfolk's infidelity. They were so glad to be home in one piece, to sit at their own firesides again, that nothing else mattered. Only a small minority of the rest went as far as breaking an engagement or ending a marriage, possibly, human nature being what it is, those who had also misbehaved, and who, for all they knew, may have left living souvenirs behind them.

As the doctor had hoped, most married life soon returned to normal and there followed a spate of legitimate pregnancies to keep him and the midwife busier than ever – the postwar baby boom, the bulge!

For the family at the castle, though, there was no homecoming to celebrate, and it very much looked as if there would be no more Bruce-Lyall babies ever again.

Part Three

1955

Chapter Twenty-nine

It had been a long day, and Ruth Laverton was glad to sit down by the bed. Her mother was dozing at the moment, but likely not for very long. She had a knack of sleeping off and on in the afternoons and evenings and being awake all night, which wouldn't be so bad, Ruth mused, if she could also have a rest during the day. It was the lack of sleep that got her down.

She looked wryly at the pillow cases on her lap. She had noticed when she was ironing that the housewife openings were burst at the seams and she had meant to sew them, but, oh God, not right now! She would have to close her eyes for a wee while; they were stinging with tiredness.

The coals in the grate were glowing comfortably, but she'd have to be careful not to fall asleep and let the fire go out. The doctor had warned that she mustn't let her patient get cold. Her patient, she thought sadly. This was the woman who had borne her, who had struggled to bring her and her young sister up decently after their father died. She had worked her fingers to the bone for them, going out cleaning to keep them fed properly, doing without things herself in order to buy clothes for them. She deserved to be nursed with all the love she could get . . . for as long as she needed it.

No resentment, no bitterness. Her elder daughter mustn't think of it as a duty she was forced to carry out. She must look on it as a privilege and be glad to be given the chance to show her gratitude for all that her mother had done for her. It would help, though, if Gladys did a bit more to help, even if she just popped in for an hour every day. Of course, she always had an excuse why she couldn't – she had to wait in for the man to read her gas meter, or the electric meter; or she had to take up a hem on the new dress she had bought for Bob's firm's dinner dance, as well as pressing his suit and ironing a white shirt for him. They were always going out to enjoy themselves and she had a bottomless pit of excuses, but give her her due, she did sit with Mum for an hour every Saturday afternoon to let her sister do some shopping . . . but only because Bob was a football fan who went to Pittodrie every week whether it was the first team who were playing a home match, or the reserves or the schoolboys. But she shouldn't criticize, Ruth told herself. Gladys had a husband to look after, whereas she . . .

She heaved a long-drawn-out sigh. If she'd still had Mark, it would have been different. She should have known he wouldn't settle down to a dull job after the war, but she had loved him so much she didn't let him see how much she missed him when he became a long-distance lorry driver. She had Colin to look after, their beautiful son who was still only a toddler when his father was killed in a road accident on a French road in 1947. They had been married for just six years, a wartime wedding, and had been in their council house for less than eighteen months.

She had been so shocked that it seemed a good idea to move back in with her mother, who looked after Colin while she went out to work . . . until the poor woman was diagnosed as having multiple sclerosis. The illness progressed slowly at first, still leaving her able to care for the small boy, but then it speeded up until she was completely bedridden and needed constant attention. She'd had to give up her own job to look after her, and there had just been the two widows' pensions coming in; there was no family allowance for an only child. Now there was this second illness, the most dreaded of all.

Becoming conscious that her fingernails were digging into her palms, Ruth inhaled deeply and tried to relax as she let the breath edge out, then rising quietly, she lifted the poker and stirred the fire. When she straightened and caught sight of herself in the overmantel mirror, her hand went to her heart in dismay. She was only thirty-six, but her reflection was that of a woman well into her fifties. Her auburn hair was lank, her cheeks were wan and hollow. There were dark circles under her eyes, the eyes Mark used to call 'cerulean blue' but were now faded and almost blank. What did it matter, she thought. Nobody saw her except her mother and sister; her brother-in-law didn't bother to come in any more – Gladys had even stopped apologizing for him dropping her off on his way to somewhere else. Sitting down again, she couldn't help thinking that Bob Mennie was selfish to the very core.

'Ruthie.'

The weak voice shattered her reverie. 'What is it, Mum?' she asked anxiously, jumping up at once and bending over the bed. 'Is the pain getting worse?'

'That's not what –' Georgina Brown, Ina to her friends, broke off and looked earnestly at the younger woman. 'Something's preying on my mind, Ruthie. I should have told you a long time ago . . . but I kept putting it off.'

Ruth took the wasted hand in hers. 'I can see it's upsetting you, Mum, so don't bother telling me just now. Do it another time . . .'

'There won't be another time.'

'Don't be silly! Of course there will.'

'I know in myself I haven't long to go now, and –'

Her heart cramping, Ruth cried desperately, 'Don't say that! You maybe feel a bit low just now, but you'll feel better soon.'

Ina shook her head. 'I know I've got cancer, and I know you know, so you needn't pretend. I can feel my strength slipping away tonight and I can't go to meet my Maker with this on my mind. Sit down, Ruthie, lass.'

Her entire body apprehensive, Ruth sat down, leaning forward so that she could keep holding her mother's hand. 'All right, but don't overdo it. If I think it's too much for you, I'll stop listening.'

With her free hand, Ina pulled her handkerchief from the sleeve of the bedjacket Ruth had knitted for her last winter, and held it ready to wipe the tears she knew would come. 'I want you to listen to it all . . . and say nothing. I've had to screw up my courage . . . to speak about it, and I don't want you stopping me . . . before I'm done.'

Her voice was gaining a little strength, but there were many pauses between sentences, even between phrases. 'I'm going back . . . to when me and Jack was wed and . . . planning on having a big family. We wanted three girls . . .

and three boys . . . because we loved bairns . . . but the years went by . . . and we'd no luck.'

Stopping to take a few deep breaths, Ina flapped the hankie to prevent any interruption, and waited a few seconds before going on.

'We'd been wed for three years with still no sign . . . there was none of that testing in them days to see if it was the wife's fault or the man's . . . and I'd given up hope when I met a woman that had been at the school with me. She asked how many bairns me and Jack had . . . and when I told her . . . she persuaded me to . . .'

The handkerchief was put to use here, but her look of appeal kept Ruth from saying or doing anything, and she waited for what she prayed was not what she had begun to suspect. Her faith in God, however, was to be severely shaken.

'I'm not your real mother, Ruthie!' Ina burst out, dabbing at her eyes. 'Me and Jack fostered you . . . when you was eight weeks old.'

Her lips scarcely able to form the words, Ruth asked, 'And Gladys?'

Ina shook her head. 'The doctor said it was looking on you as mine . . . that had stopped me worrying about conceiving . . . and that's how Gladys happened.'

'So you're *her* real mother?'

'Look, lass . . . I'm her natural mother . . . but I love you as much as I love her . . . more, maybe. She's not half the woman you are . . . more's the pity. If you hadn't been here to look after me . . . she'd have likely put me in a home.'

'No, she'd never have done that! She'd have shifted you to her house!' Feeling obligated to stick up for Gladys, Ruth

481

secretly agreed with her mother. But Georgina Brown was not her mother – any more than Gladys was her sister! She was overwhelmed by a wave of something she had never known before, not quite self-pity, nor bitterness, nor anger . . . more a sense of insecurity.

'Oh, Ruthie,' Ina groaned, 'Don't look so lost. Maybe I shouldn't have told you.'

Ruth attempted to pull herself together, but there was one thing she had to know. 'You said fostered. Why didn't you adopt me?'

'At first, we thought we might . . . have to give you back . . . if your real mother claimed you . . . but when we didn't hear anything . . . we hoped they'd forgot we had you. Me and Jack spoke about adopting you . . . but we were scared to rock the boat, and once Gladys was born . . . well, we couldn't afford it. You see, we got so much a week for fostering you, but them that adopted got nothing. And I got the money . . . for your keep right up . . . till you started working.'

'But after Dad died, you were really hard up,' Ruth reminded her, 'and you had your own child to think about, so why didn't you send me back to where you got me?'

'It never crossed my mind, lass. As far as I was concerned . . . you were mine and . . . it was up to me to . . . provide for you.' There was a long pause, the effort of the sustained speech obviously too much, then Ina whispered, 'I'm awful tired, Ruthie . . . I need . . . to sleep.'

Ruth jumped up, alarmed by her mother's extra pallor. 'I'll make some Ovaltine for –'

'I don't want . . . just settle me . . . there's a . . . good lass.'

Barely five minutes later, Ina was breathing steadily, if a little shallowly, and Ruth went into the scullery to make herself a cup of tea. Her legs were shaking as she waited for the kettle to boil, which was not surprising in view of what she had just been told. It was a great shock to learn that the woman she had always thought was her mother wasn't her mother at all, and she hadn't found out where she had come from or got any clue as to who her real mother might be. Oh well, she'd have to contain her curiosity until morning.

Making herself as comfortable as she could in the wide easy chair at Ina's bedside, Ruth shut her eyes. She had learned over the past few months to make the most of every minute's peace she got.

Not being called upon even once to lift Ina to the commode, or to turn her to her other side, or to give her a sip of water, as she usually had to do several times a night, Ruth had slipped into a deeper sleep than she'd had for many weeks, and woke to the sound of the milkman rattling bottles outside. Before her body was fully mobile, her brain told her that her 'patient' had passed away, so she was not surprised that there was no pulse when she felt for one.

She flopped back into the depths of her chair, uncertain of what to do, unsure of how she felt. She was glad that her mother was free of pain at last but wished that she'd had the chance to ask her more about the fostering. Where had she, an infant at the time, been living for the first eight weeks of her life? Who had looked after her? Had her biological mother died, or had she been a poor young girl who couldn't afford to keep her? A girl who had been abandoned by the father of her child? Abandoned by her own father as well, likely. Thrown out of her home, she may well have taken her baby to an orphanage, or left her somewhere for someone to find. Dear God, there was no end of places she might have gone to after that, so how on earth was Ruth Laverton to find her?

But she must stop this agonizing, she reprimanded herself, getting slowly to her feet again. She had things to do to show her gratitude for being enfolded in this woman's family . . . and Gladys had better do her share, too. Ruth's stomach lurched. She could foresee trouble – there was always trouble when Gladys was asked to do anything.

Bob Mennie took in hand to arrange the funeral – 'It's a man's job,' he said – and his wife, Gladys, still unaware of her mother's dying revelation, left Ruth to do the catering while she went round the house earmarking all items she was laying claim to.

Ruth let her carry on. She couldn't very well have an argument while Ina's body was still in the house, and she had no claim on Ina's things. Strangely, it was Bob who told his wife on the morning of the funeral what he thought of her callousness.

'This is still Ruthie's home,' he pointed out, 'and you're not taking anything out of here without her say-so.'

Glaring fiercely at him, Gladys nevertheless stopped her ghoulish inspection.

Ruth had been in two minds about admitting that she had been a foster child, but she was so sickened by the way

Gladys had behaved that she decided to wait until after the funeral. As soon as the last of the mourners had left the house, therefore, she made her announcement, her spirits lifting with the relief of getting if off her chest, and smiling at the expressions on the other two faces.

When it had sunk in, Gladys turned triumphantly to her husband. 'She's not my mother's' daughter, so she's not entitled to stay in this house.'

The bewildered man frowned. 'You can't throw her and Colin out on the street!'

'I'll give her time to find somewhere else, but every-thing here belongs to me.'

Bob glanced round disparagingly. 'There's nothing worth much, in any case.'

'We can sell what we don't want.' Gladys looked at Ruth defiantly. 'I'll be back tomorrow, so don't you dare take anything, and if you want something for a keepsake, you'd better ask me first.'

Their departure left Ruth sitting forlornly alone. She didn't need anything to remind her of Ina, who would always remain a part of her, as the mother she had more than succeeded in being. 'Oh, Mum,' she moaned, 'why did you have to tell me?'

After a while, she began to wonder why Ina had been so desperate to let her know. Were there letters about her fostering amongst the receipts and other important papers kept in the old handbag in the sideboard? Had Ina, in a roundabout way, given her a chance to find her birth mother, who would surely be in better circumstances now and might be pleased to be reunited with the child she had given up all those years before?

485

The old handbag, with its cracked leather and torn lining, nevertheless yielded more information than Ruth had ever hoped for. All preserved together in one thick brown envelope were three letters from a home for unmarried mothers in Yorkshire, recording an application for, the acceptance of, and the actual fostering of Ruth Bruce, date of birth 20.4.19, by John and Georgina Brown. Unfortunately, there was no birth certificate, and Ruth's disappointment was so great that she abandoned all hope of ever learning who her real mother had been, and stuffed the envelope back in its original place among the other papers.

Thankfully, Bob Mennie – the brother-in-law she had never cared for much – had succeeded in persuading Gladys not to turn her out of the house. 'Mind you,' he confided when he called to give Ruth the good news, 'I don't think she'd really have done it, not when it came to the point.'

Ruth wasn't so sure. They had never been close, Gladys always jealous of her older sister, always quick to take her spite out on her. But she couldn't run down Bob's wife to his face. 'No, I don't suppose she would.'

'Have you found out anything yet?' he enquired. 'About your mother . . . real mother, I mean?'

'Not a thing. I did find out where I was born, though – in a home for unmarried mothers in Yorkshire.'

'Well, that's something, isn't it?'

'It's a start, but they're not allowed to give out any information in case the woman concerned doesn't want to be found.'

'No? Well, don't give up hope. You'll maybe come across something else, if you keep looking. Now, are you not going to offer a starving man something to eat and drink?'

'The kettle's on,' she smiled, feeling much better for his encouraging remarks, 'and I was going to have a cheese sandwich if that'll do you?'

'That sister of yours . . .' He halted, looking somewhat confused, then grinned. 'She's not your real sister, of course . . .'

'I'll always look on her as my sister,' Ruth said truthfully.

'I could never get over the difference between you,' Bob observed now, 'but I aye thought it was not having any kids that made Glad a bit sour, if you see what I mean. Anyway, I was going to say she doesn't feed me properly, not like a hard-working man should be fed.'

'There's nothing coming over you that I can see,' Ruth laughed.

When her brother-in-law left, she washed up the dirty dishes and then took the old handbag out again. He was quite right – there could easily be something else in it, though she couldn't think what. She searched amongst the papers again, even emptying the brown envelope to see if she had missed something, but there were only the three letters she had already seen. Something urged her on, however, and she decided to clear out the whole bag; most of what was there wasn't worth keeping.

She spent a good hour opening folded sheets of paper, reading receipts, letters from Ina's old friends – possibly some who had long since lost contact with her but should be told of her passing, just the same – and ended up with three separate piles in front of her on the table: receipts for things like gas and electricity, coal, odds and ends of no importance, which could all be destroyed; receipts for larger items which were still in the house and which had better be kept; and a small bundle of letters from the women Ina kept in touch with.

Never one to procrastinate, Ruth got out the writing pad and wrote short, but friendly notes to Ina's friends. Maybe some of them had died, too, but at least those who were still alive would be glad she had let them know. The envelopes addressed and stamped, she felt like having another cup of tea and consigned the old everyday receipts to the fire while she waited for the kettle to boil.

Before she returned the other items to the handbag, she thought that it would be better for a good clean out, and pulled the lining away from the bottom to give it a shake, and as the dust and fragments of yellowed paper floated out, the lining tore a bit further and displayed the corner of another brown envelope which must have slipped down right out of sight . . . or perhaps it had been hidden there, she thought, in excitement.

Extracting this envelope, she found that Ina had written 'Andrew Rennie' on it. Who was Andrew Rennie? There was only one way to find out, so she carefully pulled out the wad of papers which she had thought to be a padded base to the bag and smoothed them out. Her mother, Ina, had said she was paid an allowance, and here was proof of it. Andrew Rennie had been the solictor who had seen to the payments which had carried on until Ruth left school and started work. Fourteen years! A young girl, as she'd believed her real mother had been, would not have had been able to do that, so it must have been her father, who had obviously been a man of some means and most likely married. Well, she didn't want to know about him. She wasn't out for any financial gain. She just wanted to discover who her mother was.

Ruth went over and over the official notifications of ten pounds paid into the North of Scotland Bank every month. It was two pounds ten shillings a week, she realized, more than a working man could have earned at that time. But she had now come across the one person who would be able to give her the information she sought. Andrew Rennie would have known her mother, and he was under no obligation to keep her name and address secret, not like the home for unmarried mothers – unless he was a great friend of one or other of her parents. Should she go and see him? He could only turn her away. She'd be doing nothing legally wrong, so he couldn't report her to the police. Oh God, she'd have to go! She would always regret it if she didn't. Whatever happened, it was worth a try.

She rose early the following day, but knowing that solicitors' offices wouldn't be open at eight o'clock in the morning, she thought she would take a walk to clear her head. She hadn't slept well, with the turmoil her brain had been in. It was a lovely day, and she enjoyed ambling along the pavements, planning what to say. She would prefer to see Andrew Rennie himself – he must be a very old man by this time – but his files would have been kept and his successor in the practice would be able to lay his hands on the information she so desperately needed. There might be the matter of confidentiality to consider, but surely not after so many years.

489

She thought it might be best not to go there before half-past nine, and because it was hardly nine when she came on to Union Street, she passed time by window-shopping at Esslemont and Macintosh's store, then crossed the street when the clock on the Town House struck the quarter-past to have a look in Falconer's . . . she seldom shopped there, either; their prices were too high for her meagre income. At half-past, she headed for Bon Accord Square, her stomach churning, her heart beating twenty to the dozen as she climbed the steps to the office of Rennie and Dalgarno.

'Can I see Mr Rennie?' she asked the young receptionist.

The girl gaped. 'There's no Mr Rennie nowadays; there hasn't been for years and years. Would somebody else not do?'

'It must be Mr Rennie,' Ruth persisted. 'He's not dead, is he?'

'I don't know. I'm not long started here, but I'll ask.' The girl picked up the telephone receiver and turned a handle on the small box switchboard at the side of the counter. In just a second, she said, 'Miss Leslie, there's a lady here asking to see Mr Rennie . . . no, she says it must be him, nobody else.'

Replacing the handset, she looked at Ruth rather accusingly. 'Miss Leslie'll be through in a minute.'

A bespectacled, middle-aged, rake-thin woman in black came out of a door at Ruth's left. 'I believe you are asking to see Mr Rennie, Mrs . . . ?

'Laverton, and it's very important.'

'Mr Rennie retired some time ago, Mrs Laverton, but I can give you an appointment with Mr Dalgarno. He is

490

the senior partner now, and he would probably be able to help you.'

Thinking this highly improbable in view of the secrecy surrounding her birth, Ruth stuck to her guns. 'It's personal, something only Mr Rennie would know.'

Recognizing that this was a woman who would not be fobbed off, Miss Leslie tutted in vexation. 'In that case, Mrs Laverton, if you leave your address and telephone number, I will contact Mr Rennie at home and let you know if he agrees to see you.'

Ruth gave her address and, although she felt at a disadvantage when she admitted that she had no telephone, she added loftily, 'Perhaps you'd be good enough to write and tell me.'

While she walked home, unable to face sitting on a tramcar with other people, Ruth recalled Gladys's reaction two days ago to being told that her 'sister' wanted to find her real mother. 'All I can say is I think you're potty! A woman who gave up her baby all that time ago won't want to be reminded of it now. She's likely married with other children and doesn't want her man to know about you.'

'I'm only trying to find out who she is,' Ruth had protested, 'and even if I do, I'll maybe never pluck up courage to go and tell her who I am.'

'What's the point of finding out, then?' Gladys had sneered. 'Are you hoping she married into money so you can claim a share of it when she pops off?'

That, Ruth mused, had stuck in her craw. Money had nothing to do with it. Suppose her mother had married the richest man in Scotland – in Britain – she wasn't looking for any hand-outs. All she wanted was to see the woman who had borne her and keep a picture of her in her mind's eye, not to make herself known. She didn't blame her mother for abandoning a young infant – the poor thing had probably been forced into it by a pitiless mother whose only thought was to avoid scandal.

The following morning, Ruth received a letter.

Dear Mrs Laverton,

Mr Rennie sends his compliments and begs your forbearance for a few days, because he is not at liberty to divulge anything without first consulting the other parties concerned. He will, however, contact you as soon as possible to arrange a meeting.

Yours sincerely,

Margaret Leslie

Ruth returned the headed notepaper to the envelope with trembling fingers. The old solicitor must have got a shock when he learned that she was looking for her mother. Ruth's stomach gave a sudden lurch. But how could he have known who she was? She had given only her married name to Miss Leslie, no Christian name, so how could he have connected her with Ruth Bruce, which had been her name at the time she was born? He couldn't even have known of her as Ruth Brown, let alone Mrs Laverton.

There was something most peculiar about this . . . unless Mr Rennie was senile. If Miss Leslie had spoken to him on the telephone and was quoting his exact words, they could have been phrases he'd recalled using years ago, meaningless now, in which case there would be little point in keeping any meeting he arranged. Yet there was something still niggling at her about the wording of the letter. '. . . *not at liberty to divulge anything without first consulting the other parties concerned.*' It fitted too well to be accidental. The other parties would be her mother and . . . her father – whose permission would be essential before he could give out any information.

After turning it over and over in her mind, Ruth concluded that Mr Rennie must still have all his faculties. He had let her know in a roundabout way that he was aware of who she was – though heaven knew how he knew – and had given her a modicum of hope that he would tell her everything in a few days.

With the second post, however, another letter arrived, addressed in the angular and somewhat shaky hand of an older person. On opening it, Ruth was surprised to read that Mr Rennie himself had written to say that he would come to see her that very afternoon at three o'clock. Wondering why he had changed his mind, she set about vacuuming and dusting her already spotless living room.

The tall stranger doffed his homburg as she opened the door. 'Good afternoon, Mrs Laverton,' he said, 'I am Andrew Rennie.'

His smile lit up his whole face, she thought, also finding herself smiling light-heartedly, although she was as tense as a wound spring. 'I guessed you must be. Come in, please.'

He sat down at the table and laid his hat down in front of him. 'I am sorry about the change of plan,' he began, 'but I decided that I should meet you in person before I –'

'You wanted to find out if I really was who I claimed to be,' she interrupted. 'Or maybe if I was the kind of person my mother would want me to be?'

493

His grey eyes twinkled at her. 'I plead guilty on both counts.'

'Tell me, Mr Rennie, how did you know who I was?'

'Shall we leave that for the moment? Suffice it to say that as soon as Miss Leslie told me that you had asked for me specifically and said that no one else could help you, I knew who you were. Well, I was *almost* sure who you were, but one look at you has cleared any doubt from my mind. You are so like your grandmother.'

Ruth did not know what to say to this, but her heart beat all the faster at the thought of the grandmother she had never known, and in all likelihood would never know, since she must be dead by this time.

As if reading her thoughts, the old solicitor went on, 'She is still alive, you know . . .' He paused for a moment, with a faraway look in his eyes, then continued, more briskly than before. 'But enough of that. Tell me, how did you find out that you were . . . ?'

'My mother – the woman I always believed was my mother – told me on her deathbed that I'd been fostered, and when I looked in the old handbag she kept all her important papers in, I found letters from a home for unmarried mothers about my fostering.'

Andrew Rennie nodded. 'Ah, yes. Brightfield.'

'I did think of going there to see if they would tell me who my mother was, but I guessed it would have been useless. It was thirty-six years ago and –'

'The present matron would have had no difficulty in tracing the details of your birth, but she would not have been at liberty to reveal them to you – not as the law stands – so you were quite right not to go there.' His long, tapering fingers raked through the thick silver hair. 'And is that all you know? That you were born in Brightfield?'

'That's all.' Her palms were sweating now, with the certainty that she was in for another huge disappointment. This old man wouldn't tell her anything more. He, too, would be bound by the law, and had probably just wanted to see how much she had found out herself.

But Ruth was off the mark, and when the solicitor started to speak again, it was as if his mind had gone back over the years. 'I always felt that Marianne was wrong in what she did.' He looked mournfully at her. 'She was your father's mother, and what she asked me to do was purely to save scandal. Even today, people ostracize unmarried girls who have children, and it was far worse then. Not only had she Melda's good name to protect, she also had her own family name to save. And no one ever knew. She left it to me to attend to everything, registering the births . . .'

Ruth's body jerked up. 'The births? More than one, you mean? At the same time, or . . .'

A flicker of wry amusement crossed the man's serious face. 'At the same time. You were one of twins. As I was saying, I had to register the births, and I found a good man and woman to adopt – but, sadly, they only took the boy.'

Ruth watched him as his mind went back to a time when he'd had to put his ingenuity to such a use as never before, nor since. His eyes were fixed on a point behind her head, perhaps on the Dinah bank her father had bought her when she was very small – the metal bust of a black 'mammy' with a hand out in front waiting for someone to put a penny into it then press the lever on her shoulder to lift it to her mouth. But Mr Rennie wasn't consciously looking at Dinah, he was remembering, and he could probably recall the events of long ago more clearly than what had happened yesterday. Even at his age – and he must be nearly eighty – he was a nice-looking man, and he must have been quite handsome when he was young. Engrossed in her own thoughts, Ruth jumped at the sound of his soft voice.

'Marianne was desperate to stop the Bruce-Lyall name from being tarnished. Her family meant everything to her, and I had hoped that she would never know what I did . . . that it would not come out until after we had both passed on.'

He raised his eyes and gave a start as they met Ruth's. 'Dear me, I am talking to myself again, am I? That is what comes of living alone for so long.'

She heaved a sigh of agreement to this. 'I've been a widow for eight years, and I sometimes speak to myself, as well.'

'You will have gathered that I do not want your grandmother to meet you and your brother, who was studying for the ministry the last I heard. It is this last, more than anything else, that I pray she never finds out, although I cannot explain my reason for that. I can only beseech you not to muddy the calm waters of the life she has left to her. Once she has gone, I will tell you all you want to know, your real name, the address of the castle, so that you may contact your mother, who, I am positive, will be extremely glad to make your acquaintance. Now, I feel rather tired, so I will take my leave of you, Mrs Laverton.'

Ruth had passed a restless night and she felt no better the following morning. Her mind was spinning like a top with what she had learned the previous day. Despite Mr Rennie's determination not to tell her anything, he had inadvertently revealed that her mother's name was Melda and that she came of a family called Bruce-Lyall, who lived in a castle somewhere, but he had asked her not to try to find them and she would have to wait until her grandmother died before she could do anything.

Having existed for hours on cups of tea, she scrambled some eggs at half-past five, and had made some toast and filled the teapot when someone knocked on her door. Dragging herself through to answer the summons, she was astonished to see Bob Mennie, her brother-in-law.

'Is something wrong with Gladys?' she asked in alarm.

'Not a thing.' He gave her a teasing smile. 'I just came to see how you were, Ruthie. You said you were trying to find out about your mother, and I wondered . . .'

'I've learned quite a lot,' she smiled, pleased to be able to tell somebody.

He accepted the tea she poured for him and listened gravely until she mentioned that the Bruce-Lyalls had a castle. 'My God, Ruthie!' he exclaimed. 'That's Lord Glendarril's place . . . I'd to make a delivery there once.' He leaned back in his chair and regarded her with interest. 'Don't tell me you're related to them? The Bruce-Lyalls are aristocracy, and if one of them's your mother, you haven't half landed on your feet. Gladys'll be jealous as hell.'

'Don't tell her,' Ruth pleaded. 'I'm not going near them yet. The solicitor asked me not to try to find them.'

'Did you promise him you wouldn't?'

'He didn't ask me to promise.'

'There you are, then. My God, I don't know how you can sit there so calmly when you could be living the life of Riley in a castle.'

'Oh, Bob, they won't want a working-class widow turning up on their doorstep. They'll think I'm begging for money.'

He leaned across and patted her hand. 'If what Mr Rennie said's true, and I can't see anybody making up a story like that, you're entitled to some of their money. Look, Ruthie, I'll tell you what. Tomorrow's Saturday, my half-day, so I'll drive you there. I finish work at twelve, so I'll have a quick wash and a bite to eat and I'll come for you about half-past one – it's not much more than thirty miles, so it won't take us long.'

'What'll Gladys say?' Ruth asked apprehensively.

'What she doesn't know won't hurt her,' he grinned. 'I'll say there's a schoolboy match at Pittodrie. I'd normally get home from the football round about quarter to six, so we've plenty of time.' He pushed back his chair and got to his feet. 'I'd better be going, before she starts wondering why I'm so late home from work. I don't want her to begin suspecting anything. Half-past one, remember.'

She made fresh tea when he went out. She had always thought of Bob Mennie as a selfish brute, but since her mother died, he couldn't have been nicer to her. And there was nothing nasty behind it; he'd never tried anything or said anything out of place. He was more than likely making up to her for the way Gladys was treating her.

Looking at the clock as she took the dirty dishes to the sink, she thought that this time tomorrow . . . she would either be jumping for joy at being accepted into the Bruce-Lyall fold, or more likely, weeping the bitter tears of rejection.

Chapter Thirty

It was unforgiveable of Andrew, Marianne fumed. If he hadn't let the cat out of the bag, she could have carried the secret with her to the grave, and would never have had to meet . . . Confronting the woman who had turned up yesterday had been like coming face to face with a part of the past she'd believed to be buried beyond recall, most upsetting. Thankfully, she'd succeeded in fooling the creature, though no doubt she'd be back demanding to be told the truth, and Ruairidh and his wife might not be so conveniently away next time.

Wait, though! Ruth Laverton, as she had called herself, could only have been wanting to get her hands on some of the Bruce-Lyall money, though she hadn't mentioned blackmail, so it might be a good idea to offer her some, to pay her to keep her mouth shut. It would have to be enough to do the trick, Marianne decided, which would be a bit of a problem since there was no cash in the coffers. The end of the war had been a blow for the mill. It was the end of the Ministry of Defence orders, and Fair Isle garments had gone out of fashion, so the mill was struggling and Ruairidh had ploughed all his resources into trying to get it back on its feet. The family, once so wealthy, was now in debt.

'With Dorothea gone,' he had said sadly, 'I have nobody to leave my money to, anyway.'

Marianne could feel the old tightness in her throat, the heaviness in her heart. Losing her dear Hamish had been almost unbearable, and Dorothea's death so soon after she'd gone to London had almost finished her. In a truly vulnerable state now, she toyed with the idea of publicly acknowledging Ruth Laverton as her granddaughter, and it took several minutes for her to discard it. She could not resurrect her son's illegitimate child and be the cause of endless scandal for him. Nor could she submit to blackmail, not that the woman had mentioned such a thing.

From the very start, when she'd first learned that Ruairidh and Melda had done something they shouldn't, her only thought had been to save the fact coming out. She had lied about the infant dying soon after birth, but only to save the family name from being besmirched. The family name, and all it encompassed, meant everything to her, more than it did to Ruairidh, more than it had to Hamish really, and she hadn't even been born into it.

Her daughter-in-law, of course, didn't care tuppence that they'd soon have to open the castle as an ancient monument and allow members of the public to roam through the place . . . except for the west wing, because Ruairidh had put his foot down about that. The family had to have some privacy, after all. But Melda would happily live in poverty as long as Ruairidh was with her. She had been devastated by Dorothea's death, and it had made her hard, fortifying her against any other tragedies that may befall her, but how would she react when, if, she learned that at least one of her first two children was still alive? She might erupt with the force of a long-dormant volcano . . . with the fire directed at the person who had tricked her into believing there had been only one child – which had died.

And yet, Marianne mused, her luck had held good so far. When that female had turned up like a nasty insect crawling out of the woodwork to disrupt her tranquillity, she had been alone in the house except for a recently engaged maid, who didn't count – it was difficult to get staff since the war; nobody wanted to go into service – and her bluff had worked. Ruth Laverton had gone away, perhaps not convinced that she was on the wrong track but surely a bit doubtful that Melda was her mother. She hadn't mentioned her sister, and she, Marianne, had not let on that she knew there was a twin, but Andrew knew and he'd likely insist on tying things up so that they'd be sure of getting their fair share of any money when their father passed on.

Sitting down at the old desk – her mind so occupied that it did not occur to her that this antique item alone would fetch a fortune if it were sold – Marianne left a message on the telephone with Andrew's housekeeper, asking him to come to see her the next afternoon – more of an order than an invitation, really. Ruairidh and Melda would not be back from the exhibition they'd gone to see in London until Monday, and Bessie always took all day Sunday off. She had to get Andrew on his own. He was older than she was, and had been very frail the last time she saw him, so it shouldn't be difficult to browbeat him into telling the woman, and the other twin, if she turned up, they were not who they thought they were. She could quite easily convince the fortune-hunters that some mistake had been made, that they were not Melda's children, that she, Lady Glendarril, had actually been there when those two doomed infants died.

Having told her solicitor which train to take, Marianne sent Gilchrist to meet him in the Bentley, and was delighted to see how doddery Andrew was when her chauffeur helped him out of the car and up the steps.

She kissed her old friend on the cheek, and was inwardly amused to see the roguish twinkle in his rheumy eyes when he slid his arm round her waist. Silly old fool! Surely he didn't still think she wanted him to . . . no, that was absurd. He hardly had the strength to put one foot past the other, never mind anything else. 'It's so good to see you, Andrew,' she murmured, squeezing his hand.

Completely under her spell already, he followed her into the large drawing room. 'D'you know, Marianne,' he said, taking a seat by the window, 'I can remember sitting here so many times over the years, talking to Hamish and wishing that I had never brought the two of you together. He took the only girl I ever loved.'

She decided to spread the jam on thickly. 'I wish that, too. I was beginning to love you, Andrew, but he was so charming . . . and I was so young . . .'

Andrew was not quite so gullible as she had thought. 'But not so naïve as you are trying to make out. You knew what you were doing when you married him.'

'He told me he just wanted me so he could have sons, but I was blinded by the prospect of the wealth he would fall heir to, the idea of being a titled lady in a castle. I admit that, but I did discover that there is more to life than wordly possessions.'

He nodded gravely. 'Yes, there is, Marianne. There is compassion for your fellow men or women, and honesty, and abiding by the rules, all of which you have totally disregarded throughout your life.'

Stung by criticism from a man she had believed loved her without question, she snapped, 'And where was your compassion for me when you spun that vile story to that awful Ruth Laverton?'

'It *was* a vile story,' he agreed, 'yet true, nevertheless. At the time, I carried out your instructions and excused your heartlessness by telling myself that you were desperately covering up the results of Ruairidh's irresponsibility. When Ruth contacted me, and I realized that she was one of Melda's twins, I was pleased that your daughter-in-law would be reunited with one, at least, even after such a long time. Poor girl, she must often have wondered what had become of them.'

He paused and turned his eyes on Marianne accusingly. 'I found it extremely hard to believe that she had agreed to their being adopted, but loving you as I did, I could not contemplate the alternative – that you had forced her into it. It strikes me now, however, that there must have been a reason why she did not search for them after Ruairidh married her. How did you arrange that? Did you tell her they had died?'

Bowing to a Fate that seemed to be determined to catch her out, even after so many years, Marianne came to the conclusion that she had better confess. 'I'm afraid I did – to one anyway, and Melda was never told about the other one.' Feeling that the atmosphere inside had suddenly become oppressive, she said, 'Why don't we have a walk in the garden? We can talk just as well there, and we can take a seat if we get tired.'

Even in the warmth of the June day, both old people felt the need of a jacket before venturing outside, and so it was another few minutes before Marianne put her arm through Andrew's and guided his tottery feet along the path from the heavy studded door of the west wing to the vast rose garden. 'My father-in-law had this laid out to mark Edward's accession to the throne,' she informed him as they turned into the walled-in rectangle, adding quickly, 'Edward the Seventh, I mean. He and Hector were great friends, and he had often come here for the shooting when he was Prince of Wales. I wish I'd been around then, for I've heard so many stories about him with young girls, and I wouldn't have minded being his Princess . . . but I'm speaking rubbish. I had my dear Hamish, hadn't I?' She stole a sideways glance at her companion and was confused to find him regarding her sadly.

'How little I knew you,' he sighed. 'I always hoped that you regretted marrying Hamish.'

'I never regretted marrying him, and I loved what the marriage brought me,' she declared, honest up to a point.

'So you . . . never thought of leaving him . . . for me?'

Marianne felt a rush of pity for him. For sixty years she had flirted with him at every opportunity, led him to believe that he meant something to her other than her man of business, and he didn't deserve such scurrilous treatment – he was truly a decent man. She changed the subject abruptly. 'I said I'd tell you about Melda and the two babies. She was just a young thing, and not the kind of girl I wanted as a daughter-in-law, and she took everything on trust. She wouldn't hear of the child being adopted or put in an orphanage, so I threatened her that if she didn't do what I wanted, I would tell Ruairidh she'd been carrying on with one of the soldiers at the camp, and it was *his* baby. Then I started thinking she might wonder how the child was and so, not long after the births – she wasn't told she'd had two and with a difficult labour she wasn't in a fit state to know – I said the baby had died and she believed me. I made her promise never to breathe a word to anybody, especially Ruairidh.'

'Poor Melda,' muttered Andrew.

'Not so poor! She was besotted with the idea of marrying into the nobility, and she talked him into it not long after he came home –'

'Melda's not like you!' Andrew broke in harshly. 'She had always loved Ruairidh; she wouldn't have cared if he was destitute, and he had always loved her. I can't believe you were so cruel to her, Marianne . . .'

'She was just a doctor's daughter, after all. Middle class.'

'And what were you before my aunts took pity on you? What work did your father do?'

She had the grace to look slightly abashed. 'He just worked in a sawmill in Tipperton.'

'Yes, so you were from working stock, and none the worse for it. Your blood instilled new life into the Bruce-Lyalls. Your sons were much sturdier and healthier than their father and their grandfather. But tell me, were you ever sorry for leaving your home?'

'I had to leave. I told you, remember, I stole some money.' And now, so long afterwards, Marianne felt the shame she had not felt at the time.

'Yes, I do remember. Five sovereigns, wasn't it, a lot in those days, more than a year's wages in many cases? Um, did you ever take anything from my aunts?'

'No, never!' She could sense a new coldness in his manner towards her which, after the long years of his constant devotion, pained her more than she could have thought possible. But she could not blame her old friend for despising her, not after all he had done for her in the past.

He had never been just a friend; he had always been a part of her that she could not do without, not a lover in the physical sense, but in a far more lasting capacity.

'Oh, Andrew, I must have a rest,' she gasped, plumping down on the wooden bench they were passing, one of several at the side of the walkway round the large pond.

She had hoped for at least a slight show of concern, but he sat down beside her without saying a word and it was some time before she ventured, in a small voice, 'I suppose you're shocked by the things I did, but will you do one last thing for me?'

'If it lies within my power,' he replied stiffly.

'Tell Melda's . . . tell Ruth and her twin, there must have been some mistake and they're not hers at all. Say I was there when both her babies died, and –'

He rose slowly but angrily to his feet, glaring venomously at her as he spat out, 'Good God, Marianne! I just do not know how you have the effrontery to ask me that!'

Turning, he took a step away from her, and she sprang to her feet to try to pacify him. The abrupt movement made a dizziness come over her, and trying to find something to steady her, she stretched out her arms. Tragically, she knocked Andrew off his feet and, feeling himself falling, he caught hold of her sleeve. Fingers clawing at empty air, it dawned on Marianne that there was nothing she could do to prevent the inevitable.

Falling heavily on top of him, her body ground the fluted tiles edging the path further into his temple, while she splashed face down into the water.

Chapter Thirty-one

The front pages of the Scottish newspapers next day carried some mention of the 'catastrophic accident', mainly along the lines that it had almost been a double tragedy and speculating as to how it had happened.

The unusual occurrence even warranted articles in the national dailies, the more sensational proclaiming in large headlines:

'SUICIDE PACT GONE WRONG?'
'ONLY DEATH COULD PART MARIANNE AND ANDREW!'
'DEATH UNVEILS SECRET PASSION!'
'THE LADY AND HER LAWYER LOVER!'

The ages of the 'lovers' were not revealed until the end of the articles, within parenthesis and in tiny print which most of the readers passed over as not worth straining their eyes for. Those who did take the trouble were left feeling cheated. A man and woman both in their seventies? They wouldn't remember what passion was, if they'd ever experienced it, which was doubtful.

In less than a week after the funeral, the public's interest had moved on to other scandals, but in an airy office in Aberdeen's Bon Accord Square, Graham Dalgarno was having problems. He had intended executing Andrew Rennie's last will and testament before turning his mind to anything else, but it was not nearly as straightforward as he had imagined. No relatives remaining alive, the old man had left his entire estate to Lady Glendarril's *first two* grandchildren. The peculiar underlining of the words 'first two' when, as far as Graham knew, there was only one, who had died since the will had been drawn up, combined with the pencilled note at the side which read 'Ruth and Samuel', made him realize that he would have to go through the Bruce-Lyall papers to find answers to the suspicions which had jumped to his mind.

Andrew Rennie had jealously guarded his right as senior partner to deal with Lady Glendarril's affairs, and on his retiral, he had given orders that any future correspondence relating thereto should be laid aside for his attention. Hence, for the past ten years, he had come in once a month to bring her files up to date, and it was only after his death that Graham had got his hands on the key to the roll-top desk and the power to handle this prestigious account. But having access to what was more or less Lady Glendarril's life history was the beginning of his nightmare!

The first document he had come across was the dowager's will, which Andrew had no doubt helped her to draw up. It was a complicated document, changed several times over the years, first stating that everything she left was to go to her granddaughter, Dorothea Bruce-Lyall, and then a codicil which noted that because of Dorothea's death,

Marianne's son, the present Viscount Glendarril, would inherit his mother's entire estate. Graham had thought it strange that no mention was made of the present Lady Glendarril, but this was something he would have to come to terms with when the dowager died.

He had discovered that the Ruth and Samuel, to whom the old man had left all his wordly goods, were not included in their grandmother's will, which, although it did seem very strange, was not something he should worry about meantime. His worry would lie in tracing them, finding out who was their father . . .

The thought which struck Graham then almost knocked him sideways. Was it possible? If so, it had been the best-kept secret ever, but then people with plenty of money could always find ways and means to cover up any indiscretions.

Graham's suspicions gathered momentum. Andrew was a crafty old beggar! He must have fathered two children on Marianne Bruce-Lyall when they were young and whisked them away somewhere out of sight! Graham had sensed that their relationship went much deeper than solicitor/client, but he had never dreamed . . .

Wait a minute! If Ruth and Samuel were Marianne's illegitimate *grand*children, she definitely wasn't their mother, and it meant that they had also been the late Hamish's grandchildren, unless . . . had he impregnated the present Lady Glendarril – the younger one – at some time? The idea of this was quite repugnant to Graham. Esmerelda – he had always thought it a beautiful name for the elegant woman, although he believed she was usually referred to as Melda – was not the kind to have a sordid affair with a man old enough to be her father. There must be another

511

explanation, but he was blowed if he could think of one. He had better put all his other commitments aside to give him the time and the freedom to search the desk for birth certificates or other documents which would enable him to wind up Andrew Rennie's estate as he had wished.

Graham searched the top left drawer slowly and methodically, inwardly thanking his late partner for writing notes to remind himself of things he might otherwise have forgotten, but nothing he came across shed any light on the matter in hand. Disgruntled, he started on the drawer underneath, but found almost at once that it held only correspondence from various tradespeople in answer to complaints Marianne Glendarril had raised, and dating back as far as when she had first become a titled lady.

At four thirty, depressed and tired, and hungry because he had gone without lunch, Graham decided against taking the contents of the bottom drawer home in his briefcase. He would leave it until the morning, when his mind would be fresher and more able to spot anything relevant.

Next day, he gave his secretary instructions that he was not to be disturbed and settled into the swivel chair again. After unlocking the bottom drawer, he saw that it contained a large tin box, black japanned like all the old deed boxes. His pulse quickened when he discovered that it, too, was locked. It seemed promising – a locked box in a locked drawer must conceal something of great importance. His fingers trembling, he took some time to find the correct key, but at last the latch snapped back. The papers he took out led him into a maze of legality – or illegality? – which would need to be sorted out before he could go any further.

His most astounding discovery in the first hour was that from 1919 to 1933, Andrew Rennie had been transferring money every six months from an account in his name with the Clydesdale Bank, but marked in his secret journal as belonging to 'Marianne'. As if this were not mystery enough, the money had been divided equally – one half going to an account with the Royal Bank of Scotland and the other to an account with the North of Scotland Bank for the maintenance of two children. The question was whose children?

If Andrew had used his own money, the answer would have been that they were his, but the fact that it was Marianne Glendarril who had actually paid would suggest otherwise. And in 1919, she herself would have been around forty, past child-bearing age. Would they have been spawned by one of her sons? The elder, Ranald, had been killed about nine months before the payments began, so he could have been the father, but that was pure conjecture.

Graham sifted through all the papers again in the hope of finding something more definite, trying to decipher all the pencilled notes which cropped up in the strangest places in Andrew's rather cramped scribbles – along the tops of pages, across corners, up or down the margins.

Nearing the end of another hour, when Graham was on the verge of giving up, something caught his eye. His dejected spirits soared as he studied the statement of interest in his hand. It was from a firm of brokers concerning a block of shares Lady Glendarril held in a tea plantation in Assam, and halfway down, between two lines of figures, was a faint insertion – so faint that it was a wonder he had noticed it: 'Ruth married Mark Laverton 21/7/41.'

Sitting back, Graham held the sheet of paper up to the window, turning it this way and that to make sure there was nothing else written on it. There wasn't, and this had no connection with the paper on which it was written. Andrew had obviously learned of the girl's marriage while he had been working with the statement, and had jotted it down to remind him. But this information gave Graham the incentive to carry on.

He set to with renewed vigour, and when, twenty minutes later, his secretary knocked on his door, he called, 'I told you I do not wish to be disturbed today.'

Jane McDonald opened the door a little and said, 'I'll get the lady to make an appointment then, shall I? When would be best?'

'You had better make it next week. Do I know her?'

'I don't think so. She said she spoke to Mr Rennie about ten days ago, and then she saw his death in the papers.'

Graham's head snapped up. 'Andrew never mentioned taking on a new client. Did she give her name?'

'Mrs Laverton.'

'Laverton?' He bounded up off his chair and practically shoved Miss McDonald out of his way in his haste to make sure that it was the correct Mrs Laverton.

His noisy entry to the waiting room startled the woman, who said, nervously, 'Mr Rennie was dealing . . . but when I saw his death in the papers, I wondered who . . .'

Feeling equally nervous, Graham cleared his throat. 'He retired from the firm ten years ago, Mrs Laverton, and since then, his only client has been –'

'My grandmother?'

He was pleased to have at least one of his suspicions confirmed.

'Um . . . can you tell me . . . what was your mother's name?'

'All I know is her first name is Melda.'

'Melda?' he gasped. 'But Esmeralda is the present Lady Glendarril and in that case, Ruairidh . . . Lord Glendarril . . . cannot be your father. They were married in – I think 1920, and you were born in 1919?'

She gave a smiling nod. 'If he *is* my father, I can't understand why they didn't claim me when they became husband and wife. I was fostered out, apparently, though I always thought the Browns were my real parents. My mother only told me she wasn't my birth mother when she was on her deathbed.'

When Graham learned that Samuel had been adopted, but had later been taken to Edinburgh by his adoptive parents, he burst out, 'Did Andrew Rennie tell you all this?'

She explained that the old solicitor had inadvertently let slip the Bruce-Lyall name and where they lived, and she told him about her visit to the castle itself. 'My grandmother was the only one I saw, and she swore there was some mistake, and she had no idea who I was. She was so convincing I started doubting what Mr Rennie had told me, then I read about his death, and I thought, why shouldn't I go and see if someone in his office knew anything?'

Graham was shocked by the dowager's behaviour. 'She did know who you were! She had authorized Rennie to deposit money in your foster parents' bank every month for your keep. Her son must have refused to marry your mother . . .' He stopped, looking more bemused than ever.

'But he did marry her after the war . . . I wonder, now? Is it possible that he hadn't known about his twins? I wouldn't put it past the old vixen to have covered up all traces of her son's indiscretions . . . and threatened your mother with some dire calamity if she let the cat out of the bag.'

Ruth brightened. 'It must have been something like that! I can't see any mother, however young and inexperienced, not telling the man she loved about their babies . . . and he must have loved her, too, or else he wouldn't have married her when he came home from the war.'

Graham hit his right fist into his left palm. 'One payment stopped in 1933, that would have been when you started earning for yourself, but the other went on until 1938. Although Samuel was legally adopted, Marianne, or Andrew on his own initiative, must have paid for a better education for him, because he was a boy. Her name had been kept out of it, so that no one would ever know that she had any connection . . .' He stopped again, frowning. 'Ruairidh would have been in either France or Belgium at the time of the births, and I wouldn't put it past his mother to have sent Melda away during the latter months of her pregnancy.'

'That old besom has a lot to answer for,' Ruth said bitterly.

His heart went out to this woman who had clearly had a hard life right from the time of her birth, and who was dressed in well-worn clothes which told of ongoing financial struggles. She had not let herself go, however. Her chestnut hair, bobbed quite short, was gleaming with cleanliness, her face had been lightly powdered or whatever women did to take the shine off their skin, and her lips were not nearly as garish as some he had seen, just

516

a little touch of lipstick. Her face was a perfect oval, but there was a sadness in her dark eyes.

Graham became aware that she was waiting for him to say something else, and said the first thing that came into his head. 'Why did you want to get in touch with your mother, Mrs Laverton? Were you planning to ask her for –'

'I want nothing from any of them!' she burst out. 'I just want to know the truth about myself, Mr Dalgarno, to see what my parents look like and what kind of people they are, and why they allowed other people to bring me up. I'm not out for revenge for being abandoned, don't think that, but I *would* like to make them feel a wee bit guilty. Can you understand that?'

'Indeed I can.' Graham seemed to make up his mind about something now. 'I hope you are not in a hurry, because I have some good news for you, something that will prevent the dowager from thinking you are after *her* money.' Noticing her bemusement, he smiled benignly. 'You are in for a wonderful surprise, Mrs Laverton, but perhaps you would prefer me to wait until your brother can be with you?'

'You've made me curious, so you might as well tell me now.'

It did not take him long to tell her of the legacy from Andrew Rennie, but it took some time for her to take in the extent of the wealth she and her as yet unknown brother had inherited. And he could see that he would have to make her understand Andrew Rennie's motive; that would be the only way she would feel free to accept such a large windfall.

'But why would he leave anything to Samuel and me?' she asked for the third time. 'Maybe he'd been given the

517

job of making sure we had decent food and clothes, but his obligation was over when we started working.'

'Andrew was a very kind-hearted man,' Graham said patiently, 'and I think he wanted to make up to you for . . . and I'm nearly sure he had loved Marianne Glendarril since he was a young man, which was why he did everything she asked of him, but what she did to you when you went to Castle Lyall must have made him see her as she really was – a wicked schemer. I can't pretend to fathom out what happened ten days ago. I do not like to think that she was responsible for his death, Mrs Laverton, yet I have the nastiest feeling that she was.'

'Oh, surely not, Mr Dalgarno! It was an accident! But I'd like to know why Mr Rennie left his money to my brother and me. He had never met us when he drew up his will.'

'He knew you would get nothing from your grandmother, and I expect he felt sorry for you, Mrs Laverton.'

'Call me Ruth, please,' she begged. 'I don't know who I am or what's happening to me, but whatever my last name was, is, or will be, I'll always be Ruth.'

'And you must call me Graham; this Mr and Mrs business is far too formal. Well, Ruth, I advise you to go home now and I will do what I can to make Lady Glendarril agree to see you. I shall also go through Andrew's papers again with a fine-tooth comb, and pray that I find the answer to your brother's whereabouts.'

After she had left, Graham leaned back with a satisfied sigh. He hadn't solved all the mystery, but he knew now how fairy godmothers felt. It wasn't the first time he had sprung an inheritance on an unsuspecting beneficiary, but it was usually a distant relative or someone who had worked for the deceased, and never on this scale. Andrew Rennie had been a bachelor all his life, had lived frugally and invested his savings wisely, and Graham had already learned, from some tentative enquiries he had made, that the sum involved would be well into six figures. Ruth and Samuel would receive an amount far in excess of anything their grandmother could have left them.

His next task was to plan the meeting. He admired Ruth Laverton. However poor she was, however much in need, she would never grovel for help to her new-found family. His opinion of Esmerelda Glendarril, on the other hand, had been badly dented. He had met her only occasionally over the years and did not know her well, but on the day of Andrew's funeral she had given the impression of being a gentle, caring person – very similar to Ruth, in fact.

It would be interesting to arrange for all parties concerned to meet, he mused, and to watch their reactions, but it would not be ethical. For one thing, Esmerelda may not have told her husband about the twins, and had she the guts to tell him after all this time? If she did, would Ruairidh believe her – would he even want to believe her? It would be upsetting for him, galling, to learn that the girl he loved had concealed the existence of their love children from him for so many years. He would doubt that they were his, and imagine that she'd had other lovers while he had been away fighting for his country, which would turn him against Ruth and Samuel.

Recognizing that a large confrontation was out of the question, Graham decided to stick to his original plan and talk to Lady Glendarril alone first. The outcome of that would decide what his next move should be.

Chapter Thirty-two

Melda couldn't think why Graham Dalgarno wanted to see her, or why he had insisted that she came to him. He could say all he wanted to say in front of her husband, surely?

Joe Gilchrist, the chauffeur/handyman who had often taken Marianne to see her solicitor, drew the Bentley to a smooth halt at the steps up to his office. 'When do you want to be picked up, your Ladyship?' he asked. 'When old Lady Glendarril used to come here, she always told me to come back for her in an hour, but if you want longer . . . ?'

Despite her misgivings, Melda managed a smile. 'No, an hour's long enough – maybe too long,' she grimaced wryly.

'Should I just wait outside, then?'

The tightness in her chest eased a little. She had a feeling that the coming meeting was to be somewhat uncomfortable and it was good to know she could make her escape at any time. 'That might be best.'

Waiting until he came round to open the car door for her – he would be insulted if she didn't – she glanced around in admiration at the raised garden laid out between the two rows of tall granite buildings, because Bon Accord Square belied its name, and was, in fact, a long rectangle. The grass looked as well kept as the lawns at Castle Lyall, and whoever had been given the job of laying out the flowering shrubs had a good eye for colour. Reading her thoughts, Gilchrist grinned as he helped her on to the pavement. 'Me and Lady Marianne always said this was one of the bonniest streets in the town. Will you manage now, or will I . . . ?'

'I'll manage, thanks.' Taking a deep breath, she went slowly up the outside steps without holding on to the handrail.

With her usual abhorrence of being late for any appointments, she took a quick look at her watch, and her heart sank. Not quite ten to twelve. Her mother-in-law would have said it was just as bad mannered to catch people on the hop by being early as it was to keep them waiting. When she reached the top step, however, she was glad that she wasn't late, because Graham Dalgarno himself opened the glass door for her. He must have been watching for her.

'Good morning, Lady Glendarril,' he smiled, taking her hand in a tight grip and shaking it vigorously.

'Good morning, Mr Dalgarno,' she replied, trying to discover from his expression whether he had good or bad news to impart.

Shepherding her up a carpeted flight of stairs, he ushered her into his private office and gestured to the high-backed armchair he had drawn in for her. 'You'll be wondering why I asked you here?'

'I've been a bit curious,' she admitted, his obvious unease making her more apprehensive than ever.

'This is very difficult . . . perhaps we should have coffee . . . No, I think something stronger is called for.'

She watched him crossing to a tall filing cabinet and taking out a gill of whisky. Back at his desk, he produced two glasses big enough to hold a generous dram, not the little tot she had expected. 'Oh, just a mouthful for me,' she protested, as the amber liquid gurgled out of the small bottle. 'I'm not a drinker.'

'You're going to need it,' he warned.

Deciding to leave the whisky until she did need it, if at all, she looked at him searchingly. 'Why did you bring me here? What is so secret that you can't tell me in front of Ruairidh?'

Graham fortified himself before saying, 'I wasn't sure if he knew.'

Her brows came down, yet her eyes remained clear. 'Knew what?'

'I may be wrong in doing this, but I thought he should know about your two children.'

Her whole face closed now. 'I am afraid you have made a mistake, Mr Dalgarno. My only daughter died some years ago.'

Seeking the nerve to carry on, he took another sip. 'It was not . . . er . . . it was Ruth and Samuel I meant.'

If he had hoped to see signs of shame or guilt, he would have been disappointed. Her eyes showed only perplexity. 'Ruth and Samuel? I don't understand.'

Bracing himself, Graham said, as calmly as he could, 'I have in my desk, Lady Glendarril, two birth certificates which name you as the mother.'

Her cheeks blanched but she did not look away. 'Oh, my God. How did you find out about that?' Before he could answer, she burst out, 'But I only had one baby, a boy who died hours after he was born!' The grief she had thought she had mastered forever surfaced without warning, and she bent her head to hide her distress.

'I knew it!' Graham erupted, making her raise her streaming eyes. 'I knew your mother-in-law had told you that your babies were dead. It *was* her, wasn't it, and you never saw the bodies?'

She shook her head and lifted the glass of spirits to her lips. Its fiery content burned its way down her gullet and enabled her to accept what she realized he was telling her. 'They gave me something to knock me out, and when I came round, she said the baby had died and it was best all round. She pretended to be sorry, but before the birth, she'd forced me to agree to having it adopted . . . and I never got to see him. Nobody told me I'd had twins. What did she do with them?'

'As far as I can make out,' Graham said gently, 'she asked Andrew Rennie to do the dirty work for her. I do not know the full story, but it seems your son was adopted, but your daughter was just fostered. When I first learned of the money which had been paid out over a period of years for maintenance, I gave Lady Marianne full credit for providing for them, but it had likely been Andrew's idea, not hers.'

Draining her glass, Melda said, her voice low and quivering, 'I can't believe there were twins and they're still alive, and you talk as if you know what had happened to them . . .'

He lifted the whisky bottle again and poured what was left into her glass. 'Drink it!' he ordered, as she gripped her lips to show she didn't want it. 'I do know what

523

happened to them, in fact . . .' He hesitated, then said softly, 'I kept searching through all Andrew's papers looking for information about Samuel, and I could find nothing until I took out the newspaper which I thought was lining the bottom drawer. It was an *Edinburgh Evening Citizen* dated October 1943, and I was about to dispose of it when it dawned on me that it must have some significance for Andrew to have kept it. It had! A small announcement inside stated that Samuel Fernie, only son of John and Margaret Fernie of Clermiston, had been posted as missing.'

Her gasp of dismay made him shake his head ruefully. 'I'm sorry, your Ladyship, I should not have come out with it like that.'

'It's quite all right. It's better that I know –'

'No, no, he is still alive! I looked up the Edinburgh telephone directory to see if there were any Fernies listed in Clermiston – on the outskirts of the city – and struck lucky with my second call. Samuel, or Sam as they call him, had been taken prisoner at Salerno, was transferred to Stalag 77 in Germany when the Italians gave up, and repatriated after the war ended.'

'Oh, thank God he wasn't killed,' Melda said, in a small voice. 'I don't think I could have borne to hear of his death a second time. Does he still live in Edinburgh, or does he work somewhere else?'

'With the money provided for his further education, Sam had gone to university in order to get a degree in medicine, but the war started before he graduated. Being a red-blooded Bruce-Lyall, although he was not aware of it, he gave up his studies and joined the Army

Medical Corps. After the war, what he had seen in the prison camps – the helplessness and hopelessness of the captured Allied servicemen – made him vow to become a preacher if God spared him, so when he came home he went back to university and eventually gained his MD. He is now touring the Army of Occupation in Berlin, but Mrs Fernie, his adoptive mother, promised to write to him straight away, so it should not be long until we hear from him.'

It crossed Melda's mind that, in view of the calling of her real and adoptive fathers, it was strange that her son should have been drawn towards both medicine and the ministry, but it would probably send her mother-in-law over the edge into the madness she had wrongly attributed to all men of the cloth. But that was a bridge to be crossed later . . .

'And now, Mr Dalgarno, what about . . . Ruth?'

'She has only recently learned that she was fostered, your Ladyship.'

'If she's angry at me for giving her up, you'll have to –'

'Andrew had told her what happened, and she's a very understanding person. I think . . . I know that you won't be disappointed in how she has turned out . . . and she is desperate to meet you.'

'As I am to meet her.'

'Good! Shall I take her to Castle Lyall tomorrow?'

The alarm which flooded her face made him say, 'No, I shall have to give you time to adjust, and I can see you are still suffering from the shock I gave you. Get that Scotch down, it should help.' While she obeyed, grimacing at each sip, he wondered why she had suddenly changed her mind about an early meeting.

'It's not that I don't want to see Ruth,' Melda muttered, as if she knew what he was thinking, 'but I have to prepare someone first.'

'Does Lord Glendarril not know . . . ?'

'No, I'm sorry to say, he doesn't. His mother threatened to tell him I'd been going with soldiers from the camp if I ever said anything to him.'

'But surely, if he loved you, he'd have known they were his?'

'I was frightened to risk it. I was very young, and I couldn't stand up to her. To tell the truth, I was grateful to her at first for whisking me off before anybody in the glen noticed I'd been a bad girl. I wouldn't have been allowed to marry Ruairidh if it had come out we'd had . . .'

'Didn't you ever feel like telling him after the war, the second war, that is? It's not such a crime nowadays.'

'It's still a disgrace, even yet, but it's not telling Ruairidh I'm worried about, it's my father. He knows nothing about this, and he'll be very hurt that I didn't tell him.'

'And your mother?' Graham prompted.

'My mother died about three years ago – she didn't know, either – and Ruairidh managed to get Dad to give up the house they moved to when he retired and come to live with us. I wouldn't be surprised if my mother-in-law had told him the whole thing any of the times Ruairidh and I were in London. She has always liked to make trouble, and she was acting really strangely for days before we left.'

She took out her handkerchief and dabbed her eyes. 'I'm sorry to get upset like this, Mr Dalgarno. I loved Uncle Andrew as much as my husband did, but – you'll find this hard to believe – it's Marianne I feel sorry for. In spite of all she did to me, all the nasty things she said over the years, I couldn't help but admire her, because she stuck to her guns, no matter what. If she got something into her head, nothing would shift it.'

Melda decided not to tell the solicitor about Marianne's obsession about ministers, not yet. She would, one day, if only to help him to understand why her mother-in-law had not let her keep her first two children.

Gathering up her gloves and handbag, she said, 'I'd better go home now, but I'll let you know when to bring . . . Ruth to the castle.'

After shaking her hand, the solicitor saw her down to her car, and stood until it went round the corner into Bon Accord Street and out of sight.

Contrary to her usual habit of sitting in front with Gilchrist when they were going home, Melda sat in the back, unable to make any small talk, unable to think of anything other than the momentous news which Graham Dalgarno had sprung on her. If it hadn't been for her father, she would have been overjoyed at finding another daughter to replace Dorrie. Her death had sent Melda into the lowest trough of her entire life, when she had sobbed for days, and kept thinking that it was terrible that she'd given birth to two children and not one was left alive – she hadn't known then that she had actually given birth to three. She'd been too distraught to speak to her mother-in-law, in case she attacked the woman in her misery. Marianne, of course, had also been at a low ebb, with Hamish having died so recently.

And now? Was she to be the cause of *her* father's death? He was quite frail these days – he hadn't been properly well since her mother's fatal heart attack, and she suspected that he would never get over the most recent shock he'd had. Apparently he had been away for the weekend visiting a friend in Montrose, and had returned on the Sunday evening about seven. Not finding Marianne anywhere in the west wing, he had gone to the rose garden, where she often took a stroll on a Sunday afternoon or early evening, and had been appalled, when he rounded the wall, to see two bodies lying half on the path and half in the pond. That would have been enough to give him a heart attack without him hurrying to see if he could do anything. Fortunately, Marianne had been able to raise her head out of the water before she lost consciousness – so she told them later – and, apart from being unable to get up off the ground, had suffered only superficial injuries, and shock.

First making sure that there was nothing he could do for Andrew, Robert had managed to lift Marianne to a sitting position and then rushed to telephone Dr Addison, the man who had taken over when he himself retired. And when, Melda recalled, she and Ruairidh arrived back on the Monday morning, both old people were in bed. It was strange that, despite Marianne's usual indomitable spirit and Robert's extra years, he had been up and about again days before she even stopped weeping. She had obviously cared very deeply for Andrew Rennie and seemed to blame herself for his death.

On arriving at the castle now, Melda hurried up to her mother-in-law's bedroom, her heart turning over at the sight of her father sitting by the bedside with one of Marianne's hands clasped between both of his. How pale and drawn they both looked, she thought, their silver heads only inches apart, their sunken eyes gazing fondly at each other. It was so unusual – they were inclined to be rather hostile as a rule – that Melda took a quick step forward in the belief that the old woman was dying.

Both turned slowly towards her now. 'Marianne's been telling me about your twins,' her father said, his voice trembling. 'It's taken her some time to get me to believe what she did to you, and I still can't understand why you didn't come and tell me at the time.'

Feeling like the young girl she had been then, Melda stuttered, 'I was s-scared to t-tell you.'

'But your mother and I would have stood by you.'

A shaking hand crept out from under the counterpane now, coming to rest on top of the other three. 'Too late to discuss the rights and wrongs of it now,' Marianne muttered. 'Everything that happened at that time was down to me. It was all my fault, and you shouldn't blame Melda or Andrew or anybody else, Robert. Just be glad that the two poor infants were taken care of. Ruth, the one who came to see me, is quite pretty, a bit like Ruairidh but with auburn hair more like I used to have, and she said nothing about her sister.'

Melda opened her mouth to correct the error, then closed it without saying anything. She couldn't help the shaft of perverse pleasure that shot through her at the idea of the surprise Marianne would get when she found out that the other twin had been male . . . a male who would be heir to the title since his parents' marriage had made him legitimate.

A grandson of Duncan Peat, whose very name her mother-in-law still hated with the same intensity as of old! And above all, a minister himself!

But her satisfaction was short-lived. She had a momentous task ahead of her – to confess to Ruairidh what she had never had the courage to tell him before, just because she had been too afraid of what his mother might do. Well, it wasn't Marianne she was afraid of now – what had she to fear from a frail woman in her seventies? – it was Ruairidh's reaction. Waiting in the drawing room for his return from the mill, she felt so chilled that she switched on the small electric fire which was kept handy for those days when it wasn't cold enough for a coal fire. What would he say? Would he despise her for being such a coward? Could he possibly forgive her? Or would he be so angry at the deception that he would turn her out?

When she heard the low purr of the Bentley – Gilchrist always drove him to and from the mill – her heart thudded, her whole body stiffened in preparation for the battle she believed would come. He entered the room, smiling as he always did.

'What have you been doing with yourself today?' he asked brightly. Her silence made his expression change. 'Is anything wrong, Melda? Has Mother been more difficult than normal, or have she and your father had another difference of opinion?'

How patient he is, she thought. Most men would have felt irritated when she didn't answer straight away, but how would he take what she was about to tell him?

'Come on, darling,' he urged, 'I can see something's upset you.'

'I was talking to Graham Dalgarno today.'

'Ah, I didn't know he was coming, otherwise I'd have been here. What did he want?'

She conveniently postponed answering the question. 'He didn't come here, he asked me to go to Bon Accord Square.'

'Something about Andrew's will?'

'In a way.' She could detect little signs of exasperation in his eyes now, and deemed it wise not to procrastinate any longer. 'Sit down, Ruairidh, I've something to tell you.'

'Has dear old Uncle Andrew left us a fortune?'

She knew the light-hearted remark was forced. She knew him inside out. 'It's nothing to do with Andrew . . . well, it has in a way, but . . .' She stopped, wringing her hands in her confusion. 'Oh, I'm making heavy weather of this. Please, I beg you, just listen, and don't interrupt.'

She told him everything, from the day they learned of Ranald's death to the day she left the Brightfield Maternity Home for Unmarried Mothers, and he interrupted only once, to ask, 'Was Rannie the father?' At her response, 'No, Ruairidh, I swear he wasn't!' he said quietly, 'I just wanted to be sure,' and leaned back in his seat again, his face inscrutable.

When she stopped, shivering a little, she muttered, 'If you want to say something, do it now and get it over with.'

'I need time to think.' He had been sitting for several minutes, head down, hands at his temples, when he gave an abrupt exclamation and stood up. 'I'm going to have this out with Mother . . . No, she's no mother of mine, is she?'

His voice was so harsh that Melda put out her hand to stop him. 'Please don't, Ruairidh dear. What's the point now, after all this time?'

'I feel like killing her! I wish she had died along with Andrew! And he was as bad as she was! How could they? Keeping something like that from me? It was cruel! Wicked!'

'I kept it from you, too,' she reminded him softly.

He drew a deep breath to calm his rattled nerves, then thumped down on his chair again. 'It was different with you, Melda. You were so young – newly sixteen weren't you? — and I don't blame you for knuckling under with her, but . . .' He stopped, shaking his head. 'What I do find difficult to forgive is you not telling me, not even after we were married . . . not in all these years.'

Melda had been hoping, praying that he had put all the blame on his mother, but it appeared that he hadn't. 'I told you what she said she'd do if I breathed a word of it.' Her voice was strained.

'But surely you knew I wouldn't have believed her? I loved you so much I'd have trusted you, whatever lies she spun about you.'

'Like you said, I was still very young . . . I didn't know what to do. And she kept her side of the bargain, so I couldn't break my promise.'

'She manipulated you, Melda! Can't you see that? You owed it to me to tell me!'

Having been on a knife edge since her talk with Graham Dalgarno, this accusation that she was as much to blame as the other two participants in the deception was too much for her. Bursting into tears, she jumped to her feet and ran out, pounding up the stairs and flinging herself on their large bed. She had half expected him to follow her, to apologize, but when it became clear that she was being left severely alone, she told herself that he had nothing to

532

apologize for. After all, she *was* in the wrong; she should have told him as soon as he came home from the war. If he'd known about the child, he might have wanted to find out if it really had died. It wouldn't have mattered if they'd had to run away to be married, for Ruairidh to give up all claim to the title and the mill.

Her laboured thoughts came to a halt. It certainly wouldn't have mattered to *her*, but she couldn't have allowed him to give up his birthright. She had done the only thing possible under the circumstances . . . but no matter how strongly she assured herself of this, it did not ease the pain in her heart, nor take the edge off her anger at . . . herself as much as his mother.

It was almost an hour later, when she had exhausted all her tears and was drifting off into a troubled sleep, that her husband came in and, thankfully, she got no time to try to make further excuses, because he swept her up in his arms and she could feel his own salt tears on her lips as he kissed her.

'I'm so sorry, my dearest darling.'

The murmured words were all she needed. She knew that she was forgiven. Perhaps they could discuss it more fully in the morning, when they were both calmer, but perhaps not. It might be best to let the matter rest until Graham Dalgarno brought Ruth to the castle. Ruth! Their daughter. And they would meet their son, Samuel, as soon as Graham could arrange it.

It was probably all for the best that they would be introduced to only one at a time.

Chapter Thirty-three

As the Ford Zephyr Zodiac sped down the main road south from Aberdeen, Graham Dalgarno could sense that an element of reluctance had crept in to Ruth's eagerness, probably a fear of rejection despite his assurances that Melda Glendarril was just as anxious to meet her as Ruth was to meet her mother.

His own mind, however, was not on the business in hand at all. It had been on Ruth Laverton since she had walked into his office three weeks ago, though it felt like a lifetime, and with her sitting so close to him, his blood was pounding, his mouth was dry. There was no denying his feelings for her, but how could he ask her to marry him? Her share of Andrew Rennie's estate would make her a wealthy woman, and she was bound to suspect him of being a fortune-hunter. After all, what had he to offer her?

His thoughts were thrust aside as he swung round a blind corner under a railway bridge and only just missed a Post Office van coming from the opposite direction. Afraid to take his attention off the road again, he didn't look at Ruth as he murmured, 'Sorry about that. I'm a bit preoccupied.'

'Me, too,' she smiled. 'I'd have felt better if my brother could have been here to support me.'

A third party was the last thing he'd have wanted, but he could understand how she felt. 'Maybe I should have put the visit off until he managed to get here, but I got such a shock when I learned who was on the phone that it never crossed my mind to postpone it. In any case, one long-lost relative at a time may be enough for your new family to cope with.'

'I'm so nervous, though. What if the old lady told them not to . . . ? What if they don't like me?'

'How could anyone not like you?' The astonished exclamation was out before he could stop it. 'I mean . . . well, you know what I mean.'

'Flatterer,' she grinned.

He was glad that she felt easy enough with him to say that. He had asked her to his office several times to discuss various points – mostly those needing no further discussion – and he had taken her out to lunch once, so they did know each other a little better now, but he'd have to be very careful. One false move and he might ruin any chance he had of courting her.

Marianne nodded knowingly at the faint click of a door closing. 'That's them going down now, Robert. We'd better start moving. They're to be here about three.'

What he had been trying to tell her for days was preying on his mind like a canker eating at him, and he could put it off no longer. She had to be told before going downstairs. 'Marianne,' he began tentatively, 'I have something to say.'

'Oh, for any sake, man! Not now!'

'It's crucially important. I should have told you long ago, but –'

'It can wait another hour or two, then! I don't want to miss anything.'

Giving up, Robert got to his feet and helped her to hers. 'Will you need your walking stick?'

'Not today. It would put me at a disadvantage.'

He could see her point, but hoped that she wouldn't fall or trip on a loose rug. She had been relying on Hamish's silver-topped cane since Andrew Rennie's death, which had had a quite drastic effect on her, so now he placed his hand under her elbow. 'I hope you are not planning anything, Marianne,' he observed, closing the door. 'Remember, we two will be there purely as spectators.' He would have liked to issue a sterner warning, but it would have made her angry, and an angry Marianne was something to be avoided at all costs.

He couldn't help but admire her as she walked stiffly at his side. Her carriage was as erect as ever although her knees were affected by arthritis, and with his spine curving with osteoporosis, she was taller now than he. Both their heads were thatched with silver – his was natural, as he'd only been about forty when the black had started disappearing – where as her once-coppery hair had faded to a horrible yellowish-grey and needed the enhancement of a colour rinse to make it silver with a hint of blue. She was still a good-looking woman, though. Her unblemished skin was practically free of wrinkles, while his was like corrugated cardboard.

Their descent of the stairs was slow, almost majestic, but he thought he had better put her in a good humour. 'You're going like a two-year-old,' he teased.

His little ploy did not work. 'This is no time to be joking,' she reprimanded him. 'God alone knows what Melda and Ruairidh will promise her. When I saw her, she struck me as being after something – and I must be there to stop it getting out of hand.'

With something of a jolt, it dawned on him that she had not been told of the boy twin, and he bitterly regretted not forcing her to listen to him before they came down. His face, therefore, as he steered her into the drawing room, was enough to warn his daughter of possible ructions.

Nothing was said for the next five minutes, each person in the room dreading the meeting which was almost upon them, and none more so than Robert Mowatt, his old secret lying heavily on his conscience. To take his mind off it, he studied Melda, who, at fifty-three could have passed for forty even under the closest scrutiny. Her dark hair needed no artificial colouring nor permanent waving. Then she turned her head towards him, and her brown eyes were so apprehensive that he gave her what he hoped was a reassuring smile and transferred his attention to her husband.

Though he was only two years older than Melda, Ruairidh's blond hair had appeared to turn white almost overnight. Whatever, it didn't detract from his appearance. In fact, the slicked-back wavy hair and the neat moustache, combined with his normally upright stance, would suggest to a stranger that he was a military man. It would have amused him to be told this, of course, because it was many a long year since he had come out of the Fusiliers.

The sound of a car drawing up outside made Melda jump up and make for the door. 'That's them!' she exclaimed unnecessarily, as Ruairidh followed her out.

Marianne looked at Robert in appeal, obviously not wanting to ask for help, but he shook his head. 'No, my dear, as I said before, we are spectators today. We will sit and watch, and we will not interfere!' He had to suppress a smile at her offended expression as she cast her eyes to heaven and snapped her mouth shut.

'Are you sure I look OK?' Ruth asked as the car glided to a standstill. 'I couldn't afford anything new to wear.'

Graham groaned at that. 'Oh, Ruth, I never thought! Why didn't you say something? I could have given you an advance on your inheritance.'

'I don't want any of Mr Rennie's money, nor any of the Bruce-Lyall money, either.'

'That's exactly what your brother said, too. How strange.'

'What's strange is that I *have* a brother, and these people will have to take me as I am.'

Longing to tell her that he would love to take her as she was, he had to be content with saying, 'They won't care what you're wearing.' He got out and came round to open the door at her side. 'Well, Ruth, this is it! Good luck!'

The heavy door was opened before they reached it, and Melda ran down the steps, her colour heightened in the same way as Ruth's. 'Marianne was right!' she exclaimed, throwing her arms round her daughter. 'You *are* like your father.' Pulling Ruth inside she gave her a tight squeeze before passing her on to Ruairidh, who, after a moment's hesitation, also embraced her and then shook hands with Graham.

'Is Samuel not with you?' Melda asked Ruth, as she linked arms with her.

'He told Graham on the phone it'd be over a week before they could get a replacement for him.'

'Oh well, it's probably better that he's not here today. I haven't told your grandmother about him yet, so this gives me a bit more time to prepare her.'

Ruth felt a slight chill wash over her. The old lady was apparently even more of a dragon than she had seemed, but she made no comment on it.

'Come and meet my father, your grandfather,' Melda said, pulling her on. 'You met Ruairidh's mother before, of course. I hope you excused her rudeness to you then, but she hadn't long lost her dearest friend. Andrew Rennie's death hit her very hard. She shouldn't have been left on her own that day, but . . . there, it happened, and that's that. Here we are, and my father's dying to meet you.' Melda opened the drawing-room door and ushered her inside.

Ruth was taken by surprise at the bear hug Robert Mowatt gave her, and he made her sit next to him when the maid-of-all-work pushed in a trolley laid out for afternoon tea. 'This is some day!' he enthused, laying two thin slices of fruit loaf on his plate, then caught Marianne's reproving eye and said, apologetically, 'You met your grandmother before, of course.'

Marianne's smile was clearly forced, and the apology, such as it was, just as evidently made because it was expected of her. 'I treated you rather badly last time you were here.'

'It's all right. I understand how you must have felt.'

'Your twin sister is not with you?'

Quite taken aback by such an unexpected question, Ruth stammered, 'My . . . my twi-twin's name is Samuel.' Then, remembering that the old lady hadn't been told about him, she said timidly, 'I don't have a sister . . . well, I thought I had, but now I've found out Gladys isn't really my sister.'

'I was right all along, you see, Mother-in-law.' Melda couldn't resist saying it. 'I did have a boy. He was the first of the two babies, though I didn't know I'd had two.' Her face darkened suddenly. 'But *you* knew there were two, and you must have known they were still alive.'

Marianne did not appear in the least abashed. 'I knew there were two, but I thought they were both girls, and I'd no idea what happened to them. I left all that to Andrew.'

In an effort to curb her arrogance, Ruairidh said, 'The less you say the better, Mother. I have only recently learned what you did, and if it wasn't that you're over seventy, I'd have thrown you out when Melda told me your actions, and the pain you caused her.'

Every vestige of colour left her face, and Robert stood up in alarm. 'Shall I take you upstairs, Marianne?'

'Leave her there,' Ruairidh ordered harshly. 'I want her to hear everything that's said. Maybe then she'll realize the extent of the damage she caused, to Ruth as well as Melda, and possibly also to . . . Samuel.'

Uncertain of what to do, Robert latched on to the last word, and gave Ruairidh a playful slap on the back. 'Just think, though. You have a son and heir at last, Ruairidh. Isn't that good news?'

'No! No!' Marianne's sharp cry startled them. 'Duncan Peat's grandson can *never* be Lord Glendarril! For one thing, he is not legitimate!'

Robert cleared his throat nervously. 'I thought you would realize, Marianne. He was born illegitimate, certainly, but –'

Graham Dalgarno broke his long silence now. 'By law, the parents' subsequent marriage legitimates any previous issue.'

There was a long, brooding pause before Marianne muttered, 'I can't remember Andrew ever telling me that, but maybe he did. Anyway, I take it that there is nothing I can do about it?'

Ignoring this, Robert addressed his next remark to Ruth. 'As a matter of interest, my dear, what type of work is your brother engaged in? Has he a trade, or a profession?'

She related what the solicitor had told her about Samuel's early career, then dropped her innocent bombshell. 'He took up the ministry after the war, and he's in Germany now.'

There was shock on all three Bruce-Lyall faces, but Marianne's was greatest. She opened and closed her mouth as if gasping for air, then let out a sudden screech of desperation, which went on and on until Robert leaped across and gave her a stinging slap on the cheek. The noise stopped instantly, and Graham and Ruth looked at each other in astonishment, while Melda and Ruairidh exchanged apprehensive glances, none of them knowing what to say or do.

They were thankful when Robert turned round and began to speak. 'I had better tell you something, all of you. I originally intended to make my confession only to Marianne, but she wouldn't listen, and present circumstances demand that I make a clean breast of it here and now.'

All eyes were on him as he returned purposefully to his seat, looked at Marianne and said, quite calmly, 'I hope you can forgive me, my dear. I should have told you this long ago, but I could not say anything as long as Flora was alive.

I couldn't bear to hurt her in any way. Yes, I am well aware that it is three years since she died, but I mistakenly thought that you had forgotten your silly nonsense about Duncan Peat and all ministers, and I didn't want to stir it up again.'

She held her hand up weakly. 'Nothing you can say will make me change my mind about him.'

'I'm not even going to try. Just cast your mind back fifty-odd years and listen . . . and don't say another word until I've finished.'

He spoke now as if he were telling a story, a story about a young wife who was longing for a child but whose doctor husband could not prevent her losing the three she managed to conceive; of another young woman married to a dour minister whose quick temper made him ill-treat her at the slightest provocation, and who made her douche every time he used her because he did not want children. Furthermore, he had become impotent over several months as a result of prostate trouble, which was why he knew that he was not the father of his wife's child.

'Grace came to me so often for treatment for bruises and cuts that I felt deeply sorry for her,' he went on. 'Unfortunately, as you are no doubt aware, pity is but a small step from love, and I began to call on her when I knew Duncan was out. I despised myself for being unfaithful to my dear Flora and tried to be extra loving to her, so I was mortified when . . . well, I'm sure you can guess – I impregnated both of them.'

Gasping, Marianne burst out, 'Oh, Robert! I never dreamed! You should have told me!'

'I was deeply ashamed, and for Flora's sake, I couldn't admit it, not even to you.'

'But good God, Robert, it was me you should have told. You know what happened because I got hold of the wrong end of the stick. It's because of you Melda had to give up her twins.'

'You covered that up too well. I didn't know she was pregnant. If I had, I'd have told you everything, I swear!'

'But you didn't even tell *her*! Not even after she was married.'

He bowed his head in abasement, then, deciding that he had to explain further, he went on, 'She looked on me as her father, and she got far more love from me than she would ever have got from Peat. I didn't want to turn her against me . . .'

The others in the room had listened to his story unfolding like a stage drama, but now Melda said, a little sadly, 'I wouldn't have turned against you; I haven't, not even now. In fact, I admire you for shielding . . . your wife. I loved her, but I didn't realize what a wonderful woman she was, taking in her husband's child by another woman and treating her like her own.'

'She *was* a wonderful woman, Melda.'

Marianne tutted loudly. 'Haven't you forgotten something, Robert? You knew how I felt all those years, yet you let me go on believing that man was her father.'

'I *did* try to give you a clue that he wasn't,' the old doctor defended himself.

'You did?' She looked puzzled for a moment, then said, 'Ah, yes, I remember. You tried to make me think it was that tinker.'

'Duncan thought it was him.'

'*I* never thought it was. I couldn't imagine Grace having anything to do with a tinker. But I *can* see her taking up with a doctor.'

The sneer on her face infuriated him. 'It wasn't like that, Marianne! You make it sound so sordid, when we truly loved each other. She, too, was a wonderful woman, putting up with that man for so long, and you have no idea how much I despised myself for what happened.'

Ruairidh had been far too astonished at his father-in-law's confession to take any part in what transpired, but he suddenly realized that he had to stop it. 'Robert,' he began quietly, 'I think we should let the matter rest there. I am glad you've told us, because it will save Mother making any scenes when Samuel comes, but I must make it quite clear that I consider you equally to blame for the heartache that was caused. And now, the subject is dead and buried and will not be resurrected again by anyone.'

He smiled at Ruth now. 'I don't know what you must think of us, my dear, but I would very much like to hear a little about your life.'

She told them that she had started work as an office girl at fourteen, rising to bookkeeper typist before being called up to the ATS when she was twenty-one. It was while serving as a clerk that she had met Mark Laverton, a young corporal in the RAOC, who later became her husband.

'We married in 1941 and we only had six years together,' she said, her eyes misting, 'though I did have his son. After Mark was killed in a road accident in France, my mother . . .' She paused in confusion. '. . . the woman who fostered me . . .'

544

'Please keep thinking of her as your mother,' Melda said quickly. 'She brought you up and cared for you . . . and I'm very grateful to her.'

'Well, she suggested I give up my house and move in with her – Dad had died a year before. It was a good arrangement, because I was able to take a job, and the extra money helped us to live quite comfortably. Then Mum fell ill, multiple sclerosis, and it developed so quickly that I'd to stop work to look after her. That was when things got tough. We only had two widows' pensions coming in, ten shillings each, and that had to cover everything, and for about four months before she died, she needed attention twenty-four hours a day . . . and it was very tiring. I don't know if I could have gone on like that for much longer.'

Graham Dalgarno had been marvelling at how well Ruth had stood up to the hardship of being left a widow with a small son, so he was pleased when Ruairidh murmured sympathetically, 'So you've had quite a hard life?'

'Not as bad as some, I suppose. It was a funny thing though, when I think about it. Mum fostered me because she hadn't had a child of her own, and she had Gladys thirteen months later.'

'That happens,' Robert said. 'If a woman has been trying unsuccessfully for a child, it is often her anxiety about it that prevents conception. When that anxiety is removed, as in your mother's case when she decided to foster you, nature takes its course.'

Something made Melda ask, 'What's your son's name, Ruth?'

'Colin. He's nearly ten.'

Ruairidh clapped his hands in glee. 'We have a grandson, Melda!'

Marianne, who had been sitting rather chastened since her son's homily, cut through his delight. 'I hope you do not expect any money from us? Tell her, Ruairidh.'

He looked embarrassed. 'What Mother means, Ruth, is that the mill was doing extremely well until the war ended. We'd been supplying uniforms to the army and air force, you see, and then . . . phutt! Nothing! And things kept on going downhill.'

'There wasn't the money going about,' Melda reminded him. 'People couldn't afford to buy clothes even after they stopped needing coupons for them, and, to be honest, after our daughter was killed, we both let things slide for a while. We're in pretty bad straits at the moment.'

It had taken Ruth several moments to get over Marianne's attack, but now she looked at the solicitor with her eyebrows raised. 'Graham, could I possibly . . . ?'

He grasped her meaning at once. 'It's entirely up to you, Ruth.'

She spoke now directly to Ruairidh. 'Apparently, Mr Rennie left most of his fortune to my brother and me –'

Marianne heard only one word. 'Fortune?' she muttered feebly.

It was Graham who leaped to his feet and scooped her frail body up in his arms. 'Show me the way to her room,' he said briskly, standing aside to let Robert go first.

Once Marianne was laid on her bed, the old doctor took a bottle of smelling salts from her dressing table and wafted it under her nose until she came round, then he ordered his daughter, who had followed them upstairs, and the solicitor to go. 'You know, Marianne,' he chided, when they were alone, 'you are the most stubborn woman I have ever come across. If you'd just sat quietly and listened like I told you, instead of interfering . . .' He wagged a reproachful finger at her. 'It's not your business who Andrew Rennie left his money to.'

'You don't understand, Robert,' she whispered. 'It's the irony of it. He always loved me, you know, and I didn't marry him because I thought he would never be rich. I wanted a husband with lots of money. I wanted a standing in society . . . but . . .' She shrugged woefully.

'It was your own fault you got nowhere in society. I remember Flora saying you told her you weren't going to mix with such a bunch of snobs.'

'Yes,' she agreed wistfully, 'that was my own fault, but I'd never have felt easy with them.'

'Still, you had years and years of being Queen of the Glen. Every man, woman and child looked up to you, and you enjoyed every minute of their adulation, didn't you?'

'Of course I enjoyed it, but that was years ago. I'm speaking about now. What have I got? Nothing! No money, a son and a daughter-in-law who'll probably never forgive me for keeping their children from them –'

'Marianne! They don't hold anything against you . . . not now.'

'Ruth said Andrew left them a fortune. If I'd married him, I'd have been rich for a lot longer than I was. Of course, if Melda hadn't let the mill run down . . . Oh, I shouldn't blame her, should I? I know what it was like to lose a grown-up child.' She stopped, looking stricken as a new thought occurred to her. 'I took advantage of Andrew. I realize that now. I played on his love and expected him to do all sorts of things for me, be there

547

when I needed comforting, and . . . at the end . . . I killed him.'

'You mustn't blame yourself for that. It was an accident!'

'It felt like I was to blame.' She looked up into his concerned face, her eyes pleading for understanding. 'Fate has played a dirty trick on me, Robert. After all my dreams of wealth and power, I've finished up a penniless, lonely old woman.'

'Stop feeling sorry for yourself! How can you be lonely with so many people around you?'

They were interrupted by a soft tap on the door, and Ruairidh held it open to allow Melda, Ruth and Graham to go in. 'We came to see how you were, Mother, and I'd say, by the look of you, you've recovered enough to hear what we have to tell you. First of all, in spite of all I could do to persuade her against it, Ruth is determined to sign her entire inheritance over to us as soon as it can be arranged. And that's not all, but I'll let Graham tell you the rest.'

The solicitor stepped closer to the bed. 'When I talked to Samuel on the telephone, Lady Glendarril, he asked if the money had originally been left to anyone else, and when I told him that before he and Ruth were born, it had been left to you, and that your close relationship with Andrew had continued until the day he died, Samuel asked me to draw up documents for the transfer of his share to you personally.'

'But I don't need his money,' she muttered. 'Not at my age.'

Robert, worried by the deep red spots which had appeared in her ashen cheeks, took hold of her trembling hand, ostensibly to steady her but actually to feel her pulse, which, he was relieved to find, was only fractionally fast. 'You had better accept it,' he advised. 'You'll have the money you always wanted and the power to save the Castle Lyall from falling into other hands.'

'The power,' she repeated faintly. 'The power and the glory, for ever and ever, Amen.'

Looking wryly at Ruairidh, Robert said quietly, 'You had better go, all of you. This has been too much for her – she was a bit overwrought to begin with. I'll stay with her for a while, to make sure she's all right.'

Marianne looked at him pathetically when the door closed behind them. 'I was a very wicked woman at one time, Robert, but I was punished for it. First of all, I lost my darling Ranald, then my beloved Hamish, then dear Dorrie. Could it be that God is relenting now? Is He giving me a chance to redeem myself?'

'It seems that way,' he murmured cautiously.

'I'm going to plough it all into the estate. I'll make sure all the debts are paid. I'm going to get back on my feet again, and take a proper interest in what's going on.'

'That's the spirit! And don't forget, there *is* a Bruce-Lyall heir, after all.'

'And Ruth's Colin is a spare,' she smiled, 'like Hector insisted on. "An heir and a spare", that's what he used to say.' She fell silent for a moment, then said, 'I just hope Andrew's clerk doesn't talk them out of what they want to do with the money.'

Robert's drawn-out sigh told of exasperation. 'Graham Dalgarno isn't a clerk, he's the senior partner now, and he wouldn't have told you if he wasn't happy about it. For goodness' sake, woman, stop wallowing in self-pity and give a man a chance to be happy for you.'

549

'I'm sorry, Robert. I know I'm up and down and I'm being unreasonable. I don't know how you've managed to put up with me for so long.'

'Neither do I.' But his eyes were twinkling.

Downstairs, Melda was weeping softly but joyfully in her husband's arms. 'I can't believe it. It's like a fairy tale. We've got two children, the mill will soon be back on its feet, and –'

'God's in His heaven and all's right with the world,' he quoted, grinning. 'Like all fairy tales, it has a happy ending.'

'A truly happy ending,' she agreed. 'Ruth's nice, isn't she? I wish she would keep something for herself, though, to buy some new clothes. Did you notice the darns on the elbows of her cardigan? And her shoes were all down at the heels.'

Ruairidh burst out laughing. 'Trust you to see that. With all that went on here today, it amazes me that you had time to notice.'

'Yes, it's been quite an afternoon. I feel absolutely drained.'

'I do, too, so we should leave the analysing, the guessing and the planning until tomorrow, and take it easy for the rest of today. Not another word!' He laid his finger on her mouth to stop what she was about to say. 'I told Bessie we wouldn't need her after we'd had afternoon tea, so what about just going to bed? We can come down later for something to eat if we feel hungry.'

'Ruairidh Bruce-Lyall! What would Mother and Father say?' Melda gave a little snigger. 'That sounds as if they were a married couple, but you know what I mean. She'd be shocked.'

'So let her be shocked.'

'Are you all right, Ruth?'

'Yes, Graham, I'm fine. It's just that there's been so much to take in, I don't know how I feel about it yet. Do you think I'm daft to give up my inheritance?'

His heart almost stopped at the opportunity she was presenting to him. Could he? Should he? Taking a deep breath, he said, 'How can I when it has given me the courage to . . . This is probably the worst place I could have chosen to . . . Oh God, Ruth, I'm trying to ask you to marry me.'

He hadn't dared to look at her, and held his breath waiting for an answer which didn't come. 'I'm sorry,' he said flatly, after a few seconds, 'I shouldn't have placed you in such an awkward position. I quite understand –'

'No, you don't,' she replied gently. 'You took me by surprise, but I think I'm trying to say yes.'

'You are? I can't believe it!' Coming to an open gate into a field, he drew off the road and took her in his arms. 'You'll only be a Bruce-Lyall for a very short time in that case; just till I arrange the wedding. Won't you be sorry about that?'

Ruth cocked her head to one side to consider, then laughed, 'Ruth Bruce-Lyall's a bit of a tongue-twister, isn't it? Ruth Dalgarno's much easier, wouldn't you say?'

But nothing more was said, or needed to be said, for some considerable time.

BIRLINN LTD (incorporating John Donald and Polygon) is one of Scotland's leading publishers with over four hundred titles in print. Should you wish to be put on our catalogue mailing list **contact**:

Catalogue Request
Birlinn Ltd
West Newington House
10 Newington Road
Edinburgh EH9 1QS
Scotland, UK

Tel: + 44 (0) 131 668 4371
Fax: + 44 (0) 131 668 4466
e-mail: info@birlinn.co.uk

Postage and packing is free within the UK. For overseas orders, postage and packing (airmail) will be charged at 30% of the total order value.

For more information, or to order online, visit our website at **www.birlinn.co.uk**